CASANOVA'S ONLY NOVEL (1788) NOW TRANSLATED INTO ENGLISH FOR THE FIRST TIME (1985).

In a letter to Count Lamberg in 1785, Casanova writes: "The title of my work is the Icosameron for the hero takes twenty days to tell his story"

"The Icosameron is one of the most curiously picturesque works in world literature." Eugenio Giovanetti in the Giornale d'Italia of April 17, 1928.

"It is certain that of such works, none exceed it (Icosameron) in singularity and interest..Casanova presenting a scientific culture very rare for its time." Dino Montavani in La Domenica del Fracessa, Rome July 5, 1885

"Among his various other works is a remarkable novel recounting fantastic adventures in a fantastic world with many anticipations of modern inventions." Encyclopedia Britannica.

The Icosameron "serves as an excellent vehicle for Casanova's opinion on everything: politics, medicine, surgery, geology, mathematics, physics, chemistry and philosophy." S. Guy Endore in his biography, Casanova, His Known and Unknown Life.

"It is a work of profound and above all, free thought. Even more, it is a most interesting adventure story...that fascinates by the deliberate wealth of interest quite apart from its intellectual content." Quoted from the 1922 preface of the German translator, Heinrich Conrad by Paul Nettl in his 1950 biography The Other Casanova.

Icosameron **means** *Twenty Days* **(ĭ·kō·săm!ûr·ŏn)**

Casanova represented the Icosameron as his translation of an English manuscript rescued from a fire which destroyed the library of the Duke of Newcastle in the 17th century.

Cover Portrait - Casanova at about 30 - Alessandro Longhi

"*Since I have reached the age of decrepitude, I have become an exhorter*"

Casanova at 63, from an engraving by J. Berka

Count Waldstein's Castle at Dux, Bohemia, where Casanova spent his last years, 1785-1798. He wrote the *ICOSAMERON* and his *MEMOIRS* at Dux.

(from a lithograph by J. von Richter)

Casanova at 26, by his brother, Francesco Casanova

Casanova at 42, from a painting by Anton Raphael Mengs

JCOSAMERON

OU

HISTOIRE

D'EDOUARD,

ET

D'ELISABETH

qui paſſèrent quatre vingts un ans chez les
Mégamicres habitans aborigènes du Protocosme
dans l'intérieur de nôtre globe, traduite
de l'anglois par

JACQUES CASANOVA

DE SEINGALT VÉNITIEN

Docteur ès loix Bibliothécaire de Monſieur le comte
de Waldſtein ſeigneur de Dux Chambellan
de S. M. J. R. A.

A Prague a l'imprimerie de l'école normale,

Facsimile of Original Title Page of 1788

CASANOVA'S "ICOSAMERON"

or

THE STORY OF EDWARD AND ELIZABETH

WHO SPENT EIGHTY-ONE YEARS
IN THE LAND OF THE MEGAMICRES,
ORIGINAL INHABITANTS OF PROTOCOSMOS
IN THE INTERIOR OF OUR GLOBE.

by

JACQUES CASANOVA DE SEINGALT

A Venetian

Published in Prague, 1788

Translated and abridged
from the original French
by
Rachel Zurer

Jenna Press, New York

Jenna Press
37 W. 8th St.
New York, N.Y. 10011

Distributed by

The Talman Company
19 E. 36th St.
New York, N.Y. 10018

Library of Congress Cataloging in Publication Data

Casanova, Giacomo, 1725–1798.
  Casanova's "Icosameron", or, The story of
Edward & Elizabeth.
  [1. Fantasy] I. Zurer, Rachel (translator)
II. Title. III. Title: Icosameron.
PQ1959.C6I2513 1985   843'.5   [Fic]   83-82006
ISBN 0-941752-02-X
ISBN 0-941752-00-3 (pbk.)

The publisher of *Casanova's "Icosameron"*
dedicates this work to

JAMES RIVES CHILDS

American diplomat, writer and Casanova scholar

Among his books are:

Casanova: A Biography Based on New Documents	1961
Casanoviana: An Annotated World Bibliography of Jacques Casanova De Seingalt and of Works Concerning Him	1956
Casanova: Die Grosse Biographie (in German)	1977
Casanova Gleanings, an international magazine for Casanova research scholars. Mr. Childs edited this publication for many years	1956–1973
At ninety years of age, his *Autobiography* was published, *Let the Credit Go*. It is the story of his life, principally as an American Ambassador and diplomat. He now lives in Richmond, Virginia. (1985)	1983

CONTENTS

CASANOVA'S FANTASY OF UTOPIA

"Three years ago in Venice, discontented with everything, the fantasy seized me to cast myself in the role of the creator of a new universe, a new human race, a new civil code, a new religion, a new means of nourishing oneself, of housing, of living together, of reproducing. . .

"The title of my work is the ICOSAMERON, for the hero takes twenty days to tell his story. . . The inhabitants are called Megamicres . . Their height is eighteen inches. . "Their life has a fixed term. . . They do not sleep; they feed on liquids and odors. There is no night with them, but it is always midday. . .

"The language of my Megamicres is music. . . They do not know old age.

"Here is a work which will assure me immortality."

Thus wrote Casanova in a letter to his friend Count Lamberg in 1785. In 1788 his *Icosameron* was published.

To Casanova's great disappointment, the *Icosameron* did not bring him the "immortality" he hoped for. (This he achieved through his later *Memoirs*). He had 350 copies of his five-volume work published for the 156 subscribers but scarcely anyone read it.

During the next 130 years occasional references could be found in the literature about this "remarkable novel recounting fantastic adventures in a fantastic world with many anticipations of modern inventions." Or, "It is certain that of such works (as the *Icosameron*) none exceeds it in singularity and interest." Still another reference notes, "The *Icosameron* is one of the most curiously picturesque works in world literature. . ."

PUBLISHER'S PREFACE

Literary historians have on occasion included mention of the *Icosameron* as a novel by the author of the *Memoirs* but no one gave it more than passing attention: no one had apparently read it.

In 1922, however, Heinrich Conrad translated, adapted and shortened the work for German readers. In his preface, he wrote, "It is a work of profound and above all free thought. Even more, it is a most entertaining adventure story - true, one that requires a thoughtful reader but it also fascinates by the deliberate wealth of incident quite apart from its intellectual content." An abridged Italian version of the *Icosameron* appeared in 1960 and an abridged French adaptation in 1977.

Casanova's biographers now began including summaries of the *Icosameron*. The first comprehensive biography, *Casanova, His Known and Unknown Life*, by Guy Endore was published in 1929. Endore comments that Casanova was influenced by the philoshophical speculations of the new enlightenment. The often ponderous eighteenth century philosophizing is reflected in the *Icosameron*. But his "dissertations are frequently illumined by flashes of brilliance which play even in his dullest writing."

In 1950, Paul Nettl wrote *The Other Casanova*. He included a chapter entitled, The *"Megamicres"* which was based on Conrad's *Icosameron* as well as on the works of other scholars devoted to the study of Casanova. The most notable is the former American diplomat, J. Rives Childs, who collected what is now the world's most complete library of works by and about Casanova. In 1956 he wrote *Casanoviana*, an annotated world bibliography of and about Casanova. (396 pages). We learned from this work that Casanova wrote 42 works of which 24 were published during his lifetime. There were 8000 manuscript pages in his files when he died.

In the section on the *Icosameron*, we find "The opinion has been advanced by competent Casanovists that it was in the face of the bitter disappointment over the lack of success of his *Icosameron*, that Casanova turned, in 1790, to the composition of his masterpiece, the *Memoirs*, a work which was to occupy him until his death in 1798."

The latest biography to date is John Masters' *Casanova*, published in 1969.

3

Referring to the *Icosameron*, the author describes it as "a philosophical -
scientific - prophetic novel" and he concludes, "The *Icosameron* was a pouring-
out of the contents of his mind and his mind was brilliant, turgid, contradic-
tory, by turns sharp and obtuse, incisive and careless."

Casanova whose name has become a synonym for the irresistible lover and
seducer of women was no mere Don Juan. Described by Havelock Ellis as a
"natural man in *excelsis*", he was an anomaly in a world burdened by religion
and sin. (Casanova's eighteenth century was already sloughing off that burden)

Keenly intelligent, audacious and resourceful, he thrived by his wits as he
adventured throughout all of Europe satisfying his enormous appetite for life's
earthly pleasures.

But his candid disregard for conventional morality did not diminish his
humanity. He was accepting and tolerant of others just as he accepted his own
often dubious enterprises without remorse. It may be noted that the women he
seduced continued to love him (as he did them) even after they parted. And
that he retained the friendship of distinguished noblemen as well.

Advancing age and poverty forced him to accept from one of these lords, a
generous offer to serve as librarian in his castle in Bohemia. Here, he retired in
1785 and here he wrote his five volume Utopian fantasy in which he shaped an
imaginary world to his desires.

His intellect was as keen as ever; his imagination and his experiences
provided a rich and lively source for the tale he told of the siblings, Elizabeth
and Edward. His opinions on family, politics, government and religion give him
a place among more modern thinkers. But the adventure story alone should
suffice to entertain a reader.

Now, more than two centuries after Casanova began this work, the *Icosameron* is at last available to the English-speaking world.

TRANSLATOR'S PREFACE

After these few explanatory pages of mine, you will be alone with Casanova as you read his science fiction fantasy. He makes very good company.

Why, you may reasonably ask, did almost two centuries pass before an English speaking public would have access to the one novel written by the author of the famous *Memoirs?*

For one thing, there are very few copies of the *Icosameron* in existence. These may be found only in the rare books division of prestigious libraries. But the better explanation lies in its unreadability as a five-volume opus.

When the present publisher succeeded in obtaining a facsimile copy of the original, exactly as it was printed in 1788 in Prague, I was given the opportunity to pursue Casanova through each of his 1745 pages. Here was an indefatigable, garrulous lecturer and story teller who wrote, just as if he were speaking, in a slack, loosely-jointed French. Critics generally agree that Casanova was no literary artist, not in his adopted French nor even in his native Italian.

In the *Icosameron* (twenty days), he repeated himself, he digressed and he indulged in minutiae. At times, he permitted himself sentimental rhetoric. And he wrote diffusely about medicine, theology, philosophy, economics and government. Throughout, he was endlessly self-congratulatory in the person of his chief character Edward.

As Edward, he gloried in his invented wealth and high station. It was a wistful substitute for the vanished world of Casanova's lusty and ebullient youth. He created a stable, unchanging and utterly predictable environment, radically different from the real world where he had led such a tumultuous, unplanned existence. But even in this 'protocosmos' where Nature was benign and unvarying, Casanova has Edward meet one challenge after another as he creates incident after incident. In his own vigorous manhood, Casanova enjoyed the struggle to master, with audacity, wit, charm (and skulduggery) the challenges of the real world. In his utopian inner world, Edward becomes the nobleman Casanova longed to be, the wealthy and generous patriarch who seems forever young and who is moreover an honest and moral man.

Aging now and isolated from company (except for rare visitors) writing became his only solace. Throughout his life, he had composed poems, plays and polemics when the occasion demanded it. Now, however, he wrote ceaselessly. It was his only occupation. The *Icosameron* and later the *Memoirs* (*History of My Life*) were the chief products of his last thirteen years at Dux where he died in 1798.

The one volume you now hold is the result of a year's effort to reduce the bulky *Icosameron* without diminishing its essential contents. Included in its pages, you will find the adventures of Edward and his sister-wife Elizabeth as they made their extraordinary trip to the inner world of the fascinating Megamicres; their experiences among these single sex creatures for more than eighty years; their own parenting of forty pairs of twins and then their strange journey through caverns and volcanoes upward to the earth's outer surface and finally to London where Edward relates his adventures to a group of lords and ladies over a period of twenty days. Here you will read accounts of Edward's startling inventions, precursors of the automobile, telegraph, airplane, asphyx-iating gas and even the fountain pen.

The religion he devised for his descendants —he left about four million of them —is spelled out in his own sacred book. No mention is made of the Crucifixion, the Incarnation or the Old or New Testaments. But he does have some interesting views on social and ethical conduct. His comments on govern-ment are spiced with humor; his remarks about men as midwives have a modern ring as do many of his other insights.

The science fiction fantasy is related in its entirety. For the rest, I omitted nothing I thought valuable for an understanding of this unusual personality. I took no liberties with his language or ideas; the lines you will read are his own, translated, I trust, to reflect his own intentions.

What then has been eliminated? To begin with, his whole commentary on Genesis in which he finds justification for the union of brother and sister, and for the possibility of an interior world, has been set aside for separate publica-tion. I cut short his long-winded lectures. For examples, he discusses the nature of light and its relation to color; he expatiates on optics and cataract removal; he discourses on theology and religion. A modern reader seeking enlightenment on these matters, will not need to turn to the *Icosameron*.

As a mathematician, Casanova was enamored of numbers and his work reflects this passion. When he describes the theaters he is building or the city he is planning, he details every single measurement. I retained only those enumer-ations which seemed to me indispensable for conveying an image, establishing a setting or furthering the plot. The reader may decide that even these figures are excessive.

Wherever possible, I eliminated sentences, phrases and words that were repetitious or trivial or unnecessarily detailed. They added nothing to the narrative nor to a better understanding of the author —except to tell us that he was given to verbosity. I noted also that in contrast, he might dispose of an important subject in one paragraph or less.

I frequently had to pull his paragraphs into shape. As I followed his rapidly moving pen, I would see that sentence number four should follow sentence number one, for example. The two intervening sentences would distract or confuse the average reader. Sentence number one, however, had aroused a train of associations in Casanova's teeming mind and apparently he set them down just as they occurred to him.

Although translating the *Icosameron* required much editing, I did not venture beyond syntactical changes. I did however add some transitional words in the dialogues among the lords and ladies who were Edward's auditors.

In the area of facts and figures, Casanova may be described as a perfectionist. His calculations are unfailingly correct. He never lost track of places, dates, weights and measurements. I came upon only three discrepancies, none of them important. He names his sixteenth and thirty-second daughters both "Rose" and he names his twenty-second and thirty-ninth sons both "Godfrey". On one occasion, he refers to the name of a Megamicran day incorrectly; on another occasion, he mentions having a Bible in Greek as well as Latin when earlier he had spoken of his one Latin Bible. These mistakes are so inconsequential that one includes them out of astonishment that Casanova erred at all.

He spent five or more years writing and rewriting the *Icosameron*. He changed from Italian to French when his first draft was two-thirds done, believing as he explained, that a work in French would have a wider readership. He was deeply disappointed that his voluminous work was barely read.

Freed from the layers and wrappings of verbiage and self-indulgent lecturing in which it was confined, the *Icosameron* speaks well for itself and for its author. His lively and inventive mind, his humor, satire and keen insights belong to the present. His views about women (whom he adored) will appear antiquated to most moderns, however. He had no doubt whatsoever that men were vastly superior beings. Casanova was enormously vain but his vanity was inoffensive and was overbalanced by the humanity and gentility of his spirit.

7

THE RETURN

In the gracious residence of Count Bridgent on the bank of the St. George canal near Monmouth, a very old couple, James Alfred and his wife Wilhelmina, were sitting before the fire. It was an hour past sunset on the fifteenth of February in the year 1615 when they saw a pretty young woman enter on the arm of a handsome young man.

The two strangers had barely glimpsed the ancient pair when they halted their steps. After a brief moment they cried out in excitement, "It is they!" and ran to them. Throwing themselves at their feet, they covered them with caresses while tears streamed from their eyes.

Bewildered and upset, James and Wilhelmina got up from their chairs to extricate themselves from this torrent of affection. In agitated tones, the venerable James asked, "Who are you to enter our house like this? Where do you come from? Is it not enough that we Catholics are always under suspicion these days? If you think we have Jesuits hidden here, you are mistaken. Tell us what you want or leave."

The young man with unmistakable sincerity said, "I am Edward your son." "And I", said the lovely stranger, "am your daughter Elizabeth." With these words, they moved toward the old couple to embrace them again.

James pushed them away and drew back saying indignantly, "How dare you try to make us believe such an impossible story? And how can you expect to keep up such an imposture?"

"Only by telling you the truth, father." Elizabeth spoke gently. "And by asking you, mother, to look at us more closely."

Wilhelmina murmured, "Dear husband, I am quite beside myself. These persons are the living images of our two children. Remember how we mourned them eighty-one years ago when the 'Wolsey' was swallowed up in the Maelstrom."

"Exactly", Edward said.

"What do you mean, exactly?" The old man was outraged. "Are you mad or do you take us to be fools? Any impostor can learn these facts. Even if there were a single doubt that they had been drowned, how do you have the effrontery to present yourselves as our son and daughter? He would have been

9

ninety-five, she ninety-three. One can see that you both are no more than twenty-five years old."

"Putting aside for the moment the matter of age, do you not recognize our features?" Elizabeth pleaded.

"I admit that the resemblance is extraordinary", said James, "but even if you showed me the marks of a dog bite on your left arm, I still would not believe what my reason tells me is false."

Wilhelmina added mournfully, "And my poor Edward had a birth mark on his right thigh."

"Here it is", said Elizabeth, "the scar that you mentioned. Look." At the same time Edward showed them his birthmark.

"It cannot be a dream". Wilhelmina spoke softly as if to herself. "We are not sleeping."

Edward said eagerly, "You will recall that when we took ship at Plymouth, all England was in turmoil because of Henry the Eighth's apostasy."

"We believe we were the only ones who escaped with our lives" said Elizabeth. "A God-given miracle caused us to enter a world where time is measured differently. We do know that we are the age you say even though we appear to be young."

James exploded. "Here is a fine fairy tale! So you spent eighty-one years in another world, a world where the passage of time does not make you grow old."

"Please, father, be calm". Edward tried to soothe him. "Get ready to hear of marvels which you would never believe."

"He is right", Wilhelmina put in. "I am inclined to believe what our children tell us."

"Wife", James said irritably, "you are babbling. I am a hundred and nine; you are a hundred and seven. After living so long and so sensibly, are we now going to rush into dotage by believing something that can not possibly be true?"

"But what we see", countered Wilhelmina timidly, "is real".

"Please allow me to continue doubting", James' tone was ironic, "at least until tomorrow". He shook his head. "This experience, this unique and unheard- of experience has completely unsettled me."

"Tomorrow" Edward agreed. "Yes, father, it is wise to wait a day. But promise you will hear us out then."

"You will hear astonishing truths", Elizabeth added, "such as no one in this world could ever imagine."

In the grip of his wonderment, the worthy old man stood motionless for a long time without uttering a word. Then he cast a glance, sometimes at his wife, sometimes at the two.

At last, overcome, he yielded to the intense emotion which overpowered and possessed him and gave way to a burst of weeping. He wife dissolved in tears and the two strangers joined them. Nothing restrained the expression of their

10

feelings. These overflowed in embraces and caresses. His emotions inspired in the old man a gayety so unbounded that he began to laugh immoderately with helpless joy.

After this, the old mother brought two chairs to the fire and had these extraordinary beings sit between them. To her they were visitors from Paradise. Where else was there eternal youth?

An old peasant woman of the household who had known Elizabeth in her childhood, witnessed the whole scene. She could not believe what in fact her eyes told her was so. Looking at Elizabeth now, knowing she was old aroused a gnawing vexation in her. This apparition, she thought, must be the work of the devil. With this idea in mind, she left abruptly to notify the Catholic priest who kept himself hidden in their village. On the way there, she told everyone the startling news. They laughed at her but curious nevertheless, they all hurried to the home of James Alfred.

Soon the apartment was filled. Count Bridgent, not knowing what to make of this hubbub, came downstairs with his wife, son and daughter.

A moment later, the priest arrived. After he learned what it was all about, he ordered everyone to be quiet. Those two persons, he said, could very well be sorcerers. If, however, they could be kept from escaping, he would promise to make vanish in smoke anything about them that was satanic. But first he had to fetch his stole, his ritual objects and his relics.

Two stalwart and zealous Catholics there assured him that the persons would not get away, unless they were ghosts. They stationed themselves at the door while the priest ran to get those weapons which, his religion had told him, were necessary to do combat with the Evil One.

Lord Bridgent, who believed neither in angels or devils, laughed heartily at all this. Milady, his wife, was somewhat fearful but their young son, ignorant of the meaning of the word 'exorcism' and charmed by Elizabeth's beauty, wanted to get at the priest and thrash him. His fifteen year old sister, impressed with Edward's good looks was upset to learn he was so old and might moreover be an evil spirit.

The two objects of curiosity quietly kept up their parents' courage and firmly dissipated their fears. The good priest soon returned with all he needed for his exorcism rites.

He made every effort to uncover the alleged sorcerers. Seeing nothing of a diabolic nature forthcoming, he thought that the presence of several heretics in the group whose bursts of laughter rang out from time to time, might account for his failure. He ordered all those who lacked faith and did not believe in the supremacy of the Church of Rome to leave. They obliged him and he resumed his rites redoubling his efforts at exorcism by certain commands and rituals.

At last when he saw that these young-old ones did not make the expected responses, such as howling, throwing themselves to the ground or uttering

11

even a single word in Hebrew, he wrote out a certificate stating they were completely human and free of any magical power. Then he begged pardon and left.

Count Bridgent, inquisitive by nature, began asking all sorts of questions. Edward and Elizabeth answered him with exactness. Milord, wishing to learn much more and realizing that the presence of a large number of auditors would complicate matters, graciously invited them, together with James and Wilhelmina, to come to dinner. They accepted. Milord offered his arm to Elizabeth while Edward offered his arm to Milady. Followed by the Deans—so were the ancient couple called—they went upstairs to the dining room. The others returned to their homes.

His other dinner guests arrived shortly after: Lord Charles Burghlei, Admiral Howard, and his friend Lord Dunspili. The latter's cousin Lady Rutgland soon came as did Count Chepstow and his friend, the Duke of Brecnok, both of these on horseback.

When Edward and Elizabeth were presented to the Admiral as survivors of the ship 'Wolsey' which had been engulfed eighty-one years before, he received them with a great burst of laughter. He remembered the event having heard the story a number of times from his family. It was his great-uncle, the Count of Surrey, who had commanded the vessel and had perished with it. Besides, the couple who were thus introduced were so young, how could he help but laugh. When he was told it was a fact, not a joke, his astonishment was no less than that of the others.

Lord Bridgent addressed Edward. "We hope you will forgive our curiosity, and more, that you will satisfy it. If an hour will do, perhaps we can hear the story before we dine."

"I doubt that three hours a day for a period of three weeks would be enough if you really want to know what happened to us since we left England. That was eighty-one years ago", Edward reminded him. "But I can begin now if you wish and I can stop at any time if the narration gets too long or if your business calls you away."

"Listening to you", Count Bridgent assured him "will be my sole occupation from now on. It will give me great pleasure." "And your sister can remind you if you forget anything", Milady suggested. "We shall forget nothing", Elizabeth said.

"You undoubtedly agreed beforehand on the details of this romance you have concocted", Burghlei said mockingly. "But I promise to pay you the same attention as if you were telling us a true story."

"What I shall narrate", Edward said, "is the truth. The only ones deceived will be those who do not believe."

"If the honorable Lord Burghlei", added Elizabeth, "will give us an account of events in England after we left, we shall give him the same credit for truth-telling which he demands from us."

"Obviously you do not know this young man", Bridgent said ironically, "or you would not expect him to instruct you in history. He has never been outside of England; he is only twenty-five years old and he has spent ten of those years hunting and tippling in taverns. He is one of those who always says, 'I don't believe you.' That, he thinks, is a mark of intelligence. I warn you in advance that he will find fault with everything you tell him. Pay no attention to him. As for the events in England, I shall give you a little summary myself. Edward, do you remember how things were when you left?"

"Yes, Milord. It was the twenty-fourth year of Henry the Eighth's reign."

"Very well", said Bridgent. "Of course, the history of England for the last eighty-one years would fill many books. But I can try to tell you briefly what were the outstanding events during that period of time. Henry wanted to divorce Catherine of Aragon in order to marry Anne Boleyn. The Pope wanted to excommunicate Henry when he divorced Catherine, so Henry became England's pope for a while. He had Sir Thomas More beheaded in 1535. Twelve years later Henry died of his leg sores and left three children. These were Mary from his marriage to Catherine, Elizabeth by Anne Boleyn, and Edward (who died at age sixteen) from his brief marriage to Anne Seymour.

"There was endless friction between the Catholic church and the new Church of England. For a while, the country was Catholic; then it became Protestant under Elizabeth who reigned for forty-five years.

"Shortly after her death in 1603, her cousin James, now James First, became king. He is our present ruler, the son of that unfortunate Mary, Queen of Scotland, who was beheaded in 1586. Our history has been full of intrigue, religious dissension and recurrent outbreaks of plague.

"And now, ladies and gentlemen, I would suggest we go in to dinner." He gave his arm to Elizabeth whom he seated next to himself. Edward entered with Milady and the others found their places. The 'Deans' sat nearest the fire.

After the succulent roast beef was cut into generous slices and served, Lord Bridgent said to his neighbor. "You should have a good appetite, I think."

Elizabeth smiled. "Not especially, Milord, but I shall try to improve. In this world, the stomach needs solid food."

"I thought that was generally true."

"In this world, yes", Elizabeth replied, "but in the world we left, one needed no teeth."

"I would think it more healthful to eat solids", said the Count. "Still, if taking only liquid nourishment is the source of your youth, I would gladly give up the pleasure of using my teeth."

"I believe, Milord", said Edward, "that there are other reasons as well. Their air is entirely different from ours. They have one season only of gentle warmth in a totally unchanging environment. And one never sleeps there."

"Well", Count Bridgent looked dubious, "being awake all the time may be fine, but I would forego this privilege just for the pleasure of waking up from a

13

good sleep. What I do like, however, is the absence of old age. Permanent youth seems to be a gift of divine grace, the lot of the blessed. Would that world of yours be the earthly paradise we read about? I wonder."

"Tell me", Lady Rutgland turned to Elizabeth, "do you feel as young in all respects as your looks would suggest?"

"I must confess, Milady, that I am less interested in events: the promise of pleasure does not excite me as it used to. But as for bodily vigor and clear thinking, I feel the same as I did at twenty."

"Happy world!" exclaimed Bridgent. "Are there no illnesses there? Are people born and do they die as we do here? How do they occupy their time? Can we all go there together?"

Elizabeth laughed. "If it were at all possible to get there, I would advise no one to go there who looks old. The Megamicres believe that the marks of age are the result of wrongdoing. They would not treat such ones well, I'm afraid."

Admiral Howard remarked thoughtfully, "Whoever conquers this world for England will be immortalized. . .I should like to speak to the king about it and offer my services. Of course," here he addressed Edward, "we would go together and share the glory."

"I am honored, Milord", Edward said soberly, "but such an undertaking is not possible. When I describe this world to you, you will agree that it can never be conquered. There are eighty monarchies, ten republics and two hundred and sixteen fiefdoms contained within, some of which are larger than all of England. Besides, what right have we to subject a free world to our rule? In addition, I personally would not wish to return evil for good: they saved my life and all my descendants live there in peace and happiness. At any rate, this interior world is impregnable. To overcome the force of gravity, to pass through the fires, the abysses, the floods—no, I do not believe it possible or desirable."

Count Bridgent made a proposal to the company. "Let us all dine together tomorrow", he said. "You, Edward, will begin your account, stopping at whatever point you think suitable, then continue from day to day until its conclusion. And beginning tomorrow, my house shall be closed to everyone but us; no visitors, no messages from Parliament, not even from the king. I want nothing to interrupt us."

Everyone agreed to his proposal. They drank glasses of punch and retired.

Before he went to bed, Count Bridgent summoned two of his secretaries. He ordered them to be ready to take down Edward's story just as he told it. They were to be seated behind a thin tapestry so they could hear without being seen. Their presence, the Count thought, might impede the otherwise natural flow of the narration.

14

FIRST DAY

The ancient couple returned to their ground floor apartment. James Alfred, after being fondly embraced by the visitors, finally fell asleep, still troubled by doubts as to whether the two were mad impostors or really his long lost children. Wilhelmina, whose emotions more readily persuaded her of their identity, could not sleep until they had talked for two more hours.

The next morning, they were awakened by the noise of a crowd which had gathered to see the unusual strangers. Elizabeth and Edward soon went down to show themselves and to speak with them until noon when they were summoned in to dine.

After dinner, Count Bridgent led Edward to a sofa near the corner where the secretaries, well-concealed, were prepared to write down his words. "Our maternal uncle", Edward began, "who had spent his life at sea would come to visit our mother after each voyage. He would tell us about all the extraordinary things he had seen and the dangers from which he had escaped. Elizabeth and I, now adolescents, would listen with intense interest. We longed, more than anything else, to accompany him on a voyage. We begged our parents so insistently and so repeatedly that they finally allowed us to go.

"Ten days after the March equinox of 1533, we sailed from Plymouth on the 'Wolsey', so named in honor of the late Cardinal and Chancellor. I particularly remember", Edward reminisced, "the rumors going about at the time of our sailing that Cranmer, archbishop of Canterbury, was about to proclaim invalid, the marriage between Henry the Eighth and Catherine of Aragon.

"The commander of the fleet", and here Edward turned to Lord Howard, "your great uncle, Lord Arthur, intended to explore the unknown lands inhabited by the Hyperboreans in that northern area of Tartary and Asiatic Russia.

"For a month, our journey went well but towards the end of April, cross winds caused us to wander for more than three weeks. Then in mid-May, with favorable winds, we reached Iceland. We dropped anchor and went ashore for supplies. Not far off, we could see Mt. Ecla erupting. Torrents of liquid lava poured from its summit continually, and the earth below remained blackened with ash and pumice.

"The people on this island, superstitious as people are everywhere, believe that the volcano is one of the mouths of hell. They are sure of this since they often see with their own eyes, bands of devils entering there, clutching between their claws, the souls of the damned. They see them come out a little later apparently in search of other damned souls.

"On the eighth day, we set sail again directly towards Greenland, pushed by a southeast stern-wind. Halfway there, we saw the Gundebiurnes Skeer, little islands inaccessible to mariners since they are inhabited by bears. Not far from here, we were shown a frightful looking monster they call Haffstramb. From his haunches up, we saw his long and pointed head, his enormous shoulders and long arms. He had no hands. Later we saw the upper half body of a creature they call Margugner. With its breasts and long hair, it seemed female. Two stumps at the shoulders ended in hands webbed like the feet of a goose. This creature was busy gobbling fish out of its cupped hands. The third monster pointed out to us by the old mariners was the surprising Hafgierdinguer whose three heads are three mountains of water. These form a triangle whose center swallows up anything which runs afoul of it.

"We arrived at the polar circle and after three weeks of calm, we entered the glacial ocean. Now heavy cross winds blew us back from the huge blocks of ice we were trying to navigate and did not cease until we were off the coast of Norway where a dead calm stopped us. We were then between the little island of Vero and the southern part of Laffouren Island.

"It was in the morning, on the twentieth of August that the fateful event began. A powerful tide was irresistibly drawing our ship to its inevitable destruction. No one of the crew doubted this. With one voice, all cried out in terror: 'the Maelstrom, the Maelstrom!'* This is a vast whirlpool, subject to such a powerful subterranean pull that it engulfs and drags down anything solid on its surface. The tide was pushing us towards this vortex, this Maelstrom.

"When the dreadful cries rang out, Elizabeth and I were standing trembling on the quarter deck near the bulwark where a lead chest was suspended. An old seaman brought this along with him on every voyage. This chest was to be his tomb should he die at sea. That way, he explained, the deep sea monsters could not get at him to devour his remains, and he could present himself whole to his Maker on Judgment Day.

"The case was large enough for a dozen piled-up bodies. Each of its six sides could be raised or lowered as one opens and closes a hinged box. I do not know, my friends, by what lucky chance the chest was open at this time. We had seen it open four weeks earlier when the owner had propped up the cover with an iron peg. We had examined the interior with curiosity.

"Each of the six sides had two round holes bored through its thickness and

---

* A celebrated whirlpool in the Arctic Ocean off the west coast of Norway.

16

then grooved. Into these holes were fitted telescopic lenses, similarly grooved. Each lens extended two inches further inside so that it could be grasped and removed at will. The outer surface was strong enough to withstand shock and pressure, as we were to learn later.

"Inside its two lateral walls, the chest was fitted with twelve pockets made of Moroccan leather, each pocket stuffed full and tied with a draw-through cord, handbag fashion. There were six bottles containing pure water and six bottles with spirits of wine or aqua vitae. The other pockets held a compass, a case for mathematical measuring, another case with surgical instruments (in the use of which I had had some training), India ink, a box of pastel colors, and tweezers of different sizes. In a corner lay a magnet of such a huge size, I doubt anyone has ever seen its like.

"In the terrified confusion, sailors were trying to lower lifeboats, hoping to escape death by rowing away from the vessel. From all sides, we heard the cries, 'We are lost' and 'there is no hope for us', and 'God have mercy on us.'

"All the cannons had already been thrown overboard. Two sailors were cutting the ropes which supported the heavy chest. Several others were tugging hard at a cable behind us when they inadvertently hit us on the back with that same cable. We had been clutching one another closely in our fright when the blow hurled us both towards the bulwark and into the open chest. Our fall removed the iron prop, the cover came down and we were imprisoned.

"We were conscious only of overwhelming terror. Speechless and rigid we felt the chest plunge into the water. We did not know what was happening to us; we were without the power to reason or feel anything but fear. A brief moment before the plunge, we could see the light from the glass openings; after the plunge we were in total darkness. Our chest dropped into the abyss, more by reason of its enormous weight than by the drawing power of the Maelstrom.

"Our lead sarcophagus continued its precipitous journey downwards. A sudden jolt told us we had reached some landing place.

"I cannot tell you, Milords, how one measures the speed of such a descent, but I do know that my watch had read ten-fifteen o'clock the moment before we sank into darkness.

"I now took from my pocket the small candle and matches I usually carried and looked at the time. It was twenty minutes past ten. Only five minutes! We remained in darkness when my efforts to relight the candle failed.

"A minute later, we felt a jarring impact and we guessed that it was the 'Wolsey' which had fallen near by.

"Cold sweat, palpitations and nausea overcame us. We vomited and though our queasiness was somewhat relieved, we suffered from the fouled air. Breathing became more and more difficult. As we sank into a stuporous sleep, we believed we were dying.

"But we came awake when the chest began to shake. A powerful blow stopped the jolting. The chest started to fall down what seemed to be a precipice of air. We were almost certain that we were no longer in water so we ventured to unscrew first one then another of the lenses from their bores. The air became freshened. Outside there was only deep darkness. The shaking began again and the chest somersaulted down the length of a precipice. For perhaps a quarter of an hour, we rolled and tumbled down, unevenly and with an occasional leap as if we were descending a craggy mountain.

"Our sweating and nausea had stopped somehow. Though we were dizzy and dirty, there was something comical in the way we were being hurled helplessly upon one another. We could not laugh about it then, but in later years, we did as we recalled our adventures.

"Our long hurtling over rugged terrain came to an end. Our movements made us think we were cleaving layers of air. We dared to open two more of the apertures. Almost all the bad odor disappeared with the fresh air. But it was frigid air which made us shake with feverish chills even after we had hastily closed all the apertures.

"Elizabeth, though she was also being tossed about, managed to maneuver out of one of the pockets, a bottle of aqua vita. We each drank hastily but then as hastily we had to get a bottle of pure water to relieve the burning sensation from the alcohol. Our chills subsided but we began to sweat copiously. We tried more of the aqua vitae. Being a little drunk, we began again to hope even though reason would deny this hope. But such is the nature of man: we know we are wrong to hope but we do not wish to be set right.

"Suddenly we were subjected to a battering of such frightful force we feared our entrails were torn from their attachments. This brutal collision of the chest with something, we did not know what, must have created a fissure because at once, the darkness gave way to light, a strange, brilliant, reddish light.

"In this new atmosphere, we began to sneeze explosively as if nature were helping us expel the over-strong air we were inhaling. The strong light assaulted our eyes and we kept them shut for a while. After we could tolerate the splendor, we looked about in every direction. That reddish atmosphere seemed actually to be fire. We had unscrewed four lenses for air but the heat was unbearable. We replaced them and we began to suffocate. We could not breathe so again we opened them. The heat was so intense, we could not hope to survive. Then unexpectedly, a dry torrid air blew inside. Our clothes which were drenched with sweat dried in less than two minutes.

"Amid all our confusion and torment, we were aware of the astonishing effect of a gravitational pull. Sometimes we were on our side; then on our stomachs. Now we were upright; more often we were standing on our heads, not unlike those acrobats they call the Jumpers of Chelsea. The chest had apparently lost weight and moved slowly and irregularly, like a lump of mud in water, neither heavy enough to sink nor light enough to stay afloat.

"The atmosphere through which we were passing was illumined by the fiery light we were leaving behind. The heat abated and our courage returned. Then

I was struck by an uneasy thought: what if we were embarked somehow on an unending orbit. Our irregular speed and movement made me hope otherwise. But still. . .

"Now we passed through a dark and humid atmosphere, then into a strange kind of rain which alternately fell from above and rose from below. After we passed this watery region, we found ourselves shrouded in night. The darkness did not prevent us from seeing what loomed ahead, an immense opaque mass. This, we decided was the earth we were wishing for. But there was no indication anywhere of a horizon. Finally, we became convinced, as we observed the plains and rocky land flee by, that the earth was not below us but alongside of us.

"The land surface was no farther than a hundred paces when the chest slowly turned over. A freezing cold again entered and I shut the apertures, except for one away from the wind. I again began to fear the endless orbiting. I suspected now that we were in the interior of the world. Shadows would be expected there; a fiery atmosphere would also be part of an interior world. We felt desperate; if the chest ever stopped, no one would open it. The idea that the interior world could possibly be inhabited by reasonable beings was too absurd to be considered.

"In ten minutes, the chest, after hitting a small rise sank into a very thick mud. An unbearable smell of sulphur drove me to shut the one hole I had left open. Our oscillating motion now resembled that of a ship at anchor in a harbor when the wind and sea are doing battle.

"With all the openings closed against the sulphurous fumes, we lacked air and we experienced the worst and cruelest heat. In our extreme distress, we hastened to the one source of help providence had left us; we drank a throatful of aqua vitae with water. Somewhat revived we thought we should ration what was left. Even though we looked at the chest as our tomb in which we were buried alive, yet nature, ever the conservator, was prompting us to gain a few more moments of life.

"The chest which had been revolving slowly and regularly took on a different motion as if it were free of the heavy mud. Its movements became rapid and violent, fierce and unrestrained. We used all our strength to brace ourselves. Backs against the side, arms and fingers interlocked, we struggled to keep steady. The chest now struck a hard object, shattered it and we found ourselves floating free and weightless. This ecstatic sensation lasted barely a few seconds but we should have liked it to go on forever. Except that unexpectedly, the enormous magnet at my feet rose on its own (hitting my elbow en route) and fastened itself to the top above our heads. In our turn, we were reversed and now we were standing on our heads, the magnet again at our feet on the top. From this peculiar position, we could see outside clearly. We were totally surrounded by a reddish light. With a strenuous effort, we righted ourselves; the magnet remained fixed to the top side.

"Of the twelve lenses, ten showed light but the two on the base reflected nothing. We could safely assume we were on solid ground. I therefore opened one of the lighted lenses. To my consternation, clear red water flowed in. Before replacing the lens, Elizabeth and I could not resist tasting the water. I can truly say it tasted better than Thames water.

"Curious about the time, I noted that it was now twelve minutes before one. Only two and a half hours had passed. It seemed that we had been suffering much longer.

"From all indications, we were now at the bottom of a river. Newly encouraged by some aqua vitae, we trusted that good providence which had preserved us from so many serious dangers might intervene on our behalf once more, we could not guess how.

"And here I must comment that it is in the nature of man to think thus, ("pejora passi") when the worst has passed. But we realized that if Fortune were to favor us, she would have to make haste; we could not hold out very long.

"Staring out into the clear water, we saw with astonishment, two completely nude red creatures swimming towards the chest. They circled it three or four times, came nearer, studied it carefully, and then touched the glass of our lens. Had they been fish, we would not have been surprised, but these two small beings were not very different from us. They appeared to be male, except from the throat down. Their foreheads were framed in a kind of bonnet which formed a narrow visor over the eyes and continued on both sides to below the ears.

"The two visitors communicated to one another by signs then went off. They returned with others entirely like them in size—about twenty inches— but of different colors. They all examined the chest.

"Hoping to arouse their curiosity, we opened and closed six of the lenses. They went away but their comings and goings appeared to us as a good sign.

"In less than a quarter hour, our chest was surrounded by thousands of them. They were of every color imaginable except for black or white. These attractive creatures, needing neither tail nor fin, swam as easily and gracefully as real fish. They agitated their little hands, kicked their legs and frisked about as if water were their natural element.

"Some of the Megamicres as they are called were communicating the news about us to the two reds. These showed surprise then came nearer to the chest. For our part, we moved the lenses in and out to indicate our presence. The two reds swam to the top, examined how the two lenses there were set in and conveyed their information to the others below. Then they left and the others, perhaps ten thousand of them, followed.

"We judged the reds to have a superior status both because of their own deportment and from the haste of the others to make way for them.

"We learned later that our appearance was considered an event of the greatest importance. They believed we had miraculously issued out of their universe which they see as an immense and boundless mire with no center.

"They decided that the chest was inhabited, as we found out later, and they planned now to find a way of speaking with us, ascertaining our needs, discovering who we were and how we had got there. Reasoning thus, they took action which saved our lives. By now, we were almost entirely debilitated because of the heat and lack of air.

"A few moments later we saw two swimmers land on our 'roof' accompanied by a group of others who darted and leaped around us. One of the two held the end of what seemed to be a cord. It was no thicker than an ordinary cane and beyond our view, perhaps long enough to reach the surface. The other one held a box with a knife, a hammer and other tools. The first Megamicre began working on one of the lenses. In fifteen minutes that lens no longer admitted light. We unscrewed the blocked lens and pulled out three lengths of cord. We could pull no more; the cord's diameter was too large to pass through.

"We assumed that the plan inside their small heads was to draw us up by these cords. Knowing this was impossible to achieve considering the weight of the chest, we felt bitterly disappointed. I seized the cord to pull it out but it was firmly glued on with some mastic gum. With a sharp knife from the surgery case, I cut the cord. It was not a cord after all but a hard hose or pipe, actually a conduit. As a puff of much needed fresh air came in, we almost cried with relief and gratitude. How had these creatures who could breathe in water, guessed our need for air? But we were wrong; they had wanted to communicate with us. And now we heard a kind of melodious sound coming from the hose. The repeated songs like the warbling of nightingales pleased our ears but meant nothing otherwise. Our would-be deliverers came back from time to time singing delightfully to us, trying to tell us something. Useless! We did not even think of uttering any words in English, but Elizabeth had a sweet voice and she tried humming a song but they did not answer. Four hours passed before their next attempt.

"Now we saw a large number of them descend on us. Some carried instruments or tools whose purpose we did not understand. They listened attentively to two yellow Megamicres in charge of the operation and they proceeded to carry out their orders. They made a total of fifty holes in both sides of our chest quincunx fashion, hammered in four inch nails, equal to the depth of the hole and put rings around the tops. Then they threaded each with a strong cord. On each bank of the river, cranes were already in place to which these would be attached. Now fifty Megamicres, two each to a cord, grasped those twenty-five cords on one side of the chest and fifty did the same on the other side.

"Two hours after they began this ingenious operation, we saw ourselves on the surface of the water which was six hundred feet deep. What first struck us was the perfectly perpendicular ray of the sun coming through the glass above our heads. Here then it was noon. We removed all of the lenses above water

21

level and the sight of the beautiful countryside at once held our interest. True, we could only see a vast plain on one side and a river on the other. The land was carpeted with low grasses and shrubs of several colors, woods of low trees and some low-lying buildings, none especially beautiful. However, the view, though uniform, seemed very beautiful to us. The very color of the atmosphere, a pale rose, pleased us and the delightful sounds we heard did not seem to come from the air, making us believe for a moment that we had entered that garden of pleasures where God had first brought Adam, the earthly paradise. We could not speak, our hearts were too full. We rendered homage to God by this very silence. Had some presumptuous fool had the insolence to say that we owed our life not to God but to a series of lucky accidents, I believe we would have torn his heart out.

"A multitude of Megamicres swarmed over both banks of the river. Seeing them all naked, my sister observed that they must be angels. They no longer communicated with gestures but their language was an harmonious singing.

"Eight or ten small boats drew near, laden with staves of differing sizes. The boatmen, working under the chest and weaving the staves together with willow-like branches, formed in a hour, a raft perfectly proportioned to the size and weight of the chest. A dozen rowers pushed the raft to a nearby basin where it was dragged over dry land in the middle of a clearing. Here, the staves were quickly unfastened leaving only those on which the chest rested.

"With beating hearts, we awaited the end of our adventure. The workers on the raft now left and another group came towards us slowly. All were nude save the two reds at the head of the procession. These wore very white cloaks which covered them in back from shoulders to heels but were open in front. A white sash girdled them from breast to loins.

"They approached the chest and carefully examined it, paying special attention to the fittings of the lenses. At a command which sounded like a gracious song, eight polychrome Megamicres took the necessary positions to form a pyramid. One after another, the two reds leaped up to the top of the chest and leaned down to look through the holes. They immediately removed themselves, holding their nose, and lamenting. We learned a year later that they had said "Oh, what a stench!" Six of the servants were given orders and they went off in three different directions. In the meantime we heard beautiful songs by one, two and four voices, and a chorus which sang a divine melody.

"Two of the polychrome servants returned carrying baskets which they raised up and offered to their masters. These took some of the fragrant herbs and flowers and put the rest into the chest through the holes. The perfumes were of a delicate fragrance such as no one here can possible imagine. They apparently had nutritive power too because in a short time, we felt strength-ened. We tried tasting them but hurriedly spit them out, the taste was so bitter.

"The other four polychrome servants returned followed by five or six hundred others who were dragging some seventy carts laden with lime bricks.

They heaped these up and formed a square well whose sides were two feet from the chest. Just before the well reached a height beyond our view, we had observed an even larger group of Megamicres carrying on their shoulders more than two hundred buckets containing a viscous red liquid. Within two hours the enclosure reached the height of our chest and then four Megamicres with knives and sticks of wood plugged all the openings except those on the roof needed for breathing. For about an hour, we heard dull sounds repeated at intervals and then silence.

"You can imagine our surprise and unease when we remained thus isolated for hours knowing nothing of what was happening and seeing no one. Impatience, boredom, hunger and finally despair that we had been abandoned deeply troubled our spirits. Yet we could not entirely believe that we had been left to die. On the one hand, they might have feared that we carried some disease, smelling as we did and by closing us in, destroy a plague. On the other hand, they might have a religion like ours and had gone to consult their priests and their oracles. Surely they would not lack theologians who would find in this apparition of a monstrous chest, sufficient material for fanciful and time-consuming conjec tures.

"After twenty or thirty hours, during which the unmoving position of the sun told us that here day and night are the same, I felt certain we were not in a land where six months of light is followed by the reverse but I formed a theory compatible with my ignorance—as philosophers have always done—. I told my sister we were in the kernel of the earth; that in fact we were the first to have arrived there. What wonders we would see if we could get out! How wise we would become! Yet of what use would our new knowledge be if we could not spread it, if we could not retrace our steps to enlighten our countrymen and others. Everything would die with us.

"Elizabeth had the good sense to tell me that my wish to communicate my knowledge arose more out of vanity; that people should be content to know the truth for its own sake. And anyway mankind would rather submit to fanciful lies than to hard truths.

"Her reasoning silenced me but I was not altogether in agreement. We are never really sure ourselves until we have convinced others of what we perceive as truth. But who knows? Perhaps things might be worse if man were freed from error and prejudice. Perhaps what we have now is what is right for us now. "At the end of twenty-four hours, our fortunes took another turn. Prepare to listen tomorrow, Milords, to facts which will surprise you and which you can learn only from us."

SECOND DAY

At noon, Count Bridgent entered the drawing room where his guests were already assembled. After the usual exchange of courtesies, he addressed Eliz-abeth. "Do you know", he smiled at her, "I spent the whole night with you both in that fateful chest. I can barely wait to see us get out."

"What your brother told us yesterday", the Countess added, "is more than anyone can really grasp; it seems impossible that you could have survived."

"We would have drowned", Elizabeth said simply, "if the chest had not been so perfectly sealed. Death was always close at hand, but God was there, too."

Lord Howard remarked thoughtfully. "You owe your lives to something, certainly. I wonder how a scientist would explain it. I surely can not."

"Edward will not be offended, I hope", Lord Howard said, "if we ask some of our scientific friends for their opinion."

"Milord", Edward replied, "everyone has a right to his opinion."

"When you speak to our scientific friends", Lord Bridgent told Howard, "be sure to ask them also about that brief ecstasy they felt. Edward thinks they might have remained in that state forever if the magnet had not jolted them out of it."

"Let me try to explain that", Dunspili urged. "The chest could not pass from one gravity to another opposing gravity without an encounter. At that point, perfect equilibrium takes place; weightlessness results and this is the so-called 'ecstasy'. The almost simultaneous movement of the magnet jarred the chest back into motion; the motion and force of the chest broke the solid body which touched it, namely the bottom of the red river. Immediately, the chest regained its weight, but this time it was the gravity of the Megamicran world, not ours. Your good fortune, Edward and Elizabeth, was due to the chance that you landed on the bottom of the river from which the Megamicres fished you out."

"I think", the Countess insisted, "that it was their prayers that saved them." Lady Rutgland agreed, then added, "But I do not think God's mercy depends on whether or not one prays."

"How do you explain that, cousin?" asked Dunspili. "First you agree that their prayers helped; then you say prayers do not affect God's mercy."

25

asily", Lady Rutgland replied. "Praying gives troubled people the confidence and assurance they need. They help themselves with this courage and they take action instead of doing nothing and feeling lost."

"I doubt", said Chepstow, "that you will find many theologians to agree with you."

"Please", Bridgent addressed the company. "Let our friend go on with his account."

Edward began: "Twenty hours after the well was built, we noticed that the roof of our chest was giving way. Little by little it was giving more and more and we feared that our skulls would be crushed if it fell. Had our liberators arrived a quarter of an hour later, that might have happened to us.

"The director of these operations was heaved up from the well to the roof. There stretched out on his stomach, he probed a wall with an iron rod. Finding it thin enough, he saw it could easily be broken into pieces before it liquefied. I learned that the reddish liquid was mercury but of a greater potency than ours. They hurriedly perforated the well four inches from the ground and allowed the mercury mixed with the melting lead of the chest to pour out, catching all of it in a receptacle. They then broke down a side of the well and propped up the whole 'roof' of our chest. When they were satisfied that the top side could hold, they broke through a side.

"Half our bodies were now visible. The two chiefs approached and looked at us with some astonishment but without fear. They must have found us agreeable in appearance.

"After a long silent examination, they spoke among themselves. Then they greeted us with a delightful song, which we guessed was in the nature of a decision. We could not understand however what it could be. Troubled by our lack of response—actually we wished to indicate our timidity and harmlessness—they offered us fragrant herbs and lovely flowers. Elizabeth stretched out her arms for them and I did the same.

"They sang a charming motet very softly and drew back, inviting us with gracious gestures to come out. When they saw we did not appear to understand them, orders were given to take down the well and open all four sides of the chest.

"At that, something happened which surprised us all. With the last stroke of the ax, the magnet which was still tightly stuck to the roof, flew straight up with such speed and violence that it disappeared in a minute, roof and all.

"Since it did not come down, everyone was convinced that it had been lost in the sun, a reasonable conclusion as it could go nowhere else. From this we deduced, rather boldly, that their sun must contain enough iron to attract this enormous magnet. We too might have ended up in the sun had the magnet possessed enough power to carry off the whole chest, not just the roof.

"This extraordinary phenomenon caused a somber silence to fall on the crowd. Among the physicists there, no one dared to suggest a natural cause for the event. People prefer to attribute such happenings to the wish of God who thereby displays his miraculous powers. The theologians present were of the same opinion. Looking very profound, they decided that God had spoken. Now the question was, what had God said?

"Only the abdala* would have the answer, they believed. He would give an interpretation and they would be ruled by it.

"As soon as we found ourselves standing there alone, we decided to walk towards the chiefs. At this, they burst into a song which lifted our spirits. Everyone now sang in chorus and the two principals danced. They were most graceful. After them, everyone danced to an enchanting song. Had we not been so tired and hungry, we could have believed we were in the garden of the blessed.

"When we faced the chiefs, we made a deep reverence as we had seen the others do. Bowing, we made a circle of both arms and touched our lips with the middle fingers.

"The two chiefs are distinguished from the rest, not only by their white cloaks and the flower garlands on their bonnets—those natural half-circles of cartilage which shade them from the sun—but also by their white slippers. The other reds wear shoes of green to match their hair. The polychromes are not required to wear any particular color. As I told you, the outer contour of their body is not dissimilar from ours except in size. But their coloration is remarkable. The reds have big blue eyes, a red iris and green pupil. Tongue and lips are also green. Their teeth are set in two rows. Each row contains thirty tiny white balls made, not of bone but of hard cartilage. Their nails and eyelids are green as is their hair. This hair, curly, almost wooly, covers the head but leaves the nape of the neck bare.

"Because of their breasts, we had thought them female. These breasts start below the neck and end in the stomach area; they are of equal size, each one with a green nipple in the center. We discovered later that they were neither male nor female. In a world which ignores the division of sexes, one can not define them, except perhaps by the term 'androgyne', a term we use more for convenience than for accuracy. Unlike the error of painters and sculptors who have represented Adam and Eve with navels, these Megamicres had none, because their method of reproduction is quite different from ours.

"We stared at them and they at us. Then several servants laid at our feet all the possessions we had had in the chest. Elizabeth and I, exhausted by our journey and by the lack of food other than the strong aqua vitae, felt we had to sit down. The grass was soft, the colorful flowers all about were inviting. Though nothing could be more silken soft than this grassy lea, one of the chiefs sang a command and in a short time, a dozen couriers brought back pillows both small and large, making very comfortable beds for us.

---

* The abdala functions like a bishop.

"At another chanted command, four polychrome Megamicres timidly approached us, bent down and placed their tiny hands tentatively on our shoes. Seeing we did not object, they removed them and after that all our clothes, except our dirty shirts. We were embarrassed, Milords, not at our nakedness—everyone else was nude—but at our dirtiness. While we were being unclothed, the assemblage sang and danced around us. We gathered they approved of our ready acquiescence.

"Another order was given and we saw jets of water rise from the edge of the basin, forming a shower of red rain, dazzling in the sunshine. They invited us to bathe and we did so with pleasure. Then ten or twelve of these dear creatures washed us from head to foot singing as they did so. They climbed on our shoulders as they washed us with the utmost delicacy. They admired our hair, the blond of Elizabeth's and even more the blackness of mine which they found an extraordinary color.

"They were particularly surprised by the difference in our physical structure, wondering at a feature of mine which was lacking in Elizabeth and noting my lack of breasts which she had. These strange defects seemed to make us inconceivable creatures.

Once the shower of rain stopped, we were gently dried with red towels, led to our beds and there massaged with invigorating herbs and flowers.

"We had barely lain down when the noise of a crowd drew everyone's attention. People were walking in front of a carriage drawn by twelve quadrupeds. These animals while not resembling our horses serve the same purpose for them. The carriage stopped near us and six persons got out. We noticed that they wore a transparent sphere on the cartilaginous head covering which I will call 'bonnet' from now on. They themselves were of different colors and they wore shoes of varying colors.

"We learned later that these were the alfas*, sent by the abdala, their superior, to get information from the chiefs about the miracle reported to him. We noted also that the alfas were old and ugly with flaccid breasts and hoarse voices.

"After they had spoken a long time with the chiefs and others, they addressed us. We got up and made the customary reverence. Then we lifted our eyes to the sun and lay down again. We had to lie on our side to avoid the powerful light of their sun. Apparently satisfied with us, the alfas wrote out a paper, had the chiefs sign it, greeted us, then left to the accompaniment of a song by those gathered there.

"We saw that our clothing as well as the contents of the chest had been placed beside us. To make them understand that we were in accord with their nudity, I tossed my clothing far away. Elizabeth, though in some distress, also

---

*Alfa or alfaquin serves as a priest or abbe.

28

threw away her skirts. The assemblage, pleased, broke into a joyous concert. Now two servants came near and measured us for slippers.

"Listening to their speech, we got some inkling of their style of language. They use vowels only; consonants are apparently too harsh for their delicate eardrums.

"They came near to examine our possessions. Though they studied our pistols carefully, they could not guess their use. Our watches interested them less; evidently they understood their purpose. Our cases of mathematical and surgical instruments interested them most though they did not understand their use. But an ivory oval frame with miniature portraits of Elizabeth and me pleased them immensely. They repeatedly looked at us and then at the painting and admired the artfulness.

"We were now parched with thirst. My sister seized a bottle, put it to her lips and then showed her disappointment that it was empty. I did the same. Upon this, the chiefs conferred, embraced, sang and then lay down beside us. It would have been impossible to understand them, had they not acted out their meaning. With embraces and delicate kisses, they offered us their breasts.

"We did not demur nor hesitate a moment. Our need for nourishment was not the most important reason for accepting this sign of their friendliness. It was also a matter of sensibility. We had to show that we were neither ungrateful, nor less courteous than they; a refusal would have insulted them, and also caused us to die of hunger and thirst. So we sucked that milk, being careful not to injure their breasts with our teeth. What an exquisite flavor, Milords, the milk of the Megamicres. It satisfies taste and smell, awakening in the senses, all the pleasures of which one is capable. We could believe the fables of mythology now. What we were imbibing was nectar, the ambrosia that gives immortality.

"After five minutes on each breast, the nipples were withdrawn, the breasts empty of their blissful contents. To our pleased surprise, two other Mega-micrans lay down beside us and then followed a third, fourth and fifth couple. This nourishing lasted an hour and might have continued had we not seen with dismay several drops fallen from the fifth couple's breast on our chest, looking the color of blood. That sight calmed our insatiable appetite and we indicated that we were now satisfied.

"Our agreeable nourishers then sprinkled herbs and flowers on us and rubbed our entire bodies. The delicious perfumes awakened in us an exquisite sensuality, a sixth sense conveyed to our awareness through nerves and blood and effected by the gentle rubbing of our skin. This sixth sense of which I can give you only an imperfect idea is the pure source which gives the milk of the Megamicres that quality of youth and health which they enjoy right up to the day of their death. That day is known to each of them. It never arrives before the determined hour unless they deviate from the rules in which they have been trained. I also learned that their final moment comes in the enjoyment of this sixth sense, an enjoyment of which we are deprived since we lack this sense. Further, our religion would frown on a pleasure which preserves youth and is experienced even at the moment of death.

"After so many sensations, new, pleasurable and abundant, we fell into a sleep, so deep and profound, that our good Megamicres could have done what they wished with us.

"Now I must tell about the situation I found myself in when I woke. Elizabeth by my side was wrapped in deep sleep. From her light breathing, I assured myself that she was still alive.

"I was totally stupefied as I looked about me. I saw a room and furnishings I had not seen before, a daylight which came neither from the sun, lamps or torches. I recalled London, our submersion, the sufferings we had endured, the new world we had entered, our reception there, the nourishment we had received and those who had cared for us. All these reflections must have taken at least half an hour and yet I was still confused after the recollection of all these bizarre happenings. I wondered if I had become deranged.

"Elizabeth awakening at this moment, came to my rescue. Together, we were at last able to orient ourselves by degrees though not completely. When we felt somewhat in command of ourselves, we looked at our watches but they had stopped.

"Seeing ourselves now rescued from despair and distress to a condition which seemed a happy though extraordinary one, we began to cry, so moved were we by our circumstances.

"Our eyes now sought the source of the beautiful light in the magnificent room where we had been sleeping. As we got up, we were delighted to find a pair of white slippers for each of us. They fitted to perfection.

"We walked about on the carpeted floor, saw the tiny armchairs and the large sofas and tables. All, however were no more than five inches from the floor, being made for the beings whose height rarely exceeded eighteen inches. Our two beds were in a curtained alcove.

"The light we had wondered about came from four nine foot squares made by joining crystal glass to steel and leaving a very slim space into which was poured a liquid phosphorescent substance. This phosphorus liquid is mined and is regarded as a precious commodity. It lit up the crystal brilliantly but without dazzle. All four steel sides were polished to such a gleam that they outshone the glass mirrors of Venice.

"After an hour of observation, we tried to find somebody but could see no doors or windows. We found our belongings in a small cupboard behind our beds but we had no clothes and were entirely naked. We were not embarrassed by our nudity, nor were we cold. But because we would be living together, we would eventually have succumbed to nature. Nature in fact did not even allow us time to think about becoming husband and wife. We became united without any conscious intent. And once it happened, we felt no humiliation or remorse

30

or even shame. Nothing altered the serenity of our feelings. We continue to love one another today as we did on that first day when we were joined as man and wife.

"God blessed our union with a vast number of descendants. There were about four million when we left. My wife was twelve when we arrived there and she remained fertile until her fifty-second year. During these forty years, she had given birth to forty daughters and their male twins.

"My daughters' husbands were always their male twins. They always believed, Milords, and I did not disabuse them of the idea, until twenty-two years ago, that nature in producing a male and female twin tied them with an inviolable bond. I was careful not to tell them that things were quite different in England and that their union would be regarded there as quite shocking. They would simply not have believed it.

"I taught them only those facts of world history that I judged suitable. I told them nothing about the Old Testament because I did not consider they had enough judgment to understand the sublime doctrines as they should be under stood. Also I did not believe myself equipped to answer all the questions they might want to ask of me. I only inculcated in them an adoration of the one God, and the holy trinity. If my descendants live righteously, they will obtain salvation just as did those antediluvians who obeyed the natural law and as did those who lived, loving God and fearing God, before the law of grace came to man.

"Believing, as I did, that after the resurrection of the eternal word the road to heaven would not be open except to those reborn through water and by the Holy Spirit, I baptized all my children and I taught them to do the same for all their children. I hope merciful God listened to my pious intention and con-firmed the validity and sacramental force of my baptizing.

"A month after their birth, I circumcised all my males and handed on this precept to all my descendants. They observe it and will always observe it. I did not however include this last precept as a divine command but simply to serve for human cleanliness. I would call this circumcision simply 'incision' because it is a removal of skin without mutilation. I believed it necessary for the sake of healthful reproduction and to guarantee against certain ills to which the uncircumcised are subject.

"If I have established among my descendants only the sacraments of baptism, confession and marriage, I must congratulate myself that I did not deviate from my duty, first because I did not have the ability to administer the other sacraments and secondly because I believed they did not need them for salvation. I did not tell them there were seven sacraments for fear of overbur-dening their understanding. I instituted prayer to God and I told them that they would obtain pardon by true repentance. Unless God sends missionaries there to perfect the work which I was able only to begin, they will have to remain the kind of christians I made them.

"During the eighty-one years we lived there, none of the infants died, none got sick, nor was there a single unfortunate childbirth. None of them believed they would ever die. When I pointed out that Megamicres die at the age of forty-eight (European) years, they replied that was not proof that Alfred's christians need die.

"In time, Milords, you will learn how it came about, this sovereign realm of Alfred's christians, and how, a hundred years from now, my descendants will be masters of that interior world, so much vaster than ours, so much more habitable, with no deserts and seas and with no territories where extreme heat and extreme cold prevail. Elizabeth and I circled their world several times so I can describe the laws and customs in some detail.

"The Megamicres themselves travel rarely first because their religion prohibits curiosity of any kind and second because their world is of such uniformity, it is not worth flouting the law. With merchants, however, travel is a different matter. Since business, not curiosity is their goal, they are free of this odd religious taboo. Further, the sovereigns of the realms profit by their goings and comings. Staging posts on land, boat transportation on the water, all are provided at convenient intervals and modest cost. Canals intersect the entire Megamicran world.

"Commerce is a relatively simple operation. All the lands are equally populated. The shortest and most direct routes are well known since geography has been taught with morals from the earliest years. Each city has available for public use a large globe showing exactly all places and distances. Merchants pursue their business with a minimum of difficulty.

"The land extends as far as the eye can see without anything to block the view. From time to time, small woods intervene to interrupt the flatness of the plains. About these woods which they consider sacred, we shall say more later. All structures are underground although a few observatories of modest height may be seen.

"The entire surface of the land is divided into square areas, each bordered by a canal. Each area of 600 feet square contains a minimum of eight subterranean dwellings whose inhabitants cultivate every inch of their soil.

"Peasant homes, small and square, have three floors, each four feet in height. On the sides are stables for their animals and storehouses for their grain harvests. Only the top floor receives natural light; this comes in obliquely through small openings under the unadorned cornice.

"But in the cities, the architecture is splendid. Especially so is the Econearcon or royal residence. It is to be found in every city where an abdala resides. Vast and magnificent, there are countless apartments, each furnished with everything that industry, science and wealth can provide of luxury and comfort. No one of the many buildings may go down deeper than six hundred feet below the surface. This point marks the beginning of the mud and mire which is considered the universal element of the Megamicres. On the surface, many gardens, woods and canals abound.

"In that world as in ours, there is "thine" and "mine", that is, wealth and poverty. For this reason, the government has built houses for the poor at the base of the city walls. They are like the peasants' houses except that they lack stables and crop storage space. One of their religious precepts demands that even the poorest among them may enjoy a dark retreat during their hours of repose. Since light is in such abundant supply, it has less value than the dark for which one must pay more. Prisoners, for example, are placed only in sunny cells unless they merit the favor of darkness.

"In several of the capitals of this world, I saw huge globes which one actually enters to study the exact replication of their world. These globes are lit by round lanterns hanging from the center which duplicate their sun. The largest of such spheres belong to the monarchs in the capital cities; they cost as much as a royal palace and are ingeniously designed and luxuriously fitted. Inside are narrow spiral staircases, covered with woven hemp cloth, which lead all around the planisphere.

"The sun of this concave world being always and everywhere at its zenith, they have no need for measurements of latitude or longitude. The circum-ference of their world is 21,380 miles; its diameter nearly 6,690 miles or 180 miles less than the diameter of our equator.

"Eighty kingdoms and ten republics, each with an area of 1,210,000 square miles make up their world. The additional 36,000,000 miles are divided into 216 fiefs, triangular in form and varying in size. No fief is smaller than 60,000 miles with 10 million inhabitants. The feudatory princes recognize the sov-ereignty of the king but on all other matters, they are the rulers including the power to make laws.

"The world from which Elizabeth and I just returned is a closed world. I believe their system of physical laws, so fortunate for them, can exist and endure only because there is no means of connection with ours. On my way back, I learned much which convinces me that a return would border on the physically impossible. But I will tell you about that in time.

"To return to our story: After we got up from our beds, Elizabeth and I thought about the many strange events, about our hosts, the milk we had drunk, the long sleep which had overcome us. We were curious about their sex, their method of reproduction. Perhaps they were male but with the physical difference that they could produce that excellent red milk they had so gener-ously given us.

"Looking about, I found a square panel with a chain in the center. When I pulled it, we heard pleasant chimes and after a minute the red Megamicre entered, followed by his companion. After a salutation of song and dance, they pushed us towards the sofa where they had us sit between them. They spoke at

33

length in their melodious language, then gave us a letter written in a number of colors. After I had learned their language, I translated the contents which I never forgot. It follows:

" 'At first, when we saw you overcome with that compelling sleep, we were not surprised; the milk you drank was enough to stupefy twenty sons of the Sun. Had we supposed you to be ignorant of these effects, we would have warned you; apparently your constitution is strong enough to with stand its effects. Among us, sleep overtakes only those who become irrational because they have overindulged. Drunkenness is forbidden both by divine and civil law. Sleepers may be robbed with impunity. No law will punish the thief. In all other situations, thieves are severely punished. Drunkenness has the further effect of aging one early and of shortening our natural life span of one hundred ninety-two harvests.*

" 'We watched over you for a pentamine (five of our days) to come to your aid if the sleep should prove dangerous. Our doctors found your pulse normal and that you were in no danger of death. We thereupon went to the abdala for advice.

" 'I was instructed to take you to my house and wait until you awoke. I was told to warn you that drunkenness is a scandal here. If you do not understand our language, you are to receive instruction at once so you can understand our laws and customs. I was to inform the king of your presence here. This I have already done.

" 'I must tell you that I as the king's representative, the Governor of this city, will take responsibility for you.

" 'As soon as you can, you must tell us why you came here, who you are, how you got here and what you intend to do. In spite of the miracle of your arrival, we are troubled by your ignorance of our divine language. This suggests that you are not a child of the great Sun, the Father of all reasoning creatures.'

"With this the two Megamicres embraced us and left."

---

*192 harvests is equal to forty-eight European years.

THIRD DAY

Everyone gathered the next day in the same room. Count Bridgent greeted Lady Rutgland who was the last to arrive. "You're late. Aren't you curious to hear the rest of this marvelous story?"

"Extremely curious", she replied. "I dreamed all night of those enchanting siblings who became husband and wife. It seemed a most natural thing."

"Only an ignoramus would be shocked", Brecnok agreed.

"Adam's children did the same you remember", Howard remarked.

"And there are classical authors", Dunspili added, "who find the union of Adam and his daughters both likely and acceptable."

"What a discovery, that world of the Megamicres!", Lord Howard said. "It does not seem so inaccessible if it takes only a day to get there. Maybe there is a secret passage."

"Edward tells us not to hope", Lady Rutgland answered him. "Still, after he tells us how he got back, we might figure out a way. . . . Meanwhile, I must say I find those Megamicres utterly charming."

Countess Bridgent agreed warmly. "To think how they nourished strangers, creatures who might even have harmed them. If only", here she addressed Edward, "you had been able to bring back one of them."

At this, Edward seemed unable to speak for emotion. Finally, he said, "We did have one Megamicran with us but he died just as we entered our world. And we owe our lives to him." He stopped. "Excuse me. I can't think of him without wanting to cry."

"Oh, dear God", Countess Bridgent murmured tearfully.

"Good Heavens!" Burghlei exploded. "All of you crying? That's really funny. So much concern for hermaphrodites! I'll wager that is what they are and I'm surprised that Edward did not suspect it."

Lady Rutgland rebuked him. "It is *your* ideas which are funny and laughable. What makes you think they are hermaphrodites? And what if they were? But I'll wager they are neither hermaphrodites, nor androgynes in the real meaning of those words. Ideas like yours are born out of prejudice, prejudice about both sexes. The Megamicres are just what they are and until Edward gives us more information, we know nothing. I find them charming and interesting and not

35

the ghastly freaks you make them out to be. . .I am far more interested in their language. It is more like music, not words as such. In our world, we read that Adam gave names to all things and we take this on faith since we know that words have only a conventional value. But with music, there is a difference. The Megamicres' language speaks to the mind and soul through some kind of sixth or seventh sense. I can even conceive that by uttering a certain sound, the object it intends to convey will become known to us even if we had not known this object before. All by way of this special sense."

Count Bridgent interrupted. "Lady Rutgland, let us now go on with Edward's story. There is so much to hear."

Edward continued. "After the Governor left, four polychromes came in. One touched a spring in the polished steel and glass reflector and a door opened. We were led into a lovely well-lighted, square-shaped room which had against each of its four walls, a green marble tub sunken and oval in shape. Each was about four feet wide and four feet deep.

"Elizabeth enjoyed a bath in one of these with the help of two attendants and I similarly attended, stepped into another tub. Water gushed from gold faucets as we washed. Then we were dried and rubbed with herbs whose delightful fragrance we breathed in with pleasure.

"Our hair badly needed attention. The polychromes tastefully combed and arranged it and left us half a dozen combs. Then two of the prettiest imaginable polychromes came in. Their coloring was so varied that we had to laugh, but with delight. They brought us each a head covering which simulated their own natural bonnet. In their environment, a covering for the head is considered indispensable. They fitted these to our heads, securing them with diamond pins mounted in red gold. Then they led us to a room and left us. Here were extremely clean fixtures which were intended to serve our natural bodily needs.

"When we went out, we found our hosts in still another room. They were seated around a table singing and playing instruments. When we entered they rose but continued their singing and gestured to us to sit down.

"Two yellows and two blues entered when the music finished. They brought four notebooks, two with writing and two blank. A large inkwell held seven small bottles of different colored ink and next to the inkwell, they placed thin pens made of light wood. Each pen had seven tiny tubes ending in a writing point. They were so designed that one point at a time could be used. The ink capacity of the pen allowed an entire day's writing.

"Our first language lesson began. On the first page, we saw six signs, each of which was repeated seven times in different colors. These were the six vowels which make up their alphabet. One of the teachers read the alphabet slowly and clearly. It consists of forty-two vocalizations in groups of seven, since each vowel can be sounded in seven different tones.

"It was a seven note scale but ordered like the diatesseron of ancient music;

36

one major, one minor and one half-tone major. Starting with the first note of the octave, the 'ut', one leaped to the fourth note, to the seventh, to the third, to the sixth, to the second and then to the fifth. This was the preferred order, demonstrating that it was a singing language, not music itself.

"I repeated the sounds after the teacher, and Elizabeth imitated me. She received many compliments for her voice which they preferred to mine. After a third try, they marveled when we read the alphabet without help. The books were closed and the teachers left, well pleased with us.

"Later Elizabeth delighted our two friends, the Governor and his mate, when on a whim, she began to sing an Italian aria. At its end, they hugged her repeatedly. Enthusiastically, they took up their instruments which resembled a lute and a flute. Elizabeth agreed to sing the aria again and I joined her in a counter tenor. The Governor's mate also sang, a melodious solo a cappella.

"A chime announced two visitors, two vermillions who were cordially greeted. All six of us then left. We first went up a wide staircase whose risers were only an inch high; then we entered a courtyard where a handsome open carriage awaited us. Twelve splendid quadrupeds in triple harness were attached to the conveyance. These animals resembled Danish greyhounds but they were smaller, perhaps fourteen inches high. They were all violet in color and seemed to be males. Our coachman was a velvety amaranth (bluish-red) in color with a wooly green head.

"At a rapid trot, they carried us to the cathedral. We descended a gently inclined spiral ramp which circled the temple five times before the entrance was reached. Here the interior rose two hundred and forty feet. Phosphorus lanterns lighted the way. Three hundred feet in diameter, it would have been a perfect sphere except for a large area one fifth the size of the temple which was distinguished by a floor made of square tiles of colored wood. From the center hung a luminous globe six feet around. This together with the five hundred lamps set like jewels above each of the loggias created a scene of great splendor.

"The lamps illuminated maps of the five hundred cities of the kingdom. Under the globe, in the center of the artfully paved floor, there seemed to be a kind of well or pit surrounded by twenty-four columns each two feet apart.

"After a brief fanfare, we heard a symphony of instruments issuing from below while twenty-four Megamicres were simultaneously rising up out of this hollow structure. They wore red cloaks covering their shoulders and chests up to the elbow and open in front. Above their natural cartilaginous bonnet, they wore a yellow cap and on their feet, were slippers of the same color. They all looked quite old.

"After them, forty-eight Megamicres of every color except red came out of the well. Each held a round lantern above his head and each carried a sheet of music. In orderly fashion, they stepped behind the first group of twenty-four and began to sing. At the same moment, the huge globe opened from the bottom and we saw emerging, a Megamicre standing on a gleaming semicircle. He appeared to be a statue made of gold or gilt. Above his head, he held an enormous red ruby. It was the abdala himself. He was lowered little by little until he stood firm, about ten feet above the ground. An armchair with steps, like a throne was raised up to this height and the abdala seated himself.

"A concert lasting an hour began. Each song had a refrain in which we all joined. Then the abdala sang the euphony. He was now lifted upward to re-enter the globe; the alfas returned to the pit.

"We stayed where we were looking all about us. The religious assistants or oblates went about with their great gold plates, gathering offerings of flowers and herbs. When these were burned, the temple was filled with fragrance. Suddenly all five hundred lamps went out at once, leaving only the big center globe alight. It seemed like a miracle and was so intended to be regarded. Actually there was a device which triggered the simultaneous darkening.

"Everyone now left. We got into a carriage and drove along straight wide streets lined with houses and shops and protected from the sun's glare by canopies overhead. These streets are excavated from the hard rocky earth and are not otherwise paved. This same material is used for both exterior and interior of the houses. It is a porous but very compact substance like stone.

"At the Governor's palace, we stepped out of the carriage and came into a large room filled with Megamicres of every color. The Governor and his mate sat on a double throne. The reception which lasted three hours gave us an opportunity to observe the manners and customs of this happy people. Everyone stopped to look at us but we pretended not to notice. We were sorry we could not understand the comments they made about us which amused them so greatly. When they laugh, they appear even more charming. Our good-natured demeanor won their respect and we took good care to keep it, knowing full well how important it was.

"Meanwhile the Governor was busy judging cases. Not even the Megamicres agree on everything. Wherever reasoning beings exist, vanity, bias and difference of opinion also exist. After the hearings, we went in to dine. Their settings consist of plates, spoons and vials of crystal. The plates may be made of gold, porcelain, pottery or wood. Beside the spoons are laid finely woven napkins of red hemp cloth.

"Five dishes were served, one at a time. The soup is a semiliquid puree which tastes of no familiar legume for it is flour cooked in water. The delicious and different taste of each of the dishes is due entirely to the variety of its fragrant seasonings.

"Once the food is on the table, it stays warm because each plate has a hollow bottom containing hot water. Equal portions are served to each guest; rarely does one ask for a second helping no matter how flavorsome it is. Without seasonings, the food is tasteless and actually unwholesome. Even the very poor will not eat unless the dish contains some herbs, no matter how ordinary or cheap. The rich distribute these as charity. With the herbs, the flour dish becomes palatable enough so they can derive the nourishment afforded by the milk. Sucking of the milk which takes place between mates lasts only a minute each time. After five such brief intervals the dinner is over. For dessert, each person gets a small basket of herbs, the vial is opened, a pinch of red powder is sprinkled on the herbs and instantly they begin to burn. An azure blue flame fills the room with a delicious perfume which induces a spirit of gayety in the diners. It should be remarked that the drinking of pure water is an offense against divine law. The water in which the flour is cooked is exempt.

"And now, my friends, you know how the Megamicres eat. You know more in fact than we did when we sat down for the first time. Then all eyes were attentively fixed on us. After the first dish, when the exchange of milk took place between the Megamicran and his inseparable*, they stopped to see if I would make a move to suck at Elizabeth's breast since they reasoned she would have a supply.

"We were quite put out of countenance and felt embarrassed and ashamed. They thought I did not approach her because I was not endowed with breasts to return the milk. But the Governor after a word to his mate had two blues come in who provided Elizabeth with milk. They then gently directed my head towards Elizabeth's breast. When I resisted, they seemed mortified by my reluctance. They also were surprised that I seemed to be waiting to be nour-ished as Elizabeth had been.

"My behavior caused a considerable amount of talk between the Governor and his friend and the whole gathering voiced their opinions too. We learned later what had been said. But now, the Governor sent for nourishers who let us suck their milk after each dish.

"The dinner lasted twenty minutes longer than it should have but did not detract from the merriment. After the perfumes had filled the room, servants gently rubbed each diner with the fragrant herbs. We would gladly have foregone this experience but we felt we had to do as they did.

"A digression here about the flour which is important but secondary to their essential diet of milk. This flour derived from round red grain is perfectly ground and harvested every three months along with hemp.

"Harvesting takes place on the last day of the year. Sowing takes place on the second day of the beginning of the new year And on the third day the people go to their temples to worship. These three days are their only holidays and the only time when they use their six hour daily repose period for merry-making.

After working for fourteen hours, they rest for six. This constitutes the twenty hour Megamicran day. On the holidays, there is revelry with carnivals, masquerades and public entertainments during those three six hour periods.

"Grain is one of the principal sources of wealth; land is another and

---

*The Megamicres live in pairs throughout their lives. They are born at the same moment and die at the same moment.

39

phosphorus a third. The preparation of grain is considered an art. Those cooks who devise seasonings, essences and new recipes are among the most respected and also the wealthiest in the country. They are not merely cooks but pharmacists, chemists and botanists. To practise their art, they first have to be approved by the College of Physicians.

"Returning to the discussion which the Governor had with his mate and friends, we later learned its gist.

"When they first laid eyes on us, the Megamicrans were less impressed with our size and coloring than with the fact that our bodies had a different conformation than theirs in certain important aspects. I, especially, surprised them. Unlike them, I had a navel but no breasts. They wondered how nature could produce a creature without the necessary vessels for nourishment. As for Elizabeth, she conformed better but how was I to nourish her as she could nourish me? They did consider that perhaps we could live without milk or obtain it from some source unknown to them. But if not, I had no right to accept from Elizabeth what I could not give back. They did not think it likely that they could furnish us with ten Megamicres each day to keep us fed. In their eyes, we were two monstrous creatures towards whom they had no obligation and who moreover would never be of any use to them.

"As for Elizabeth and me, we had no idea that in order to feed us, ten Megamicres would have to fast each day. We did not know that they had milk enough only for their own needs. Further we did not know of their custom which makes it anathema to accept milk without returning it, unless one does it out of need or donates it out of charity. That first day we had been fed by rich Megamicres who had voluntarily fasted. Those who fed us the following days were paid or were under some penalty and constrained to do so.

"But none of this troubled our mind at this time. After dinner, we left the room and went out to the large garden. It had twelve avenues covered above with tapestry held up by columns. These columns were of a design and structure that Vitruvius, the famous first century architect would never have recognized. They were beautiful however and well-planned. Next to each avenue ran another one equally wide but uncovered where elegant lawns were planted with whimsically arranged foliage, tiny exotic plants and exquisitely lovely flowers, all tastefully intermingled. Nor were these avenues separated as they are among us with hedges which restrict the view and deprive the eye of the beauty of the gardens on either side. Here only tall slender evergreens separate the avenues. These pines are laden with pine-nuts, a delicacy which the Megamicrans lacking our teeth, ignored until, much later on, we showed them how to prepare and enjoy them.

"A large open boulevard, four times larger than any of the other avenues was planted with trees, eighteen feet high, the tallest to be found in their world. Except for the pines, these are the only trees that bear fruit.

"And here live the serpents who feed on the fruit. The branches and foliage make a very comfortable resting place for the serpents which the Megamicrans consider their natural enemy. But they have been taught to leave them alone. They have also been taught that the trees are sacred and its fruit forbidden to any but the serpents. If these creatures' repose is troubled, they may descend from the branches and kill the Megamicres. The trees are regarded with awe and it is a whim of the wealthy to own a good number of these serpent-sheltering trees.

"They bear seven hundred and twenty fruits each harvest to provide each of the two snakes with two fruits daily. Each harvest consists of one hundred eighty Megamicran days. A Megamicran day is equivalent to twelve European hours.

"The serpents reproduce by laying eggs about the size of turkey eggs. These they vomit out a little while before their death. (When later I examined these creatures, I could find no sex differentiation.) They live twenty four Megamicran years (six of ours) and when they die, they simply fall out of the trees and are buried in the lime pits at the border of the garden along with the fruit skins and ordure. Thus these useless snakes are scrupulously cared for.

"In appearance, they measure three feet in length and six inches in diameter. Their skin is scaly and spotted. Yet they have a human expression, gentle and even seductive. A whistle they emit is so piercing that on hearing it, the terrified Megamicrans grind their teeth, feel their limbs tremble and their hearts freeze.

"One would surmise that the Megamicrans would hate these cursed monsters. The contrary is true. The fearful actually revere them. How often does helpless hatred become with time profound respect and often adoration! When a feared object may not be destroyed and the violent emotion of anger and hate is not purged, then that emotion becomes a heavy burden. That burden is then discharged by metamorphosing the violent emotion into a gentler one, like worship or adoration.*

"We left the garden after our stroll, charmed with the warbling of a thousand different species of birds. There it is a criminal offense to cage a bird. Megamicrans are sure that birds have language and some have succeeded in communicating with them. My own children were never able to do this.

"The outer door of the garden gave on a wide street and here the company took leave of one another. Our hosts invited us into their handsome open carriage. We saw no beast attached to it yet the Governor was able with some devices to make it move, go right or left and stop at will.

"All the rich here drive these carriages, charging and recharging them as we do clocks. They can take long trips since the terrain is flat and they need not trouble about obstacles and inclines. They need only take into consideration

---

* Translator's note: Compare with psychoanalytic concept of identification with the aggressor.

41

the weight of the passengers to determine what amount of power is required to keep the vehicle in motion.

"We drove to a wide street where shops devoted to every kind of art and craft lined both sides. I saw carpentry shops for woodworking and the construction of furniture. I saw tin factories, the shops of farriers, blacksmiths and locksmiths; places where implements needed by carpenters, wheelwrights, coopers and laborers were made and sold. I saw hatchets, saws, pincers, billhooks and edge tools. There were shops for the making of optical goods and medical instruments, others for making scissors and penknives, still others for diamond cutting and porcelain making. Special shops made sofas and chairs of velvet and cabinets of fine inlaid wood. Then there were the weavers, the toy makers, the manufacturers of glazes and enamels. The bookshops and stationers' stalls showed a profusion of paper, pens, inkwells, ink of every color, as well as manuscripts. Printing was unknown.

"Stores sold the syrups and essences that gave a thousand different flavors to the flour dishes. Glassmakers specialized in making lamps and lanterns with containers for phosphorus for the rich.

"Commerce is conducted by direct exchange or with money. Money is in the form of small ampules of phosphorus. One ounce of liquid phosphorus costs twenty-four ounces of red gold. One ounce of red gold costs twenty-four ounces of silver. Silver is the smallest coinage used among the Megamicrans.

"After my observations of their commodities, I concluded that the cost of living there is not high. Work opportunities are plentiful and only those are poor who do not wish to work. But these are few since the Megamicran hates nothing more than boredom.

"At the end of that beautiful and busy street, was a large plaza which we had to ascend since it was situated on a level higher than the street. Our carriage would have had difficulty making this ascent, though it was slight, had not the Governor, by moving a device, caused iron spikes to emerge from the wheels and prevent it from sliding backwards.

"We left the carriage to walk to the lumber yards where boats of every description were being made. We looked at the warehouses where carpets intended for every possible use were being fabricated; enclosed areas where cable and cordage of every degree of thickness up to an inch and a half were manufactured.

"We examined laboratories designed for physics experiments and for the study of mechanics; public schools for the study of pharmacology—these focussed on culinary aspects since pharmaceuticals were not needed by the healthy Megamicrans.

"The only method of obtaining credit by those who spend heavily is to mortgage their lands, houses and gardens. If they fail to meet the terms of repayment, they may lose their collateral. Or if the matter is disputed, an interest of no more than one percent on the amount owed is permitted. The payment of interest upon interest is not allowed, nor is compound interest permitted. The moral code there frowns on mortgages generally as tending to deprive heirs of their inheritance.

"The wealthy possess horses whose upkeep is extremely costly. They con-sume grasses, age early and die of biliousness. Presumably because of this bilious nature, they utter not a single sound in all their life. When the horse dies at forty-eight Megamicran years, he is buried in lime like all other animals.

"Back in our carriage, we came to a river which we crossed in a raft. We found waiting for us on the bank, a twelve horse carriage which took us to a palace. Here in a brightly lighted room, the abdala flanked by two alfas, greeted those assembled and seated himself. His whole body gleamed as it had when we saw him at the temple. We remained standing with the Governor who ad-dressed him in a very grave tone of voice. Later, I was to learn that the subject concerned our nourishment, and the abdala as head of the church had to be consulted about this matter.

"The abdala rang a set of chimes and shortly afterwards twelve mitred alfas appeared. An hour later, we were summoned back and the Governor was given his answer. We returned home. Our host seemed satisfied and they left us, this being the period of rest for all.

"Once alone, Elizabeth and I discussed our unusual situation. The matter of food was uppermost; our position as petitioners for food, our loss of self-esteem as recipients of charity and our image of ourselves as beggars, all this troubled us deeply.

"Though this was the time for rest, we found to our surprise that we were not in the least sleepy even though we were lying on very comfortable beds. We got up and began to study our new language.

"We did not see our hosts until the next day when they came to our room accompanied by many others of their household. After the usual fifteen minute concert, we seated ourselves at the dining table. We noted that our hosts' faces lit up with joy when ten polychrome Megamicres, sent by the abdala entered. Five stood behind Elizabeth's chair, five behind mine. They looked somewhat frightened but then cheered up when they were graciously welcomed. In one Megamicran day which consists of twenty hours, of thirty-six minutes each. we would be nourished by ten of these creatures. Because of the miraculous nature of our arrival in a chest whose roof had flown upwards into the sun, our persons had become the concern, not of the civil but of the religious body.

"The hierarchy begins with the supreme pontiff whom they call the Grand Helion or Great Spirit of the Sun. He interprets the will of their God. They believe he is powerful and immortal even though he had a beginning. He has a kingdom and jurisdiction as well over four large and four smaller fiefdoms. (His realm was very distant from where we found ourselves.) Each realm, republic

43

and fief has an autocephalus* in its capital city. These serve as ministers of the Great Spirit. And in each city, an abdala presides and reports to the auto-cephalus about religious concerns. It was after consultation with his auto-cephalus, that the abdala arranged for ten ecclesiastical prisoners per day to serve as our nourishers.

"The Megamicres, superstitious and religious, hesitate before any undertak-ing and seek religious advice. It is to the abdala they turn. His advice or oracle takes twelve hours of contemplation. God gives him this counsel when he is asleep. The pious abdala therefore must gorge himself with milk in order to fall asleep. The rich who seek an oracle, pay for these extra nourishers to provide the milk which puts the abdala to sleep. Sleep has the effect of aging the sleeper and contributing to attacks of apoplexy. Among the Megamicres, there are those who oppose the practice of drunken sleep and there are those who regard it as an example of piety. For our part, we were well served by the milk and by the flour dishes. We ate for ten, using five times as much milk as did the Megamicres.

"Fifteen days after we came to their world, as we were strolling with our hosts in the garden, we were astonished at the sight of a huge bird flying towards us. As it approached, we were even more surprised to see a winged horse, mounted by two Megamicres, stop at the garden gate. The Governor ran to greet them and we followed spurred by curiosity. The riders dismounted, our friend kissed the tip of the horse's wing and had him led at once to a special stable whose door he locked, after stationing two guards there.

"After a customary greeting of song and dance, the two horsemen and the Governor and his mate retired to his study for more than an hour. From there, they went to the abdala's palace, then back to a dinner to which had been invited the most distinguished Megamicrans of the city.

"We watched all this with attention but without understanding anything. We suspected however that we were the subject of their interest. They touched us all over as they carefully examined us. After dinner, the two travelers went with our hosts to visit the river where we had been discovered in our chest.

"On their return from the river and after the herbal messaging and perfumed vapors, the Grand Geometer and the Grand Geographer plotted the course of their return flight; the horse was led out up to the ramp, his wings released, the riders mounted him and flew off accompanied by the cheers of a huge crowd.

"When we learned the language, the Governor told us the visitors had been the royal secretary and his mate who had brought a dispatch from the King at Helion concerning us. It recommended that our needs be fully provided for in case the abdala skimped on our nourishment. The Governor was to provide more at the King's expense, until the oracle of the Great Helion was made

---

* Functions like an archbishop or a patriarch

known. Meanwhile we were to apply ourselves to learning the language as quickly as possible.

"While some intrigues went on about us as to whose jurisdiction we were to be under we lived quietly studying the language and often joining our hosts when they went swimming. We learned also to swim, though not underwater, and eventually the time came when we were grateful to God that we had learned this skill.

"Among the wealthy nobles were some who had built for themselves underwater retreats where they spent some of their hours of repose. I had a strong desire to study the anatomy of Megamicres to learn something about the mechanism which permitted them to breathe in water. I was curious too to learn about their method of reproduction. But the study of anatomy was forbidden absolutely. In line with this prohibition was their unwillingness to kill any bird or fish. Even when they went hunting, they would let the dog catch the game, bring it to them, and then they would caress and free it.

"The first thing we learned when we had an adequate knowledge of the language was that the people feared and hated us. This hostility was spread by those among them who still, against all religious injunction, believed in dual-ism, that is, that there are two Gods, one of good and one of evil. These believed we could only be two monsters sent by the Evil Power, enemy of God, from the dark abysses of the earth and that we were bad omens, not emanations from the Sun. Their reasoning was not to be mocked; it exists in our world too and often with harsher consequences. Luckily not all believed so. But the alfas also put us in a bad light when they refused to give oracles to poor Megamicres, protesting that our consumption of milk prevented them from having enough for them-selves. They aroused the poor, the superstitious, and the bigots. These latter are the most dangerous of all people in all the world.

"The abdala himself did not like us. He ordered that we should be provided for the period of only four harvests (one European year). During this time, we would be under church rather than secular jurisdiction. He thought the Great Spirit would not approve of the welcome we had received since we were of no use and were expensive to maintain.

"We came to the realization that to live happily in this world, we needed to make ourselves needed or at least very useful. We began to think along those lines."

FOURTH DAY

When the company met, Burghlei addressed Edward. "We are all grateful to you for telling us your story but I have one comment to make if I may. This morning, while I was taking my tea, I figured out that you had spoken three days and had covered only fifteen days. At that rate, as I calculated, it would take sixteen years to recount the events of eighty years. I'm not a busy man; I have the time, but what of the others? Maybe some of us might die before you get to the end."

"I'll keep that in mind", Edward agreed. "I can't tell what details are superfluous; to me they seem equally important."

"You must not leave anything out", Bridgent said firmly. "The honorable Count Burghlei will simply have to submit to his boredom for the next sixteen years if your story takes that long to tell."

"Please", Burghlei said, "you must not take my little jokes so seriously. I would even find the story instructive if certain questions, certain absurdities . . . ."

"Do you mean those flying horses?" Lady Rutgland inquired.

"Yes, yes", Burghlei said. "I would find those horses enchanting if only I could believe in them."

"I am sorry, milord", Edward said, "that you have some doubts. Had I known, I could have cleared them up earlier. Let me describe them in full.

"These four-footed birds whom I call flying horses resemble our horses only in that they can be saddled. They have small pointed heads. On them are bonnets like those of the Megamicrans except that they are three inches wider, somewhat higher on the head and permit only forward vision. Their mouths look like those of greyhounds.

"They are thin and light and covered with feathers. Their tail, forked and rigid, does not add to the speed of their flight but serves to keep the body in perfect equilibrium. Four wings attached to the top of their legs are short, thick and powerfully muscled. Two forward wings measure three and a half feet long; two rear wings are five feet long. The front wings push the air with vertical vibrations and in reaction, the earth sustains the horse's horizontal position. The rear wings beat the air behind horizontally, thus assuring forward

47

movement. Speed depends on the power with which the bony part of the wings can make the feathers agitate the air. These feathers are of different size, the larger ones supporting the smaller, while tiny feathers cover and protect the wings close to the body so no air can penetrate.

"When the horses draw back their wings, they contract; when they push them forward, they expand. The power of the leg muscles, like those of the chest, is perhaps a hundred times stronger than that of animals that do not fly. The extraordinary stability of the flying horse is due to the one factor; that the strength with which the wing beats the air equals the resistance of the air.

"These horses walk slowly and with difficulty on ground. They are not allowed to reproduce until they are too old to be useful for flights. They fly in a straight line over an area parallel to their body and never for less than a hundred miles. During flight, they can neither raise, nor lower themselves, nor make a turn.

"The animal is made to follow a pre-set path so that his master is always sure he will go where he wishes him to. The runway is a ramp, fifty paces long and two paces wide. One end of the ramp rests on the ground, the other is raised in proportion to the length of the flight. The rise never exceeds five feet. Five feet of height allows for a trajectory of a thousand geometric miles. This is how the owners of the horse assure themselves that the message will arrive at its destination. Riders are not always required. A letter fastened to the horse's neck will suffice.

"For example, if the king of realm 90 wants to send a letter to a neighboring king, he consults the chart to determine the distance. Then, knowing the greatest diameter of the curve for this straight-line distance, the course is plotted. He now knows the distance and the most direct route to his addressee. Nothing is easier than to adjust the ramp to the height necessary to follow that course and complete the exact distance required.

"Setting the direction by pointing the ramp is the task of the Great Geographer; raising the ramp is the task of the Great Geometer. These two lead the horse to the top of the ramp, untie his wings and immediately flatten themselves on the ground since with the release of the wings, departure is instantaneous, whether the horse is alone or mounted by one or two Megamicres.

"At the other end, the chief receiving the message, gets exact instructions for sending the horse back. Should the horse deviate from his course because of faulty direction, the Geographer would be condemned to die in prison; should the horse deviate because of faulty elevation, it is the Geometer who would have a like fate.

"The accuracy of the flight also depends on the placement of the horse's head. His nose must be perfectly aligned with his point of destination. To insure accuracy, the ramp is marked by a very straight green line. A long straight needle attached to the tip of the horse's nose must line up perfectly with this green line. Certainty is thus assured. Most important in this maneuver is a rod, marked off by almost imperceptible, microscopic points, which is used to determine the angle of elevation. All sovereigns who use this courier service possess such a precise measuring instrument. It is called the royal perpendicular.

"In this equestrian operation, one circumstance will be fatal. Should two kings send a message to one another at the same time and to the same place, the shock of the encounter would kill the horse and any of its riders. So far, this has never happened, but no means for preventing such an occurrence have been discovered. The horses' speed is uniformly forty miles an hour; the maximum weight they may carry is one hundred pounds. No trip may last longer than twenty-five hours.

"One Megamicre who made a twenty-five hour trip told me that when he was halfway through, that is at the highest possible elevation, he observed that the atmosphere, fifty miles below, was of a brighter red than his surroundings, nor was the heat greater or less. This would suggest that their sun is not fiery though it is the source of light."

"And now", Lady Rutgland said to Count Burghlei, "do these details about the flying horses satisfy you?":

"Marvelous", Burghlei replied. "I admit it."

Milady addressed Elizabeth. "I keep thinking how hard it must have been to learn the Megamicres' language without anyone there knowing English."

"Very hard", Elizabeth confessed. "Actually, it was our children who helped the most. The language itself is very difficult but one also has to have a very finely attuned ear." She sighed. "It takes an unbelievable amount of practice. The phrases are different perhaps because they are all vowels and there are not too many of these, and to catch meanings, one has to look straight at the speaker. Meanings depend on the gestures and the facial expressions. We finally learned it but even our children could not grasp all the nuances; they would have had to have the throats of nightingales. There is another factor which people our size could never master. The Megamicres use graceful movements which contribute more to meaning even than their gestures. But this grace seems to be related to their size. We are too big.

"We had less trouble learning the mute language they use in water. It is a gestural language perfect of its kind and capable of expressing everything visually and in pantomine. Naturally it is a poor language and has no intrinsic value since it depends on a give and take relationship."

"And now", said Bridgent, "I see Edward is ready to take up his story."

"Our good hosts", Edward said, "were our only real friends. We had some noble acquaintances but we could not count on them. And we were constantly aware that our fate depended on the decision of the Great Spirit at Heliopolis. His oracle would come at the end of the fourth harvest.

"Meanwhile, the time passed pleasantly enough. After each fourteen hour period of Megamicran time they rest for six hours. After this rest, the new day begins announced by twenty blows struck by the town crier. They all appear joyful and refreshed after time spent in bathing, grooming, perfuming and praying. We too followed their regimen but instead of resting, we kept busy studying the language and devising musical instruments. We sold many of these, receiving precious herbs in return. Our health was perfect.

"We noticed with surprise that among the multitudes, there were no old people other than the alfas. Nor did we see women or children. How could we have guessed that there is no aging, that there exists only one sex (although there is a kind of marriage) and that signs of pregnancy are nowhere visible?

"We continued with our language study and in the space of one month we learned to read and copy. As time went on, we learned the names of everything around us. Our teachers drew pictures of things that were not at hand. We wrote the English equivalents alongside their word sounds. Along with learning verbs and abstract nouns, we imitated their special gestures indicating praise, blame, admiration and the like. We copied their facial expressions, the movement of their arms, hands and heads as these represented their habitual customs of greetings, courtesies and manners. We were delighted to note the absence of masculine and feminine articles and of synonyms.

"In one year, we learned the meaning of twenty thousand words and we could communicate in more or less mangled Megamicran. It took us four more years to add another ten thousand words to our vocabulary, thus completing the total of their dictionary words.

"The first speaker in a company sets the conversational tone. This is the key note which determines the meaning of a great number of words. Once begun, this tone must be maintained. A change in tone may be regarded as rudeness or may occasion laughter. Usually the head of the household makes the decision regarding the tone. At court, only the king sets the keynote. Should he be busy elsewhere, half a day may pass without a sound being uttered. Communication then takes place in sign language.

"Some explanation of their language is required. It may be described as based on seven notes, unaccompanied, without restriction of time or beat and composed of arrangements of both dissonance and consonance. It has nothing in common with formal music which depends on counterpoint.

"Their music teachers are their poets. For them music is authentic poetry; it speaks to the soul. If God had a language, that language would be music. As we have said, their six vowels became forty-two by reason of the different coloration of each. These forty-two sounds are the base upon which a vocabulary of almost thirty thousand words is formed. Yet their language with fewer than half our words is richer than ours. The pauses, the gestures and the caesuras are worth thousands of epithets.

"Eloquence among the Megamicres depends on clear, concise and harmonious phrases and sentences. A gentle manner of address, together with the pauses and gestures affects the success of the orator. But they deplore an arrangement of words which will make their speech sound like a prepared musical composition. They say that the orator who sings rather than speaks does neither. Among us, speakers who employ such an artifice are like women who paint their faces.

"And in their music, Milords, you will find no libretto. Their great music teachers who are their great poets burst into laughter when I told them that we combine words with music. They found this bizarre. They asked if words added to the beauty of the music or vice versa. When the music is beautiful, I told them, one can forgive the words. But if the music is bad, the most beautiful words possible can only sound bad. They expressed pity for our sad situation.

"They are natural musicians and those who study it further are superlative. The ear is not the only conduit of music to their souls. They absorb music through the skin of their entire body. If they are dressed in cloaks or mantles, they take them off to fully enjoy the sound and to open every avenue which will allow the sensation to enter their being. Music assures them of the reality of the existence of their soul.

"This instinct for harmony makes them unable to understand why war is more natural to us than the exercise of intelligence, reason and peace. They can understand how one nation angered by another nation's actions might demand payment of damages or failing that even make war. But they can not see how men can attack one another in cold blood. Nor can they understand how men can blindly engage in carnage without knowing why they have been so commanded; nor why those who are massacred by a monarch's orders are then honored for it. Death in battle, they think, must always be an ugly death.

"I told them that a king has the right to send his subjects to war against their wish. They refused to believe that a king who should be like a father could possibly send his children to be killed.

"When I told them about the existence of slavery, they laughed out loud. This could not possibly be true, they said, for how can a person believe he is not his own master? To be a slave, he must be convinced he *is* one. It is a physical impossibility, like trying to place inside a solid globe, another one of equal size and nature.

"The Megamicres' world is divided into 80 monarchies, each of equal size; ten republics, also of the same size, plus 216 fiefdoms, both large and small which are under the sovereignty either of the monarchies or the republics. The kingdoms are not all equally wealthy because of their differing natural and industrial resources. However, money value, cost of living, the buildings and materials are everywhere the same, as is the language and religion. There is one religious head who allows each to think as he pleases about the nature of God and the soul, provided one follows religious laws and cult practice and does not try to institute any new religion.

"There is a general code of law but each sovereign has municipal laws. The criminal code differs throughout with regard to penalties but the definition of wrongdoing is everywhere the same.

"There is a Council of Five Hundred which meets once every twelve years. The king will call them when a new law is to be passed or an old one abolished. In cases in court, judges give their decision in writing without consulting with one another. Minority opinion judges are required to pay a heavy fine. In this world when cases are tried and lawyers present their sides, the voice of eloquence is very effective.

"We were understandably interested," continued Edward "in knowing how many months and years were passing in this world of perpetual daytime. From the commencement of our stay, we began measuring our time against theirs. Luckily we had our excellent watches. It seems to be man's nature to measure time. Just as the earth is the realm where the body of man roams and explores, so is the imagination the realm where man's sense of time may roam.

"We noted that the Megamicres are practical and sensible about the way they measure time. Our year begins quite haphazardly. The first of January bears no relation to the sun or the moon or even to religion. But their year begins on the day of sowing and ends on the day of harvesting. Their year has one hundred eighty days divided into four periods of forty-five days each, a season they call the greenwood fire. Each season consists of nine weeks of five days each. They call this five day period a pentamine, or a resurrection. Each day has twenty hours, each hour has thirty-six minutes, each minute thirty-six seconds. Each second corresponds to the beating of their arteries. Their clocks are called pulse watches, or pulsometers.

"The greenwood fire, the name given to a Megamicran month of forty-five days, has its origin in a green shrub without leaves or branches which comes out of the ground on the first day of their year and attains the height of a Megamicre in forty-five days, or in nine resurrections (pentamines) of the black worm. This shrub catches fire after the universal rain lasting two hours. As soon as its ashes cool, the shrub pushes back its root into the ground. Then at the end of forty-five days, it burns once more. The process is repeated and goes on forever.

"In their world, the rain falls four times every Megamicran year, or every four harvests. This rain does not serve to water the earth, but rather to refresh the atmosphere. Here is how it happens: three hours before the end of their month, a gentle wind arises. Within an hour, it becomes strong, then it calms down. Before it stops altogether, the entire surface of the earth is covered with fog, which rises gradually and eventually conceals the sun. Then a soft red rain begins to rise from the earth as if it were issuing from the many spigots of a man-made fountain. It continues to rise for almost two hours, never redescending. The air gradually clears, the sun shows itself again, and in ten minutes, the earth is as dry as it was before the rain. When this rain begins to fall, the

Megamicres come out of their homes to welcome it. They drench themselves in it, rejoicing in the delightful bath and in the beautiful spectacle it provides.

"Theologians have constructed the theory that the rain is earth's homage to the creator Sun. The water is earth's offering, hence drinking of water is forbidden to the Megamicrans on religious grounds.

"The five day period, or pentamine, which they also call the resurrection of the black worm, derives from the unusual fact that this insect emerges from its egg at the precise moment that the greenwood shrub catches fire. The cycle is continuous and infinite. The emerging black worm becomes a butterfly, the butterfly a dead insect, the dead insect becomes dust, the dust becomes an egg, and from the egg emerges the black worm. The time between each change always takes twelve of our hours, and the process goes on ad infinitum.

"The Megamicres' name for a day is "metamorphosis"; their days are called, in order: Chrysalis or Cocoon, Butterfly, Death, Dust, and Egg. The second and fourth days, namely Butterfly and Dust, are considered their days of sadness. On these days only do they cremate and bury their dead. On the day of the Egg, the newly adult Megamicres come out into society and are formally joined to their mates. The nobles do not always strictly observe these rules.

"We had been living among the Megamicres for eighty-seven days (our time) and we could make ourselves better understood by then, when the Governor's mate asked Elizabeth whether we could have children. Although Elizabeth was then pregnant, she pretended not to understand. The Megamicrans were as puzzled about our mode of reproduction as we were about theirs.

"You can imagine, Milords, the thoughts that crowded our minds as we thought of the event due in some months. Elizabeth's growing abdomen was a daily reminder. How would we feed ourselves? How would we bring up our child? We did not care to guess what the abdala, the Governor, the people, would make of it. All we could say at the end of our troubled discussions was, 'God's will be done. '

"An interesting and curious aspect of our situation was the utter absence of any sense of remorse or wrongdoing, even though we considered ourselves good and informed Christians. On the contrary, we even felt that we had been obedient to the will of God by becoming husband and wife. Nor was this the result of subtle and specious reasoning; we felt that an unknown power was producing in us, this sense of total security about our union.

"The more my wife's belly enlarged, the more attention she got from people who saw her. Those who liked us became alarmed; those who felt enmity were pleased. The doctors all concurred in the opinion that she had been attacked by a rare disease which eventually would be fatal. They disagreed on the nature of the disease but were united in the prognosis. The superstitious looked at her in horror, seeing in her condition which they regarded as a disease, the punish-ment for some enormous crime. She must have eaten some of the forbidden fruit of the serpents. They said that when a Megamicre ate one of their fruits, the serpents would leap from the tree, spring upon the guilty one, force him to the ground, and spew into the victim's mouth their poisonous wrath. In fewer than three of their years, the Megamicre would die, showing the same symptoms which Elizabeth did. Such persons would not be honored by cremation but would be thrown into the lime pits. Our hosts believed this and were grieved. They pitied Elizabeth, believing she had committed some crime out of ignorance. When I told them there was nothing to fear, they pitied me.

"The matter became serious enough for the Governor to seek advice from the oracle. Here was the answer: 'If God has not ordained that the healthy giant die of this or of another disease, the swollen giant will be cured before the third greenwood fire.'

"Here was a safe prophecy. Whatever the outcome, the oracle would not have lied. When this answer became known, everyone looked on me as a dead giant. No one expected Elizabeth to be cured. If she died, as they expected, I too would die, having undoubtedly partaken of her crime. And if I survived, they would perhaps arrange for me to die, if only to safeguard the glory of the oracle. But, had I had any fear for Elizabeth's well-being, this oracle would have given me some anxiety. But I knew that childbirth was not a sickness, and pregnancy less so.

"Toward the end of the ninth month, her belly had become so big that she secluded herself from everyone but our hosts. They came daily for long visits. They were in despair, so Elizabeth, always light-hearted, cheered them by singing little arias. Astonished and confused, they would leave, still believing that her end was near.

"I would take a walk by myself in the garden every day. This surprised everyone since, except for the alfas, no one let themselves be seen without their 'inseparables'.

"It often happened that I saw the serpents as I strolled along. At my appearance, they would retreat, whereas when they noticed a Megamicre, the serpents became bold and menacing. To be sure, the Megamicres were half their size while I was at least twice their size and six times as heavy.

"The first time I ventured to take one of the fruits, their hissing brought the gardener running, so I tossed the fruit quickly to the foot of the tree. If the gardeners had discovered my crime, I would have been in a bad situation.

"On the last day of their year, our hosts took leave of us to go celebrate their three day holiday of the harvest. An hour after their departure, my wife, who had been in labor for two hours, gave birth, first to a male child, and then to a female child. Despite my inexperience, I made an excellent midwife. Common sense and tenderness instructed me and I acquitted myself wonderfully well. There is no easier task when delivery is normal. Elizabeth most happily paid tribute to nature in this first delivery and for all the forty years during which she made me the father, each year of a twin, one a boy and one a girl. This occurred with all my children, and all my grandchildren, up to the sixth generation. Then an unexpected happening took place and nature adopted another system, another style of uniting my descendants. Still, the birthing continues to be uncomplicated and no descendant of mine has any idea that childbirth can possibly be hazardous.

"Presenting to their fatigued mother the charming twins, our feelings were too great to express. We were both ecstatic. The great emotion we felt could only be assuaged by a flood of tears. This gift from heaven lifted our grateful hearts to God. Our hearts, pure and innocent contained no idea that there was reason for remorse or that there was any taint of a religious taboo.

"I hastened to the bathroom, washed my infants, and took care of their needs such as any capable midwife might have done. Then I baptised them with water in the name of the Father, the Son and the Holy Spirit. I gave them the names of my father and mother, my dear parents, whom we had no hope of ever seeing again.

"Finally, I placed beside their mother these precious pledges of our tender love and eternal commitment. I covered them up to the shoulders with a cover of brilliant purple.

"In those first important, sacred days, we saw no one except our nourishers and the two valets who brought us the food dishes. We easily kept from them the sight of our new borns and also the decreasing size of Elizabeth's abdomen. Elizabeth was delighted when she found she had a supply of milk to nurse the babies.

"How can I explain to you, Milords, the astonishment. the incredulity of our two returning hosts, our guardian angels, when they saw, on coming into our room, the two infants lying on the bed, on either side of their mother, those beautiful children, almost the same size as the hosts themselves? They were speechless as they looked at James with his curly black hair like mine and at Wilhelmina, a beautiful blond like her mother.

"They ventured at last to ask us to explain this phenomenon. Elizabeth arose nimbly, and holding the infants in her arms, said 'These two creatures who were developing in my belly for three years, these are our children. I present them to you; embrace them and take them under your protection.'

"Our hosts then kissed our dear little ones a hundred times, put them back on the bed, sang and danced before us, and with joy shining in their eyes, kissed us over and over. They swore their most solemn oaths that they would always love our children as tenderly as they did their own. But their glances at Elizabeth's belly indicated their confusion at the manner in which two such well formed infants could have emerged without leaving any mark. We determined not to enlighten them but rather to imitate the actions of the Megamicres, who themselves maintain a reserve in all matters. So we pretended we did not understand the purport of their glances.

"The Governor did inquire how the children would be nourished since we would now have two more mouths to feed. In reply, Elizabeth began to nurse them. At this sight, the joy that overcame these noble friends cannot be described. Elizabeth, to complete their joy, had the infants suck five times, as is the Megamicran custom. Now the Governor and his mate were truly gratified, feeling that we concurred with them in religion and custom and, like them, we were truly children of the Sun.

"A moment of anxiety clouded their happiness when a few drops of milk appeared on the purple sheet. Elizabeth soothed their concern easily by explaining that in our nature, blood was red, milk white, contrary to the Megamicran physiology. They were pleased to be given this information and were relieved by the explanation. They also were pleased when Elizabeth explained that our infants needed to sleep in order to grow; they had seen the babies sleeping and were upset at this other strange characteristic of our race.

"They finally left with feelings of serenity and joy. We saw them as they went off in their carriage two hours later. We learned that the Governor had spent the intervening time in his office writing to the king of the realm, explaining the extraordinary circumstances of the supposed malady and of its result, the birth of two little giants who were being nourished by their mother's milk.

"Our hosts went to the abdala to tell him of the event and to ask for an oracle. This arrived the next day with a letter to be read to us, word for word. If the giant father of the new born has been provided with nourishment for them, he must acknowledge this benefit as a sign of the power of the Great Spirit. His minister expects him with his children on the day Egg of the following pentamine. Disobedience of this order must be punished by a lack of that nourishment. This was the content of the oracle, in which pride and ignorance were mingled.

"Speaking briefly with my wife, I said that even though the threat about her milk was clearly stupid, nevertheless we should go; we would otherwise be deemed ungrateful and blasphemous. I know that he counted on our obedience; if we had the temerity to scorn his oracle, he would arouse the religious bigots against us. Of all people, religious fanatics are the cruelest, the most implacable.

"The Governor was deeply pleased when I told him that Elizabeth and I would obey this command of the abdala. In turn, he arranged for Elizabeth to be spared the frequent ceremonial visits she had had to endure since the birth of our infants. It may be noted that they had slept a good deal until she weaned them. After that, they slept not at all, nor did any of my children for the rest of their lives.

"On the appointed day of Egg, we left with our children in a carriage, and in fifteen minutes were at the Temple. A large crowd, which had heard of the miraculous event (embroidered a hundred fold as it was told and retold) gathered to see us but were kept back by servants. People everywhere are curious to see some interesting sight. Later, they will report the event as they imagine they have seen it. They may go away as ignorant as when they came, but now they have the right to talk about it as bonafide spectators.

"The abdala awaited us, seated on a throne under a grand violet canopy. He was adorned with gold, wearing a mitre and gleaming slippers. Seeing that my wife's belly was no longer swollen but of normal size, he inquired how the swelling had subsided. She replied that her belly had held the developing babies she was presenting to the abdala. She told him courteously that they were conceived of me, that they needed to be nurtured for a length of time inside her body, that the possibility of having more depended on the will of God, that no, her husband would not bear children, of that she was sure. All this she told him in adequate Megamicran. From time to time, the abdala would lift his eyes up to the phosphorous globe and intone something in the nature of an affirmation to the Great Spirit.

" 'How do you think you will nourish these creatures?' he asked. "With my blood, which in my breast has become milk so I can feed them," Elizabeth replied. At these words, the abdala rose and sang a verse of an ancient prophecy. ' The blood, having become white as milk, will become a substance white as blood and we shall see issuing from the earth's recesses, an unknown and formidable race.'

"A hundred voices rising from the temple vaults sang the same words. We were surprised because they seemed to us to contain the truth. We shivered a little.

"The abdala asked if the infants would wake up and take some of his sacred milk. My wife seemed not disconcerted by this unexpected demand but said in a straightforward way, that she was sure they would, and would accept this favor with gratitude.

"I confess, my friends, that I was afraid that her words would be given the lie by the infants. In my heart, I accused her of overboldness. But both infants woke, sucked at the flaccid breast of the prelate for the prescribed five times and did not cry or protest. The entire assembly in the temple was struck with wonder, unable to interpret this event as a good or evil omen.

"Now the abdala touched a device with his foot; a door opened and he ordered us to follow him. We entered a sacristy which had a gold basin at floor level, filled with water. He had us immerse the babies up to the neck. Meanwhile a choir sang for five minutes. Four alfas then appeared to dry and perfume our poor little ones. To our great joy, they did not utter a cry. On the advice of the Governor, Elizabeth asked permission to kiss the sacred throat of the abdala. He granted this signal favor to both of us and after this, we took our leave.

"In every part of town, the talk concerned itself with the remarkable events, the birth of the twin, Elizabeth's return from sure death, the mystery of our origins and functions and especially the behavior of the abdala towards us and the infants.

"We knew, however, that the prelate's graciousness was not sincere; it was a calculated step. Had the infants refused his milk, we would have been dispatched as nothing less than children of the devil; it would have demonstrated

57

our difference from them and have increased the fear and hatred of the superstitious.

"Elizabeth was regarded more kindly; she was seen as the fertile producer of milk, but I was regarded as useless. That interesting part of my anatomy was only an ornament and until I too could produce, I could only be an object of scorn. But there was still some belief that eventually, my belly too would grow, and for this reason I was not entirely given up. The idea of two sexes is not an easy one to grasp by people all of whom are of one and the same sex. In time, they learned their error and accepted the fact that the laws of nature in our world differed from theirs.

"Throughout our stay at the Governor's, their house was always filled with strangers who came from far away to look at us and the children and to marvel at their birth and their size at birth, and wonder why Elizabeth's breast had filled with milk to nourish them.

"We found it a great burden. Fortunately the visitors who besieged the house were constrained by law and custom not to make inquiries. We did nothing to enlighten them. This is a precept which I always kept myself and impressed on all my children. I hope that our secrets continue to be kept. Silence being an article of religion of the Megamicres, our own reserve in not questioning or answering questions made them respect us. Nor did they by any ruse attempt to wrest our secrets from us.

"The nudity which is characteristic of them also guards their innocence and modesty. Clothing, which often makes a prurient imagination more so, is lacking here and so is any effort to have recourse to shameful fakery. The naked body, when it is a common, matter-of-factual reality, removes the need for deception.

"And now, Milords," said Edward, "I should try to explain more exactly the nature and upbringing of a Megamicran couple. They are two individuals engendered at the same time and born two months later at the the same instant. They pass their whole lives together and they die together. The parents engendered them as they were both engendered by their own parents.

"The Megamicran couple spend their first twelve years in a type of enclosure or cage where everything is provided for their needs. This cage is divided by a separation of wood or metal or strong willow wands. Each Megamicran has his own niche, though he may spend time in his mate's niche. They talk and amuse themselves, and they study.

"Raised in this fashion, seeing each other constantly, told from the beginning that they are to belong to one another, their affection reaches such a degree as is impossible for us to imagine. Their education too is designed to heighten their affection for one another so that when they are formally joined when they emerge from their cage, they are more than eager to be 'inseparables'.

"Megamicres do not believe in teaching their young anything for which they have no real inclination, since they believe that success will result only if the student has a genuine taste for the subject. The young are educated in religion, music, geography, civil and criminal law, and in the elements of all the sciences: physics, chemistry, natural history, botany and agriculture.

"They memorize a short religious catechism about which they may ask no questions for they are told that not even the wisest can understand the mysteries. They thus blunt any initiative and inquiry. These two creatures, united by nature, leave the enclosure only to become more intimately united, one spirit in two bodies. After leaving the cage, they are informed of everything needful except for the natural history of their birth. When they inquire about this interesting subject as children do in all worlds, they are told that curiosity is a crime when the subject does not directly concern them. They are told they were not involved in the birth process. This serves to rein in the curiosity of a child in whom a fear of crime has already been instilled.

"The engendering parents lead them to a table where they are allowed for the first time to eat with the rest of the family. They observe all and say nothing. The only thing which distinguishes them from the others is that they cannot exchange their milk. That occurs only six or twelve hours after they are joined.

"The two Megamicres are compelled by their very nature to love one another. This sentiment is brought to the highest level by their education. In this happy state they are then led by their parents into the chamber where they will seal their perpetual union. To one of them is said: 'You will have the right to command and dominate in the outside world. ' To the other: 'You will be in charge of the house and its maintenance, for you are more handsome than your sibling. ' Then 'Bring forth noble offspring and be one flesh to love one another always.'

"After the ceremonies, they are left alone, the parents never doubting that nature and instinct would do their work. The next day, the parents return, and if they are devout, they go to see the abdala to kiss his breast. Then the alfas lecture them on their religious duties, after which they return to their apart' ment. "At the end of two greenwood fires, they ask their parents to visit. They then deliver into their hands, two eggs the size of hen's eggs which have come forth simultaneously from their mouths. These eggs come out from a matrix in the breast by way of a passage between esophagus and trachea; it begins apparently at the opening of the upper stomach. The muscle, (like a ring), from which the eggs emerge first dilates slightly and then contracts after the ejection.

"The parents take these eggs with the greatest joy into a room where they are immersed in a red liquid in a basin. The liquid maintains an even natural heat. The incubation period lasts as long as two more greenwood fires, then the eggs are lightly tapped and broken, and two small Megamicres issue from them. If they are red without stripes of any other color, everyone rejoices. It can happen however, that one is red and the other is not. In this case, there is no rejoicing but embarrassment. The family must inform the abdala for reasons which I will tell you later. If they are of the same color though not red, there is neither rejoicing nor sorrow. Sterile by nature and hence bastard, they will find occupations according to their ability, whether in science or the arts or in trades. Those who are born multi-colored, also sterile, will serve to amuse others. These polychromes are brought up in the cage like the others until they are twelve, but they are given instruction only in religion and geography. They are sent out after that to work in suitable jobs, as farmers, laborers, or porters. They may be sent to offices where valets or servants are registered. In short, they work at jobs for which advanced instruction is not required.

"Megamicres," Edward went on, "know exactly when they will die. In our calendar, it is at the age of forty-eight after eighteen months of repose; in their calendar, the age is one hundred and ninety two, of which six Megamicran years are spent in retirement until death.

"Some of us here would consider it a misfortune to know; I think otherwise. Some think that death after a long illness is preferable to sudden death. They say that the illness gives one time to set his affairs in order. Agreed. But the Megamicre, knowing the date of his death, has his affairs always in order. Why does a person who wishes to be ignorant of the day he will die, find sudden death such a calamity? The Megamicre, knowing the date is fixed, does not have reason to fear its inevitability. We are in fact, cowardly enough to be glad of our ignorance, even though we are all certain to die. But the Megamicres thank God they know. We live each day in the shadow of death; the Megamicre is untroubled. The Megamicran couple leaves the world of society six harvests (a year and a half) before death and gradually arrives at that moment when they take their last nourishment from one another and expire. This, in brief, is the life style of the Megamicrans from birth. They live for 48 of our years without ever suffering illness.

"Among us, the life span is said to be seventy. You do not believe, I think, that we live longer than they do. Even without the three years in the cage, without the year and a half of retirement, they still have forty-three and a half years of active, healthy living. How many of us can count on so many active years? In our world, if we begin at age fourteen to savor life and end at sixty when our senses grow duller, only forty-six years remain. Throw away sixteen years lost in sleep and we are left with thirty. During these thirty years, we endure heat, cold, rain, wind, fog. We are subject to colds, toothache, and those ills we bring on ourselves through unwise habits in addition to those sicknesses which nature bestows on us from time to time, through no fault of our own. Add war, famine, and pestilence as well as many other misfortunes. Not a shadow of any of these sorrows ever occur in that other world, a world however, from which I was able to get out, thanks to God."

FIFTH DAY

They were all seated at the table when Countess Bridgent addressed Edward's father. "Does it seem to you, Master James, that your son committed a wrong when he married his sister?"

The old man replied wearily, "Milady, I try to be as faithful to my religion as I can. When I believe I have sinned, I go to confession. As for those faults committed by others, I can not be a judge. God's wisdom is beyond man's comprehension. I am not capable of reflecting on the subtleties of good and evil.

"The Creator's first precept was that male and female should be united; no qualifications were placed on it. Perhaps He needed to people the earth quickly. After that, limits were placed; then the church forbade marriage between relatives.

"In Edward's case, I would not classify his action as right or wrong. Even if his action were a voluntary, calculated one—which it was not—I can not call him culpable. Had he by specious reasoning or by wilful restraint of his natural instincts, chosen to live in celibacy, I believe he would be tacitly condemning the actions of our ancestors Adam and Eve."

"My dear James", Countess Bridgent said, "you have argued superbly. Even Rome would have to do some hard thinking here. And you, dear Wilhelmina, what do you say?"

The ancient mother spoke timidly. "You know, Milady, that I have limited experience and knowledge. Still I have always heard that a marriage which produces so many progeny must be one blessed by God. To think that through my two children, I have as many descendants as there are people in all England! I would beg your ladyship to make this news known to Rome. I hope that our Holy Father will find some way of conveying his benediction to our poor children. His blessing would make all the marriages valid and legitimize all the offspring. Because we must admit that they are all bastards and I feel terribly guilty."

"Please, gentlemen!" Countess Bridgent looked sternly at the young men at table. "Stop laughing!" She turned to Wilhelmina. "Let them laugh, dear friend. You are absolutely right. I promise to tell Paul V about this. He will do what he can to remove any obstacles on the path of salvation for so many people."

Lord Howard tactfully interposed a question. "Do you know, Edward, what area those eighty kingdoms and ten republics represent?"

"Each state, Milord", replied Edward, "is eleven hundred miles wide and eleven hundred miles long. About one hundred twenty million Megamicres live in each."

"Why, that number is about the population of China", Howard marveled.

"In that interior world", Edward continued, "there are as many marriages as there are couples, whether noble or bastard. Only the nobles, or reds, can reproduce. But of the fifteen pair they engender, only one or two pair are reds. These can reach the highest positions in society.

"The first born, if they are not red (but not polychrome either) are considered a privileged nobility. They usually occupy positions in the religious hierarchy except for the position of autocephalus which is reserved for a red. If a family has the misfortune to have not a single red pair, they have to leave their possessions to the nearest relative.

"Their ideas of nobility differ from ours. Since *all* Megamicres must perforce be born of reds, we would judge the offspring to be noble as well. Still no bastard ever aspires to be superior to a noble. Each knows his role. A red would never behave ignobly to a bastard nor would a bastard ever be impertinent to a red. Thus by mutual agreement, authority, respect and submission are maintained.

"With the privilege of procreation granted solely to reds, nature has prevented the proliferation of population with its attendant disorders. Their scientists maintain that in ages past, all Megamicrans could reproduce. Then their god, the sun, took a hand and limited this role to the reds. Red is said to be the sun's favorite color.

"On those rare occasions when it happens that of the new-born couple, one is red and one is not, the family must find a red to match their one as well as a mate for the bastard. In this unhappy situation, the family notifies the abdala who notifies other families who may be similarly afflicted. When a match is found for the red, a new family tree begins. Both sets of parents must turn over a fourth of their property and income to the children. Other benefits accrue from this pairing but the one grief arises if the birth dates do not exactly coincide. Then they will have different dates of death.

"Before I continue with my own story, I ought to tell you about the Megamicran modes of love making so you may compare them with ours.

"With us, taking a lover does not have to be a problem necessarily. But among the Megamicrans, it is a very serious matter. I do not speak of those rare cases when two couples fall in love with one another's mates. Even though society looks askance here, yet this double reciprocity can be full of delights. It may even be a source of mutually profitable business enterprises. But this turning around of four hearts and heads, completely and unanimously, occurs infrequently.

"Their definition of beauty, it should be remarked, is not confined to the lips and eyes and figure. It starts from the feet and goes to the top of the head. The face, as a portrait of the character and personality, will be seen as beautiful if those qualities are beautiful; if not, the face is considered plain, no matter how superficially attractive. It is not entirely so among us. Women here know how unfair it is to be put in the shade by the empty charms of some pretty little face.

"Until he knows that he is the parent of a pair of reds who will assure the family succession, no Megamicre ever reveals that he is beginning an affair. Once established, he can ignore gossip and be free to indulge his amorous fancies. But the object of his passion has to have certain qualities if he wishes society's respect. The lover must be already an object of admiration, established in his own menage, witty, talented and handsome. And no older than ninety six years of age (twenty four of our years).

"The enamored one gives parties, dinners, concerts and precious herbs to his beloved. He writes poetry or, if he cannot, he engages a poet to write for him. If the suit is successful, the admirer and his admired exchange kisses, intimate conversations and songs. When after dining, the ritual rubbing of the skin with herbs and perfumes begins, the 'inseparable' of the one being courted may go to sit near the 'inseparable' of the gallant and suggest that they engage in this ceremony together. The enamored one, though he is overcome with joy, pretends not to be and he engages in mutual skin rubbing with his beloved as if he were giving tit for tat. These games of love making are usually carried on by nobles who are already settled and have parented red heirs, as we have said before.

"High society finds it amusing to watch a green, yellow or other colored Megamicre engage in ardent courtship of a red. This mad creature spends money wildly in an effort to seduce the object of his love. The reds do not spurn their invitations and even invite them in return. Because the sterile colored Megamicres are harmless and often charming, they keep up the affairs. They explain that the bastard admirers are very wealthy. Whether this is true or not, no one knows; discretion is the rule.

"I myself found that the greens are more seductive than the reds. They are extremely pretty with their pink colored hair, nails, eyebrows, lips and tongue. Their eyes are large and well-shaped. The bright green pupils and red iris sparkle from out of the white background. They are well formed creatures who are also interesting to be with. They usually get whatever they want. The reds say that the greens are somewhat devious and hypocritical and that these traits may be observed from the way they dance. I did note that they do not dance very often. Mechanics and phonics (poetry) seem to be their special forte.

"Rich reds frequently entertain very pretty non-reds in their underwater retreats during their hours of repose. No one finds fault with this; no one sees these actions as scandalous. Each person may amuse himself as he wishes so long as he does not harm others.

"The time was now approaching when the answer from Heliopolis was due. The king of this state, called Realm One is also the supreme pontiff of the universal religion. He is a unique being whom no one other than his ministers has ever seen. He is described as a red of youthful appearance, without an inseparable, born when the world began. This would make him 32,634 Mega-micran years old. In his service are three hundred and twenty million ecclesiastics of every degree. The explanation for this number is the fact that the population contains so many non-reds. This pontiff-king has dominion over five hundred million souls when one includes the subjects of his kingdom.

"Besides being worried over the contents of the oracle to come from the Great Spirit, the problem of obtaining food for our infants who were now being weaned was a source of great concern.

"It was my habit always to pass an hour or two alone in the garden. Here I would give myself over to these gloomy thoughts. True, my wife had told the abdala she was feeding her infants with her blood and this mollifying statement had kept him quiet. But the time was near when her statement would no longer be true.

"The sight of those trees was continually before me; I coveted their fruits. One day, I yielded to this irresistible desire and plucked several of them. I was convinced they were not poisonous but rather good and nourishing. As I tore them off, the serpents hissed but then retreated. I was more interested in these huge figs than in the serpents. I bit into one. Finding their taste delicious, I continued to eat, using at last my teeth which had had no exercise for a year. Then I threw the skins at the foot of the tree and picked another. If I had obeyed the demands of my appetite, I would have devoured a half dozen. But I remembered the sleep which had followed the drinking of the Megamicres' milk the year before. I was also afraid of being discovered.

"I wrapped the fruit in my red handkerchief and made my way to the garden gate which was near our apartment. On the way, I encountered two poly-chromes who were hurrying to find out what the hissing of the serpents meant. When they saw me, they understood. In their opinion, the very sight of my face would be enough to anger the serpents. Had they known the real reason, they would have made things very bad for me.

"As soon as I entered our apartment, I told Elizabeth everything and put the fruits in front of her. Shocked into a thoughtful silence, she at last recovered and smiled at me, saying, 'It is not Eve who gives her husband the forbidden fruit this time.' She took the figs and ate them avidly. When she had finished she said, 'I want to be part of everything that happens to you, good or bad.'

"Ever since she had begun nursing the babies, she had been suffering from hunger and had lost weight. Our food supply had not been increased when we

64

became four. Our good host would not have allowed us to suffer but we were unwilling to impose on his generosity.

"Our nourishers arrived six hours later but we found we had not so much need for the milk as on the preceding days. We knew now that, however we obtained it, food would no longer be lacking. The next day, I made sure to make the caretakers aware of my presence when I went to the garden so they would know why the serpents were hissing. I ate one fruit and picked two for Elizabeth.

"In ten days, she had recovered her health with the daily diet of fruits which I brought her. She weaned the children and conceived again at the end of that day. I was always careful to bring the skins back to the trees. I also took fruit from neighboring gardens. By this time, we had gotten our hosts used to the idea of our eating alone. After dinner, our providers would leave and we would save some of the soup dishes for the children. Five figs sufficed to nourish them both and to substitute for the breast milk. We too were adequately fed now but we had always to be on guard for fear the supply would be interrupted. We were not happy about it.

"Finally, the messengers came back from the sacred court in Heliopolis with the oracle which would decide our fate. This oracle which was delivered to the abdala, decreed that the matter concerned civil not ecclesiastical authorities. We learned from our host who came at once to bring us the good news, that though the abdala was enjoined to keep watch over our behavior lest we do something to taint the religion of the children of the sun, we were nevertheless free of the jurisdiction of the religious authority. We were now required to go to the capital of the kingdom to find out how we were to be provided for. Before allowing himself to get too involved in our affairs, our king, the king of the Realm 90, wanted to make sure that his dignity would in no way be compromised by complaints or accusations made by the abdala.

"In the world of the Megamicres, the throne and the altar maintain a mutual harmony by adroit maneuvering on the part of both. The church wants the public to know that the monarchy is in accord with its policies. While their strength lies only in the power of the pen, the king knows well how formidable a weapon that can be. The king wants no encroachment however on his royal rights. He carries out his own policies but is careful not to speak against or issue decrees to irritate the church and provoke them to use the pen and influence thereby the masses to take their side. The government avoids quarrels by avoiding confrontation. Thus a surface harmony is maintained.

"Until we were to journey to the capital city, five hundred fifty miles away (a twelve day trip), the abdala continued to send the providers and I continued to take the forbidden fruit.

"A terrible accident happened during this time which had very bad consequences for us. Two violet Megamicres were attacked and strangled by

65

serpents in the garden of the mines president. (I had often stolen fruit there.) The accident threw the whole city in a panic. The last such recorded incident occurred eight hundred years ago.

"The parents of these violets hastened to consult the oracle. Their sorrow for their well-loved sons was considerably mitigated when the oracle declared the serpents' anger rose from the fact that their tree was neglected and in need of cultivation. The parents had feared that their children had been in some way culpable. Public opinion now favored the dead victims.

"The ecclesiastical court under whose jurisdiction any matter concerning sacred serpents would come, lodged a complaint against the president of the mines. They took testimony from witnesses, excluding any testimony which might be favorable to the accused. The ecclesiastical court explained that they needed no favorable witnesses in order to start criminal action. (The consistency of this reasoning speaks for itself!)

"The court found that the president of the mines had been guilty of neglect. His garden was to be sold at auction with one third of the proceeds going to the parents of the two violets. One sixth of the remaining two thirds was to cover the costs of the case.

"This judgment was lenient but the other lords and nobles who owned gardens considered it harsh. Supervisors of kitchen gardens whose office was a civil service one, were afraid that they too might go on trial if such an accident happened within their jurisdictions. More important was the fear that the serpents' anger could cost the lives of any or all of the Megamicres.

"Veneration for serpents arose from a belief in a prophecy which was said to be as old as the world. 'The well-being of the Megamicres will end when their wicked treatment will irritate a people of another species larger, stronger than themselves and nourished by them.' The Megamicrans interpreted the 'species' to be none other than the serpents whom they themselves were nourishing by caring for the trees which provided their food. The number of gardeners was redoubled and ordinances passed for the careful upkeep of the trees.

"Three or four days after this, Elizabeth and I, alone, saw two handsome reds coming towards us. Their manner was courteous but very sober. We learned that these two were the very ones who had first come upon us in the chest in the river. They had come to warn us, they explained, that we were in grave danger. I had been seen by the gardener of the city archivist taking fruit from the tree. The gardener had reported this to the president of the tribunal dealing with crimes. This president was none other than the grandfather of the two friendly reds who had come to us out of a feeling of affection as our rescuers.

"These young friends felt obliged to warn us even though they would be severely punished if it came out. The information had already been given to the abdala and we were to act with care. We were thunderstruck but we did not lose our head nor our courage. We immediately told the Governor who was painfully astonished by the detailed confession of my crime. He considered the situation, conferred with his mate, then decided on a unique expedient; he would go to the abdala and accuse me as one who had confessed a crime. He could not lie but he could keep to himself those facts that would be injurious to my case. Since the religious oracle of the Great Spirit had given up jurisdiction of our persons, he, the royal Governor would declare me prisoner and take responsibility for me. With our admiration and gratitude, he left at once to see the abdala and to denounce me as culpable to be kept prisoner in his home.

"The abdala, however, responded that he could have exercised this right, if he had been the first to report the crime. As it was, the abdala had a warrant ready to have his guards conduct me to the ecclesiastical prison. He and the Governor argued at some length but the abdala insisted that since I had disobeyed a law involving a religious matter, I was subject not to civil but to religious law. The case was referred to the College of Jurists, eleven red couples who passed on matters of jurisdiction, from which there was no appeal. These learned masters of jurisprudence listened to both sides and handed down their opinion in writing. Six decided in favor of the abdala's contention, five for the king's. The five had to pay the usual fine which is required of losers and the case was decided. The Governor's demand that he be allowed to escort me and to see I was well-provided for in prison was unavailing.

"Our friend returned with the news of our cruel sentence. He also sent a courier to the king and the prime minister asking for help. The answer did not arrive until three pentamines had passed. Our Governor's request that the winged horse be used as courier was apparently not heeded. He assured us that the king would not abandon us, and that my wife and children would be cared for by him and his mate. At this, Elizabeth burst into tears and declared that as an accomplice, she would accompany me to prison. She gratefully accepted their offer to care for our innocent children. The Governor wanted to bring us to the temple and hand us over since he did not wish to have the abdala's guards come to his door. We agreed and set off. He left us with the guards after embracing us warmly.

"Four multi-colored Megamicres then came to bind our feet with cords and thrust us into a prison which was to be extremely uncomfortable for us. It was only four feet in height and six by six feet in size. The floor made of wood, served as our bed. We could only crouch or lie supine. Without pillows or books or writing materials and without any visitors, our situation was painful. Once a day, five rough inmates came to provide milk for us and to bring the five soup dishes, all of them having a disagreeable taste.

"No comfort was permitted; we had no furniture of any kind. The enclosure was subjected to perpetual daylight. Our only solace was in being together. You can imagine, Milords, how time dragged. We were uneasy about our children and wondered whether we had sinned in giving them life. We wondered how they would survive without us in a hostile world.

"Delivered over to the arbitrary superstitious cruelty of a prelate jealous of

67

this power, and to the hatred of a deluded people who believed us guilty of the death of the two Megamicres strangled by the serpents, we could not hope for pity. Rather we would provide a sacrifice to calm the people who feared the anger of those snakes.

"Our sufferings, the tedium and our anxiety made us wonder if we were going mad. And the pitiless perpetual daylight worsened our condition. Tears would come to calm somewhat the cruelty of torture.

"Man being by nature a counting animal, we counted our days by the appearance of our bad-tempered nourishers. We better understood now why the name of 'Eumenides' was given to the Furies. By terming the Furies 'Eumenides' (which means well-disposed or gracious), it was hoped to propitiate their wrath. We too had to propitiate our providers, bad-tempered as they were. We depended on them for our survival.

"On the day called 'Dust' of the third pentamine of our stay—we had spent thirteen indescribable days already—, a gray-brown Megamicre opened the door of our prison and ordered us out. We followed him, walking on all fours like animals. At the end of the corridor, we tried to rise but our legs gave way. The gray-brown ordered some polychromes to open a room to which we dragged ourselves. It was a large bathing room filled with Megamicres of every color. When we came in, they all took to their heels. This precipitous flight of the prisoners impelled us to laughter.

"It is not uncommon that when we pass suddenly from a condition of turbulent feeling to one of relative calm, the first things we see in our new state, provoke unexpected reactions in us. A stone hurled into a stormy sea has no effect on it. The same stone thrown into a quiet pool forms circles which extend to its very edges. The sudden flight of these multi-colored inmates made us laugh. We were pleased that we had not lost that sense of humor which distinguishes man from beast.

"A half hour in the bath restored our strength enough so that we could walk out into the courtyard where an open carriage awaited us. We got in accompanied by two couples who sat facing us while four polychromes sat behind between the wheels. The gray-brown without his inseparable had a seat behind the coachman.

"Eight horses harnessed to the coach moved at a slow pace through the town. An unruly crowd followed us to the outskirts of the city with shouts, insults and curses. After five relays to change horses, we arrived at a hotel. There, the gray-brown standing with a yellow whom he had called as a witness, read a statement: 'You are hereby forever banished from the diocese of the abdala of Alphapolis. If you are ever found there again, you will be imprisoned for life.'

"Then the gray-brown went away and the yellow said in almost identical words that we were banished from the diocese of Gamapolis, apparently the town where we now found ourselves.

"We tried to rent a room from the innkeeper but he turned his back when he learned we had no money. We went out and began to walk, following the main highway. No one had the insolence to follow us. The rabble who had witnessed the treatment accorded us seemed frightened of us.

"Here we were, free after a fashion, poor as painters, homeless without our children, obliged to die of hunger since we could not eat the fruit we saw on all sides, the fruit which had brought about our misfortune. We were not yet ravenous enough to succumb. The thought of going back for our children was frightening remembering the dire punishment, the merest thought of which made us shiver. We entrusted ourselves to God's providence and pursued our way.

"Everyone we encountered slunk off as soon as they saw us. We passed through several villages, however, without being insulted and at the end of five hours, utterly exhausted, we reached a hamlet. It was the day's end we knew, because we heard the trumpet announce the hour.

"We needed rest and food but had no means to obtain either. We did encounter a red couple who were taking a walk towards the river. We stopped and exchanged courtesies. Tired and hungry, we longed to be offered rest and food but we should have had to ask, to make our wants known, in short to beg. This we could not do.

"We then made our way to a grove of trees we had seen at a distance where we hoped to rest, face down, to avoid the rays of the sun. I pulled a nut from a tree and broke it open with a stone. Inside, I found hard yellow berries and I broke these open as well. Each held a quantity of oily seeds, pistachio green in color, which tasted like pine nuts.

"We spent three hours cracking them and eating them. Luckily our teeth were strong because the seeds, though edible, were quite hard. We had never heard of these nuts before but we guessed that the cooks here could make some excellent dishes of them by expressing the juices of their seeds.

"After a rest of five or six hours, we felt refreshed and able to continue our travel on the main highway out of the borders of Gamapolis. We hoped we would not be banished from the next state.

"We had been walking for almost an hour when we heard loud sounds coming from a distance. We turned to look. A convoy of carriages riding post haste was approaching. We thought of seeking a hiding place; we were ashamed of being seen, if the truth must be told. We concealed ourselves behind a small rise as best we could. To our surprise, we observed that the carriages, twelve in all, had stopped at the spot on the highway from which we had run to hide. Two reds from the first carriage were running about, looking from right to left around the very hillock where we were.

"Elizabeth was the first to recognize them though they were nude, not wearing the cloak they usually wore on state occasions. She ran out from our shelter and I followed. They had seen us. They ran towards us and leaped on our necks, speechless not only because they had been running but even more with the joy of finding us.

"We ran back with them to their carriage. Arriving breathless, we beheld our children, James and Wilhelmina. We thought we would die of joy on seeing them both. They were seated on purple cushions being held by four green Megamicres. Elizabeth fainted and I thought I would too, except that I kept my head lowered to avoid losing consciousness. We both recovered and took the places of the greens, who took another carriage.

"The Governor ordered the postilions to stop at the best inn in the first city we came to. In less than half an hour, we were there. No one had spoken; we were too overcome with happiness as we covered with kisses and embraces our smiling little darlings whom we had lost hope of ever seeing again.

"After we were alone in a large beautifully lit chamber, our host said, 'Nothing could have been crueler, more inhumane and extraordinary than the treatment you were put through by the abdala.' Then he told us of the events following our imprisonment, prefacing his remarks by saying that the least the abdala could have done was to postpone our arrest until he had the king's report if only as a mark of respect. Further, persons who are exiled have the privilege of returning home to gather up their belongings before being forced to leave. But the abdala showed not a zeal for justice but evidence of hatred. He cut the food allowance, did not allow bath privileges which the most ordinary inmate is allowed every five days. 'I knew none of this', added the Governor with outrage 'until yesterday, a half hour after you left the city. My hands were tied until the courier to the king came back. The king disapproved of the abdala's action and ordered me to conduct you to his court, not as guilty persons but as persons of rank whom he wished to have near him. I then went to the abdala and read out in public the king's letter so all would know. The abdala said he was not concerned. It was up to me now to carry out the king's commands.

"'I took steps to find out what road you were taking and I brought everything along you would need, carriages, servants, your possessions and most important, your children. I would urge you to let us take care of them. No one in the world is a better friend to you than we are and we love your children dearly. We shall send them back whenever you wish. They shall lack for nothing in the meantime.'

"Restored to life by the Governor's account even though we would be parted from those dearest to us, we told him about our experiences. When he heard that we had eaten the seeds of the anaze tree, he was troubled. Megamicres do not dare to eat these because they cause a fatal colic in them. Perhaps, be reassured himself, our greater size protects us from these effects.

"I did not need to ask Elizabeth how she felt about entrusting our children to the Governor and his inseparable. We had no doubt that in them we had unfailing and generous friends.

"We were deeply pleased when we learned that our coach held all our possessions from the chest, as well as our watches, rings, portraits, and tools and equipment, both for painting and for making musical instruments. He introduced us to the twelve colored Megamicres who would take charge of our expenses on the road and who would deliver us to the king's courtyard.

"In addition, he gave us letters of recommendation to his friends, the greatest of the nobles in the capital. He told us that the king of Realm 90 was a most generous and affable monarch, well loved by his subjects, well educated in the sciences, and on the throne from an early age. He was now seventeen years old. He and his mate had not produced a red couple as heirs but they had fourteen more opportunities. This king was furthermore extremely wealthy since he came of a thirty-two hundred year old lineage.

"In finally parting from us, the Governor warned us not to repeat the crime we had committed. It was considered to be the gravest of all since it carried with it the destruction of the whole population which depended on the good will of the serpents for their salvation.

" 'When I consider, dear friends, that your future in this world of ours depends on making for yourselves a firm base of acceptance and love, I am deeply troubled. I can not see how this will be possible. You need to be nourished but you can not nourish others. Generosity is a constant virtue, true, but it prefers to find different objects or persons on which to be bestowed. And the object himself would be irked always to be the recipient of generosity. The fact that you reproduce, makes your situation even more precarious. Consider also that our people do not know you nor where you come from, nor of what use you can be now or in the future.

" 'Our theologians say you can not be our brothers and that you are monsters sent to our world to punish us for our sins. Even I, I admit it, find it unlikely that people who have not been endowed by their creator with the simplest benefits can be loved by their God. And if God does not love you, how can you expect his children to welcome you? They can only fear you.

" 'I foresee with a bitter heart that very soon you will be required to leave. There is only one way to avoid such misfortune: you must use all your ingenuity to discover the secret which will make you useful in our world, even necessary. Then it will not be so difficult to muzzle religion or reduce it to silence—or even make religion speak on your behalf.

" 'Farewell! I have opened my heart to you and I feel more peaceful. I would wish to have you live among us, loved and respected. Write us often.'

"Dissolving in tears, we embraced them tenderly and in gratitude. We placed our children in their arms. The sight of these four well-loved creatures consoled us somewhat, since we knew they were bound to one another in a nuturing love.

"In eight days, we were in the capital of Realm 90."

SIXTH DAY

"I was thinking, cousin", Countess Bridgent addressed Lady Rutgland, "that the Megamicran parents might have had some plausible reason for calling their non-red offspring, bastards. Some physiological reason, perhaps. I wonder if color depends on what their parents were thinking at the time of conception."

"Do not ever believe that", Burghlei broke in. "The mind has nothing whatever to do with the foetus."

"But those birthmarks we sometimes see on babies", Milady protested.

"A popular misconception", Burghlei said positively. "Anyone who believes the imagination can produce a visible mark is mistaken. And", he added, "anyone who thinks he can read character in a person's face is also mistaken."

"What annoys me, Milord", Lady Rutgland said impatiently, "is your tone of voice. How can you be so positive? You should learn more about the power of the mind on the body. Look at people's faces. You have seen them grow white with fear and red with embarrassment. And what about expressions of hatred or horror or approval? The mind can not operate outside of man, just as man is nothing without the mind. The two are interdependent; they make up a unit.

"Because the scientists do not yet understand the connection, they prefer to deny rather than to deal with the problem; it's much easier that way. They also say that metaposcopy, that study of character by reading faces, is a deception. I do not think that is always so. How do you account for the fact, my dear Burghlei", she added mischievously, "that everyone who looks at you knows what sort of character you have?"

"I didn't know that". Burghlei was taken aback. "May I ask what my unsuspecting face is telling the world?"

Lady Rutgland smiled. "That you are a very likable fellow, after all, Milord."

Countess Bridgent asked the company. "And what did you think of Edward's offering the forbidden fruit to his wife?"

Dunspili answered. "I thought it very amusing. I was reminded of a writer who insists it was the fig, not an apple, that Eve gave to Adam."

"All we are told in the Bible", said Lady Rutgland, "is that Eve gave him a fruit. It could just as well have been a pineapple."

73

Count Bridgent turned to Edward. "You arrived at the capital in good health, I presume."

"Yes, Milord. The traveler finds every convenience. The highways are beautiful; there are inns every ten leagues and post horses are always available. We covered seventy leisurely miles each day.

"The capital Poliarcopolis presented a magnificent sight to our eyes. We descended very gradually for twelve hundred feet. At the end we were only twenty-four feet below the level of the surrounding countryside. The downward slope is flanked on either side by red marble staircases of four hundred steps with one inch risers, for the convenience of foot travelers. Around the capital, the walls rise twenty-four feet and may be entered by no less than ninety-six gates. At the base of the walls, the government has built almost five thousand homes for the poor.

"A wide esplanade winds around the whole city, serving as a quay for its large canal. The canal is a perfect polygon of twenty-four angles, each angle marked by a single-arch stone bridge. To the left of the bridges, pedestrian walks have been built; to the right and a little lower are roads for vehicles. On the other side of the canal, the quay makes a circle from which radiate ninety-six avenues which divide the sectors where the population lives and works. Each avenue ends in a plaza with arcades, sparkling fountains and shade trees. Statues of the royal couple in gold are mounted on cenotaphs. A weekly market is held in each square.

"These ninety-six quarters are the suburbs of this magnificent city. In each quarter, ten thousand infertile Megamicres live comfortably and work at their trades. They have access to the twenty-four temples below by means of a stairway for each quarter. The clergy lodge in the temples and the nobles and wealthy live in palaces, each separated from one another by little woods in this huge area.

"Bordering this large open area, one can see, towards the city's center, palaces rising twenty-six feet high overlooking the shops, houses and squares, bridges over canals and many intersecting streets.

"Standing by itself on a thousand foot square rises the royal palace. Within its circumference can be found all that art and nature can combine to provide the palace and its grounds with luxury and magnificence to enjoy life's pleasures.

"As we entered the royal courtyard, two dozen polychromes had to push back the crowds who gathered there, agog to see creatures of our species. These multi-colored Megamicrans conducted us down several stairways to a room where they left us. Here four noble reds received us graciously and presented us to the royal couple.

"They were seated on a wide sofa and both looked at us intently. Their bonnets flashed with fiery gems; sheer cloaks fell to their heels over a bare-shouldered tunic of a green gold cloth. The monarch who wore a gleaming plume above his head-dress was leaning back; his mate sat at the edge of the sofa but with a seemingly nonchalant air. Their attendants stood motionless, keeping their eyes fixed on us.

"At a gesture of the king, a piece of instrumental music sounded. Its strains gave us a feeling of joy and courage. A second gesture brought a vermilion Megamicre forward. With a serious mien, he read a speech to us which said that we were now in the presence of the king who had sovereignty over our persons and our life. We were to answer all questions exactly and truthfully. These were the questions: Who are you? Where do you come from? Who sent you? How did you get here? How do you plan to get back? How is it you can not provide for yourself? Why did you not bring the milk for your sustenance? How do you expect to be fed? Do you worship God? Did that God create you? What is your religion? How old are you? How long do you have to live?

"Other questions concerned our children, our method of reproduction, our plans for the future, and the most important question as to why we violated their laws by eating the forbidden fruit and thereby provoked the anger of God against a people who had treated us well.

"I was given the paper on which the questions were written out so I could answer them all. The same vermilion took down my replies in short hand.

"My answers gave the history of our experiences from the time of the shipwreck until our rescue in the river. We did not know our way back but would gladly return if they showed us the way, we said. I also described our life on the convex part of the earth, our belief in the one God who had created us all and our conviction that God had intended his creatures to enjoy the fruits of the earth. We never thought we would be envying the lot of the cursed snake, a creature without a soul, whom the Megamicrans fear. True, we feared God but only because we first loved him. We could not love God simply out of fear.

"As for the future, we did not know how we would live. We were fashioned differently being of two sexes with only the female having breasts for the nourishment of the young.

"We offered our skill and knowledge which might be useful to the state. We would be happy to contribute to the glory of the benevolent monarch. We also hoped to convince him that the fruit is a suitable food for creatures like us and that we would not offend God or Nature by partaking of it. We would however rather die than have any harm befall our benefactors. At some future time, they might believe that the serpents, who do not worship God and are not reasoning beings, are not only useless but the most formidable enemies of the Megamicrans. This was my explanation, Milords.

"Accompanied by beautiful music, we were escorted to an upper chamber where we found every comfort including our belongings. Poor as they were, they were precious to us.

"The polite Megamicre who had conducted us to our apartment informed us that the king had arranged a hundred providers for us. He had sent back, for the nourishment of our children, those providers who had accompanied us here. We were also told that five soups of the finest quality in addition to the necessary flowers and herbs would be served us daily. We would not hear from the Great Spirit at Heliopolis for some time, he said. In the interim, we were to make no attempt to eat any of the sacred fruit on pain of death.

"Left alone, Elizabeth and I congratulated ourselves on our present good fortune. I was well pleased with the answers I had given the king inasmuch as I had not lied about anything. Now we had to put our minds to work to see how we could make ourselves, if not necessary, at least not useless.

"Our providers took care of us admirably and our soups were delicious. We recognized that we were mendicants who did not have to beg. It often happens at court that beggars, never called by that name there, actually forget they are indeed beggars.

"I passed the time in writing and Elizabeth studied the mandolin, a skill at which she became marvelously proficient in time. We had not asked permission to go out. Elizabeth was by now getting close to her confinement. Seven months had already passed. Our only grief was missing our children.

"We did not want to have visitors though we could have had many. It seemed wiser that people should talk little about us at this time. Though we were well-placed now, we felt out situation was still precarious, and being at court, we feared the envious and we dreaded traps. So we kept to ourselves as we awaited Elizabeth's delivery time. Meanwhile our polychrome servants entertained us delightfully.

"But one day we were pleasantly surprised by a visit we never expected. The same two red Megamicres who had discovered us and saved our lives and then warned us of the abdala's action, came in singing and dancing. After the warmest greetings, such as I can leave you to imagine, they told us that the Governor had become a great friend of theirs, had procured the position of Chief Gardener here at Poliarcopolis for them and they had been settling in this past pentamine. I could hardly wait for news about our children.

" 'How is the Governor?' I asked first, out of politeness. 'And how are our poor darlings?'

"They assured us the Governor was well and the children even better. They were the delight of the whole family who called them 'little giants.' They added soberly that though the children appeared happy and well-nourished, they had not grown much.

"When we laughed at their solemnity, the couple looked surprised until we explained that the rate of growth was much smaller among us and that the children would not attain adult height until sixty Megamicran years had passed. They now were only four of these years.

"They wanted to deliver the letters of introduction the Governor had given us to the nobles here but we said we would wait until after Elizabeth had given birth. She would not be able to make return calls in her condition.

"We also learned that our habit of reserve was regarded as praiseworthy by the king and his counselors. A request for an oracle had already been sent by them and a decision was hoped for which would allow us to settle down. We would bring enlightenment and information, it was believed, for the public good and to the advantage of the realm. Our friends added that persons like us could initiate an epoch that would make this monarch's reign an illustrious one.

"We were deeply pleased that we had friends like these at court. Nothing argued better for our future. The Governor, we felt, had managed to assure himself that we would have good friends here.

"My wife was happily delivered of a twin, a blonde male and a brunette female. I baptised them and two days later, she began to nurse them. The king wished to see the new-borns and for the second time, we were led into his presence. They caressed the infants and were pleased to see Elizabeth nurse them with what they called her blood, even though we assured them it was milk, though white. Smiling, the king then said that our blood must be made of milk, since it was red like their milk. The physicians present agreed with him. I said that color was not a determinant and that I could argue equally well that the Megamicres' milk was blood, something I did not believe. The physician said I was using sophistry; that I did not know the first principles of color origin.*

"I politely disagreed saying that color did not determine substance and I would be ready to argue this point before his colleagues. The king indicated he would like this questions discussed openly and he asked his physician to think about such a debate.

"We now made the acquaintance of the important personages to whom we had letters from the Governor. Had we introduced ourselves earlier, our reception might not have been so cordial. Now, however, we were on good terms with the king and had a position of sorts. As often happens, the great lords are eager to serve you when it appears that you do not need them.

"They paid us so many visits that we had only the hours of repose to ourselves. But we continued our practice of keeping to ourselves as much as possible while we waited to hear from Heliopolis the outcome of my answers to their questions.

"Meanwhile, I discovered a way of providing nourishment for my wife who lost weight when she was nourishing the infants. I asked our friend the Chief Gardner to provide us with a quantity of those pine nuts of which I spoke to you, Milords. In his position, he could get them easily. These were plentiful and cheap and were bought mostly by artisans to make alkali for the use in dyeing carpets.

"Crushing, cooking and diluting the seeds, I concocted a syrup which proved

---

*Translator's note: Casanova here indulges his penchant for using ancient Greek —in this case, "Chroagenesis".

delicious and nutritious for Elizabeth and in later years for all my daughters when they were nursing. Taken at other times, however, this syrup caused indigestion. Taken by the males, it caused a very dangerous effect, the more so since its ingestion would only make them laugh. In time, I forbade the syrup to all my males and you will note that I actually had to include this prohibition among my religious precepts. I knew that forbidden fruit is very tempting but luckily the effects of taking the syrup showed. Embarrassment and shame at discovery had more effect than any conscientious scruple.

"Eight or ten days after the dialogue with the king's physician, a green beadle came to invite me to a meeting of the College of Physicists. He left a notice of the meeting and departed, after skillfully executing a dance, pirouetting five times on one foot with great charm. On the day of the Egg of the following week I was transported to the College by a handsome carriage which the king had provided for my use. In a large room, beautifully lit by a hundred phos-phorus torches, all the scientists were gathered: physicists, chemists, engineers, doctors, botanists, mathematicians, apothecaries and cooks. All the learned men of the city were present. Besides them, the autocephalus came and after him, the king.

"After each head of the various branches of science made a speech, I was called on to speak. I spoke at length in very simple terms and with illustrations about color. The gist of it, was that color has no quality in and of itself but is a property of light. I lectured on the principles of optics, the effect on objects of refraction of light, of reflection, of the speed of light as colors are perceived by the mind. I spoke about the fact that objects do not have intrinsic color. I ended my discourse by saying that the differing appearances of color of our blood and milk do not affect their substance and function, that we shared the same qualities and that we were all true brothers.

"Our friend the Chief Gardener came to visit the next day. Everyone, he said, wanted a copy of my dissertation and the scribes were busy working on them. He congratulated me and said he would send one to the Governor.

"When the oracle finally arrived from Heliopolis, the king summoned us and read it aloud. We would be required to prove the divinity of our mission by a miracle, the validity of which would be passed on by the College of Physicists and it would then be decided if we could be useful. A fuller explanation of our religion was expected without however our having to reveal any mysteries if these are considered secret. Finally, if we could stop the hissing of the serpents, we could take their fruit. From that time on, we would no longer be permitted legally to suck the milk of the Megamicres. After a superb tone poem by an excellent orchestra and after the distribution of flowers, the meeting was over and we returned home.

"Our friend the Chief gardener was there to invite us to dinner at his home the next day. The dinner was a brilliant affair. All the nobles, friends of the

Governor, were assembled there. Among them was the brother of the autocephalus elect, and heir to the post upon his brother's death. But the latter,
over-zealous in pronouncing oracles was always in a drunken sleep. The
brother, who was also a dinner guest, was fearful that his brother might die
before his time, of an apoplexy and that the post of autocephalus would be
granted to another by the king.

"We had already left the table and were awaiting the distribution of the
perfumes when a blue (the color of sad news) Megamicre appeared to tell this
brother that the autocephalus elect was dead. The news struck the brother and
his inseparable like a thunderbolt. We tried to console them with the usual
comforting words but the grieving pair took leave of us with a mournful song.
We accompanied them so as not to leave them alone with their sorrow. It is
otherwise in our world here when friends, on the pretext that they can not
endure your suffering, abandon you in your grief. There the whole company
went along to the home of the autocephalus where we saw desolation and
despair depicted on every countenance.

"Six physicians of the highest rank, two greens, two jonquils and two lilacs
were examining the autocephalus who was not quite dead. Relatives and
friends sprinkled their milk on the dying man; his mate was dissolving in tears
as she gently massaged his body. The doctors, using incomprehensible scientific
terms, gave him no hope. In less than an hour, they expected his end.

"I asked permission to help and my friends told me I could do anything I
thought might succeed. I then asked Elizabeth to wait for me; I would soon
return. Once at home, I took my surgeon's instruments, some dried flowers and
told the most faithful of our nursemaids to care for our babies in case I should
not return for eight hours.

"The people had barely noticed my departure nor my return. I listened
silently, like the others to what the doctors were saying. The lilac doctor, after
having gently tapped the body in five different places, called his colleagues.
They did the same, then sadly asked for writing materials. That said everything. The mate now gave free rein to a torrent of tears. The certificate of death
was written and then signed by all six. Two theologians present declared to the
six alfas who were sitting quietly in a corner that the autocephalus designate
was a holy martyr in that he had died out of pious inebriation. Without that
ardor and zeal with which he had rendered many oracles, he would have lived
to his natural end.

"The physicians were leaving since they had nothing more to do when I
approached the mate and asked in a simple manner, whether I might examine
the body. The mate, in some surprise at my request, asked the physicians their
advice. They replied that they saw no reason to refuse.

"I approached and rubbed the body wherever I thought I felt a pulsation.
After fifteen minutes, I began to repent of a step which I feared would make me

look ridiculous. At that moment, I felt a weak though unmistakable pulsation at the bend of the elbow. I said nothing about this but asked permission to be alone with the body.

"The doctors looked at me with scorn but the family thought they had heard the voice of God. The brother with whom we had dined asked the theologians if it were permissible. They replied that the matter was of such consequence that it would be a crime to refuse. The brother then turned to the doctor to ask if there was any hope and received in reply the remark, 'Weak minds often console themselves by hoping for the impossible!' After this dictum, he went out followed by his colleagues. Everyone sang a lovely hymn and went away. "I asked for hot water, soap, vinegar, linens and bowls. I shut myself up with Elizabeth to help and asked that no one enter. Elizabeth looked at me with the greatest astonishment fearing I had taken on too much but I had no time to lose discussing this. Megamicres knew nothing of phlebotomy or bleeding and its usefulness in certain cases. They thought blood might be the seat of the soul and cutting into a dead body could be sacrilege. A corpse is owed the homage of a funeral pyre in their thinking.

"I prepared linen, a bowl and some cord. I heated the strongest herbs and steamed the nape of his neck with its vapors, at the same time that I gently rubbed his temples. I felt a pulsation in the neck after the heated perfumes were applied. I turned the body on its side. Placing a large cloth underneath, I had my wife hold the bowl to receive the blood while I searched in vain for the jugular as I massaged his neck.

"Determined to risk everything on a body already given up for dead, I felt anew for every pulsation I could find and marked the spots with a green pencil. I thrust my scalpel in superficially, and made some incisions. A small quantity of blood came out and then stopped. I washed the wound; the skin closed so well that the incisions were not even visible. Elizabeth threw the blood away and washed the bowl. Then I immersed the sick man's feet in the solution I had heated. This hot remedy applied for half an hour resulted in a light pulsation behind the left ear. His lethargy continued however.

"Emboldened by ignorance, I tried another incision using only my finger to find the place where I felt a throbbing. The same quantity of blood came out as before. I became frightened because the Megamicre showed no sign of life at all for a full quarter of an hour. I thought I had killed him. But after renewed massage and perfuming, I let him rest. In a couple of hours, I perceived the same pulsations and I saw that a steel mirror which I held to his mouth had become clouded. My hope mounted. Two hours later, the pulsations diminished but I redoubled my efforts and felt that the throbbing in the elbow was now the same as when I had first observed it.

"Now I felt I really knew nothing. I could not tell whether the bleeding had been useful or fatal. Again I made an incision. This time to stop the bleeding, we made a tight compress out of a handkerchief; Elizabeth cut off a lock of her hair and we used it to bind the compress.

"An hour later, we were gratified to see the patient slowly begin his rhythm of breathing. Elizabeth had noticed that his lips seemed to be seeking nourishment. I diluted half an ounce of syrup of pine nuts and soaked the end of a cloth for him to suck. He fell asleep. Then his body began to sweat and soon resumed the natural perspiration which brought a uniform dry warmth to his body. He remained in this drowsy state for two full hours. We did not touch him. But now his pulse was normal and we could remove the compress. I saw no scar. My wife kissed him and he returned the caress. She sang to him and he fell asleep again. I judged my patient out of danger now and that his complete awakening was not far off.

"I thought I ought to use some stronger perfume vapor with which I rubbed his temples. This was effective; he opened his eyes and after staring at us, said he knew who we were. Then he asked what we were doing there.

"In a very gentle voice, Elizabeth told him he had been very sick and we had been with him for thirteen hours to help him recover.

" 'Where is my inseparable?', he asked in a languid voice. At this, we believed we could call in his family. I put away my instruments. Elizabeth seated herself on the bed, comforting him, while I stood by looking at them.

"The first ones who witnessed this sight were his mate and his brother with his inseparable. They remained fixed, immobile, unable to utter a word. When he asked his family why they had left him, they ran to him, overwhelmed him with caresses. Then they leaped on our necks, covered us with grateful kisses, until impelled by emotion, they threw themselves face down on the carpet before us. We at once pulled them upright to keep them from performing such a sacrilegious act. This was their adoration posture when once a year, the autocephalus pronounced the ineffable name of their god, the sun, in the temple.

"I explained we were only puny mortals and that it was God, creator of the universe to whom they owed the life of the autocephalus.

"The mate had the carillon played; its sound could be heard everywhere. At once, the room became filled with those in the house: masters, servants, friends, all in a confusion of inexpressible joy. The servants, of their own accord, ran out into the street to carry the incredible news. The two principal couples of the family went in person, one pair to notify the king, the other to tell the reigning autocephalus about the miracle, a story these eminent persons would not have believed had it come from another source.

"With nothing more to do, Elizabeth and I prepared to leave. I addressed some words to the gathering: 'The autocephalus elect, who was given up for dead yesterday is actually sure to recover, provided he maintains a healthful regimen. Here is the recompense we ask from you. You must recognize that his recovery comes through the grace of the God we worship and who has created us all; we have only been the instruments of his mercy. Under the care of his physicians, the autocephalus should be cured in a pentamine. He should no longer allow himself to sleep, except if the Great Spirit at Heliopolis orders him to do so.'

"After these words, my wife and I embraced the recovering autocephalus and bowed to the assemblage. They followed us to our carriage singing the hymn which they chant in the temple on their festival of the new year.

"Home alone, Elizabeth and I pondered on the grace granted us and we thanked God with tears full of gratitude. We no longer had doubts about our future in this world. I now saw how I must frame my reply to the oracle at Heliopolis.

"The next morning, our friend, the Chief Gardener reported on the events which had occurred after we left. When they heard the news, the doctors, theologians and alfas all came at once to the house to see for themselves that the autocephalus was alive. But then a serious altercation between the doctors and the theologians took place, the former declaring that a miracle had taken place and the dead man had been resurrected; the latter denying that he had ever been dead. The doctors were outraged that their diagnosis was questioned. They demanded a hearing before the king's tribunal on the charge that their professional qualifications were being questioned.

"When the Chief Gardener finished his report, a handsome amaranth with green cheeks approached, asking us to choose a day when we could appear before the College of Physics. We agreed on a day of the pentamine following. Ten minutes later a violet came with the same request but this time for the Faculty of Theology. Dust day of the following pentamine was chosen.

"These two appointments, far from troubling me, assured me I would have ample material for my answer to the Great Spirit. As for the physicians, they had to uphold their claim that the autocephalus had been dead and that I had therefore performed a miracle. As for the theologians, I did not worry about their superstitious ideas. They had imprudently attacked the physicians and they now needed to retreat from their position and still keep face.

"When we appeared at the first appointment, all the members rose and courteously offered us chairs which they had made expressly for us. They inquired first whether I had cured the autocephalus or had resurrected him. I replied, 'If the autocephalus elect was not dead, then we cured him; if he was dead, then we resurrected him.'

"They asked us to leave the room while they deliberated. In an hour, we returned and were given a certificate which said in effect that we had performed a miracle.

"We asked that a clause be added and they agreed. In it, we attributed the prelate's recovery to God. In doubting us, the theologians had offended not us but God. Our religion, however, requires that we pardon any offense against us and that we ask God to pardon the offender as well.

"So the affair ended. Our declaration was posted all over and our religion was now regarded with respect by the populace. The precept of pardoning enemies seemed particularly sublime to them.

"For our appointment to meet the theologians, we went to the cathedral since the reigning autocephalus himself was going to preside. An orator, speaking for the council, said it was their opinion that we had worked a miracle since we had restored a soul. We had further questions to answer however:

(1) we had to prove the existence of an exterior world.

(2) we must explain why we had a right to eat the sacred fruit.

(3) we had to reveal those mysteries of our religion which we were permitted to.

(4) we had to show that the fruit was necessary nourishment.

"Finally they would agree to give us the fruit if we would pluck it without causing the serpents to hiss. If we succeeded in this, we had permission to take the fruit and they hoped that the temporal power would give permission as well. Tomorrow I shall tell you how I answered the questions."

SEVENTH DAY

"My dear Edward", said Count Bridgent, "I admire your integrity. You knew you had not performed a miracle but like a true gentleman, you never said you did."

"If he had not dared to work on the body of that autocephalus as he did, the prelate would surely have died." Lady Rutgland remarked. We can not say positively that he raised him from the dead, but we can truthfully say he restored life to him"

"With one reservation", Burghlei's tone was mocking. "No one can give life to someone who is alive."

"No sophistries, please", Count Bridgent interrupted. "Please go on, Edward. We shall all pay attention."

"I left off yesterday", Edward said, "when I was to reply to the questions put to me by the council of theologians. They wanted me to give proof of the existence of an exterior world.

" 'What better proof do you need". I asked them, "than our presence? You know that though we were not born here, we did come from a place of light, since we can see. We take nourishment and we bear children. We are aware of right and wrong, of the possible and the impossible, of the difference between matter and spirit, exactly as you are aware. I can well understand that the idea of an exterior surface is inconceivable to those who have lived forever inside their own world. In the same way, the idea of an interior world would be inconceivable to those who never leave the convex surface of the earth. But we are here, two reasoning creatures like yourselves to convince you that there is a world of light elsewhere too.

" 'If we told you we came from another globe, you would be right in treating us as impostors because all those worlds with which the universe swarms are separated by such vast distances of space that it is impossible to journey to them. But our convex exterior is no more than about two hundred and twenty leagues away from you.

" 'You must know, holy fathers, that our religion also forbids us to lie. We would be ill-advised to displease God, who we hope, will inspire in you, humane and generous feelings towards us.

" 'As for your question about our right to eat the fruit: we regard the earth as our mother. It is a law of nature that the mother must feed her children and permit them to take from the earth what they need for sustenance. After God created the world and man, he told man that whatever the earth produces belongs to him. As descendants of the original couple to whom God gave this right—we now number almost two billion—we believed we had a right. This fruit now serves only to maintain the cursed serpents, your most feared enemy, useless creatures without soul who strangle and poison innocents from time to time.

" 'Nevertheless, we shall not touch the fruit anymore, except under the conditions you have set out. Keeping the serpents from hissing is a hard task but we trust that Providence will show us a way so we can gather the fruits without that hissing which terrifies those who hear it.

" 'As for our religion and liturgy, I can only say that we worship God simply and purely. This God whom we love and fear can only be the same immaterial, all-powerful and immortal God who also created you.

" 'We promise to use our ability and understanding for the benefit of the world to which God has sent us and we shall always respect the dominant religion.'

"I concluded by asking that a study be made and a report published concerning the phenomenon of the flight to the sun of our lead roof with its magnet when we first arrived in their world. After such a report made by the physicists, I wanted the theologians to study its religious implications. Then I would ask for an oracle and an interpretation by the Great Spirit to whose judgment I would bow. My request was granted.

"When we returned home, we found many visitors. They kept coming day after day so we had no time for ourselves except during the hours of repose. We remedied this situation, on advice of our friend the Chief Gardener. We notified all that we would welcome visitors on the fifth day of the pentamine but that we were occupied the other four days with important business. The noble reds, being accustomed to free access everywhere at all times, would have been affronted without such an explanation. An interesting fact is that we too were considered to be nobles because we could reproduce.

"In this connection, I had a long conversation with the king one day on the subject of fertility and reproduction. He was astonished to learn that everyone in our world with some rare exceptions was able to reproduce. He assumed that all our people were therefore nobles. I tried in vain to make him understand that the ability to reproduce did not confer nobility. It baffled him to hear that a nonentity, a fool and a rogue could engender offspring since this quality was a gift of God and a sure token of nobility.

" 'If everyone is fecund', he said, 'how can your world have room for its population?'

"I told him about celibacy and he laughed at me. He said that must surely be

86

an invention, a fabrication. I mentioned then that some of the celibates had concubines. I might have won a point there but I lost it when I told him that the offspring of such unions were bastards, but they were also fertile. Many of them were virtuous and learned besides. The king argued that celibacy, in any case even if practiced would not cause any significant loss of population. He seemed more interested in the reason why people took a vow of chastity. Would not such a vow be displeasing to God who urged man to be fruitful and multiply as I had told him?

"I said that in obeying the precept to multiply, man also derives the greatest possible physical pleasure. Therefore, by abstaining from this pleasure, the celibate is offering God a sacrifice of something very dear to him.

" 'Wonderful', said the king. 'A gift does entail sacrifice. But a gift must also have two characteristics: it must please the recipient and it must not be taken back by the giver. When God tells man to multiply, is he pleased with a gift of celibacy? And when the celibate takes a concubine, is he not taking back that gift? He has not sacrificed his pleasure when he produces children outside of marriage,' the king continued. He wondered whether God did not punish them when they broke the vow of chastity. I replied that the so-called celibates violate the vow in secret. Upon hearing this, the king abandoned the subject of celibacy altogether. 'Tell me, what other means do you have of limiting population?'

"I told him about wars, pestilence and early death. The fact of war struck him as unnatural, unacceptable and monstrous. He deplored pestilence and plague. But I observed that my description of earthquakes and other natural disasters and their consequences alarmed him greatly. He concluded that our world was a sorry place to live and he felt pity for its inhabitants. He thought our world might be a place of exile to which we had been banished for committing some frightful crime. I was sorry I could not tell him about Adam's sin and how he had been turned out of the place of delights where God had intended man to live.

"While waiting for the report by the physicists, I used the time to experiment with sulphur, saltpetre and carbon. I had taken it into my head to make gunpowder of which these are the sole ingredients. You will learn later how my experiments came out.

"During this time, too, my wife had come to term and she gave birth to our third twin. We had called our second pair Richard and Anne; these we named Adam and Eve. We informed the king and the autocephalus of this happy event and were gratified to hear from the king that he was providing a hundred more nourishers. He was also presenting us with a beautiful house of thirty furnished suites and a garden besides. Two months later, the autocephalus elect with his entire family paid us a visit. His family included ten reds, all charming in appearance unlike the prelate who bore the sad signs of age on his face and throat because of his holy debauches.

"He sang and danced, though badly, and then his entourage performed a pretty ballet for us.

"He said that since he owed his life to us, he and his entire family wanted to assure us of their enduring friendship and he begged us to accept a memorial of their gratitude. At these words, sixty-four Megamicres entered the room bearing a luminous globe. It was a map of their world with all its square-shaped monarchies and triangular fiefs ingeniously represented on the convex surface of this gleaming sphere. It stood on a pedestal of solid red gold with a statue of Elizabeth on the right and of me on the left. Both statues were made of pure marble, more transparent even than our alabaster. Between the statues was the figure of the autocephalus elect, molded in red gold, sitting upright on a bench fashioned of yellow gold. In his upraised right hand, he held a huge ruby, cut into twenty equal triangles at which he was gazing. It was a masterly work, akin to one of those groupings in classic Greek sculpture.

"We were stunned at the sight of this gift and overwhelmed with feelings of gratitude. We expressed these as best we could, but within ourselves, we were troubled knowing we could not refuse, without being impolite, a gift of such magnificence. A refusal might suggest that we felt above the donor. We had this treasure placed on one side of the room. We sang and danced in honor of the autocephalus and then brought out our children so they could view the work. Our older children were now fourteen European months in age. The infants were then brought out and Elizabeth nursed them the customary five times.

"When, in answer to his question, I told the autocephalus that the children were fertile as were all of our race, he exclaimed, 'Happy race, beloved of God, who because of their virtue produce only nobles.' Later, he asked a favor. He wanted to know, if there was in our doctrine, something which could explain where his soul had been during the time he was dead. When he slept he knew his soul remained in his body, but when he had been resuscitated, he had felt only that he was emerging from nothingness or perhaps from a heavy sleep. I could not discuss the matter with him at the moment, but I said I would talk with him, in a pentamine, about the location of his soul when he was in that state of unconsciousness.

"The fame of the extraordinary gift spread throughout the city. The prelate, as rich as he was pious, had kept the globe a secret even from his own family. He had spared no expense in the construction of this work, his tribute to the mercy of God.

"The Chief Gardener was the first to visit, drawn more by his friendship for us than by curiosity. He first congratulated us on the beautiful house the king had given us and then kept looking with admiration at the globe. He would value it, he said, at half a million ounces. That sum, Milords, would bring a yearly interest rate of thirty thousand pounds sterling.

"People kept coming all the time to see the masterpiece. One day we were pleasantly surprised when the king appeared with his inseparable. We tried to thank him for all his generosity but he graciously motioned us to silence. He asked to see our nurslings. Then he looked at the sculpture declaring that the autocephalus elect deserved a crown for the work.

"Later and quite hesitantly, he asked whether we could have saved the prelate had we not seen him until the following day. We would have had no hope, I said, had we seen on his body any signs of the beginning of bodily death, that is some corruption of the flesh or total absence of life. The king thanked me for the information, excused himself since curiosity is considered an offense, and left. He said he was glad for our presence in his kingdom.

"We received a letter the next day signed by those two unfortunate theologians who had been demoted for saying that no miracle had taken place. They asked for an appointment and we arranged to see them on Cocoon (or Chrysalis) day. Bereft of the insignia of their former rank, they arrived shamefaced and penitent. They conveyed their wish to repent in song and music of mournfulness. In reply we told them (though we did not grant them the courtesy of song) that we knew they had not acted out of hatred or malice but out of zeal. We offered them whatever assistance we could.

"Upon hearing this, they said that we only, could intercede to have them restored to their former rank. Without giving us time to reply, they had four polychromes bring in, one apiece, four huge volumes which they presented to us. The only others extant, they said, were the originals kept in the secret archives. These volumes contained the history of their world from its creation until the time of the great-grand-father of the present king. The books had been a legacy from the father of one of the theologians, a learned red who had made his son swear never to have a copy made.

"After this visit, we had some peace in our household. But on visiting day, we had to endure eight hours of comings and goings while the Megamicrans examined the globe, perhaps just to say they had seen it. It was to this wearying experience, however, that I owed a happy idea. Elizabeth immediately approved.

"I would consecrate the globe to the great metropolitan temple. When I wrote to the king about this idea, his reply was indirect. His words were: 'You wished me to be the first to admire the magnaminity of your soul.' I took this to mean he approved.

"I drew up a formal document turning over the precious sculpture to the temple. The document was registered by the king's chancellor and copies sent to the autocephalus and me. The prelate replied that he would write his superior at Heliopolis and asked meanwhile that the sculpture be kept covered until its unveiling on the second day of the following year. I had already sent the treasure to the temple.

"On one of his visits, the Chief Gardener reported about the people's reactions. There was general astonishment about such an unusual act. It was

89

incomprehensible that persons would give away their whole fortune, especially persons who might die of hunger were it not for the king's generosity. Some thought the act was heroic; others, more practical, that we must be crazy. Our friend suggested that we should pay a formal visit to the reigning autocephalus who had allowed the memorial to be placed in the temple without awaiting permission from Heliopolis. We agreed with him and wrote for an appointment.

"On the day fixed for the visit, Elizabeth and I with our four children rode in a splendid carriage provided by the king who also had his gentlemen-in-waiting accompany us in three other coaches. Preceded by a concert of clarinets and followed by a band of kettle drums, trumpets and horns, we made our way very slowly, accompanied by the joyous acclamations of an immense crowd which lined all the streets along our route.

"The autocephalus who had not expected this grand entrance did not have time to receive us with the customary pomp. He greeted us, however, at the door of a huge room surrounded by a crowd of Megamicres of all colors and of all levels in the ecclesiastical hierarchy.

"He seated himself on a raised throne. Elizabeth with the infants and I with our two older children sat on either side of him at a somewhat lower level. A very melodious vocal and instrumental concert followed by two other songs with refrains by the choir and orchestra preceded the talk by the autocephalus. He praised the sculpture offered to God; he praised the autocephalus elect for his trust in us, knowing we would present his gift to the temple. For it was to the Being of Beings that he owed his recovery but he had to give the treasure first to the instruments of God's mercy, that is to Elizabeth and myself.

"After his oration, he asked my wife why the infants slept and whether they had pretty eyes. Thereupon she nursed them the accepted five times, they opened their eyes and looked up at him. I judged this to be a good time to speak on behalf of the stricken clerics. I was the only one, he declared, whose plea he could not deny. The theologians, however, could not hope for his favor until after the dedication of the globe and after they made public confession.

"The prelate rose and made an announcement. He said that Elizabeth and I would now have the privilege of entry anywhere without having to be announced. The king alone has this right, by birth. We then asked and were accorded the favor of kissing his sacred breast (as we had been advised by the master of ceremonies).

"After baskets of flowers were distributed and burned, we all left with the sound of music and with the fragrance of perfume.

"Once home, I wrote to the two theologians telling them they were to appear on the fourth day of the following year for their hearing and judgment.

"I also wrote to the autocephalus elect about the question he had asked regarding the presence of the soul in life and death. I told him first that God had created the soul immortal and the body mortal. The soul does not leave the body until the body is perfectly dead. In his case, he was not perfectly dead else I would not have tried to restore him. His soul was therefore still in his body but he was confused when he woke from his unconscious state. The organs of memory, constricted and compressed when he was in his death-like lethargy, could not function. Had he been dead, his immortal soul would have returned to God. As it was, his soul never left his body.

"The same day that Elizabeth weaned our infants, we went to live in the beautiful house the king had given us. As for the garden, the autocephalus, though well-disposed towards us, thought he ought to provide four gardeners of his own. They were to watch out for the safety of the serpents. Our friend, the Chief Gardener, told us the king could not take offense at this precaution since the care of the serpents was under the jurisdiction of the church.

"On the second day of the new year, the dedication of the globe took place with the greatest pomp; there were immense crowds there. Also the two theologians were restored to their previous rank. When they came to thank us, I thanked them in return for the four volumes which made delightful reading during my hours of repose.

"Owners now of a spacious and lovely home, we worked at making it as comfortable as we could. The servants were given quarters on the top floor. I took the apartment below and I settled my wife on the third floor where, adjoining her own, were apartments for the children. In her quarters, she set up a laboratory to make essences and a studio to work on her musical instruments.

"For myself, I had access to the garden via a small stairway. I turned some rooms into laboratories and I had a large forge built on the ground floor which had natural light. The apartment below the forge was kept unoccupied because of the anvils.

"The mandolins which my wife designed had become the favorite instrument of all classes. We gave them away as presents but the gifts we got in return were worth twenty times more than the instruments. We received furniture, diamonds, metals, lamps filled with phosphorus, steel mirrors and other valuable furnishings.

"She taught some of the more adept servants to manufacture the mandolins. They were delighted to learn a trade. Some of them opened shops afterwards and became well off. But Elizabeth's mandolins with her name on them were still more eagerly sought.

"Through an ancient text given her by the Governor's mate, my wife learned the art of extracting the essence of the sweetest smelling flowers. By a process of slow fermentation, she learned how to draw one drop of liquid scent which rubbed between the palms gave enough perfume for a Megamicre.

"She also learned how to mix elixirs each of which had different healing properties. Some strengthened, others tranquilized, some revivified the body and stimulated memory. Others improved the voice, aroused gayety or courage. Some even consoled the sorrowful. Her most successful elixir which I named

91

'Nepenthe'* created a perfect balance among all the humors of the body. It was a true specific against boredom and sadness.

"We were rich, yet we would have been poor if we had had to support ourselves, maintain the house, pay for the servants and providers. When I had to tell the king my wife was once again pregnant, I felt embarrassed. It was time to extricate ourselves from dependence on our generous king.

"I spent a whole year trying to master a skill quite different from my wife's. I was determined to learn how to make gunpowder. There was only one way to make the serpents stop hissing when I gathered the fruits: I had to kill them.

"With the help of the Chief Gardener, I obtained every variety of sulphur, all white. I had red saltpetre and a good amount of gray carbon. I knew only that these three ingredients would make what I wanted. I had learned this fact from my father whom you see sitting there. But I knew nothing more.

"I spent seven long painstaking and often dangerous years in experiments. But I finally succeeded. How many times did my efforts seem useless but I never really gave up hope. It was trial and error. My wife who feared for my health tried to persuade me to abandon the enterprise but I could not be prevailed upon to stop. I would be renouncing hope. If you want something very much, the hope of achieving it will keep you going.

"One day, after countless trials, a mixture for which I had little hope, flared up. I was overjoyed. The powder flashed quickly and went out in smoke when I put a fire to it. I almost burned my face, it was so unexpected. I repeated the experiment and again it was successful. The powder was a pale pink in color. When I discharged a pistol, it went off without the slightest sound. I thought it was a miracle until, four months ago, I was told by an expert at the arsenal in Venice, that it is no miracle. Noiseless gunshots are a fact here, too.

"By the time I had learned to make gunpowder, I already owned more than a thousand pistols of every size that my smiths had made. They must have been curious about these pieces of ironwork which seemed to have no utility but they never questioned me. I will speak later about this matter.

"Having arrived at term, my wife gave me my fourth twin whom I named Robert and Pauline and the king provided a hundred new nourishers three months later.

"Five months after their birth, the oracle from Heliopolis arrived. My copy came with a letter especially addressed to me. The oracle declared that the divinity of our mission was undeniably established by the miracles, by our probity and courage and by our moral behavior and that we were owed, if not divine honors, certainly the greatest one could tender to mortals.

"The oracle further stated that the forbidden fruits belonged to us as did the trees in our gardens; that we would surely find a way to keep the children from becoming terrified by the frightful hissing of that accursed race. We had

---

* From the Greek "without sorrow" (possibly an opiate).

complete liberty to use such means as we thought proper in order to achieve this end. The autocephalus withdrew his guards from the garden.

"The letter addressed to me came from the minister of the Great Spirit. The contents astonished us. We were being presented with the sovereignty of Fief One, 1375 leagues from our present dwelling. This fiefdom would belong to us and our heirs in perpetuity; we would live there as sovereigns, free and independent. The certificate of this investiture would be bestowed on us after the secular holidays and was a manifest of the Great Spirit's special benev-olence and favor towards us.

"My wife and I were stunned. I saw myself become a prince. I could not aspire to any greater fortune. But we would need the consent of our king to whom we owed so much. We had already decided to write for an appointment when we were notified that the autocephalus would visit us the next day. The king sent his courtiers to be present at our house as a courtesy to the auto-cephalus and a number of valets came bringing the throne for the prelate as well as musicians and bearers of flowers. The king's guards, on their horses, kept the crowds in order and made a path for the monsignor. We watched and were quiet. We had not been informed of this preparation.

"At the precise hour arranged for the visit, the master of ceremonies had us go with him to the door of the house to receive the dignitary. We ushered him in with the prescribed singing and dancing up to his throne. We listened to a fifteen minute concert in his honor. Then the autocephalus spoke to us. He told us what we had already read in the oracle but in addition he said we were to receive 200,000 ounces as a gift. A throne would be prepared for us at the temple where the secular initiation rites were to take place. There we would have to chant the hymn of homage to the sun, along with all the other faithful.

"We returned to our house, beside ourselves with bewilderment, but we shortly recovered our reason. The minister's letter, the ceremonial visit, the speech of the autocephalus, the alteration in our circumstances from depend-ence to sovereignty, all unexpected, unforseen and unwanted, had positively stupefied us.

" 'Two hundred thousand ounces', said my wife, 'is even more than the intrinsic worth of the globe; the gift of the fiefdom can never be compensated for and certainly can not be reasonably be refused.'

"She was right but the gift had a price: We had to give homage to their sun god. The Great Spirit had arranged for the homage to be offered before the certificate of investiture was given. We would have to sell our faith. We would be required to give obeisance to a religion whose beliefs we knew to be false.

" 'It is a question of selling our happiness', I told Elizabeth. 'We could not live with ourselves or respect ourselves again, knowing that to obtain the fief, we would have to be cowardly and false.'

"This, Milords, is what this homage entails: 'We adore you, immortal sun. It is you, God visible by order of the invisible God who took us out of nothingness

93

and who now maintains us, who in the most brilliant and beautiful form, remains motionless in the center of the marvelous world you have created. Pardon us our sins and give us the courage to commit no more. Reflect that our souls are immortal as part of your immortal essence. Be mindful that you can not commit our souls to eternal damnation, without damning to everlasting infamy, a part of yourself.'

"Elizabeth shed a few tears. Then she said thoughtfully, 'We shall not appear at the temple and chant the hymn of homage. Someone with no religion might accept this gift and be happy, but religion is priceless and I do not envy those who lack it.'

"The next day we went to the court. The king and his inseparable greeted us, saying at once that we would drive in his carriage to the temple followed by his whole court. I was at last able to explain that we could not accept the title and gift since it meant that we would have to become idolators. We would have to lie, I told him, about our beliefs if we pronounced the words of the hymn. 'We shall not go', I concluded.

"They were aghast. After a long silence, the king advised me to write to Helopolis about my decision after I had showed him and the autocephalus what I had written. Then he left us sadly and we returned home.

"I wrote to the Great Spirit at Heliopolis explaining the reasons for our decision and asking for his understanding and blessing. I told him we could not consider the sun as immortal, much less a god. We believe that the sun was created and we do not know that he is immortal. I went on to say to the pontiff at Heliopolis, 'We cannot declare that the sun pulled us out of nothingness; we cannot ask the sun to pardon our sins and we cannot expect mercy from the sun. We do not believe our souls are part of the sun nor do we fear punishment in the after life from the sun. All our hopes and fears derive only from that immaterial God who has created the sun, who has created you and all that exists.' This response of mine to the Great Spirit marked the beginning of a coldness between us which was to last many years.

"The secular festivities took place a month after this. The whole city gossiped, each telling the story as it suited his fancy. Except for our good friend the Gardener, we had few visits.

"Six months after the festival, Elizabeth was delivered of our fifth twin whom we named William and Theresa. She weaned them the first day of our sixth year. Eight days later, in the company of the Chief Gardener, our two oldest children, James and Wilhelmina, returned to us. Though they were only four years and three months of age, they were the size of nine year olds. The Governor's letter touched us as he wrote how grieved he and the whole family were to separate from the children. They had brought him much happiness and were adored by all their friends.

"James, dark-haired and Wilhelmina, blond, were exceptionally beautiful. They were astonished to see us and retreated at our approach. We devoured them with kisses and hugs and we spoke English to them which they could not understand. They began to grow accustomed to us, especially after they met their brothers and sisters whom they surpassed in size and age.

"In one year, they spoke English perfectly under the tutelage of their mother. She also taught them christian doctrine. This they learned by way of a very short catechism about which I shall speak later.

"We informed the king about the arrival of the oldest children and asked to present them. The royal couple was delighted at the sight of these charming creatures, who were entirely at ease and spoke Megamicran and conversed in Megamicran in a simple, naive yet lively fashion so as to make them laugh and admire the 'little giants'. They told the royal couple they were hungry and approached to be suckled. We ran to stop them, asking pardon and making excuses for this boldness, but, smiling at the little innocents, they said they wanted to permit this. Before we left, the king asked that the children be sent to him sometimes when one of his courtiers came to call for them.

"In time, Elizabeth presented me with Theodore and Frances, our sixth set of twins. We were by now rich enough to take care of our needs. We thought we would relieve the king of the cost of the wet nurses, inasmuch as we had taught many of them trades. We could hire the ones we needed at a lesser cost. The king agreed to this, giving us a pension of ten thousand ounces per Megamicran year.

"At the beginning of our seventh year, my wife arranged two apartments next to hers to accommodate all our family. At the same time she set up one room, near mine, for our first two male children to be under my charge. She did not want them to have contact with their sisters with whom they already seemed to be in love. I approved of this idea. On the first day of each year thereafter, one more male charge was placed under my care. Elizabeth taught the girls her skills while I taught my sons the art of smithing and tool making, as well as the manufacture of gunpowder.

"We rarely went out. We spent the next four years quietly, to the point that we were seldom talked about. Our tasks, and the education of our children made time pass quickly enough. Our friend the Chief Gardener dined with us once a week. We did not attend court except when summoned and that was infrequently. Our oldest children went more often but never of their own accord. During these years our family was increased by Henry, Charles, and David and their sisters Judith, Barbara, and Jeanne.

"At the beginning of my tenth year there, I told James and his sister Wilhelmina that I would join them in marriage on the first of the following year. To please my wife, I made it a rule that the first of the year was the only time when they would be permitted to marry. This rule was always strictly observed by my descendants until there had to be a modification in later years. Twin brother and sister would marry at nine years and three months of age. Their physical development equalled that of fourteen year olds.

95

"The marriage date chosen was the anniversary of our waking up in the Governor's palace. We calculated that seven hundred twenty Megamicran days equalled three hundred sixty of ours. So it happened that all the women gave birth on the same day.

"In a world where the rules of nature never undergo the slightest variation, it is possible to arrange matters so perfectly."

EIGHTH DAY

"We should like to have you say something in Megamicran; would you oblige us?", Countess Bridgent coaxed.

"I shall", Elizabeth replied, "as soon as my husband comes in. You would not want me to speak to myself?"

"Yes, yes", Lady Rutgland urged. "We won't understand anyway, but do say something to us."

Obligingly Elizabeth spoke,

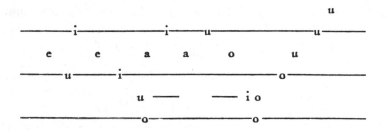

"And I", Burghlei gleefully said, "shall answer. Listen: Oeiau oi aiaia oeueiau. So there."

"You are a scoffer", Elizabeth smiled. "an amusing one, to be sure. Ask me a question in English; I shall write it in Megamicran. Then when Edward comes in, he will answer it."

"I was only joking", Burghlei protested. "I believe the language is real." But he nevertheless dictated the sentence: "We are all curious to know how you returned to this world." Elizabeth wrote it down in Megamicran.

"Here he is, just at the right moment", Elizabeth exclaimed as Edward came in. "Here", she said, "read this and give your answer to Lord Charles Burghlei, who needs to be convinced."

"You ask", said Edward after reading the sentence, "how we returned to England. Will you keep this curiosity of yours alive until a later time? Right now, I can only tell you that our voyage home was even more agonizing than our journey there."

"And I am curious to know", Countess Bridgent said reflectively, "whether our missionaries, if they get there, would administer the sacraments; whether they would look on those little creatures as having an immortal soul?"

"But without immortal souls", Dunspili objected, "they would be nothing more than little beasts."

"Nonsense!", Lord Howard said firmly. "I would not regard you or myself or the whole human race as beasts, even if the idea of an immortal soul is pure fiction."

"Edward", Count Bridgent called to him, "what do you say on this matter? What do you think of your Megamicres?"

"Exactly what I think of myself", Edward answered. "Since I am a reasoning being, just as they are, and since reasoning beings are assumed to have souls, it must follow that they do too."

Edward continued, "When I made christians of the Megamicres, as you will hear later, I did not plan to make them christians like us. Our religion does not quite fit their needs. My chief aim was to detach them from superstitious beliefs and to make accessible to them our superior morality.

"Even my children do not know what the word 'christian' means. I never explained its derivation. I did tell them about salvation and that it is achieved by good works and faith. But I did not inform them about all those christian verities, to believe in which, requires faith. I never told them about original sin, nor its aftermath, redemption. I never spoke of the deluge, nor of the written law which came after the natural law. I tried to make the path to salvation an easier one for them by teaching them only what I considered necessary for eternal salvation.

"Since the richest are those who need least, I may safely say that my descendants are richer in their religion than we are. There are only three or four beliefs they have to take on faith. These may puzzle them, perhaps, but they are not totally unacceptable.

"The principal dogmas of the christian faith which I passed on to them are: belief in an immortal, immaterial God, creator of all; a providence from which flows the ever active mercy of God and His infinite goodness; the need of repentance for sin and the need for prayer to strengthen virtue.

"In addition, I inculcated the doctrine of the immortal soul and belief in an afterlife of bliss or sorrow. Heaven i described as being granted a vision of God, than which there is no greater happiness; Hell I described as the deprivation of that vision of God with its attendant despair carried to the most extreme desolation. I did not give them any information about purgatory or angels. I would have been at a loss to explain the many confusing questions they would have asked me.

"No one I think will contest their right to be called christians. If some church fathers can say there have always been christians in the world, citing Socrates and Cyrus among them, surely no one will refuse this designation to my children who have all been baptized and who live according the the spirit of God.

"It does not matter that they are ignorant of the history of baptism; it is enough that I know it. I shall venture to tell you further, Milords, that none of my descendants will ever read either the Old or New Testaments. I did leave a copy there, but it was in Latin. If it had been in English, I would have burned it."

"I see that you did not ignore the importance of baptism. You recognized that 'in Adam, all have sinned.' But I think you should have told your children about Adam's fall", Dunspili said.

Edward shook his head. "Adam's disobedience and its consequences are not clear to us. And to tell the truth, I am too ignorant of doctrine and dogma to meddle with it. I would be afraid to disseminate more errors. It is better, I think, to know nothing of the mystery of the incarnation, for example, than to have an incorrect or false understanding of it.

"I gave my children a code of behaviour. They must abstain from lies and also from the truth when a third party would be injured by it (without helping the cause of innocence). They must respect their superiors; love their neighbors; observe the law of the land they inhabit; love and help the Megamicres. Theft is prohibited; withholding wages due is prohibited. Humiliating an enemy is an offense for which pardon must be begged. Topping the list of offensive behavior is the act of anger when it results in an impulsive and hurtful action. No one may ask to be exculpated on the ground that the action was involuntary, there is no such thing.

"I have taught my children that adultery is a crime. Reciprocal respect between husband and wife is a 'must' for a good marriage. A haughty tone of voice is forbidden, only gentleness must reign.

"Persuasion may be used but forceful argument repels without convincing. The husband may not use his superiority as a man to take advantage of his wife except when the welfare of his family demands it.

"Curiosity about other people's affairs is forbidden. Satisfying the indiscreet curiosity of others is just as bad; it makes one a party to the indiscretion.

"Baptism, I told my children, was a divine precept and a requirement. Circumcision was a non-religious precept but it was also a requirement.

"As for confession, I told them that God can penetrate into the minds and hearts of sinners to determine the sincerity of their repentance. Without genuine contrition, words alone as in open or public confession are not accepted by God. If it should happen that Roman Catholic missionaries get there, abolish open confession and substitute auricular confession, God alone knows whether this would be more fruitful for the soul's welfare.

"What you have told us in such detail", said Countess Bridgent, "spoke to my heart and mind. I wonder now if you would tell us something about that unseen Great Spirit who has lived so many thousand years."

99

"Milady", responded Edward, "that is probably a piece of deception. I always avoided any mention of the subject. This mystery of the Megamicres has become an unmentionable state secret. If it is an error, neither church nor state are interested in correcting it. There is nothing to be gained politically by denying the immortality of the Great Spirit. On the contrary, it might be dangerous. The two powers, spiritual and temporal, find it to their mutual interest to perpetuate this belief. People are not permitted to question or inquire."

After dinner, Edward resumed the story of his adventures. "The incumbent autocephalus had died and our resuscitated friend was now occupying his seat. It was a propitious time, the king advised, for us to have our business with the court at Heliopolis concluded through the good offices of the present autocephalus.

" 'Your family keeps growing', he reminded us. 'In a hundred harvests there will be almost three thousand of you to feed.' He added that our survival would be in jeopardy if we had to depend on the costly providers alone. He was exactly right, of course. The same thoughts had been troubling us every single day. I still had no way of taking the serpents' fruit without having them hiss and I could not pay homage to the sun.

"When we visited the prelate, as the king had advised, we were received with pomp, affection and even veneration. He sympathized with our plight and believed we should be allowed to pluck the fruits. Later, privately, he told me that the matter of obeisance to the sun would no longer be insisted upon if we could demonstrate to the Great Spirit that our existence had a significant value for his state. I told this to our king who said he would bring to the sacred court at Heliopolis whatever he could cite as evidence of our contributions to the state.

"In the interim, we spent our time usefully working at diverse occupations. My wife's enterprise, that of making essences, had become an important business. The sale of her products had spread to adjacent and far off kingdoms as well as throughout her own state. We employed more than five hundred Megamicres as orders multiplied. We took in more than a hundred thousand guineas a year.

"Our children's education was of prime importance since we knew that the quality and nature of one's character depended on education. At age four, they already knew how to read but teaching them to write properly and correctly was an endless task. The seven colors of the Megamicran alphabet required the use of a 'Dutch' quill. (This had to be plunged into hot sand after each use, so infinite time and effort were needed.) For this reason, the use of scribes was costly and copies took long to make.

"I conceived a new way of writing that would be easier and quicker. Using musical notation, I drew three parallel lines and placed the letters on, above or below them and utilized the spaces between. The letters no longer had to be distinguished by the colors; red, orange, yellow, green, blue, indigo and violet. Their positions with respect to the three lines served the purpose. I did this for all forty-two vocalizations in their alphabet.

"The new system met with the approval of the king. When he adopted it, the courtiers and the judges in his courts were obliged to follow suit. Within two European years, the system had become standard. The alfas held out for a long time until their oracles approved its use. The scribes first lost money but the increased volume of work compensated them for the loss. They however cursed and complained, little knowing that another blow was in store for them. The ink merchants were also aggrieved and wanted to sue us but the king laughed them out of court.

"When I saw that my system of writing had won approval, I turned my attention to setting up a paper mill. I remember", here Edward addressed Count Bridgent, "the one I had seen in Lincoln which belonged to your grandfather.

"With the king's permission, I bought a house in the country on the bank of a river. I built a dam and a mill gate and provided the factory with all the equipment needed to turn old linen into pulp and finally paper. By experimentation, by immense effort and the expenditure of much money and the exercise of patience, I succeeded in producing a fine grade of paper.

"I never had to account for anything I chose to do. My workers executed my orders and my four oldest sons were always at hand to supervise. The king visited often but restrained his curiosity. When I was satisfied, I wrote the king that I had a small gift for him.

"At the appointed time, I presented the paper. It was extremely fine, a pale pink with a beautiful sheen. The monarch was astonished at its beauty and perfection, wrote on it and regarded it in silence. I said it was up to him to make the paper popular. In fewer than ten years, I assured him, it would provide a most profitable source of income for his realm.

"And in a short time, the paper became a popular success. The retail store I had opened at the factory was too far from the city. Without my asking, the king gave me a spacious place on the main street. I placed a trustworthy and competent Megamicre in charge of the store.

"The king lost no time in sending to the sacred court at Heliopolis a dozen cases of our paper and a case of the most precious of our essences as evidence of our usefulness. He wrote that this was a small hint of our talent which the state could not afford to lose.

"My wife was now weaning our tenth pair of twins, Simeon and Faustine. The next day, which would be the beginning of our eleventh year in Protocosmos, I united our first twin James and Wilhelmina in marriage.

"The wedding feast was truly magnificent. We laid twenty-four settings on each of twenty-four tables. We also had our 1400 paper mill employees served. (I had made this a day of yearly paid holiday for them.) Sitting with the reds at the tables were a few colored Megamicres. These bastards were well-educated, respectable and rich. They were in business and in the clergy.

"The king had his master of ceremonies, an orange-red Megamicre, present us, after the customary songs and dances, with two beautiful cloaks, red for me and blue for Elizabeth. They were fastened at the neck with diamond pins. In addition, my wife was given a garment the color of her blue sleeved cloak which fell from throat to mid-leg and was open on both sides. Elizabeth cherished this tunic because it concealed her belly when she was well along in her pregnancies, not a pleasant sight.

"At the table where the bride and groom were seated, the hilarity of the Megamicran guests was unrestrained. The compliments they paid our poor children remained unanswered; they seemed struck dumb. They looked at one another and then at us, and at the entire company which tried in vain to extract a word from them. They appeared to be drunk with happiness. They ate nothing and as they confessed later, they longed to have the dinner over with.

"When the repast was over, the perfume massages began. Knowing that this ceremony made my wife uneasy and observing that the guests were already overheated, I addressed a few words to the assemblage. I told them simply that the ceremony of massage was forbidden on wedding days. They laughed at this but obediently confined themselves to embraces which to us seemed unobjectionable but which I could see, upset the young couple.

"We enjoyed a charming concert, the reading of a poem by the chief poet and a walk in the garden. Then the trumpet announced the hours of repose and everyone filed out.

"When all the guests had gone, we led the bride and groom to another room where all the family save for the six youngest attended. Elizabeth and I sat and the couple kneeled before us. We laid our hands on their heads and said the words together which became the formula for all future marriage services.

" 'We unite you in marriage in the name of God the Father, Son and Holy Spirit and ask Him to confirm our blessing. You have become inseparables, to keep order and peace in your home by diligence and gentleness. You have in two bodies a single will. We order you to multiply and raise your children as you have been raised.'

"We told them to rise. After they kissed our hands, we embraced them tenderly as did their brothers and sisters. Then we led them to their new quarters where after more embraces and blessings, we left them alone.

"We too retired to our apartment to rest. We removed our new garments with which my wife and I were very much pleased. I liked the way the cloak made my face look. By now, my beard which I had let grow since I was fifteen was very long after ten years. I had resisted Elizabeth's urgings that I cut it. It served a useful purpose in my role as patriarch of my tribe. Every eldest son had to do the same but the other males were required to be clean-shaven.

"The next day, we brought our children whose faces shone with joy and contentment to receive the best wishes and congratulations of the auto-cephalus and the king. Then we brought them to the house we had provided for them. The place where our fine paper was sold was situated here. I told James he was to supervise the business and that one tenth of all the profits would be his. I left him free to manage his own affairs, retaining only the right to advise.

"The paper mill was not my only interest. The greatest part of my time, I spent in my forges. Here I had a surprising number of firearms made of the finest metal, all beautifully constructed and designed. Only my wife knew the purpose for which they were designed.

"During this year, I perfected the manufacture of gunpowder. In my garden, I had had a shelter built expressly to keep the powder. It took patiently repeated experiments over a long time, to enable me, hitherto ignorant of the art of pyrotechnics, to devise a powder of such high quality. Perhaps the ingredients there were superior. I do not know. Suffice to say that the powder defied improvement. I realize that chance played a great part in the discovery of those ingredients needed to make gunpowder but without the science, the judgment, the patience and perseverance of man as he struggled to combine them, we would not possess this extraordinary substance. Whether gunpowder has added to the happiness or wretchedness of the human race is another matter. Even if this substance should cause the destruction of the world, its invention will be no less a tribute to the power of the human mind.

"Having foreseen that not only I but all my descendants would need to establish a solid base in this world, I realized that we must have natural nourishment in order to survive. The fruit of the sacred trees would provide this. We had to destroy the serpents to obtain this source of sustenance. This was our goal for the future. Meanwhile I learned to temper steel and to work iron so ably that at the end of six years, I yielded to no smith in skill.

"Both my paper manufacturing and one-color writing had become popular and I was emboldened to take a further step. I turned my attention to setting up a printing press. I knew next to nothing about printing but ignorance had not deterred me before. I trusted to reason to be my guide, to experimentation to teach me and to patience to keep me hopeful. I would have been wasting my time with seven-color printing but with one color, there was hope for success.

"This printing press, Milords, was more difficult to achieve than the making of gunpowder. Although the latter effort had taken more time, at least I had enjoyed the work. Here, endless detail was necessary. My instructions to the workers were not clear to them. The workers had to understand typographical composition with its basic letters, accents, punctuation, capitals from the molds I made. I also struggled to get the right ink. Comprehension came finally and when they had become skilled printers, they found it easier to read reverse writing than normal print. In spite of a hundred difficulties and as many failed experiments, I was at last able to print out an essay on a small press which I kept in my own room.

103

"Our eleventh twin, Jean and Tecla, were born and on the same day my dear daughter Wilhelmina bore a twin, a dark-haired male whom they named Edward and a blond female they called Elizabeth. On the first day of my twelfth year there, I married Richard to Anne and their nuptials were celebrated in no less grand a fashion than had been James's and Wilhelmina's. I provided an apartment for them in the same place which housed the first married pair and I gave Richard the second ten percent from the proceeds of the business.

"About this time, the king and the autocephalus received the oracle concerning our future. We were permitted to establish ourselves in their world and to eat the sacred fruit if a council of five hundred abdalas so decided. The abdalas were to meet two harvests from now and to debate whether a race which denies belief in the sun may have entry into their temples without joining in the hymn of homage and finally whether the sacred fruits may be permitted them.

"In the interim, I prepared my arsenal of pistols. If the council's decision was unfavorable, I would have to kill the serpents anyway and avail myself of the fruit. I also spent time writing out the precepts of our religion with an interpretation. When it was done, I sent a copy to the autocephalus requesting he make it available to the abdalas at their council meeting.

"I conferred with the king about setting up another paper mill in one of his border cities. When he suggested the city where our good friend the Governor ruled, I was delighted and tried to thank him with a song of praise. He laughed at my clumsy rendition. Since I could not go myself, I sent Adam and his bride. Though very young, Adam was competent. He would, besides, take experienced architects and engineers with him.

"Elizabeth had given me our twelfth twin, Matthew and Catherine, and was pregnant with our thirteenth; during that time I set up a printing establishment such as could not be surpassed in all Europe.

"The printworks had five hundred presses and employed five thousand Megamicres working in every capacity. Our production possibilities were enormous. I needed to spread the concept of one-color printing since the color alphabet was not yet out of use. To convince everyone of its superiority was not easy. Even when it is proven simpler and more efficacious, change is resisted. The simple and superstitious among those of the religious establishment held out longest.

"I waited to tell the king about my achievement until I had perfected the process. In the interim, I had been training my fourth son Robert. He would be supervising the printworks after his marriage at the beginning of our fourteenth year in this world. During this time, Elizabeth had given birth to our thirteenth twin whom we named Louis and Charlotte.

"The council of the five hundred abdalas had been meeting twice weekly in stormy sessions. Even though they knew the king favored us, they would not have been impressed except for the fact that the king generously defrayed all the expenses of their meetings. And they knew they could expect further tokens of his generosity if their opinion coincided with his.

"At the conclusion, this council issued two of three pronouncements: Since the Sun had manifested favor to us by drawing up the lid of our chest to himself, we could establish ourselves in their world and we could have entry into their temples except on days when the sacred hymn of homage to their Sun was chanted. The council wanted more time to consider the third point.

"One early morning, conferring with the king, he showed me a letter from the Governor of Alphapolis praising Adam, his application to work and his general popularity. Though I heard from Adam regularly, I said nothing, remembering the axiom which advises that one should not appear too knowing in the presence of a king. The king was interested in having the decree of the council made public. For this he would have to employ ten thousand writers in a costly and time-consuming task. He took me to the grand hall where there were ten thousand scribes writing down the words dictated by the chancellor who stood on an elevated platform. Many lights blazed on this grand spectacle.

"I asked the king to make me his official copyist. I would guarantee to have ten thousand copies of any decree, up to four pages, ready in one day. All would be in clear, legible one-color writing and all would be identical with the original.

"The king, astounded, was silent for some minutes. 'Even though I do not understand', he said, 'I agree; you are already my copyist. But do you know what you are undertaking?' I told him calmly that I did. 'Your promises appear absurd', he replied, 'but I prefer to grind reason underfoot and put my honor in your hands.' He said he needed two thousand copies for distribution the next day to the abdalas and for the public at large. I said I would need the original today written in one color.

"Shortly afterwards, his minister actually gave me the edict. I needed no wings to make me fly to my printing press. I chose blue ink, costliest, but it stood out best on the pale pink paper. I had the king's coat of arms drawn on the original and in nine hours, the work was drying. There were fifteen hundred single sheets and five hundred booklets. Together with the time needed for collating and packaging, the entire procedure took sixteen hours. I paid the workers extra for using their hours of repose and I myself went home to rest for two hours.

"I took a carriage to the palace where the royal couple were waiting to offer me more time. Instead, I bowed and offered them the package. They looked at the sheets and at the booklets, observed the beauty of the ink on the pale paper with its coat of arms and remained speechless. It is deeply satisfying to see amazement coupled with delight. The king finally spoke. 'For my peace of mind, you must tell me whether this work is of divine origin.' I replied that the work was not divine and I invited him to see how it was done and would always be done since I was the royal copyist. At this they abandoned their dignity, fell on my neck and kissed me in spite of my beard. They were intoxicated with joy.

"The minister was called in. He was sure it was a supernatural doing and he said so. The king coolly told him it was the work of one man and ordered the copies distributed at once. He added that he was dismissing all ten thousand scribes and proofreaders. Other work would be found for them. He further ordered the minister to draw up a document certifying that the noble giant Edward Alfred was named chief of the bureau of scribes and secretary of state.

"The next day, the king visited the establishment. He was struck by the construction of the rooms where the presses were. I had dug out the land so the heavy equipment could rest solidly, just as I had done with my forges. They had natural light all the time. He was even more pleased when my son, Robert without having forewarned me, presented the royal couple with a poem of praise. It was pure music, created by the best poet in the city.

"With a sure hand, Robert placed the type—the king was interested in seeing the letters in reverse—and ran off a hundred copies. He let them dry, then presented them to the king. I was afraid that he might have made some mistakes but there were none. He had also used a costly new ink of a luminous lacquer. I was further taken aback at this boldness when I heard him ask the king for a favor. I looked at my wife who was also dismayed.

" 'Speak', said the king. 'It will be granted.'

"Robert then asked permission to place a sign on the door of the building declaring it to be the 'Royal Printworks.' This, said Robert, would please his father. The king, gratified, said that now everyone would know the plant belonged to him but that I would be the royal printer, secretary and owner of all the land on which the building stood. Moreover, I would be reimbursed each harvest by a pension of a thousand ounces.

"Now all my family accompanied by the Megamicran workers sang in chorus, the poem of praise. Beside himself with this charming salute, the king ordered that two thousand ounces be distributed among all my people.

"The first printing caused a sensation. Not only the people but even the clergy insisted on seeing the work as supernatural. Our friend, the auto-cephalus, asked me in good faith to explain this marvelous species of writing. I concealed nothing, asking only for the king's permission. He said he would not stop me from showing the printing plant to anyone I pleased. The autocephalus was satisfied and could assure the clergy that the work, though divinely ingenious, was entirely natural.

"My wife gave birth to Leopold and Sophie, my fourteenth twin, and all my married daughters gave birth the same day."

NINTH DAY

"I noticed", Countess Bridgent addressed Edward, "that you included the words, Father, Son and Holy Spirit, in the marriage service but you gave your children no explanation of the 'trinity'. Weren't they curious?"

"When I had them learn the catechism", Edward replied, "I told them that this concept was a mystery beyond comprehension and that they must believe it under pain of eternal damnation. Since a mystery is something that can never be proved, it must never be questioned."

He then continued with his story. "The council was now ready with its final decree. In summary, it stated that in the sixty-one Megamicran years in their world, we had always behaved in irreproachable fashion except for the time in Alphapolis when we had taken the forbidden fruit. But we had expiated that crime. We were now free to use this nourishment with the condition still in force that no frightening sounds result. This decision was in accord with the oracle of the Great Spirit. Should we not succeed in silencing the serpents or inducing them to share the fruit, Megamicres will have the right to refuse to give or sell their milk to us nor will the clergy require that they do so. The giants, the decree concluded, will have to die of hunger, leave this world or war on the serpents. This latter eventuality would cause the greatest of disasters. The holy council requested an answer within the period of the next greenwood fire.*

"I published a reply which I distributed far and wide. I notified all that beginning on the first day of our sixty-third harvest in this happy realm, none of the giants would take any milk from the Megamicres. As religious head of my tribe, I would punish any offender from censure in light cases to excommunication in the most flagrant. The Megamicres would no longer hear any hissing from the reptiles, our common enemy, as we took the natural nourishment due us as children of the earth.

"The king and his inseparable were both astonished and overjoyed at this manifesto of mine. They did not inquire how I hoped to achieve my goal and I had to restrain myself from telling these dear persons my plan.

---

*A greenwood fire equals one season of forty-five Megamicran days.

"I summoned my married sons James, Richard, Robert and William as well as Theodore who was to be married the beginning of the next year. I excluded all the women from this conference except Elizabeth for fear they might let the secret out, not out of malice but for the opposite reason, high spirits. No, the matter was far too delicate; the success of this enterprise depended on secrecy. I told my five sons I was about to reveal to them a matter of the gravest importance. I asked them all to swear on our sacred writing that they would rather die than betray this confidence. They all swore and listened raptly.

" 'Tomorrow, two hours before the day begins, you will come here and practice firing pistols', I told them. 'You will fire at two circles, eighteen feet distant and two feet off the ground. When I see that you have become skilled so that your shots never miss the target in both circles, we shall then kill all the serpents in the six trees in the garden of our paper store. We shall gather them in barrows and throw them in the lime pits.'

"My dear sons did not miss a day of practice. They also developed skill in adjusting their aim as I placed them closer or farther away from the circle targets. At a distance of eighteen feet, they never failed to hit their mark. The day came when we were to put our plan into execution. The produce from the paper store garden, the gardens behind our house in the city, our print works and paper mill gardens would provide us with nourishment for five years. And I would acquire other gardens in the meantime.

"I admit I remained uneasy. The Megamicres are opposed to killing and moreover they are superstitious about drawing blood. The clergy would find our strategems very disagreeable and I still had to deal with a king who loved me and whom I would not wish to cause any grief. Still, on the day planned, we got our double-barrelled pistols ready, put on our shooting jackets, as I gave my sons a final speech. I told them to be quick and accurate before the serpents had time to hiss. We were all to stand, each in front of his tree and when I called out for them to fire, we had all to do so at the same instant. We kneeled, said a prayer, and were ready.

"When I said 'Fire', all the pistols went off simultaneously and soundlessly. At the foot of each tree lay two serpents, a total of twelve in all. We got the barrows, threw the snakes inside and brought them to the ditch. Our greatest problem was cleaning the blood where they had fallen. Their blood was red like ours. We were surprised that the Megamicres did not know this. In thirty thousand Megamicran years, no one apparently had ever wounded a serpent. We covered the stains with earth, cleaned the barrows and put them back. Returning to the trees, we found two eggs which we buried in the lime pit.

"The serpent parents, of whom there are two to a tree, produce from their throats, a large egg, ostrich-sized every twenty-four harvests. Shortly after the egg emerges the parent serpent falls dead to the foot of the tree. In two harvests, the hatched snakes become adult-sized and produce eggs and the cycle continues.

"We proceeded in the same fashion in the days that followed to clean the gardens of my paper mill, printworks and town house and provided ourselves with a substantial amount of food.

"On the first of August I gave a great banquet at which, for the first time, I openly ate five fruits while the Megamicres sucked the prescribed five times. This astonishing circumstance brought to the banquet table somewhat less gaiety but considerably more respect and thoughtfulness. We were looked upon as creatures whose nature was not quite comprehensible.

"The next day I went to see the king. (Elizabeth was at home because I had instituted a law which forbade women to leave their homes during the last three months of pregnancy.) My request to the king was that I send my five sons to Alphapolis to show Adam how he too could obtain nourishment from the figs and from the pine nuts. At the same time, I told the monarch, I had a plan which could be very profitable for commerce in his kingdom. If he assented, my five sons could, with Adam, go to his border cities to establish paper mills and printing works. We now had more orders than the factories here and at Alphapolis could fill.

"The king listened to my proposal with the greatest attention and gave me his approval. Then he congratulated me on having overcome the problem of the hissing serpents. Some among the people, though, were fearful lest they return and do some mischief. He himself, he said, had always loathed them and would like nothing better than to be rid of them all. He had made his position known to his minister and the autocephalus, both of whom had been upset about the disappearance of the snakes. But he had assured them it was God's grace which had sent our race to help the superstitious rid themselves of their weakness.

"I thanked the king and his mate for their confidence in me and swore I would never leave their kingdom without permission. As I left, the king gave me a document and his mate handed me a packet for Elizabeth. When I returned home, I gave my wife her gift and read my document. This was a certificate from the College of Magistrates exempting all my houses from any search such as the government may make of individual dwellings.

"My wife's gift consisted of an order conferring on her and all female descendants from the age of twenty-six harvests the right to wear the 'ex-omide'* as the garment of the nobility was called. Elizabeth was beside herself with excitement and gratitude. She ran about the room like a madwoman. She wanted to harness the carriage and go thank the king's mate. She kneeled in prayers of gratitude to the true and almighty God. In the fever of excitement, she included a prayer to the sun god as well.

"When I tried to quiet her transports of joy, she became annoyed by my coolness. 'Can't you understand what a wonderful gift this is? I never said

---

*Probably from 'exomis' (Greek Antiquity), a garment with one armhole, worn by lower classes, slaves and sometimes by women.

anything before, but this general nakedness, this indecent and shocking nudity has been the sorrow of my life.' She asked that our daughters be summoned. an hour later, they were all with her. With great enthusiasm, she told them about the 'exomide' and the nobility it conferred. Their lack of response shocked her. Wilhelmina politely said she did not care to be more noble than her husband. As for wearing the garment when she was pregnant, she said she would but that it was a small matter. Our youngest simply said that clothing was a bother.

"At this, we burst into laughter. Elizabeth seeing the indifferent reception given to the 'exomide' was finally able to smile at her own disproportionate view of the matter. But in fact, the introduction of this extremely attractive garment worthy of comparison with the most coquettish European style led my daughters, little by little, into a spirit of coquetry, something which is impossible among a people who go about completely nude.

"The obligation I felt about a source of nourishment for my son Adam and his family without recourse to the Megamicres' milk kept me in an uneasy state of mind. I had many somber thoughts about the danger of using pistols. I had been fearful here. How much more dangerous it would be in Alphapolis if the effort failed. The abdala who had put Elizabeth and me in prison still presided there. What if the slaughter of the snakes failed, in spite of the skill and best efforts of my sons? I felt apprehensive. Secrecy was of the utmost importance. The unexpected entry of a gardener, the sight of the barrows or blood could reveal the secret. The color of the blood would suggest that we, the giants, belonged to the same cursed race.

"These sober reflections made me decide to find a way of killing them without spilling blood. I studied this matter until it was time for my females* to give birth. They all delivered successfully as usual. To my fifteenth twin, I gave the names Andrew and Esther.

"You will need less patience, Milords, to hear the account of this new enterprise than I needed to accomplish it. In my employ, I had some able chemists who were also trained in mineralogy. One of these, son of the autocephalus, a parti-colored Megamicre, gave me some advice. When he saw me try to set fire to a reddish substance I had picked up in a sulphur mine, he warned me to stop. This substance would never ignite, he said, but would emit a deadly smoke. I later guessed that the substance was arsenic, having once heard it thus described by a Venetian. It was the most powerful of all metal poisons and not even a hundred sublimations would decrease the acridity of this volatile smoke. Any solid matter, he said, that does not ignite but only emits visible fumes must be anti-life.

"Fire is the primary vivifying force of nature. Life is only movement and movement is caused by the fire of nature, that grand creation whose existence is the result of a first cause, namely the incomprehensible God.

---

*Casanova's exact word.

"Wishing to test what my sage Megamicre had told me, I allowed a small quantity to rise from a bowl in which I had ignited a bit of this substance and held two birds over it. They dropped dead at once. If we could dispose of the serpents in this way before they had time to hiss, we would not have to bury them in secret or account for their manner of death.

"I put a quantity of this reddish substance in a crucible and covered it with an air-tight lid. To the lid, I attached four hermetically sealed pumps with pistons. A pipe with a valve on the lid let me open or close the lid as needed. A brazier of burning coal under the crucible fired the substance. When the crucible was full of gas and then forced into the pumps by the pistons which my sons worked, I opened the windows, removed the brazier, extinguished the fire and detached the pumps. These I sealed tight with pitch.

"Now it was time to figure out a way of firing this poisonous smoke directly into the faces of the serpents so they would suffocate immediately. I had no clear idea of how to manage this.

"Such, Milords, is my style of working. I need a challenge. Once I am involved, I do not retreat. Those who insist on a well-thought out plan with every problem solved before they undertake a difficult enterprise will be at a loss if an unforeseen difficulty does arrive. Such unimaginative engineers are incapable of coming up with a last minute expedient and they give up. To succeed, a man must be not only an excellent and prudent planner but he must know what due to give to chance. A courageous man will throw the gauntlet to chance and advance in the face of danger.

"I had to try out the effectiveness of the arsenic smoke. Two hours before day began, alone in the garden, I placed two cages made of circles of brass wire twelve feet above the ground and two feet apart. They held six live birds in each. With my rifle loaded with gunpowder and cylinders of gas, I aimed at a distance of twenty-seven feet. I had some anxiety that the longer distance—our previous measure was eighteen feet—might burn out the powder before the poisoned smoke reached its target. My fears were unfounded. I fired and the birds dropped. To make sure they were not simply overcome, I returned the next day. They were indeed dead, all twelve of them. Now I could try the poison gas on the serpents.

"Because my house was already free of them, I bought a house at auction. The two gardens had four trees in each. I had my four sons come there; I sent the gardeners off on a pretext to my printworks, and we loaded our rifles. We killed eight serpents in one garden and the same number in the other. Now we called our gardeners back and I ordered them to throw the sixteen creatures into the ditch. They were frightened and insisted they had to get proof from the neighbors that they had heard no hissing. I told them to do whatever they had to and we all left.

"On the next day when I visited the court, the king told me that the people already knew of this new development. Before, they had feared the serpents

111

would return to wreak vengeance. Now, seeing them dead, they were baffled. Seeing them dead without injury was a further cause of wonder. Never since the world began had serpents died of other than natural causes. The autocephalus had already sent a courier to Heliopolis to tell the Great Spirit of this extraordinary event. He might attribute it to some divine power we had. I assured the king that my power was not divine but that God had helped me. Then I kissed his hand and told him my sons would be leaving for Alphapolis and the other border cities in the second pentamine of the new harvest.

"When the time came, the five married couples set off in fifteen carriages. I had sent along presents for the Governor, chests of firearms and munitions, a hundred knapsacks for the men, fifty exomides for the married women, all designed by Elizabeth, and two hundred containers with the special syrup my wife had created from pine nuts. This syrup also preserved the figs which they took along for their trip.

"Three pentamines after their arrival, I received word that Adam and his family no longer had need for the Megamicres' milk. Robert had bought a house with space to include a printing press. This he set up in the space of two harvests.

"The Governor loved all our family members but his joy at having with him, James and Wilhelmina, whom he had raised, was immeasurable. My children did not wish to visit the abdala and I did not care to press them. Pardoning those who have hurt us is fine; loving them is another thing. The Law requires only that we return good for evil but we need not love those who are repugnant to us. And to indicate our scorn for them is not a crime.

"During four European years, my children established paper mills and printing presses in all the four border cities of the realm. They destroyed the serpents in all the houses they bought. When they departed, they left capable and honest Megamicres in charge of the businesses.

"When they returned to the capital four and a half European years after they left, they numbered seventy-six. Adam, his wife and fourteen children came back with them; the five couples had produced eight children each and my wife returned the ten infants who had been left in her care. My own family increased in the same proportion during those four years. Elizabeth gave birth to four pairs of twins* and we married four pairs on the first of the year.

"The king ennobled the fine young people who had done so much for his realm. They were honored with the gift of the red cloak and a pension of two thousand ounces. We were all rich now. Our establishments were profitable and we had in addition an income of forty thousand ounces as pensions from the king.

"Three months after their return, all my married daughters gave birth and my wife gave me my twentieth twin. I began to prepare for the festival of our

---

*See listing of eighty children of Elizabeth and Edward.

twenty-first year in that world. In addition to the marriage of our eleventh twin, we would also be celebrating the marriage of our first grandchildren, Elizabeth and Edward.

"We spent ten peaceful years (European) in the king's favor and in the enjoyment of everything desirable. During this time, my wife gave me ten more twins; I gave the nuptial blessing to twelve couples on the anniversary of our thirty-first year there. One of the couples was my great-grandson, James' grandson. We now numbered 922 persons.

"We had not spent these years in idleness. I had increased the number of my forges considerably. I experimented to produce a high grade metal to use in making cannons of every calibre. I invented all sorts of firearms which my children worked on. I forged three bells, a gift to the king and under my direction, a tower was built to house them. These bells now were used to announce the beginning and end of each day and to call an assembly. The bells could signal the day, hour and place for such assemblies and eventually were regarded as the very voice of the monarch.

"About the time I created the bells, I was taken by a fancy to print a christian almanac. It contained twelve of our months, constituting seven hundred twenty Megamicran days. Each day was titled with the name of a man or woman. I did not describe these as saints' names—it would have confused my children—but here my sons and daughters could look for names they wanted for their new-borns. Besides recording daily duties, this almanac also contained the activities of the Megamicres, their metamorphoses, their greenwood tree burnings, their rains, harvests, holidays and the relationship which existed

"At first, this almanac was a modest little booklet, but with time and because of additions and the inclusion of articles, it became so interesting and informative, that we put out two million copies a year, half of which were distributed outside the kingdom."

113

TENTH DAY

Dinner was nearly over and the guests were talking among themselves. "I like the idea", said Lady Rutgland, "of the husbands acting as midwives. I suppose, though, that when the women of the family grow up, they relieve the men of this responsibility."

"On the contrary", Elizabeth replied at once. "Husbands regard this as their right. They believe their wives should deliver into their own hands the fruit of their mutual love. This custom has now become the natural way of life for all of them."

"I can understand that very well", Lady Rutgland mused. "Any custom that is long established comes to be regarded as a natural law."

Lord Howard, pursuing his own thoughts, said he was troubled by the arsenic smoke that Edward had invented. "Think of it", he murmured, "those poisonous fumes can serve no purpose in our world, yet they could be used to commit atrocious crimes."

There was a pause and Edward resumed his narration. "With the increasing numbers in my family, I decided in the thirty-first year of my stay there, to establish seminaries for the education of the children. For the youngest ones from the time they were weaned at age one until their fourth year, I had a separate seminary which I called the Micropedia* and for those from age four through eight, I had built a seminary nearby with separate quarters for male and female. This seminary I named the Megalopedia*. Then for fifteen months, still in separate quarters, in the seminary called the Ephebus*, I had the children educated until they were united in marriage. Elizabeth supervised the females, I the males.

"For nurses and caretakers, I had chosen the finest workers. These I recruited from the attendants at the hospices of eternal rest. Here the Megamicre and his inseparable spent the last six of their allotted 192 harvests, removed from the world, seeing no one but each other and slipping into death in a state of the utmost tranquillity.

---

*See Glossary of terms.

"A further word about these hospices may be interesting. In the capital of Realm 90, there are twenty-four of these places of eternal peace. Although the couples who retire there continue to nourish one another with their milk, their other needs are attended to so they can spend their last days without any responsibilities whatever.

"The hospices are well-run and scrupulously clean. In a city of a million and a half couples where the hour of birth and the hour of death are known exactly, there is virtually no likelihood of administrative error. Forty-eight couples are born each day; forty-eight couples die each day. When one couple dies, another enters the hospice to occupy the room just vacated.

"Returning to the Ephebus; I required all to adhere to a strict code of behavior. Lying was forbidden although in some cases abstaining from the truth was not punished.I forbade loud talk, angry gestures and making faces. We had to distinguish stubbornness from resolute firmness and timidity from prudence. There were penalties for yawning, immoderate laughter and crying. Spitting was prohibited; this habit was one all Megamicres found particularly distasteful (they habitually swallowed their precious saliva). Every pentamine, rewards were given for good conduct.

"At this time, the king called me to court to show me a decree which offered me Fiefdom one in the kingdom of Heliopolis on the other side of the world. Twenty-five years earlier, this offer had been made with the condition that we offer homage to the sun. Now I could practice my own religion. I was to reign with all the privileges of a sovereign, enjoy its revenues, make laws, destroy old, and build new edifices and coin money. I was not to interfere with the religion of the Megamicres who were to recognize me as their ruler. All the buildings that had belonged to the late ruler who had died without issue, were to be mine. In addition, I was also to enjoy possession of a great palace bordering the river and a garden which contained ninety-two trees.

"In return, I was to build paper mills, printing presses and a foundry in the capital and four border cities for the ruler. These were to be paid for and owned by him. I could build forges and presses for myself. A specified time was set to accomplish these projects.

"I studied the contents of this decree. I could envision myself as an independent prince, assured with my family, of a great fortune. But I would have to leave my king. I asked for time to think about this munificent gift. The king granted this freely and invited me to go with his inseparable to look at the Fiefdom on his great globe which they call the Microcosm. The globe, which was on the lowest floor of his palace, was about six hundred feet in diameter. He opened a door and we were exactly in the location of his realm. High above this brilliantly lighted concave interior was a lamp representing the sun.

"The eighty square-shaped monarchies, each of equal size, were admirably depicted. Each capital was in the centre of the realm and the smaller cities were all equidistant. The ten republics and the 216 triangular fiefdoms were each

116

differently colored. The king showed me Fiefdom One which consisted of three hundred cities and 60,000 villages. The distance by carriage from Realm 90 would be 25,000 leagues. 'You told me that one of our leagues measure four hundred of your feet', said the king, 'so you can estimate the distance.'

"The king was able to show me the entire Megamicran world while we stood immobile on a dais and the sphere gently rotated by means of his adroit maneuvering of red gold hooks which punctuated the whole concavity.

"This Microcosm had been cleverly designed; it surpassed even the great one in Heliopolis. The king said regretfully that he had not traveled there. 'In your world', he said, 'it seems to me that you should all travel. You can observe the many varieties of nature and from your telescopes, you can see the distant stars. To read a letter in the light of your moon, how beautiful that must be, my dear Edward, how grand! Compared to you, we are insignificant, yet what a pity it is that you also have war, pestilence, famine and sickness. I would give my kingdom to make one trip there with you but I would not want to live in your world.'

"Returning home, I told my wife about the decree. She too had misgivings because we were never again likely to encounter a king like ours.

"At this time, an event occurred which had interesting consequences. For the last ten years, my wife had in her employ on orange-red couple whose character and talents were beyond praise. The more dominant of the two, a Megamicre of whom she was very fond, had been slowly losing sight in the right eye. The disease which causes this was not uncommon among them and was the more to be feared as the other eye soon loses sight too. There was no known remedy and no case known of an afflicted individual who had recovered his sight.

"My interest was aroused by the case and even more by my wife's strong feelings about the Megamicre's misfortune. I knew nothing about the functioning or the anatomy of the eye, but I did recall that an oculist in the city of Lincoln had restored sight to the Baron Frederick Athins by removing his cataract.

"Keeping my intentions secret, I determined to learn what I could from animals whose eye structure was not unlike ours. I used a pig-like creature that farmers employ to dig out with their snouts, certain seeds which make a base for fine perfumes. I had already examined our employee and had observed an opaque mass covering his eye. It was my plan to operate on the Megamicre only after I had worked successfully on the animals.

"Over the years, I had increased my supply of surgical instruments chiefly for my own satisfaction. I had lancets of every shape and sharpness. I even had what is called a 'speculum oculi.'

"With the help of two of my sons, Henry and Louis, I worked on one of the animal's eyes, cutting in different areas and at different depths. Of the three experimental pigs, only one lost the sight of the eye where I had pierced too

117

deep. The others were fine after a week. The next day I operated on three more and after another week, I was delighted to find them well with undamaged eyes. I was now ready to operate on the Megamicre.

"Aided by Elizabeth and my two sons, I removed his cataract, bandaged his eye and kept him quiet in a room for forty hours. When his bandage was removed and the healthy eye covered, he found to his overwhelming joy that he could read a sheet of paper with colored characters on it. He and his mate praised and thanked me extravagantly and somewhat incomprehensibly. And so I became an oculist and a miracle man sent by their sun for the welfare of his children.

"News of the operation spread. The autocephalus offered a hymn of thanks-giving for the miracle, unduplicated since the previous miracle when the previous autocephalus had been restored to life.

"My wife had just given birth to our thirty first twin and the time had come when I had to answer the Great Spirit about his offer of the fief. I consulted with my king, asking him what he considered important in the art of governing.

" 'Your subjects will love you', he replied, 'if you can provide a flourishing economy, comforts and satisfactions. You must give them a sense of enjoying freedom even if this is only a phantom liberty. You will argue that in being just, you will not satisfy everyone and I agree. But the art of ruling requires a skill whereby you can be liked even by those you have to punish. Be slow to "hurl thunderbolts" and swift to reward. Increase if you can their privileges. Reform burdensome laws. Permit liberty of conscience and ignore accusations against persons unless they come through legal channels. Watch out for the greedy rich. Forbid usury and make life easier for the poor.

" 'You should try to make yourself liked but you need not therefore become too familiar with your subjects. Do not present yourself as an ordinary man; your subjects need to believe that you are above the common man.

" 'Almost all rulers have reserves of gold or other precious metals. But woe betide the state where the wealth of its subjects depends on gold. Not gold but industry, commerce and a reasonable cost of living are important. An excessive supply of money can cause the cost of living to rise in a short time. Commercial prosperity depends on a free market but it should be watched to see that it does not get out of control. The merchant himself will control it if it gets out of hand. Imports should be encouraged because they invite exports. A sluggish circula-tion of money affects credit and leads one to believe that the country's ills are due to a lack of specie. The fact instead is that gold is locked up in the coffers of the rich. Seeing it brings no profit, they hold on to it waiting for a better time. Or they may think of passing it surreptitiously to a foreign state.

" 'A time may come when the ruler has to institute new regulations in order to correct certain abuses harmful to the general welfare. Those who profit by the old rules will cry out against the new. They will complain and even try to destroy the reputations of the reformers. A good ruler takes this in stride; he remains unperturbed, knowing the storm will pass. When the public gains by the new edicts, even the opponents will eventually benefit.' The king talked of the advantages of allowing a tariff-free importation of goods, low property taxes and an accounting every twelve years of the country's revenues and expenses. 'These two should coincide. If revenues exceed expenses, then the monies should be used to beautify the city and provide comforts for the populace.'

"He concluded his talk with the assurance that we could if we wished accept the fiefdom with our sons as proxies. We decided to send our five oldest sons, their wives and families, to take over the fief in Heliopolis.

"Returning now to the event which had excited the interest of the people, I found myself besieged by crowds of sufferers who wanted help. To control this disorganized visiting, I published two or three thousand announcements stating I would examine patients on two days each pentamine, namely Dust and Butterfly*, in the morning hours in the great hall of the paper mill. I wrote further that since no mortal is infallible, I would need two certificates, one from the office of the autocephalus, exempting the patient from any ecclesiastical censure and the other from the College of Physicists declaring the person incurable. I would charge nothing since we were all children of the same God.

"The next day, I examined twenty Megamicres of whom seven were red. Three were ineligible but I could operate on four when they brought their certificates. Of the colored and polychrome, I excluded three. Among the colored, one was a member of the College of Physicists and one was a surgeon. Henry and Charles were with me as I worked, learning the procedure of examination and later of the operation.

"The work, two days of each pentamine, became my principal activity. But I was uneasy; the slightest mischance could bring failure. My reputation would suffer in spite of my successes and my conscience would trouble me if I rendered someone incurable who might have been cured. I became very selective. Surgeons need to have special qualifications besides anatomical knowledge. A steady hand, perfect vision and exquisite judgment should be joined to a character in which caution, care, and a habit of keen observation predominate. Youth is a desirable characteristic.

"I had enlisted five grandsons to join Henry and Charles. They all worked in the country experimenting on the animals and all were enthralled with the chance to perform what seemed to them miracles. By now I had many pigs with vision in only one eye.

"In the space of one European year, all had become adept in their technique. I had restored sight to nineteen nobles; Henry and Charles were operating on non-reds after trial experiences with polychromes. By now, our mission was very old; we had lived in their world for one hundred twenty-four harvests.

---

*See Glossary.

From two people we had become a thousand or more. The Megamicres attributed our life and multiplication to the influence of their Sun.

"Now in my thirty-second year, I decided to give the king my final decision about the fief in Heliopolis. I told him that my wife and I were determined to remain his subjects; that we could not bear the thought of leaving a king to whom we and our whole family owed our fortune and our lives. But since such a great gift as a fiefdom could not conceivably be refused when it was so honorably offered, I was sending my five sons to take over the investiture by proxy. They would discharge each of the conditions and they would be provided with all the means necessary to carry these out. I explained that I would divide the fief into five parts, one for each son and his family. James would be the chief.

"The king and his mate were silent for a while, then said that our own feeling of gratitude was surpassed by the gratitude which he, his court and all his people felt towards us. Our decision to remain was the greatest gift he could receive.

"When I returned home, I received the royal secretary who had brought seven indigo-blue mantles, each with its diamond fastening. These were for my oculist sons and grandsons. In addition, in recognition of their work, each was awarded a yearly pension of one thousand ounces.

"We continued our examinations as before. One day, Henry approached me as I was examining a noble in my office at the paper mill. He was leading a jonquil whom I had pronounced curable. Henry showed me the certificate from the College of Physicists. It was different from the usual statement. It said of the jonquil, 'It is not impossible that he may recover his sight since he is not incurable.'

"I wrote an answer to the College and had the jonquil's mate deliver it. My note stated that if the College considered the Megamicre curable, then I yielded the cure to them since it was their right to do so. I took the precaution of having my note printed and posted.

"The College in turn sent an order to the printworks where William was in charge, for a thousand copies of a circular they wished printed which stated that my cure proved that the blindness was indeed curable; hence they could not be expected to sign a certificate declaring the person incurable. I had already disproved that. I replied with a statement, phrased in friendly and moderate terms, declaring that I was suspending any further operations, yielding this function to the rightly and legally appointed physicians who were in charge of this kind of service to the people.

"The matter became a subject of heated controversy. After a week of inaction by the physicians, the blind, left in limbo, appealed to the courts for an injunction against the doctors. The civil tribunal ruled on their suit, ordering the College to provide capable oculists to perform the operation, free of charge.

120

If they failed to do so in the period of one harvest, the College would be abolished.

"The complainants also charged that the physicians were guilty of deceit in that their certificates contradicted one another. For the crime of deceit there, the punishment was life imprisonment."

ELEVENTH DAY

"The physicians and the blind people were quarreling fiercely when we left them yesterday", Count Burghlei said as dinner ended. "To speak honestly, I think Edward should not have asked the doctors for certificates."

Edward defended himself. "Milord, I believe you too would have asked the College for those releases. In my position at the time, I needed an umblemished reputation before I presented myself to the Great Spirit."

"I think I would have laughed at this thirty thousand year old Great Spirit of yours', Count Burghlei retorted.

"Not if you were expecting to become a ruler in his domain", Dunspili answered him. "Whether the Great Spirit is real or a fake, Edward acted sensibly."

"What impressed *me* yesterday", Lord Howard said, "was that sound lecture of the Megamicre monarch on the duties of a king."

"King James should have had that lecture read to him", Chepstow remarked. "It might humble his pride."

"Let's leave the King as he is", Count Bridgent interposed hastily, "and find out what steps the tribunal took against the doctors. Poor devils, I confess I feel sorry for them."

Edward took up the account. "When the doctors were accused of lying, they told the ecclesiastical body they had really believed the malady was incurable. Later when they recognized it was indeed curable, they indicated this on their certificates. But at no time had they lied. The tribunal of the autocephalus thereupon absolved them. The royal tribunal, however, ordered them to start curing the blind in a specified time or face abolition. They were in despair. In the College, doctors blamed surgeons and surgeons blamed doctors.

"Meanwhile, the blind, angered and upset, waited for the time set by the court for operations to commence. Already two greenwood fires had passed and the third was nearing its end without any word. Outraged, the people were preparing a mock funeral for the doctors when we received an order to print an announcement that a certain Doctor Aaaau Eooo Eiiio was ready to operate on those individuals who had been declared curable by the Christian giant Alfred Edward. The doctor would operate three times a week in his office beginning on the third day of the following harvest. Six Megamicran couples were invited to be present to view his work.

"This put an end to all the talk. Our friend, the Chief Gardener was one of those invited to attend. He said he would report to me. I said I wished the work to be successful. It would not detract from the merit I had already acquired and would leave me free for many affairs of the greatest importance. And I would be relieved of a great burden.

"Before I had heard from the Gardener about the cataract procedure which he witnessed, I learned from my son William at the printing press that he had received an order to print a thousand copies announcing the news that the jonquil had been operated on successfully. Fifteen minutes later, my friend the Chief Gardener came to tell me what he had observed of the procedure. From the details he gave me, I admit I thought it faulty. Instead of removing the glutinous mass on the cornea, the surgeon with a rounded lancet, had pushed the substance into the corner of the eye.

"I called my sons in and told them what I thought. I enjoined them to secrecy saying that while we could be pleased at another's success, we did not have to offer them our own technique. The first obligation was to our own self-preservation and honor. Still, if they were asked, they should say only, 'We wish that time will confirm the success and sagacity of the wise surgeon.' I drew from my oculist sons Henry and Charles the unwilling admission that they hoped he would not succeed. I lectured them soundly on their ignoble thoughts.

"At the end of two greenwood fires, the reputation of the doctor was at its zenith. He had restored the sight of fifty blind persons among whom were nine reds. We had, during this time of the doctor's popularity, been excoriated for our harshness in demanding certificates from the College. The surgeon had written a long paper about the anatomy of the eye and the cataract procedure. He blamed us for our secrecy when we operated. I printed a reply, but it was read by fewer than had read the doctor's report. I recalled that the 'Analects of the Protoplast'*, those four secret and ancient volumes which the disgraced theologians had given me as a gift for having their positions restored, contained passages on anatomy. One of these, on the anatomy of the eye, had been copied word for word by Dr. Aaaau Eooo Eiiio in the paper he had published. Later when I asked the king to have the ancient texts published, he refused, explaining that the contents were supposed to be kept secret lest the sacred truths therein be abused. I did not pursue the subject.

"Suddenly, the admiration for the doctor took a fatal plunge. An unhappy accident put an end to the adulation. A rich young gridelin (bluish-red) Megamicre became blind again. The report was first denied, then two new

---

*From the French 'protoplaste', or first man.

124

cases were discovered. A blue with only one cataract had consented to have both eyes operated on. In four weeks, the unfortunate wretch was totally blind. A red suffered an inflammation; he was cured of this until cancer attacked the eye and he died. Every day new cases were found of supposed cures which had failed. Now everyone cried out against this crime. The blind individuals said they had been assassinated by the imposter—that is what they called him—and they sought redress. Complaints began to pour into both tribunals, civil and clerical. Law suits were filed, witnesses examined. Each day more complaints came in because, outside of one or two, all who had been operated on had become worse than they formerly were. The physician publicly offered to re-do the operations, but he was answered with insult and invective.

"A pentamine later, the religious tribunal sentenced the physician to excommunication, perpetual and irrevocable. The royal tribunal condemned him to life imprisonment and gave notice to the College that if, in the time of one greenwood fire, no one had undertaken to plead for the accused, the College would be dissolved.

"Custom there forbids a defendant whose culpability is recognized from hiring a lawyer or getting friends or relatives to plead for him since these are supposedly corrupted by money, friendship or obligation. The defender can only be a hostile or totally indifferent stranger. The prosecutor (who is called advocate paradox, because he takes the contrary position) determines if the defense qualifies under those terms.

"We were discussing the matter one day in our family when my grandson Sebastian, one of my ablest oculists, said he doubted anyone would take on the defense and he was sorry for the poor physician's plight. Time was indeed running out and the defendant seemed doomed. I told Sebastian that feeling sorry was not enough. And the public would not believe him unless he took positive action. I recommended that he take on the defense himself.

"Everyone was taken aback by my suggestion. For a full three minutes, no one spoke. Then Sebastian kneeled to kiss our hands and ask for our blessing and left with his wife. So we were not surprised the next day to hear that he had gone to the prosecutor. The fourth day of the following pentamine was set for the trial. A public announcement informed all that Sebastian would be the defender in open court of the doctor. I noticed that Sebastian's name was preceded by the word 'noble'. The king, I soon learned, had conferred the diploma of nobility on him and had sent him the green cloak with red sleeves which proclaimed his lofty status.

"The king sent us tickets for the loges where the nobility sat. I permitted the women to attend with their husbands though they were in their last months of pregnancy. This occasion merited an exception to the regulation requiring them to remain home. There were two hundred and ten of us, accounting for one fifth of our total family. The College of Physicians had asked for a hundred tickets so they could sit in the circle reserved for the accused. When this news spread, the whole city wanted to attend. Eighteen to twenty thousand spectators were able to get in.

"As we entered the door, we passed the line of physicians. Their heads were lowered and their hands were clasped on their breasts below the medallion of their College. The last in line, head very low, was the poor accused oculist who, in token of his grief, had speckled himself with every color from head to foot. We had trouble restraining our amusement at this sorry spectacle.

"The king was presiding because this was an exceptional case. After he was seated, Sebastian took his own place with the oculist on his left and the prosecutor on his right. Forty judges, all reds, sat in a semicircle on one level; the king's courtiers sat above them.

"Sebastian, a handsome seventeen year old, dark-haired, five feet nine inches tall and well-proportioned, looked very serious and dignified in his cloak of nobility. He was endowed with a beautiful voice and superlative eloquence. He had learned from our religion that persuasion was always more effective than a forceful, coercive manner. He rose to speak.

"He began his argument by relating the history of the affair. The doctor, he said, had studied his subject well before beginning the operations. The article he wrote on the anatomy of the eye attested to this. His mishaps had been caused by unforeseen circumstances. No one hereafter would wish to become a doctor if the law made him responsible for accidents, even those that lead to death. The Megamicres in this case were motivated by revenge, but God alone could exact vengeance. He asked them to show pity towards one of their brothers who had hurt them believing he was helping them. He stepped down from the rostrum.

"The prosecutor took his place. He praised Sebastian for his virtue in defending the accused. He agreed with the maxim that only to doctors may the law permit killing of patients without punishment and also experimenting on the suffering sick poor, even if these experiments caused the death of the ones experimented upon. But in this case, the crime was not the suffering he had caused by his unfortunate operations, but the crime of pride and jealousy when he wrote out the insolent certificate which made the noble giant Edward suspend his beneficent work. The prosecutor continued by praising my work and my forbearance in contrast with the arrogance of the doctor who further had his head turned by the adulation of a fickle public. As for vengeance being God's, the prosecutor declared that the divine will is carried out by a law which punishes the transgressor when he harms the general welfare.

"It was Sebastian's turn. Holding his trembling client by the hand, he said, 'You see before you an innocent subject who begs that you absolve him and, with head bowed, begs the whole country to forgive him.' Sebastian had the doctor kneel and prostrate himself. 'And along with him', continued Sebastian,

126

'the whole College, their hearts filled with remorse, also prostrate themselves and in tears ask for mercy.' It was a stunning spectacle to see the whole body of physicians throw themselves face down in supplication. The applause that filled the vast room made very clear to the council what the public wanted. The bailiffs cleared the room and all returned home.

"We dined with James, praising Sebastian for his masterly defense. In an hour, an officer of the king brought us a copy of the verdict. The physician and the College were absolved and restored to practice. Had Sebastian not brought off his dramatic finale, the poor doctor and the whole College would have lost.

"The day after the trial, the unhappy oculist, having washed off the multi-colored make up, came to see Sebastian. My grandson greeted him cordially and in reply to his thanks, said he had only obeyed my advice in defending him. But he was happy to have been useful. The oculist told us that he had experimented on horses' eyes before operating. When my wife suggested that the College should establish a school of anatomy, he was horrified. But he bowed deeply, sang us a courtesy song and left.

"From all sides now, there came pleas for help. I posted a notice that my house would be open to all who had become blind again after the operation. As they visited, I found many to whom I could restore sight, others were inopera-ble and there were some whose vision I could repair by a medical regimen.

"During this period, our wives all gave birth and I was given my thirty-second twin. I now presented to the king my plan to send my five oldest sons and their families to Heliopolis. I realized I would need a full European year to prepare. I fixed the date for their departure for eight days after our new year festivities. This would be the start of my thirty-fourth year in this beautiful world. By this time, the number of patients needing operations had diminished. I had given up certain of the unhappy creatures as uncurable. Henry and Louis cured the others. I could now apply myself to preparing for the journey. Only my wife and the king knew of the plans. The king asked for the exact date so he could help facilitate this long journey.

"My sons learned for the first time about the fiefdom when they received from the king, mantles of nobility as heirs of a feudatory prince. They were amazed to have such a fortune fall upon them as if from the clouds. And, incidentally, they learned a lesson in restraint and self-discipline when they discovered I had kept the news about Fiefdom One a secret for two and a half years.

"In line with our new status, we disposed at auction of our possessions such as the stores, the factories, the paper mills and presses as well as our inventory of essences, musical instruments and paper. These were taken over by Mega-micres trained and capable of managing these businesses. It would have been unseemly for princes to work in retail shops as salespeople or as accountants.

"I could not part with my laboratories, forges or gunpowder plants. I had my sons work as smiths, an occupation for which I set them an example. Jupiter, master of the forge, is not derogated when he puts his hand to the anvil nor is his son Vulcan a less glorious smith.

"My chief occupation that year was the design and construction of an entire city in a vast area which I acquired with the king's permission. A second project was the construction of a theatre. I first had ten thousand trees planted. These also served as park area for the two seminaries nearby after my sons eliminated all the serpents with the poison gas.

"With the labor of 25,000 pairs of polychromes, a large palace rose up, twenty stories high, right in the center of my land. Radiating out from this center, ten thousand square houses were built, separated by four avenues. I had a twelve foot wide canal constructed to run its course around the entire area. On a boulevard alongside, I built a hundred large houses, each three hundred feet wide with a garden of equal size. I planned this city expressly for my families; those Megamicres who lived there were in the position of foreigners.

"I built a billiard room beneath the tennis courts (which were covered by canopies against the sun). In the billiard rooms were all necessary items like cues, long handled mallets and balls of Acorus wood. My seminarians found much recreation here in their free time. The tennis and billiard games became very popular with the nobles. I had to have many made in proportion to their size. There were so many orders to fill that I left the work for them to do even though I owned the rights of manufacture. The Megamicres became exceptionally skilful in these games and began to gamble on the outcome.

"The king passed a law against this gambling. When I asked if he thought it could be enforced, he assured me that he would never pass a law that was unenforceable. In his law, players could engage in matches only with opponents who were their proven equals. The playing of billiards was not outlawed, but the practice of handicapping in the case of uneven players was forbidden. Secret agreements, when discovered, were subject to severe penalties. When the element of chance thus became small, the game lost interest for gamblers but continued as a pastime.

"I learned, in conversation with the king on another occasion, that he would be interested in attending our ceremonies, but he had not proposed this as being an intrusion. I assured him we would be more than pleased if he, his mate and a hundred couples of his court would honor us by attending our new year ceremonies and festivities. At the next open court, I invited him publicly as if on my own initiative. Such is the delicacy of the Megamicres about seeming to be curious that I made my invitation a public one. For his part, he acknowledged me as a feudatory prince and soon had a military guard placed around my houses and seminaries as befitted a sovereign prince.

"Regarding my second project, the building of two theatres, I concentrated my energies on one for the time. Here I hoped to honor the king with a play written by me and performed by my children. This would be given on the day of our ceremonies.

"I took one corner of my palace, an area 50 by 120 feet, for this purpose. It was almost fifty feet high with room for rows of wide steps like a Roman amphitheatre. Sixteen rows of loges or boxes were elevated about four feet above, six of which were for us and nine rows for the Megamicres. The royal box was in the center and two balconies on either side were to accommodate the nobles of the king's court. The stage started four feet up from the ground floor seating area and rose gently over its seventy foot length until it was eight feet high in the back. This four foot rise made for optimal viewing and corresponded in height with the last row of the amphitheatre.

"Under the floor of the orchestra, I placed hollow open ducts made of a metal alloy to carry the sound evenly to the loges. From the vaulted rounded ceiling, hung a large chandelier with two hundred phosphorus circlets to light the theatre. Each box had in addition its own luminous torch.

"By the first of October, all our women gave birth. My wife presented me with my thirty-third twin. At the end of this same month, my theatre was finished. By the middle of December, I had already rehearsed many times behind closed doors, the two plays I had written, until I was sure that my children knew their parts perfectly. A prompter was not necessary.

"I asked the king to place a thousand royal guards at my disposal and to invite to the festival, after dinner, eight thousand noble couples and a thousand bastard couples. He was surprised, but said the guards would be available. He wondered why I would need so many guards at a party of twenty thousand Megamicres to be held in open country. I told him that the nine thousand couples were not to arrive until ten-thirty o'clock. The marriage ceremonies would begin at eight-thirty and only the king and his court would be there. The whole festival would end at the fourteenth hour, the end of the day."

TWELFTH DAY

"That young Sebastian is a marvel", Lady Rutgland remarked. "It would give me a lot of pleasure to see him."

"As he looked then? Or as he looks now?" Burghlei said disagreeably. "If I calculate correctly, he is sixty-six years old. Isn't that so, Madame Elizabeth?"

"Exactly so", she replied. "But to tell the truth, he looks younger than you do."

"Well", murmured Bridgent, "that answer should hold the honorable lord."

"I agree he must look young, just as you do yourself, Madame, but it is not the real thing." Burghlei turned to Lady Rutgland. "Isn't that so, Milady?"

"The appearance of youth is not the same", she agreed. "But in your case, you would not even have to look youthful; your juvenile speech would be proof enough."

"And there is another slap for the lord as good as the first", Lord Howard added softly.

Burghlei was stung. "An argument with a sharp-tongued woman gives me the greatest amusement", he retorted, "because I can always end it."

"How is that?" asked Chepstow.

"Simply by conceding defeat."

"Enough." Count Bridgent intervened. "We are here to listen to Edward."

"Excuse me Count", Burghlei persisted. "Edward is certainly our friend but since he has listed all his titles for us, should we not address him as 'prince?' "

"I thank you, Milord", Edward said quietly, "but when we left that world, we left our rank there too. As you would lose yours if you went there."

"Of course", Countess Bridgent soothed... "Now, Charles, I must speak to you seriously. Stop your dull jokes or go away."

"I prefer to stop them, Milady."

"Then let us finish our dinner", Count Bridgent said. "I am impatient to get to Edward's theatre and see the plays his children performed."

"There is one matter among the other marvels that astonishes me", Lady Rutgland said. "Edward went there as a very young man. True he had had a good education and he was clever but, as he admits, he had no experience in the arts and not much more of science than would be expected of a fourteen year old. Yet over there, with no books to help, he became an artisan, an architect, an engraver, a chemist, an alchemist, a mathematician, a theologian, an excellent oculist, a poet and a great politician. Here we have one man doing what it takes many men to do working cooperatively."

"And I", Count Burghlei added, "keep wondering about the learned words and phrases Edward uses in discussing some of the Megamicran affairs. They surely did not know Greek so he must have supplied them himself in his narration. Did he learn them before or in the half year since he returned here?"

"I learned a little Greek in school, Milord, but I also read a great deal in physics and in the arts. I remembered the technical words used in these English works so I developed a considerable vocabulary."

"Do let him go on now", said Lady Rutgland.

Edward took up his story. "At the appointed hour the king arrived with his court. I had arranged three tables, under canopies, within a circle. Elizabeth and I sat with the king, his mate, the autocephalus as well as royal princes, ministers from four neighboring kingdoms and ambassadors from the court of the Great Spirit. Outside the circle, but alongside, I had a hundred settings for other reds and some of color who were attached to the court.

"After the banquet which lasted an hour and a half, I requested the king's permission and I united my fifty couples in marriage, beginning with Renaud and Egeria, my twenty-fourth twin. I married them two by two as I intoned the beautiful wedding service in English. My wife delighted the auditors by repeating the words in Megamicran.

"When the ceremony was over, the couples received congratulations and were presented each with a ruby which the king suspended about their neck with a ribbon. The seminarians were presented to the king followed by five hundred and fifty younger students down to the age of three years. The very youngest, six hundred and thirty-eight to be exact, remained in their schools.

"By now, since the theater would be full, I led the king inside followed by his court. I told him that an entertainment to last three and a half hours awaited him. We went down a carpeted staircase of a thousand steps with one inch risers, circling until we reached the theater itself. The first view he had was of corridors illuminated with phosphorus lamps. Up a short flight of steps, a pair of doors opened and the king found himself in his beautiful loge which was as high and wide as twenty-four of the others. The orchestra started playing as he entered. He looked around amazed at the construction of the theater and the multitudes in the amphitheater below. Beyond the orchestra, a huge curtain hung, stretched inside the length of eight columns, which all gleamed with light.

"He had his courtiers, princes and ministers take seats in the two empty balconies on either side while he and his family occupied the royal box. Clearly, he expected a vocal and instrumental concert. He commented that the sound of the music seemed augmented and improved rather than diminished in the large area.

"Suddenly to everyone's surprise, the great curtain went up. At this unex-pected sight, everyone applauded loudly but the tumult ended abruptly when they saw on stage a tall red who appeared to be a Megamicre. He was pulling containers, metals and money out of his strongboxes. This was the miser, the chief actor of the play. The villain of the piece was a fraudulent alchemist who had convinced him that he could turn base metal into gold by the use of a powder he was working on, known as a 'powder of projection.'

"The three acts were concerned with the miser's credulity as he turns over his wealth to the fraudulent alchemist, the noble sons' efforts to dissuade the greedy father (who also fails to give them the money they need to procure positions), the use of spies to uncover the villainy and the eventual resolution when the miser sees that the impostor is about to abscond with all the treasure he has given him. The alchemist confesses all, is sentenced to life imprisonment and the sons force the miserly father to supply them with the money they need to procure suitable positions.

"The play was a great success. There was much laughter at the miser's credulity, at the medical jargon between the physician and the miser and at some dialogue between the inseparable and a foolish valet.

"At the king's request, I conducted him to a seat in the circle near the orchestra. When his subjects caught sight of him, they broke into vigorous applause.

"The farce was about to begin. The chief actors were two six year old seminarians whom I had transformed into perfect—if over tall—Megamicres by painting them red and coloring their hair green. I had added the necessary breast formation. These betrothed reds were annoyed with the attentions of their two enamored tutors whom they rebuffed and mocked. Offended, the tutors plan revenge. Donning serpent skins, they terrify the couple as they stroll in the garden. They are rescued by giants who discover the serpents are fakes. The tutors are then pummeled by the two young reds. For a final punishment, the four giants toss the miscreants high in a blanket a dozen times. This last action, especially, provoked outbursts of laughter from the audience.

"The play was over, the curtain lowered and the finale music played. This music was in the nature of an apophony* which together with a true proslam-banomenos** told the audience that the entertainment was over.

'The king was very much pleased when I invited him to go backstage. When he remarked that all our actors were male, I said I believed that the Megamicres

---

*'Apophony' from Greek for off-sound.

**'Proslambanomenos', a term used in ancient Greek music referring to the note of lowest pitch in the tetrachord.

preffered the males of our race. He agreed. (I remember an early conversation with him when he said he thought males were more interestingly formed and superior in other ways. 'Male giants', he had said at the time, 'are structured to give pleasure; females to receive it.' The matter, I recall, was a bit too delicate to pursue.) After the king and his countries had inspected everything which merited inspection, he told me he had never enjoyed anything more than that day's entertainment.

'The hours for repose sounded and we all left.

'The many activities I engaged in to make the spectacle a success had not kept me from thinking about the long trip which my five sons and their families had to take the following pentamine. They would be carrying with them all the arts I had instituted and all the knowledge they had gleaned. Certain matters I kept secret including the method of obtaining the poison fumes from arsenic. My wife had taught our first daughter Wilhelmina the special recipes for making essences. And I had included in their trunks, models of paper mills and printing presses and some mechanical devices on hydraulics.

'More than thirty of my offspring had become more expert than I in foundry work. They could cast bells of various sizes all of excellent workman ship. Five were competent oculists among whom was my dear Sebastian. In all, they numbered nine hundred and ten persons; in addition they were accompanied by an equal number of Megamicran servants.

"I filled fifty chests with firearms, twenty-five with gunpowder and the same number of chests with cylinders of arsenic gas. Another chest was filled with type plus a hundred small bales of paper. They also carried with them expensive household goods including phosphorus and costly carpets.

"In planning this voyage, I knew I would have to buy at least eighteen houses along the route so the caravan could halt, provide themselves with fruit from gardens they owned and rest.

"When I spoke to the king two days after the entertainment and showed him how many persons with their baggage I needed to transport, he smiled and showed me a paper. It was the copy of an order he had sent to all the staging posts on the direct route to Heliopolis. He had provided for our departure a caravan of four hundred carriages to accommodate our travelers. He knew without asking how many would be departing and he arranged also that they should go through the countries of eight kings who were friendly to him.

"En route, as a token of friendship for my king and for the sovereigns friendly to him, I arranged that the carriages stop for ten day periods in each of their capitals so the oculists could serve any among them who suffered from cataract blindness.

"The route also included the border city of my dear Governor who had helped raise our two oldest children and had given so much help to Adam. I had expected to buy houses along the route but the king had foreseen this. His ministers had arranged to buy twenty-four houses for stops at three pentamine intervals during the three hundred and sixty days the trip would take. Such was the goodness of the king.

"I charged my children and especially James with the need for diligence, good management and exactness. And above all with generosity. Generosity is the most important way of making others well-disposed toward you but this must be determined by one's means. There is a middle road between prodigality and stinginess which may be difficult to follow, but I suggested tilting the scale on the side of prodigality, however slight so as to give the appearance of generosity. James needed to hear this because he tended to be overly thrifty.

"I ordered him to spare nothing in the building of seminaries, houses, theaters and most important, temples. These latter, however, were not for immediate construction. Establishing the giants' religion was still some years in the future.

"Among other points in my counseling, I advised James to employ capable Megamicres and not be stingy with their salary; a meritorious worker is never paid enough. I told him to encourage the system of one-color writing, to build many presses and above all to have a care to keep the cost of living down; to encourage industry and commerce and provide the people with as many comforts and pleasures as possible.

"The day of departure was a day of tears for all, especially for me and my wife. Gathering all the emigrants to say farewell, I told them that I delegated my authority to James until the time that I came to the fief myself. An immense crowd saw them off. In this world, we could see them as they rode off for a distance of eighteen miles with the naked eyes. Here the farther away an object is, the more elevated it becomes.

"After they were gone, I began to plan the entertainment I would give the king on the new year. It would be a fireworks display. I had already spent ten years on this project, planning and experimenting. Among my children, my twelfth son Matthew and his son Joseph had shown special aptitude in this area. They were so devoted to the study of pyrotechnics, I felt sure I would succeed.

"In an area in my park where excavation had already proceeded, I had a theater built such as European architecture has never conceived. In this world, the cost of excavation and disposal of fill is primary. I had to have the dirt transported far away because the nearby countryside had already been covered by earth over the centuries. The fill had to be so disposed as not to form any mounds but rather be reasonably flattened out. The Megamicres are excellent at this work.

"Since a builder knows that two cubic feet of land gives six of fill, he can tell almost at once what it will cost. Knowing the cost however does not bring the price down. I spent a fortune. The dirt filled three million carts and I had only twenty thousand. You can see how many trips it required.

"I realized that to make a fortune for myself and my posterity, I had to win

135

the Megamicres' respect by means of some dazzling achievement. A beautiful fireworks display would surpass all my previous productions.

"The theater I built for the display measured four hundred eighty feet in depth. Cylindrical in shape, it had an inside circumference of more than two thousand feet and two hundred forty more feet outside because I had squared off the exterior. The triangular spaces formed by this squaring of the exterior, provided areas for public convenience.

"I provided forty-four entrances, equidistant from each other, with the same number of wide staircases. Inside stairs led to the 378,784 seats of which 40,000 were designed for the giants, the rest for the Megamicres.

"If a fireworks display could have been presented in the open as we do here, I would not have had to spend eleven million ounces of gold to build this vast edifice and hire more than 200,000 Megamicres. My workers had no idea what I wanted to do. They could not see how it could be a theater for plays since viewers who sat behind the actors could not see the performance. But such speculations did not trouble them as much as the continual noise coming from the rooms below where the giants were working at what they did not know. No Megamicre was admitted there.

"The whole city was talking about the rumbling noises. Being ignorant of the cause, they invented one. The most popular story was that we had decided to break open a road back to our own world. They believed us capable of anything. While on the one hand, they were upset that they might lose us, on the other hand, they feared that the extraordinary excavations we presumably were making, would bring a disaster to their world. God alone knows what effect such an aperture might do. Their rivers might flow into the opening and release an enormous mass of mud from the abyss which would in a short time, smother and suffocate the children of the Sun.

"Seeing us so busily engaged in this mysterious work and not daring out of courtesy or from religious scruple against curiosity to inquire, the fearful, the superstitious and the politicians presented a petition to the College of Physics to inquire whether such an aperture could or could not have fatal consequences.

"The College, having had an unfortunate experience with us only a few years earlier, was at a loss as to how to handle this inquiry. They did believe that an opening in their world might engulf them, but they were not sure what we were doing. The current president of the College resigned. A new election was called and I, as a member, was required to attend. To my consternation, the voting results showed that I had been elected for that year. I had to return the next day to make my acceptance speech.

"Imagine my surprise when the secretary handed me the petition to answer. I saw now why I was elected and I had to restrain my amusement. I wrote out my reply and then read it aloud to the body. They all signed it at once and sent it off for printing.

"I had written that all of us at the College agreed that an opening in the surface of the world would drain it of the waters which now give it life. And it would permit the entry of foreign matter alien to our earth's weight. This would upset our whole system which is in a state of perfection just as it is. This statement was highly praised and my opinion lauded as infallible.

"When I returned, I told my dear technicians the whole story. They found it amusing and continued to work secretly and earnestly as before. The noise continued, made necessary by the heavy hammer blows on the rockets and by the pounding of hard substances in the cast-iron mortar. We were pressed for time. The great machine had to be ready the next harvest. We pushed ourselves and gave up much of our rest.

"We worked only in the underground rooms. In one room, we broke up, sifted and mixed substances; in another we made firecracker tubes, glued them and let them dry at the stove. In another room, we kept powder and other combustibles in glazed earthenware pots so they would not spoil in the air. In still another room, we kept carbon, saltpetre, iron filings, sulphur, sawdust, quicksilver and many resins and powders. We had ordinary sieves and fine ones according to our needs.

"All the rooms underground were interconnected. Entrance was forbidden to all Megamicres. People began to think it very odd that we pursued our activities even after the public declaration issued by the College.

"My wife gave me Denis and Eugenia, my thirty-fourth pair of twins."

THIRTEENTH DAY

"I read somewhere", Lady Bridgent said, "that Adam's first earthly abode was called *Paradise* because the word means the place where one sees God."

"And some clever fellow actually invented a Latin phrase 'parans Dei visum', meaning just that; he abridged it into *Paradise*." Lady Rutgland scoffed.

"That seems possible, wouldn't you say?" Milady inquired tentatively.

"No, my dear cousin, it does not. The word is of Persian origin and it means a garden of pleasures. Then the early church writers called it the sojourn of the blessed and gave it a religious meaning. Everyone tried to guess where on earth it was situated. Some said it was on the highest mountains. Three or four writers taking an example from the Jewish philosopher Philo set it in the heavens. Those who said it was merely a spiritual concept were censured. Origen placed it in the third heaven, even though Paul, who said he was transported there, has nothing to say about Paradise. Tatian, the second century church writer, said Paradise was not on the earth's surface but on earth.* So I must put it *inside* the earth and state that we are the first to learn that the Megamicres live there!", Lady Rutgland concluded, triumphantly.

"And we shall pay them a visit", Count Bridgent said, "as soon as we find out what route to take. In good time. And here is Edward ready to go on with his narration."

Edward readily resumed his story. "When the notice I had signed as president of the College was posted, the citizens were satisfied. The frightened among them calmed down, but when the underground rumblings continued and even grew louder, their fears were revived. The people thought I had been making fools of them; there there was little time to lose. They hastened first to see the autocephalus and then the king. I was ordered to appear the next day and again in three days at the king's court. I was able to satisfy both councils

---

*Translator's note: Casanova's own footnote states he found all the data cited about Paradise in a book he read at Count Waldstein's library. Written in English, the book was titled "A Discourse of the Terrestrial Paradise" and was printed in London in 1666 by James Flecherus.

that no harm would result from the noises. These, I promised, would last no longer than three more greenwood fires and the results would enchant the entire city.

"During this same year while I was preparing the fireworks show, I had been building a small theater expressly for the king. Within the grounds of the royal palace, I chose a space two hundred and forty feet square and I surrounded the whole area with a twenty-four foot walk. At much expense and labor, I had trees planted and so shaped that they curved over towards one another. The walkways surrounding all four sides of the theater formed a continuous promenade with overarching trees. These, I made sure, were free of serpents.

"The pit seated four hundred; there were four rows of boxes, an orchestra area below had room for sixty musicians with thirty spectators on either side. I had a gallery built which reached the ceiling. The boxes were separated by grilles of highly polished steel with a column of luminous phosphorus in front of each. The ceiling and floor of each box was covered with mirrored plaques as was the wainscoting.

"Six gleaming columns flanked the stage and supported an equally luminous cornice and corbel under the ceiling. Between these columns I had built loges, each just big enough for one couple. They could view the performance without being seen. The stage curtain was made of a fine single piece of tapestry which could be rapidly raised and lowered by a mechanism. Beyond the wings on either side, I constructed small dressing rooms for the actors.

"A new feature was the three room apartment which I attached to each of fifteen loges for privacy and which had free access either to the theater or to the street at the whim or wish of the box-holder. The cost was two million ounces of gold. The king's treasurer respectfully reproached the king for this outlay. In reply, the king, while acknowledging the expense, declared that those who saw the theater estimated its cost to have been five million ounces.

"The king asked me to teach the princes of his family the roles so they could perform the farce. I agreed on condition that the tossing in the blanket be done by my four giants for safety's sake. All went off perfectly the day of the performance. Only the 'elite' attended. Not counting the royal family, there were six hundred spectators. Everyone laughed a good deal. Even the most staid among them would have enjoyed being tossed in the blanket if their dignity could have been preserved.

"Everyone found the theater a perfect jewel. Its construction, its luxurious materials, the arrangement of the apartments were all admired. But the taste and harmony of the whole impressed them even more than the luxury of its appointments. The king preferred the small grilled loges for single couples which I had built adjoining the stage. He enjoyed the privilege of seeing and not being seen and he kept the distribution of the tickets in his own hands.

"After the play, everyone followed the king as he toured the walk which surrounded the theater. Covered as it was by the overarching trees, the light of the sun came in only as a reflection in hints of red and green color, a sight to enchant the eye. Everyone had his eyes fixed on the vault of the trees and no one dared believe that they were actually free of serpents.

"The promenade became so popular that guards were needed to attend the crowds that thronged there. In the evening when the king held court with his nobles, no others were allowed admission. The autocephalus, who found himself walking there very often, named it 'The Tranquillity of the Soul'. This became its permanent name.

"The day after the entertainment, I received a letter from James. He was then about two thirds along on his trip. The letter contained some details I wanted the king to know. James notified me that the ruler of one of the kingdoms he was passing through had received an authorization from the Great Spirit permitting the destruction of the serpents. James had had one hundred and sixty of my sons use the arsenic fumes to destroy six thousand serpents in all the king's gardens. In grateful recognition, that ruler had conferred citizenship on all the giants and had given them enough land on which to build a city if they wished to stay.

"I showed the king my letter and asked if he wished to learn the secret of getting rid of the serpents. I knew he very much wanted to know but could not bring himself to ask. He agreed and we made plans for the following day. At the small cottage the king had chosen, I told my five sons to be ready with the necessary equipment. I sent the gardeners away and I examined the trees. While we waited for the king, I loaded six guns with the cylinders and as a precaution I loaded six pistols with soundless gunpowder in case of an emergency.

"We saw the king and his inseparable approaching us in a carriage which moved swiftly without horses or coachman. Without being impolite but also without giving them a chance to ask questions, I gave them both double-barrelled pistols about six inches long. I told them that these weapons were like lightning fire which brought death to enemies of the peace and security of the human race. To destroy these enemies, they had to keep the pistol steady and the arm raised and pointed in the direction of the body one wished to pierce. A small flash leaping out when the trigger is pressed would tell the marksman that the enemy was dead. Though I was sure they would not need to fire, they could use it in self-defense if need be, just as God orders man to do when face to face with the enemy.

"When they were a distance away, my sons and I placed ourselves in front of our respective trees, took aim and, at my command, fired. Twelve serpents fell dead without a single hiss being heard. I walked slowly with the royal couple to observe the dead serpents. They were upset, I could see, and I was troubled for them. But when they looked and saw the creatures motionless, they recovered.

First putting down their pistols—I admired this thoughtfulness—they expressed their feelings in song and dance and many embraces. Unmindful of the scratches to their delicate skin, they covered my bearded face with kisses.

"They were now ready for the next step which was practice firing. I had constructed two papier-mache serpents for this purpose. Holding their pistols as instructed, they aimed and fired at the counterfeits which I had placed in the correct position. They were astounded when they saw the holes their weapons had made. (I had used the special powder for a soundless charge.) When I presented them with the pistols as gifts, they were all joy and gratitude. Pressing these miraculous contrivances to their breast, they seemed stunned. The king said he was especially glad to be the only one among all the Megamicres to own such a treasure.

"With some hesitation, he commented that the real serpents we had killed had no wound or holes. I explained our use of the poisoned fumes and showed him the discharged cylinders, some of them still smoking. The happy couple returned to their palace and we too returned home.

"I decided to present an opera as a prelude to the fireworks display. My son Lawrence translated the work which I had written in English into the native tongue and the greatest poet in the city put it to music.

"The subject matter had given me some concern. I could not use our own mythology; I had to draw on material familiar to them which was also of heroic stature. I finally decided on the circumstance that the royal couple had not been blessed with red (noble) children to succeed them. They had already parented eleven pairs but none of them were reds. By this time, the chances of having heirs were very slight indeed. The king and his mate never spoke of this affliction and no one else dared make mention of it.

"Since this was to be an opera and since my daughters and grand-daughters had the most delicate voices, I chose the best musicians among them for the parts and made them up as red Megamicres.

"The stage setting represented the 'Sojourn of the Blessed'. In the rear, the columns of a peristyle were each painted with flowers and covered with luminous phosphorus. A sun in the background threw out rays of phosphorus and gleams of simulated diamonds. The result was dazzling.

"Three acts, each lasting a Megamicran hour, dealt with petitions to the personifications of Mercy, Justice and Grace, imploring them to grant the royal couple their dearest wish, namely a royal succession. At the end of the opera, my seventeenth twin, Daniel and Louise, appeared as themselves, without make-up, nude and with Louise's long blonde hair falling over her shoulders and back, singing a duet in which prayers for a noble succession was mingled with a recital of the virtues of the royal couple. They sang of the people's grief in being deprived of successors to such a noble pair. And they appealed to God's mercy to grant this favor.

"Sublime instrumental music was heard, then a chorus of voices and a concert of clarinets. Following this, a voice issued out of the sun's center. All the actors fell prostrate as they heard this pronouncement: 'The royal couple will not be dissatisfied when they go to their eternal peace.' After a vocal and instrumental symphony, the actors withdrew and the curtain came down.

"I could not have asked for a greater success. The profound silence of the spectators, the tears which the king could not restrain as he listened, the respectful attitude of the autocephalus who gave me his hand to kiss and who declared he had truly been transported to the sojourn of the blessed—all these marks of success did not calm the apprehension I felt.Two days from now, the eggs would break out and the oracle chanted in my opera would be tested against the event. True, the oracle was cryptic and obscure regarding the color of the new-borns, but the audience seemed to believe it foretold the birth of heirs to make their king happy. How great would be the derision I would have to endure if they turned out non reds!

"Yet the king, talking to the poet, author of the opera, said, 'Your oracle is infallible, for in adoring only the will of God, I shall end my days in perfect peace.'

"The opera over, we walked to the great theater. It was already full. Two hundred of the king's guards and an equal number of my own were posted at the doors as we entered. Corridors and staircases were brilliantly lighted. The extraordinary sight of this new vast theater filled with multitudes of his subjects dazzled the king. The applause of half a million subjects, clapping their hands to greet him provided a more agreeable sound to his ears than any music could. The most beautiful moments in a monarch's life are those in which he receives the clamorous plaudits of a joyous public. This is triumph!

"The theater was alight with forty-eight thousand lamps. These were small tinplate boxes which contained a substance, a mixture of rock alum and powder, which gave out a heavenly blue flame when exposed to air. The lamps were designed to give light for two and a half hours. At the end of that time, they would all go out at once.

"At ten o'clock, I had had all the boxes opened simultaneously. I contrived this by having a Megamicre at each of the one hundred forty-two rows stand, cord in hand, ready at a signal to lift the lids of the three hundred tinplate boxes in each row. The cord connected all the lids and controlled them. Now at twelve-fifteen, they would shine for fifteen more minutes. Then they would go out, all at once.

"During this time, the king was trying to guess the purpose of this huge eight-sided machine which stood in the middle of the floor. It rose twelve stories for two hundred and forty feet. Each story decreased in height from the bottom one of forty feet to the top one of eighteen feet. The machine was designed so that each of the half million viewers could see the display. It stood on a floor of sand mixed with damp earth and was crammed with fireworks.

"My forty giant pyrotechnicians were all inside. By means of ninety-six breakneck stairs, they could go up and down wherever their presence was needed. A total of forty thousand fireworks, the stationary and soundless kind that flared steadily in place studded the entire outside surface of the machine in an even distribution.

"I asked the king, as soon as the lights went out, to open a small box I gave him. This held two line rockets (fuses on a long cord) which I had amusingly disguised as five inch polychromes. When he released one of these, he would start the fireworks display. At that moment, the lights did go out plunging the entire theater in an abyss of darkness. Instead of becoming fearful, as we here might, the Megamicres burst into roars of laughter. It seemed like a good joke.

"The king, remembering my instructions, opened the box. The fuse caught fire and flew to the quick-match. This started the lighting of forty thousand fireworks on the machine's surface. Applause broke out as the lights flared for nine minutes. Now darkness followed and the king's mate hastened to light the other line-rocket. Again the fuse took fire and now from the base of the machine to its summit, a display blossomed forth of every shape to dazzle the spectator. Architectural forms, showing arcades, terraces, moving and colorful doors, porticos and peristyles flashed from the machine and delighted the eye.

"Now the brilliantly lighted machine hurled out with enormous noise, fiery tracings of cannon and mortars at the very moment that an orchestra concealed inside, struck up a booming volley of sound from kettledrums, trumpets, fifes and cymbals. This salvo of artillery had barely stopped when the machine shot forth for a full quarter of an hour a succession of serpentine forms, stars, showers of fire and rockets. The smoke was instantly dissipated through vents in the ceiling. The smell of sulphur was masked by perfume so that the theater was filled instead with a pleasant odor.

"Another charming effect was achieved by the intermingling of Catherine wheels, cypresses, egret plumes and fountains of fire, all flashing with color. Everyone had a view of my forty Cyclops inside the machine as they raced up and down through the floors. They seemed to be moving through flames, their naked bodies blackened to moderate the effect of the heat. Red kerchiefs bound their hair under brimmed hats.

"The spectators, ecstatic about marvels never before seen, could not imagine any further ones. But then suddenly, on each of the machine's eight sides, two suns appeared—sixteen in all. Each sun had twenty-four revolving wheels. These wheels turned at varying degrees of velocity and force and sent out rays of ever-changing color. Clearly visible in the center of each sun were the outlined figures of several life-size red Megamicres who turned and tumbled, embraced and suckled one another, danced and frolicked as if they were alive, so well-designed were they.

"When the suns went out, little flares appeared on the surface of the machine. On the top of each of the eight sides, on their very summit, two red Megamicres could be seen by all. They bore a globe on their shoulders on which was written in flaming characters, the words: 'The best of kings must also be the happiest.'

"At this sight, five hundred thousand voices took up the message, proclaiming the words aloud. I caught sight of the king and his inseparable. Stirred by strong emotion, they sat with head bowed, hands over their face.

"After another salvo of artillery fireworks followed by the release of a stream of eight thousand serpentines, the machine remained in darkness except for the two red Megamicre images on top holding aloft the globe where the nine words still flamed. The darkness lasted only a minute when a line-rocket in the form of a winged horse flew out of the machine to light the quick-match which in turn set twenty thousand of the stationary fireworks alight. These circles of light illumined the theater so the spectators could leave.

"Without the many doors I had constructed, the crowd could not have left so soon. They were further hastened by the sonorous voice of my son who called out from the topmost floor of the machine, 'Children of the Sun; the spectacle is over; you can go home!'

"I approached the king. He looked at me as one who is just waking from a profound sleep. He said then that he and his subjects had seen what no one else ever had or would ever believe.

"I was satisfied that no mishap or disorder had marred my festival of the new year. My sons, exhausted, left too tired to be revived by the praise and admiration. Though I had not worked, I too was extremely fatigued and went home.

"The autocephalus sent a description of the opera to the court at Heliopolis. He had it printed for all the world to read. Regarding his account, Milords, nothing seems more curious for us here than this description by such a wise literate Megamicre, as was the autocephalus. I translated his words and I will give it to you in writing. I can only say that the author did not lie since he believed he was telling the truth in describing what he had seen. Yet what he saw was not the truth but the appearance of truth. What he witnessed, we can not believe. But he believed. We find in some ancient history, unbelievable accounts which are no less true to them than my opera was to the autocephalus. Man is the only creature who has the privilege of not telling the truth and not lying at the same time.

"Two days later, the royal family including distant relatives, the ministers, the autocephalus and all the nobles gathered at court for the new-borns to break through their shells. The event was due in five hours. The eggs were in

145

their bowls which rested on a beautiful pillow under a handsome canopy. The king and his mate were in an adjoining room as was the custom, talking with good humor to those courtiers and nobles who were not required to be present at the examination of the new born.

"At the anticipated hour, the eggs broke open. The little ones were found, after the most careful scrutiny, to be perfect reds. Joy, whether sincere or not, appeared on the faces of all present. The king who heard the news in his room at the exact time, by way of a device arranged between him and his prime minister, at once whispered to the Chief Gardener to go out by another door and notify me; that he would await me the following day at the first hour.

"Then the autocephalus and his entourage came in carrying the newly born to the royal couple saying, 'Your succession, Sire, is immortal.'

"We thought we would die of joy when we heard this important news. We kissed the messenger, our dear friend, a hundred times. In an hour, the whole city, made aware of the event, gave itself over to extraordinary demonstrations of joy. Not only did the foolish and the superstitious attribute this happy event to my great power, but even the sensible ones.

"I sent a hundred thousand ounces of gold to the chief almoner of the autocephalus for distribution among the poor, enjoining secrecy as to the donor. My precaution was futile; everyone knew.

"The next day when I came to see the king and his inseparable, they did not give me time to congratulate them. Being alone, they leaped into my arms and covered me with caresses. When we were calm and seated, the king made a speech. In summary, he said that during the 132 harvests I had been with him, he had had more than enough proof that God had granted me exceptional powers as demonstrated by all I had done. Everyone in his kingdom, he first of all, believed that I could do anything I wanted to. Though I could reign in Heliopolis if I wished, yet I preferred to stay in his kingdom, and spend mighty sums of money for the realm. He attributed this to our strong affection for him. To keep me and my family with him, he wished to bestow on me Fiefdom 216, his own property, and half the size of Realm 90.

"It was a land rich in natural mineral resources, like phosphorus, red gold and diamonds, besides the many semi-precious minerals there. He believed I would be like a father to that nation and see to their happiness. He said I would be invested with the land the next harvest and that either I or any one I designated could take over. He said further that he wanted me near to guide and counsel his offspring. In twelve harvests, they would have left their infancy and be ready to learn from me, ways to bring happiness and well-being to their subjects.

"How could I reply to these warm and generous sentiments? Bending over his hands, I shed tears of gratitude and tenderness. I told him his increasing generosity could only increase my obligations to him but never my affection.

That had already reached a peak of devotion. I swore I would never leave him and that I would serve the new princes with my counsel and strength, if they wished this of me.

"Two months after this, I heard from James that he and all with him had arrived safely at Heliopolis. All the wives were in their eighth month of pregnancy and were comfortably lodged in a palace whose four gardens he had already cleared of serpents.

"The king showed me a letter from Heliopolis for my attention. It contained the approval of the Great Spirit for all the gardens to be rid of serpents provided the clerics and the local owners agreed. The autocephalus here already had a copy. I had barely finished reading this missive when the consent from the autocephalus of this realm arrived. He too granted approval.

"The letters were ordered printed. Ten thousand copies were to be printed each day and distributed world-wide to total one hundred thousand. The king was first to ask that his garden be cleared. My next order came from the autocephalus himself. I turned this task over to my sons and grandsons who gleefully undertook thus hunt. I entrusted the chest with the poison cylinders only to Theodore. Before the next harvest, other nobles too had their gardens rid of the cursed pests.

"To the surprise and pleasure of the Megamicres, I announced that the giants would pay ten farthings for ten figs from the cleared trees. The gardeners were especially glad of this. I told James to publish this notice in the fiefdom of Heliopolis. I expected he would make some objections to paying and he did, but I was not too concerned.

"At the beginning of our month of April, the king with his own hands invested me with the ownership of Fiefdom 216, a land even larger than the one at Heliopolis.

"I sent Theodore, my sixth son, with his family of one hundred thirty, to take on responsibility for governing. He was accountable for everything. He was to divide the land into five parts just as we had done in Fiefdom One. Ten of his children were also, like him, skilled in the arts and crafts I had taught them. In three years, he built a printworks, a seminary and a little theater where his children performed for the nobles. He cleared out all the serpents from the gardens of the upper nobility as well as his own. In consultation with me, he lowered taxes and sold property to rich merchants. At the end of six harvests, he sent me thirty million ounces of gold with which I paid my debts. He managed the other four areas of the fief so well that when I sent four of my other sons there, they found their tasks smoothed out and everything running well.

"During these three years, nothing more outstanding occurred. I busied myself with my artillery; this was a costly but pleasurable activity. I now had an immense quantity of firearms and I was especially proud of my cannons made of silver and tin, each with its own gun carriage.

"During this time too, I had had so many houses built on my land that I could now take care of fifty-thousand families. And my dear wife gave me my thirty-fifth, thirty-sixth, and thirty-seventh twins*. In my thirty-sixth year there, I united in marriage Basil and Angelica and in my thirty-seventh, Lucian and Ernestine."

*See listing of eighty names of Edward's and Elizabeth's children.

FOURTEENTH DAY

Edward resumed his story after dinner. "With the birth of those much desired princes, the king seemed like another being. True, he had always been charming, but his happiness seemed to expand those qualities he had of affability and generosity. Court was a place where his own joy communicated itself to all around him.

"For example, at all the crossroads, in all the public parks and even in the royal ccourtyard, there were story tellers who gathered people around him. These sages told tales which seemed meant for children and were so understood by the uninformed. But for those listeners who penetrated their inner meaning, they conveyed profound truths in the guise of fables. Ingeniously created as simple stories they interested and amused those who did not grasp their subtleties. These sages would disguise themselves as polychromes to attract and amuse the crowds. Our friend the Chief Gardener went daily to the most renowned of these circles. From him I got the idea of founding such Academies in my fiefdoms.

"Every Cocoon day, the royal court presented a play in which the Megamicres performed. And at the beginning of every harvest, I put on an opera and play in which my seminarians performed before audiences of twenty thousand.

"Meanwhile, the young princes, now five harvests old, were beginning to meet friends of the family. They retreated at first when they saw us—they were only nine inches tall—but later we became their favorites and we visited them weekly.

"Their teacher, for many years a professor of sublime* geometry, saw his primary duty that of teaching them to think for themselves. In our discussions of what he termed moral philosophy, he would say that ideas are not innate but gained through experience and study. Before man can arrive at a generalization, he must acquire a knowledge of particulars, sometimes through trial and error.

Even experience is not a true guide in helping distinguish true from false since judgments are often fallible depending as they do on the senses. We spoke

---

*Sublime geometry is an obsolete term. It referred to advanced geometry having to do with curved lines and conical figures.

of the danger of sophistry which will often use paradox to end an argument without solving it.

"That year, I took leave for eight months planning our return for Elizabeth's accouchement of our thirty-ninth twin. I was going to visit my new fiefdom with my seventh, eighth, ninth and tenth sons together with all their family members. My sixth son Theodore was notified to expect us. We had only to cross the river at the border of Realm 90.

"We left in mid-January, six hundred and seventy-six of us, in four hundred carriages for us and another hundred carts for our baggage. With us were a number of Megamicres who held reputable posts in our fiefs. This time we did not have the problem of provisioning as we did when James left for Heliopolis. We carried along our firearms.

"In eleven days, we easily covered eight hundred and sixty English miles. En route, we met numerous gatherings of people who greeted us with demonstrations of pleasure. We were also greeted by numbers of blind who implored our help. I promised these I would operate without charge after examining them when I got to the capital.

"My capital was a very rich city because of its commercial resources. Situated at the confluence of two rivers, it provided merchants with excellent transportation everywhere. The houses of the nobles were not so grand as those in Realm 90, but there were more of them. The population stood at half a million couples.

"My palace though of good size was not sufficiently large for us. But since it stood at the edge of the city walls, I was able to enlarge it without encroaching on my neighbors. I also added two magnificent Ephebuses* to the seminaries.

"I laid the foundation for a christian temple without explaining its purpose. Five European years later, however, I saw it completed. In the four other states, I laid down similar foundations. Each capital, I named after the son who governed it. I visited the mines which were rich indeed but poorly run. I left instructions for their care. Returning to the capital of Fiefdom 216, I established the custom of putting on a play each harvest. I hired those Academician story tellers as professional performers. This helped develop among my subjects an interest in dramatic poetry.

"Three weeks after returning to Realm 90, Elizabeth presented me with our thirty-ninth twin and, as was usual on the first of the year, I united a pair in marriage. Nothing outstanding occurred in the following year until in October, Elizabeth gave birth to our fortieth and final twin. We also celebrated a marriage.

"The celebration of this marriage was combined with a feast to honor Elizabeth's glorious career. A splendid dinner, a play and fireworks made the occasion a gala one. Elizabeth said that now she had become a man since she

---

*See glossary of terms.

150

could bear no more children. She asked me to complete a temple for the worship of God.

"The best place for this temple would have been Heliopolis, but I could not in honor leave my benefactor king. He still had fifteen harvests to live of which he would reign for only nine more before he retired for six harvests to the hospice of eternal peace. We would not leave him until after that time.

"In the interim, I laid the foundations for a superb temple on my own property here in Kingdom 90. Our land was called the city of the giants since we alone occupied it. In this, the forty-second year, I divided my family into forty tribes after my forty twins. In that same year, I lost my dearest friends, the king excepted. These friends whom I shall never forget were inestimable treasures.

"The governor was the first. He wrote a long letter six hours before he said goodbye to the world, advising me not to send a reply since he would not receive it. The second to bid us farewell was the autocephalus who had shown us so many tokens of friendship in writing to the sacred court on our behalf. The last to retire, an unexpected blow since we thought he was the king's age, was our dear friend the Chief Gardener. It was he, swimming out of his underwater retreat, who discovered the chest where we lay dying. To him, we owed our lives.

"One must, of course, recognize the role of divine providence. But should one give less recognition to a so-called secondary rescuer? Without him, divine providence would have played no role at all.

"The cruel loss of these three dear friends plunged me into an abyss of grief. I passed three days in my room, seeing no one except Elizabeth. Herself afflicted with sorrow, she observed its effects on me but dared not console me. I would not answer her or I would ask to be left alone. I thought I had found peace in this solitude. It was the only way, I told myself, that I could find a measure of satisfaction.

"Ten pentamines passed. The more I fed my melancholy, the more attached to it I became. I congratulated myself that I had found the secret for curing sorrow and ensuring that I would not have to suffer any new ones. My wife was becoming desperate. She no longer knew what to say to our children who understood nothing of the matter, nor to our friends nor to the daily messages of the king.

"As he told me later, he did not know what to think. In a society where curiosity was not only bad manners but a civil offense, he could not ask me why I had withdrawn myself. Knowing me well, he did not think I was angry with him. So he took an unusual step. He paid me a semi-public visit. A public visit required formal notice and a private visit would have resulted in being told I was not in.

"Imagine then, Milords, the effect when I heard the unexpected sound of the royal fanfare, just fifty paces from my door. Elizabeth dropped her work and I my pen. Dressed as I was without coat or head covering, I ran to the door. The royal couple could not help bursting into laughter at the sight I presented. I bowed and retreated until a servant brought me suitable attire.

"The king then entered the apartment, greeted Elizabeth and in a gentle voice said, 'You have abandoned us.'

"At these words, Milords, the dear creature you see here, my angel and my all, let her sorrow break its bounds. Her tears poured out in a torrent. Unreleased they would have suffocated her. Her tears astonished me; they seemed neither appropriate nor reasonable. The king and his mate also looked surprised and turned to me as if for an explanation. The king's mate remarked, 'Some great sorrow is causing her this pain.'

"Those simple words struck hard. In an instant, I recovered my senses. I saw with sudden clarity the extent of my own weakness and the wrong I had done. This insight renewed my sorrow but this time, the many tears I shed cured me as they brought relief.

"The king held our hands; his mate dried Elizabeth's tears. They implored us to speak freely, assuring us of their love. My wife, sobbing, told them that we had lost three very dear friends within the last three greenwood fires*. She could say no more because of her tears. I, too, was overcome with weeping.

"Our loving friends remained silent for a full half hour, restraining their own tears. Observing this effort on their part helped calm the storm in my heart. I was the first to break the silence, ashamed that I had inflicted on the king this gloomy aspect of myself. I asked permission to visit him with Elizabeth. He very warmly invited us to dinner, together with our two opera singer children at his country house. We accepted with thanks and notified our grandchildren of the honor done them.

"At the dinner, which was delicious, the young couple, who were to be married, were flattered by the occasion and comported themselves well. I knew the king had given this dinner to cheer us up and so that I could return to my normal way of life.

"The king, who was moving rapidly to the end of his worthy career, was neither sad nor reflective. He told me he was gratified that he had enhanced the happiness of his subjects. He felt he had brought glory to his reign and a unique epoch which people would always recall. He said that his last six harvests would be spent with his inseparable in the retreat of eternal peace where they would recapitulate together the events of their happy life. During his final eight Megamicran years, I saw him almost every day, sharing his joys and celebrations; the young princes were always with him during this time. During this period, he heaped gifts on me. The last and most costly one was a present of a pair of flying horses and an equerry to care for them. This was a rare and precious gift, but since I could not use them because of my weight and since

_____

*See glossary of terms.

152

their upkeep was too dear, I assigned the horses in trust to all the successors of Fief 216.

"Custom forbids the expression of any condolence when a Megamicre goes to the retreat for his final days. I was forced to spend the king's last day with him in the gayest possible conversation. A half hour before departing, he commended his children to my friendship and in turn told them to consider me their guardian spirit and to rely on my counsel and caution in urgent matters. I was too choked to say anything. When they rose to go, I wanted to take their hands and kiss them. Instead, they leaped on my neck and covered me with caresses. I returned home broken-hearted in despair that I had to appear in court the next day and show no sign of sorrow as etiquette demanded.

"Royal princes become rulers without any ceremony as soon as the parents retire. They hold court but there are no festivals. After the period of retreat ends and the royal couple die, a pentamine must elapse and then all the nobles come to render homage to the new king and his mate and festivities may begin again

"To honor the new royal couple and pay our respects to our late friends, the worthy king and his mate, I spent five months preparing a spectacle. It was ready in my forty-sixth year when I would also be celebrating the marriages of thirty-eight couples. Travelers from nearby kingdoms and also from distant fiefdoms arrived bringing their families with them. The opera I had written concerned the accession to the throne of the young princes. In a dramatic finale, all the chiefs of state offer thanks. Then from the great globe onstage, brilliant fireworks shoot forth and inside are seen two life-size figures perfectly reproduced of the late kingly pair, a veritable apotheosis.

"Everyone applauded loudly. The young king expressed his appreciation publicly. His mate added a profusion of enthusiastic words. Two days later, two bonnets arrived, one with a huge black ruby in the center, the other with a magnificent red one, both bonnets bordered with diamonds. The gems weighed sixty carats each. The king also sent me fifty thousand pounds of phosphorus to use for lighting the theaters.

"When I visited the king to thank him for the lavish gift, he told me that four rulers of neighboring fiefs wished to talk with me about having four of my tribes settle in their lands. He invited us to dine with these rulers in his country house.

"We were twenty at table, including the four sons and their wives who would be involved in the move. The negotiations were entered into. The giants would bring their expertise and in exchange would get land, money and all rights to build including christian temples. After some consultations, it was agreed that my sons would spend the next three European years under my tutelage to improve and add to their skills for the enterprises they would have to undertake. During this time there were sixty-four marriages including three of my twins and sixty-one of my grandchildren.

"After the time agreed upon, the four tribes departed for their new homes. The tribe of Jean and Tecla numbered six hundred and forty; Matthew and Catherine had five hundred and thirty family members; Louis and Catherine included four hundred and thirty-eight persons in their tribe and Leopold and Sophie had three hundred and sixty-two. On that one day, my family was diminished by nineteen hundred and seventy persons.

"It may be of interest to note here that since the figs had become available, the Megamicres, after overcoming their initial fear, had found them good to eat. As prepared by the skillful chemist-cooks, they were a delicacy. I must admit I was displeased by this turn of events. The Megamicres had their own source of nourishment and we, in our ever increasing numbers, depended largely on the figs. I was uneasy too, that by neglecting their natural source of food, some harm might be done to their health and we might be blamed.

"I consulted with the autocephalus about the matter. He said with some bitterness that he was aware of this state of affairs and found it scandalous. Some of the Megamicres were actually paying the poor to take their milk from them so they could eat the figs. He asked me what I thought he could do to control this but all I could do was warn my gardeners against selling any figs to the Megamicres.

"After this, the autocephalus issued an edict which he called the 'ur-bitorbe'*, which had come directly from the Great Spirit forbidding the use of figs to Megamicres. Cooks or chemists who used it—except for giants—would be excommunicated. And every Megamicre who died from having ingested too many figs would be damned forever.

"This edict created a stir and for a while it checked the consumption of the illicit figs. With the passage of some years, however the edict was ignored until finally the sacred court forgot that they had ever published it. The general attitude was that if the Megamicrans got sick, they deserved the punishment.

But the cook-chemists had made a good thing out of the prohibition while it was in force. They demanded double pay for making fig recipes for the Megamicres. Some material gain was due them, they said, to make up for the spiritual loss they might suffer in being excommunicated.

"At the beginning of the fiftieth year, I united in marriage the last of my forty twins, namely Tancred and Clorinda*. We had a very brief ceremony because this was also the time for a pair of Megamicres to be born to the royal couple. Two reds issued from the shells and assured the succession, to the delight of the king and his mate.

"Eight days later, I offered them a fireworks and opera entertainment as a token of my joy at the happy event. I had spent a whole year preparing for this

---

*Casanova uses the word 'urbitorbe' meaning "to the city and to the world" in imitation of papal edicts.

*See listing of Edward's and Elizabeth's eighty children.

154

presentation. Twelve of my seminarians had to be trained in acrobatics since my farce required that they seem to fall from the skies to play a trick on a pair of superstitious dolts who wished to safeguard their gardens and serpents from the giants. I had a series of platforms built one above the other to reach a height of one hundred and twenty feet. From this summit, my young giants, hair streaming on their nude gleaming bodies turned one somersault after another to the delight and astonishment of the viewers. Both the farce-opera and the fireworks were successfully performed before huge audiences.

"After this entertainment, I undertook my serious work. My aim was to prepare the ground for a solid establishment of our religion for present and future generations. We now numbered thirty-three thousand, three hundred and fifty-six and it was not difficult to see that we would increase by one fifth or so each year. I would begin to solidify our religion by going to Heliopolis.

"I gathered together my twenty-six sons and their wives in Realm 90 and assigned to each a responsibility for managing one or another of the enterprises. Andrew I named as my chief steward with all my authority. The others would supervise the schools, the industries, the forges, laboratories, fireworks and gunpowder manufacture.

"Our journey to Heliopolis was a pleasant one. On the four and a half month trip, I was puzzled to find that figs were available to us at every stop until I remembered that James had taken this same route clearing the gardens of serpents along the way. At Heliopolis, we were greeted by two of my grandsons who were functioning as ambassadors to that capital. The older grandson Edward notified the minister of my arrival and sent a messenger to James and my other sons to meet me.

"I found the minister a brilliant and spirited red who reported that the Great Spirit congratulated himself on having given me the fief. Never had the state been better governed, he said, and it was continuing to get even better. As for the building of our christian temples, the minister said the Great Spirit would not withhold his approval but asked that we show him our liturgy first. Would we be willing to tell him, if not the mysteries, at least the ceremonial of our faith. I assured I had always intended to confer with him before taking any action.

"I would have the material for him in a few days; I did want permission however to build a temple outside the walls of the capital where my ambassadors to his court and their families could go to worship. The minister was pleased with my reply and promised he would report everything to the Great Spirit without forgetting a single word.

"I now set to work writing out the precepts and ceremonials of our religion. 'Our temples,' I wrote, 'must always be clearly seen from a distance. No matter how deep the foundation, the dome must always be visible. The temples may be lighted only by the beneficent rays of the sun to remind christians of God who created light. They are built as squares with a row of columns on one or both sides. They must be open every day from the first to the eighth hour. Mega-micres may always enter and even attend service of the giants.

"The giants' year consists of four harvests divided into twelve months, each month consisting of twelve pentamines. Each first day of the month will be a holy day to be observed with solemn rites all the years until the end of the world. At these rites, the men will never dare to be seen with covered head. Women on the other hand must always wear a white veil to cover the head and face. In the temple, the male giant must never cover his visage since he is the glory of God; the woman must always be veiled since she is the glory of man.

"I went on to describe the sacrament of marriage and the sacrament of baptism and the prayers to be used in rites of repentance and absolution. I defined divine law in the following twelve articles:

1. Worship only God your creator. Never swear by him because he is too great to be used as witness to merely human truths. Never try to understand his nature. Such understanding is even beyond God's own nature. Even God cannot duplicate himself.

2. Love your neighbor as yourself. Look on him as another reasoning being, hence as an immortal soul. Do not deceive him or steal from him. Do not withhold his wages. Do not flatter him or shame him. Disarm your enemies by kindness offered in humility. If they persist in enmity, pray for them but be on guard lest you become a victim of their hate and jealousy. By exposing yourself to their ill-will, you become their accomplice.

3. Obey the father in your family and respect those who are older than you. Observe the laws of the land where you live. Be thrifty but guard against avarice. Do not abstain from charity on the pretext that people are ungrateful; this may well conceal your own ill-will.

4. Defend your life, your rights and your honor with all your power but never in a spirit of anger. The person in a rage will always make mistakes. If helpless and oppressed innocence calls upon you, defend it; be its shield and be a refuge for the persecuted and unfortunate.

5. Be faithful to your wife. You are the master of her body and she of yours in perfect equality. Reciprocal respect and friendship are required. So too is agreement on all matters except that a man may keep something secret if it is so indicated but the wife may not keep anything secret from him. Voices should always be gentle and calm. Loud tones, always hateful indicate haughtiness and domination. Gentleness will be passed on to your children. A woman must know that man is her superior without having to be reminded of it.

6. Guard against gluttony. All sorts of food are placed on this earth for you but if you are intemperate in food or drink, God will shorten your life. All the pleasures of the senses are yours, except those that are illegal or which can damage the health of your body or mind or stir up criminal desires.

7. Use your eloquence to persuade rather than to beat down your opponent. Forceful argumentation repels. It is to understanding what chains are to the body. Persuasion is like a grooved and oiled screw which easily enters the spiraled nut while forcible argument is like the nail driven into the wall by a hammer.

8. Refrain from repeating unpleasant facts already well known which, by their repetition, can do more harm. Never pry into the affairs of others and never satisfy indiscreet curiosity. Flee the person who asks too many questions: he is a dangerous tattler who will make false conjectures and draw false conclusions. 9. Administer baptism to obey God. Perform incision (elsewhere called circumcision) to obey your parents.

10. When your fellow man expiates his sins in public confession, do not listen. It is enough that he be heard by God who alone has the right to forgive transgressions.

11. Never neglect the education of your children for it is the only way to success. Do not show favoritism; it causes harmful jealousy.

12. After your daily rest, kneel and pray for guidance so you can learn to obey God's laws. Thus in the after life, you will be worthy to share in his eternal glory.

"These precepts, a copy of which was intended for the Great Spirit, I gave to my most linguistically capable son to render into Megamicran.

"I explained that as the oldest member of my family, I would serve as Pontiff. The succession would pass to my oldest son James with the rule remaining in the primary tribe.

"I set up rules for the organization of temple services including the use of Megamicran musicians and a poet. I established a hierarchy of positions ranging from priest to chief priest, to ethnarch, patriarch, and pantaphilarch (pontiff).

"I prescribed the garments to be worn by temple officials which would distinguish one from the other either by color of the robe or the color of the borders.

"On the main altar of the temple, a cube would stand with a cross on top. On each face of the cross would appear a red gold circle. Within the circle would be an equilateral triangle made of precious stones. This cross would be uncovered on the first of each month, only twelve times a year. This emblem or symbol of God would present an inexplicable problem to the mind to show that it is also impossible to explain God.

"I now awaited the time for my official and formal entry into Heliopolis and my meeting with the Great Spirit."

FIFTEENTH DAY

Dinner was over but Count Bridgent's guests continued to argue. Had matter existed before Creation? Or had God who alone had no beginning or end created matter out of nothingness? Was 'nothingness' possible? Was it dark empty space or was that too a form of matter.

They agreed that the questions could be argued but not answered.

The death of the king of Realm 90 interested them. The Megamicres knew the exact day of their death. Would we here be better off if we also knew? If we knew, perhaps we would not waste our allotted time in inconsequential activities. As it is, we prefer not to know. We reject the thought of death and delude ourselves into thinking that we will never die.

Everyone agreed that the answers would not be found at the dinner table and Edward was asked to go on with his story.

"On the day set for our official entrance into Heliopolis", Edward said, "a hundred handsome carriages with high open tops and four windows drawn by twelve horses each, appeared in the courtyard. They took us and our entourage to the outskirts of the city where a dozen more superb carriages built expressly for us were waiting. Elizabeth and I were courteously escorted into the handsomest one. My carriage was followed by those of my sons, my grandsons and two hundred more couples, all my grandchildren. Five thousand of my subjects, some on horseback others on foot preceded or followed us.

"To get to the court, we crossed half the city, a distance of four English miles. The palace of the Great Spirit was in the exact center. Perfectly straight streets, intersected by square plazas were all canopied over to shut out the glaring light of the sun. Lining the streets to left and right of us was a mounted guard of fifty thousand Megamicres armed with sabarcanes, a type of blow-gun. The population of the city was three million with fifty thousand servants and attendants attached to the palace alone. (I ordered an ounce of gold to be given to each of the mounted guard.)

"When we arrived at the court, twenty-four masters of ceremony led us into a room where we were sprinkled with perfume. Then we entered another room, gleaming with phosphorus light where we were presented to another twenty-four personages seated on a semicircular, elevated dais. In the middle and somewhat higher than the other seats was a throne. One of the masters of ceremony told me that we were now in the presence of the Great Spirit although we would not be able to see him.

"Told that I could address him for he was there to hear me, I uttered an appropriate little homage. Then I was permitted to sit.

"The king's chief minister replied. I could not make out his words because he spoke so low. In another room, the same minister presented me with a large sheet written in colors which I read and signed, in which I acknowledged the Great Spirit as suzerain of my fiefdom and interpreter and executor of the will of God.

"This document with a seal of approval gave me permission to build a temple on the outskirts of the city on land I owned. The declaration further said that nothing was unknown to the Great Spirit. He had at once recognized God in my emblem. The triangle in the circle within the square described the existence of the otherwise inconceivable trinity better than words could. The vertical upright of the cross signified creation; the shorter horizontal crosspiece signified man.

"After some perfuming and a concert of rather mediocre music, we returned home. We spent the rest of that year receiving and returning visits. I worked at the foundries, improving their efficiency. I noted that bells of the greatest dimension were cast there.

"I left Heliopolis in my fifty-second year to visit Fiefdom One. Here I concentrated on establishing a better fiscal policy and on making regulations and laws for all five governments. Inspecting my mines, I realized I would have to be careful about the amount of wealth I took out. Because they were immensely rich mines, I had to restrict the production, knowing that the value of the metals would diminish and the prices of commodities would rise if I put too much on the market. I had to consider that with a rising cost of living, the poor would be the ones to suffer.

"To regulate our religious practice, I first named James as patriarch; he would succeed me as pontiff. Then I made my four other sons all ethnarchs. I had the law of christian doctrine printed and distributed gratis. Everyone except me said that I had received the law directly from God. I did not wish to lie but I did nothing to refute this belief. I allowed the report to circulate; it could only be useful. It was enough for my conscience that I knew.

"James, an excellent man of fine character and quite a theologian, was convinced the book was divine. Otherwise, he argued, God would have forbidden me to publish and proclaim it. How could I undeceive him? The whole edifice of belief might crumble. Those theologic writings of James were responsible for many curious particulars of religion which came to be believed by my descendants. Such ideas would never have occurred to me; I could never have imagined them.

"I did not tell my sons the origin of the word 'christian' but that did not stop them from finding fifty explanations, one more fanciful than the other. I said nothing; I took the attitude that anything emanating from piety was permissible, providing basic dogma was not challenged. I did not teach them the Old Testament nor even the New (which I had in Greek* and Latin) so as not to burden them unnecessarily. I would have had to theologize on that odious and almost incomprehensible 'first sin' of Adam with its consequences of evil, misery and death. How could I explain that the whole human race, yet unborn had sinned in Adam? How explain that this sin required the incarnation of the word? How explain this second person of God in corporeal form, which is not pure spirit since it is flesh, which can not be material yet which requires space, something which is in contradiction to the ubiquity of God.

"No, I could not theologize. But if my children obeyed the law which I left them, they would be eligible to go to the 'sojourn of the blessed'. The being of beings would not condemn them for not knowing what they had not been taught.

"Before leaving Fiefdom One, I set down the regulations for temple service, its prayers and ceremonial rites and the duties and authority of the hierarchy. I prescribed which vestments were to be worn and I initiated the practice of chirotony**. Dressed in my pontifical robes followed by my five sons, in addition to a great number of my subjects, I consecrated the temple. Kneeling, I placed my hands on James' head and created him patriarch, intoning the rights and duties required of him.

"In the matter of baptism of the Megamicres who wished to become christians, general sprinkling of water by the priest on a multitude would suffice since they needed a different baptism, one more of intention than fact. They, after all, had entered the world without sin and could have eternal salvation without baptism at all.

"It was time to return to the capital of Realm 90. There we found everything in good order, even more beautiful than before. Andrew had carried out my instructions admirably. We paid our respects to the king and we met the young princes. Celebrations followed including fireworks and the performance of an opera I had composed.

"Elizabeth and I left again with our usual retinue. I explained to the king that we would be gone for forty harvests to establish a temple in my other fiefdom as I had in Heliopolis. I placed Andrew in charge as before over the remaining twenty-six tribes.

"In fifteen days, traveling at leisure, we arrived at Fiefdom 216 where

---

*Translator's note: One of Casanova's rare errors. The Bible he brought with him was in Latin only.

**Translator's note: Casanova frequently used words of Greek origin. 'Chirotony' means the stretching forth of hands in blessing to authorize an investment to ecclesiastic rank.

Theodore and Frances made us heartily welcome. For our part, we shed tears of happiness to see them and the beautiful family they had raised. Well educated, the children showed many talents.

"As for Theodore, his competent management of construction, finances and education had produced revenues which far exceeded the huge outlays I had made. Not only could I pay banks the money I owed but I was able to buy land and houses. The income from these properties sufficed for the ever-increasing numbers in the twenty-six tribes I had left behind.

"When we left the temple, I remarked to Henry that according to my calculations, I should have performed seventy-six marriages. He replied that two pairs of his grandchildren were in no condition to be married; they were dangerously ill.

"You can imagine what an effect this news produced. Living in a world where for fifty-five years, no one had ever been ill, I became profoundly upset.

" 'What is this sickness', I demanded 'and why have you kept it from me?'

"Henry tried to excuse himself. He did not wish to disturb me in my preparations for the consecration services which I held this morning. I glanced at my wife who showed me she approved of Henry's reasoning. Henry went on to say that the sickness was a mysterious one. 'All four of them show the same symptoms; they have not eaten in eight days. They do not talk; they cry; they shake as if with convulsions and after they do fall asleep, they awake with inflamed faces and with a feeling of lassitude which keeps them in bed. My wife Judith never leaves their side and their parents are with them constantly, always in tears!'

"Elizabeth was frightened. 'We must go to them at once.'

"The coachman drove rapidly and we sat there sunk in melancholy. My imagination conjured up a thousand gloomy thoughts. Was this a warning, an omen that all my descendants were to be destroyed? Had I committed the sin of pride in publishing God's law as I did? I prayed that any punishment should fall on my head, not on the innocents. Such, Milords, was the state I was in. I discovered that the bravest soul quickly becomes a prey to fear when his happiness, so assured and so long-lasting, suddenly becomes threatened.

"We went to the Ephebus where the sick lad was sleeping. He was burning with fever. In the next room, convulsive shudders shook the other lad. In the Parthenon where the girls lived, the scene was repeated. Elizabeth, pale as death did not say a word. I felt stupefied. Fever, convulsions, stiffening, stretching, yawning-I did not recall hearing of such symptoms. For a moment, I thought of bleeding them then dismissed the idea with a shudder. No one ventured to speak to me, not even my wife, so deep was my despair. Elizabeth did not suggest her essences in which she usually had such faith.

"I believe, however, that God had sent me there at that exact moment so I could save them. Had Henry given me this news before, I would not have been in a proper state of mind to consecrate his temple. God had some plan for me. So be it. I would endeavor to do his will. 'If these creatures must die', I murmured to myself, 'then I will die too. Yes, this Ephebus will be my tomb.'

"I ordered everyone to leave me alone with Elizabeth. The sick boy Eustace woke. He looked at me with a languid expression and tried to bring his lips to kiss Elizabeth's hand and mine. We embraced him tenderly and told him God had sent us to help him. He had to trust us. He looked at me, pressed my hand and sighed. Finally he said he would do what I asked. He swallowed a small dose of the emulsion. I did the same with all the others and arranged for them to be together in one room where Elizabeth and I could observe their symptoms. We sent the parents home and kept only the Megamicres in the anteroom. Elizabeth and I arranged to eat and sleep in the same room.

"I at last came to the conclusion that their illness had no physical basis but was a product of their mind and senses. Some hurtful agitation had caused their condition and I had to find a counter agent to cure it. It was not a disease of the mind like melancholia for which there is no cure. I had to find the hidden reasons for this despair, reasons which these innocents did not know themselves.

"Nourishment which consisted of syrups of juneberry and clover which my wife had prepared, helped a little. Being in the same room also seemed to improve them. Still they had fever and did not eat enough.

"When I mentioned marriage, I noted, if I were taking their pulse at the time, that the beat doubled in rapidity. I wondered if this were due to precocious desire, impatience to be married. Perhaps I had made a mistake in putting them all in the same room. When I asked if they would prefer to go each to his or her own room, they each said they would die if we separated them. The fourth day passed with some improvement but they continued to have fever, be somnolent and yawn. They were very thin and weak.

"Convinced now that the cause of their ailment was love, I began to observe with amazement that Eustace did not look at his betrothed nor she at him. Then I asked Hilary if when cured he would want to marry Anne his sister or wait a year. He said he would prefer to wait. All four gave me the same answer. Verifying with their mothers that the affianced couples did not seem interested in one another, I realized that the young people did not wish to marry their twin.

"I addressed them all saying I wished only their happiness and restored health. I would not unite them in marriage, I assured them, until they themselves asked me. I removed the screens which separated their beds and saw with pleasure that they began to talk, each one centering his attention on the cousin, and they began to eat again.

"By February, the couples were restored to their normal health. I took them with their grandparents Henry and Judith on a tour of sixty cities in Henry's state. Then in December I gathered my traveling companions together to tell them I was leaving for my capital to be there on the first of my fifty-seventh

163

year. I advised Henry and Judith that they were to unite in marriage, not only the expected eighty-nine couples but two more. These would be the two pairs of cousins, Eustace to Anne and Hilary to his cousin Ursula. In the future, I said, marriage would not take place between sister and brother but between cousins. God did not wish marriages where love was not reciprocated. Henry and Judith were stunned but the four lovers threw themselves at my feet pouring out expressions of joy. For my part, I was delighted to bring happiness so easily, the more so as my own early upbringing had made me believe that marriage between cousins was more suitable than between siblings.

"The following year, on the fifth of October, I received a memorable letter from Henry telling me that his granddaughter Ursula had given birth to a single male child while Anne had been delivered of a single female. Poor Henry was frightened and so were all the other members of the tribe. They assumed this unusual occurrence was a punishment from God. What aggravated his chagrin was the fact that all the young people in the Ephebus actually rejoiced at the event. He asked me what to do in a matter of such grave consequence. (My poor Henry was the best child in the world.) I sent a reply by the same messenger telling him that the news of the single births was welcomed with much joy by his mother and myself. He was to celebrate the births in the temple on the first day of the year with solemn thanks to God. He was to publish my letter so all could know my will, which was to be his own and his children's. Further the newly born cousins were to be betrothed and married when they reached puberty. I sent him and his wife our affection and blessings.

"Elizabeth and I discussed the astonishing news. The distress of the parents and grandparents was understandable since they had believed that marriage between siblings was the only true and natural kind. It was the only kind they knew. The young people however could see the advantage in having only one child to care for at a time. Further, they would enjoy belonging to two families, their own and their husband's. For myself, I found the event very gratifying. I had begun to worry about the huge increase in our population. God had found a remedy for us by decreasing in half the rate of our growth. And I learned later from Henry that the single birth children were both taller and heavier than each twin had been.

"In time, the news of marriage between cousins spread all over the fiefdom. Requests for information were sent to me repeatedly. I had to make an official statement. In my fifty-ninth year there, I promulgated a law for my entire race of giants declaring that henceforth only cousin marriages were permitted. My law forbade, even anathematized, marriage between brother and sister. Copies were sent to every state where my tribes lived.

"Over the years, Elizabeth and I visited our children everywhere and were happy to find them well and flourishing. On January 8th of our sixty-third year in that world, I heard from James in Heliopolis that Megamicres who frequented our temples were demanding baptism by the thousands. They found our law and liturgy and the simplicity of our sacred book very attractive. The sun was no longer god to them but the megaphosphorus. And they were no longer paying the alfas for oracles.

"It was this fact that fueled the hatred of the clergy against us. The abdalas too sent many complaints to the sacred court and even the autocephalus visited the court to declare that in twenty years he would be a shepherd without a flock unless some remedy were found. These events, James wrote, were the reasons for calling an ecumenical council to be held in the middle of our sixty-fifth year. We were summoned to attend, not merely invited. Earlier, I had been notified of this meeting which I was to attend with my two patriarch sons, but not until now did I understand the reason it was called.

"Since there was no pressing need to be there now, I went instead to visit Republic 80* My king had requested my help in curing the duke of that principality of his blindness. With me on my trip were four competent oculists.

"Twenty days of travel brought me to the capital of this country, the most renowned of all the ten Republics. The city was large and well-planned; the buildings were beautiful. But the people were quite different, unique in fact in their way of thinking.

"Literary people, I noted, all wore spectacles whether they needed them or not. Nobles in government wore garments resembling Roman togas. The common people would never allow themselves to be seen without their long knapsacks. Clock dials were all made to show the hundred hours of a pentamino instead of the daily twenty hours of a Megamician day.

"As for the manner of speaking, they seemed infatuated with eloquence. Nature had endowed them with a portion of wit, a facility in conceptualization and a degree of fluency. They used these qualities in argument. They appeared to be arguing logically but actually they used sophistry. Proceeding from a false premise, often a paradox, they inevitably came to a false conclusion. Yet they termed them axioms. They were bold and self-confident in manner and re-garded opposing opinions with scorn. They had a reputation for audacity but never for courage. If they had no hope of winning an argument, they abandoned it. They were opinionated but they would retreat if they had to prove their contention. An incredibly bad method of education had instilled pride in themselves, a pride which they had not been taught to mask. It showed itself as rudeness.

"They boasted that they enjoyed a liberty as republicans which made them superior to nobles in a monarchy. Yet this vaunted liberty was used mer-etriciously to foster license. Under the guise of liberty, oppression, violence and despotism could be carried on.

---

*Translator's note: Some of C's comments on this created state are reflec-tions of his feelings about the Republic of Venice from which he was exiled and which he never ceased to love.

"Because their form of government had always existed, the leaders wanted to conserve it exactly as it had been in the past. Any dissidence by thoughtful reformers was met with abhorrence, persecution and open ridicule. The party in power regarded as rebels those who found fault with the government and who tried to remedy these faults. Very few dissidents were stoic enough to withstand this persecution. They disappeared from the public eye and no one dared to inquire about them. Fear imposed silence.

"Those in power, the so-called conservators of the state, could take summary action without legal process. Any attempt to alter a single line of the constitution was considered an attack on the state. To them, the constitution was a magic manual, a talisman whose power would vanish if a single word were changed. If it has lasted until now, they said, it will last until the end of the world.

"The conservators did not realize that constitutions which preserved republics also brought about their downfall when they failed to conform with the times. The old legislators, almost all hidebound, appeared to me to scorn any new doctrines and to have only one obligation, to see that the state would survive in their own lifetime. Worrying about the state was too troublesome. God would provide for the future. They made easy matters difficult, and difficult ones impossible. To remedy one problem they created another.

"They believe, it seems, that long deliberations make for wise decisions, not realizing that delay in taking action can do more harm than good. And if they entrust an important matter to a capable person, they limit his powers so it is almost impossible for him to succeed. Then they hold him responsible for the failure. In choosing a person for a job, they will assign him to a task inappropriate to his qualifications, e.g., a chemist may be assigned the job of editing a code of civil and criminal law.

"The whole country appears to be in the hands of councils with the result that administration is uneven. The management of its resources is inept and the public in general is as poor as the individual. When I left, business was declining each day. The legislators did not seem to know how to stimulate competition, nor how to encourage merchants by providing capital. The government did not reap because it did not sow, being always fearful that its harvest would be taken away.

"As for religion, it is given only lip service here. The superficialities are observed in public but precepts are not followed. The government, jealous of its temporal power, always puts obstacles in the way of edicts emanating from Heliopolis.

"Young people engage in licentious behavior. Fidelity is not expected or adhered to. Megamicres have trysts with the inseparables of others and it is not uncommon to see them promenade with mates other than their own. Marriages are made between Megamicres who do not care for one another.

"The government spends much revenue on espionage. The result of having so many informers in their employ is a sense of distrust everywhere. The honest man is afraid to open his mouth for fear that his words will be misinterpreted.

"If it is true that simplicity is one mark of perfection, then this government is far from perfect. Such, however, is the power of habit over a sheep-like people that, not only do they not complain about their bonds, but they even adore the tyrant.

"Ten days after my arrival, the ambassadors from Realm 90 and from Heliopolis presented me to the duke who was head of the Republic. The duke who was blind must have said something gracious to us, but none of us understood him. The next day two nobles and their mates came to attend us and see to our needs and comforts. The two mates, very pretty but hare-brained creatures, kept us amused with their prattle. They made fun of everything pertaining to government politics including their serious inseparables. They were frankly licentious, often asking questions which made us blush. Apparently it was thought fashionable to hide nothing. Our reaction, far from disconcerting them, only made them laugh.

"We understood later that the nobles, on the pretext of entertaining us and seeing to our comfort, had been secretly commissioned to report our conversations. They could not believe we had come to the Republic out of simple curiosity. They assumed we had some plans of great importance and they had to discover what these were.

"A messenger from the Duke told me I had an appointment with him for the seventy-second hour. This would be Dust day at twelve. When I arrived there with my wife and my two oculist sons, I examined him, judged him to be curable and set the hour of the operation for the first hour of the next day. He asked me to postpone it. Later, I learned that he had to obtain the consent of a committee of 'conservators' and they had refused. He then had to submit his request to the Council of Seventeen. I could not understand why they would not want the duke to have his sight restored. I was told that every matter had to be voted upon.

"The Senate met, there was a debate, one Senator speaking for three hours, another for two. The Senate was divided, the session recessed, taken up again and the final vote was twenty-eight opposed, one hundred eighty-eight in favor. However, a seven-eighths approval being needed, the duke lost.

"I admit, Milords, I was in a fury of anger. I found it monstrous and unbelievable and I said so in a loud voice. The two noble attendants behaved icily towards me but their mates thawed them out, by saying everything impertinent they could think of.

"Since I knew that among the Senators, thirteen suffered from cataracts, I went to visit them on my own initiative. My noble attendants went with me. I found ten curable and arranged to operate on them. In three pentamines, my sons and I did a good piece of work and sight was restored to the ten.

"On the day of the hearing, the cured Senators voted in favor, the measure

167

was passed and then I operated successfully on the duke. He, in gratitude, awarded me a grant of nobility. I refused many rich rewards but gave to my two attending Megamicran couples, a gift of ten thousand ounces of gold. The Senators, not to be outdone, bought a piece of land six hundred feet square and had a palace built on it with a garden of two hundred trees. They sent me the deed of ownership.

"I had just decided to leave when a noble carrying an introductory letter from the minister of my king in Realm 90 was announced. His message, a secret one from the duke of Fiefdom 202, adjoining the Republic, bore an offer to bestow land rights on one of my tribes if they would come to settle there. At his death, they would succeed to the property since he had no heirs. No conditions were imposed. The feudal prince wrote that the Republic did not know of his offer. I asked the messenger to return the next day."

SIXTEENTH DAY

Talk at the dinner table centered on Edward's revelation that cousins not twins would now marry.

"I must admit", Countess Bridgent sighed, "that I feel more comfortable about that.... And it does halve the birth rate."

"The birth rate is still too high", Lady Rutgland said, "but I think the future will bring changes to reduce it even more."

"What do you foresee, Milady?" asked Elizabeth.

"Nothing specific, but I suspect that in time the same vices, misfortunes, sickness and poverty we have here, will come to them too."

"Now that's a pretty safe prediction!" Count Bridgent said lightly. "But we should hear from Edward what really happened."

Edward continued. "My wife and I discussed the offer. There seemed to be no risk involved so I accepted tentatively with the conditions that my four hundred married couples would have all rights as citizens and grants of land, free and clear. They would bring the same skills and services that my other tribes had brought to other realms where they had settled.

"In twenty days, the envoy brought back the document signed and sealed. I commissioned him to find a house for me in the fiefdom and gave him ten thousand ounces in bank notes of the Republic for this purpose.

"Then, unexpectedly, we received a visit from a senior senator of the Republic. He came at the ninety-seventh hour. This was during the time of repose of the day Egg. Without apology, he said that visits at certain hours were less likely to provoke unwelcome curiosity. 'We know', he said, 'that you are about to conclude an agreement. We think you have not given this careful consideration. The duke who offers you this land has no successor and his fiefdom reverts to us at his death. He has accumulated vast debts because of his extravagance. These must be paid out of his unmortgaged holdings and the fief he proposes for you is one of them. Break off the negotiations. You will not regret following our advice but you will see this as a token of our sincere friendship.'

"I was startled. Here was my private business, now become public. What he said about the duke might be true, I could not be sure. But I did not believe that the senator was really concerned about my best interests. I thanked him and replied that, if as he said, we had not carefully considered the agreement, we would surely not wish to break it off the same way. I would go to the fiefdom to look into the matter myself. The senator professed satisfaction with my answer. I knew that if he had really been pleased, he would have assumed an air of cool indifference. Republicans make a point of appearing inscrutable; they think it is good politics.

"I wrote to the minister in Realm 90 asking that a counselor on foreign affairs be dispatched to meet me in Fiefdom 202 to help me. Before my wife and I set out, we had another visit from the same senator. This time he gave me a document with the seal of the Republic. Word for word, it was a replica of the one I had received from the envoy of Fief 202. It even had the name of the son for whom I had planned it. This new grant set one condition; I was to give up my interest in 202. I expressed my liveliest gratitude and assured him I would not fail to write him from the capital of the fief. After urging me to keep my word, he left.

"In twelve days, my wife and I were at the capital of that fiefdom. My secretary and the counselor I had requested were already there. The house the envoy had bought for us was beautiful. When I looked at the furnishings, I realized that more than twice the sum I had given him for the house had been spent on these alone. I acknowledged with a smile the magnitude of the gift and told the envoy I would accompany him to court the next day. I spent an hour in the gardens ridding them of serpents. My wife and some others who had by now grown fearless, kept me company.

"The ruler of this fiefdom was a magnificent spendthrift. With his inseparable, he had succeeded to the throne at a very young age. They shared the same inclinations. They preferred the friends who encouraged them in their fondness for amusement and their excessive spending.

"Although he had inherited a vast fortune, accumulated through the thrift of his forbears, his extravagance, it was said, had forced him to relinquish possession of many of his domains when his personal fortune was exhausted. His ministers' chief occupation was raising money so he could satisfy his passion for spending. His subjects became very rich when they bought his properties and leased his revenues.

"The moral depravity there was even worse than in the Republic. Honor and modesty were regarded as a sham; violence and extortion were unchecked and justice was for sale. Even the clergy despairing of making any headway, had thrown off the mask and were living by the same standards. Why bother, said the alfas, and they actually took the lead in mocking the oracles and the people who believed in them. The pursuit of pleasure raised the cost of living. Labor was expensive because few were willing to work yet work needed to be done. It was not surprising in a country functioning like this that the necessities of life cost dearly.

"Games of chance absorbed the populace. Gambling can be tolerated when only the usual risks have to be faced. But here, dishonest maneuvering tipped the scale of fortune unfairly so that one heard daily of whole families being wiped out.

"The duke's mate had died of apoplexy eight days after a pair were born to them. One was a yellow, the other a perfect red. To succeed to the throne, the red would have to be united with another red of royal lineage of the same age. Such a union had not been achieved nor did anyone even know the whereabouts of the little prince. Those hostile to the duke said he had sold his child to the Republic for a considerable sum and that the Republic had put him to death. No one dared ask the father though he must have known what happened. I myself did discover the truth some time later. I shall tell you about this when the time and circumstances are suitable.

"In other respects than his excessive spending, the duke was charming and accomplished. No one could be more polite and solicitous. He greeted me not as an equal but as one might receive a supreme being. He gave celebrations in my honor for nine consecutive days (as if he had read Homer) and did not bring up any business matters until the tenth day. He introduced us to all the dignitaries of the court and invited us to his private dinners.

"The guests at these intimate dinners were the most charming creatures imaginable. There were never more than five or six of these each without his mate. The duke was surprised and his charming guests felt rebuffed and chagrined when, as politely as possible, we refused his invitations. But the truth is we had been finding ourselves in embarrassing positions when these fascinating creatures approached us with dangerously enticing caresses. I could laughingly ward them off, but my wife found nothing to laugh at.

"At our first business conference, the duke gave me an accurate report of all his finances. He showed records of his indebtedness and revenues. He would have to pay death taxes before mortgaging these revenues. He showed me the holdings which he controlled absolutely and finally showed me his treasure of diamonds. His loss of credit was due, he said, because he had farmed out his feudal revenues for the next sixteen years at high interest. The usurers argued he was not a good risk. This was a pretext, he said. 'Nature, if not abused', he told me, 'assures me of ninety more years. You do not see on my face those ugly signs of aging which come from a dissolute life. My pleasures are not of such a nature that I worry about dying. No one will challenge your tribe's right to the land since I will cover all my debts before ceding over the land.'

"I thanked the duke for sharing these confidences with me and told him my counselor would handle all the details. This capable counselor did examine the data and found nothing amiss. the negotiations were brought to a satisfactory conclusion in two resurrections.

"I saw the land which was to be my children's and found it large and delightfully situated near a river which after a course of ten miles flowed into one of the largest rivers of the fiefdom. This natural resource would prove useful for extending commerce.

"I returned to the senior senator of the Republic his document of donation, using in my letter, the politest words of thanks that I could devise.

'Three pentamines later, we were back at Alfredopolis. In a week I would consecrate the temple and appoint Andrew as exarch. By now Alfredopolis had become celebrated, not so much as the city inhabited only by our race, but even more as the cradle of our people.

"On the first of January, I consecrated the temple and also united in marriage four hundred fifty-six cousin couples.

"In January, I received a renewed offer from the senator of the Republic. As a mark of esteem, he said, he presented the duchy to my son Ceasar and his tribe, but this time without any condition. I called in the two couples, Ceasar and Rose and Daniel and Louise, and informed them they were to take the lands in the Republic and the fiefdom and settle there with their families. They would leave the first of March. I warned them to watch over their families so that none of the corruption would infiltrate their tribes since the state of morals in both places was deplorable.

"About this time, I had been working on a world globe which I planned for a private room in my palace. I wanted my children to have a true picture of the earth. From a map in my atlas, I had two of my grandsons, skillful in such work, paint a representation of the world on the circular wooden surface of this thirty- one foot globe. I covered the globe with glass—I had manufactured glass from a mixture of sand and alkali salt—leaving a space of one sixth of an inch between wood and glass. In this space I introduced liquid phosphorus to light up the sphere. The eighteen foot pedestal on which the globe was mounted held the four life-size statues in red gold of the royal pair and their heirs. I wanted to embellish the statues with gems of which I had an abundance. Besides enamels, I had diamonds of several colors, eight huge rubies for the eyes and a quantity of garnets, beryls, topaz, amethysts, superb opals, emeralds, sapphires and smaller rubies.

"One day, alone in my little forge, I was finishing a glass sceptre which I had cast. In order to ornament the sceptre with precious stones, I wanted it very smooth so I was polishing it vigorously with a small pad. I held it steady against a great slab of pitch which I used as a table. It was then that I came across a discovery which pleased me very much. As I was polishing the glass, I saw a little heap of gunpowder, six feet to my right, suddenly catch fire. I stood stock still, thanking God that the heap of powder—which I had used in another experiment—had not been any larger. At the same time, I wanted urgently to know the reason for the surprising accident.

"I reached out to pick up the paper on which the gunpowder rested. Between that and the glass sceptre, a small iron rod happened to be lying. As my hand approached the rod to move it out of the way, my whole body felt as if it had been pricked all over by numerous pins. When I repeated my action, the same thing happened. A hundred possible explanations passed through my mind, all of them absurd since I knew nothing of electric fire.

"I had tossed the rod some distance away. When I went to pick it up, I felt no sensation. but when I put the rod back where it had been before and I started rubbing the glass sceptre, the same tingling returned when I touched the rod, prickling me from head to foot.

"I spent eight to ten days concentrating seriously on hundreds of experiments, using different materials and methods in different combinations. What I had seen had to have a cause and I was determined to find it. I was Oedipus wanting to understand the riddle which nature, the true Sphinx, had put to him.

"I finally came to the conclusion that the iron rod permeated with electric or fluid fire, disturbed the air around itself and created this phenomenon. The air alone, agitated by a substance susceptible of being penetrated by electricity could set fire to inflammable substances. To convince myself, I made a wheel which when turned rapidly and energetically near glass, became a source of this fluid fire. I needed to turn the wheel only two or three times to generate this electricity and impregnate the whole rod at once.

"Curious to see how far this phenomenon could go, I stretched a brass wire for 2000 feet across my park, making a few turns here and there as I suspended the wire on more than a hundred stakes placed at intervals. My grandson held the wheel with its glass tube at one end. I waited at the other end. As soon as he turned the wheel I felt the sensation.

"I tried another experiment with a sheet of paper. I held it in front of the rod without letting it touch. I turned the wheel rapidly and the paper was drawn towards, then pushed away, by the electric fire. The same thing happened with a sheet of gold. I thought I would make every possible use of this great discovery, but first I wanted to try another experiment.

"With the help of my grandson, I set up wheels with glass tubes five miles apart from each other. At each end, I suspended sheets of gold. At a prearranged time, my grandson seeing the sheets flutter at his end, turned his wheel as I had done. And now the sheets of gold at my end also moved back and forth. Our messages had come five miles through the brass wire which connected us! The action of the electricity in the wire had set the sheets in motion. The speed of this force was as quick as thought or at least as quick as light.

"I decided I would take credit in the king's eyes by making a present of this discovery to the young princes both of whom were devoted to the study of physics. Following the same procedure, but this time placing a basket of dried herbs in the king's chamber where it was attached to the brass wire, I had the king turn the wheel. His sons in a cottage five miles away saw the sheets of gold flutter; at once they turned their wheel four times and before the eyes of the king, the basket of herbs caught fire and perfumed the room.

173

"He was thunderstruck and wondered if he were seeing a miracle. I assured him that the action we had taken was not a miracle even though the nature of the universal, invisible electric fire was unknown.

"The time had come to leave for Heliopolis. I left Andrew in charge of the twenty-four tribes and went to see the king to make my farewells. With his own hands, he gave me a certificate which declared that Alfredopolis was an independent principality. I had always longed for this favor but had never dared to ask.

"In ten days, I arrived at the capital of Fief 216 where my five sons awaited me, Theodore as patriarch, the other four as exarchs. I heard from Ceasar and Daniel that all was well. I visited the seminaries to see the single-birth children. The oldest were not quite four but they were tall and handsome and appeared to be more like ten year olds.

"The law I had passed which forbade marriage except between cousins had an unexpected effect. A new way of thinking had taken hold. Unlike the twins, the cousins had a greater interest in the happiness of their partners. From this arose the cultivation of purer and more refined ideas of behavior. The twins, knowing their marriage was fixed and certain, had perhaps felt less need to please their mates. The cousins, though they said nothing about it, seemed to feel themselves superior to their parents and destined to produce a race which being taller would therefore be more intelligent. Young people think this way when they are still raw material, unhoned by the grindstone of experience. Yet the greatest men are often enclosed in small bodies.*

"We left our state in a magnificent convoy and arrived at my fief in Heliopolis after four and a half months travel. Everywhere, the beneficent effects of good governing were visible. On the last day of the year, I visited the Ephebus and met in the garden the sixteen hundred and ninety cousins who were to be married the next day. And on that next day, the first of our year, I joined eight hundred and forty-five cousin couples in matrimony. Elizabeth and I made no effort to restrain our joyful tears. On that day, my patriarch son James in the temple outside the capital baptized eight hundred Megamicres. I admired his boldness since we knew that this matter was foremost on the council's agenda.

"By the end of March, the council fathers began arriving. In the interim six month period before the start of the sessions, my sons and I studied our doctrine and made commentaries and interpretations of our law. Then on the last day of September, we entered the great palace. The first session was to begin the next day. From that time on, we were sequestered for two European years. Our servants could go out to do errands. We could not leave.

"The council room was wonderfully luxurious. Phosphorus lighting, pre-

---

*Translator's Note: An interesting comment from Casanova who was much taller than average.

cious stones and beautiful marble lent richness to the furnishings. The seats for four hundred voting members all had arms and were of equal size, except for the thirteen chairs which formed the semicircle of the tribunal. Above this was a niche, curtained in gold mesh. Inside, a large dais covered with jewel-studded cloth of gold, was reserved for the Great Spirit who could see all but not be seen. A huge globe adorned with large rubies hung from the ceiling in the middle of the room.

"Each council father wore a white cloak, a green chiton-like garment beneath, and green shoes resembling brodkins. Above each head floated a halo. I do not know how they managed this but it was clearly visible. The council president had a nimbus around his head, like those we see in paintings of the saints. All of those present were reds, by nature or by artifice. Tinting oneself red was permitted only to high level clergy.

"The president's opening speech declared that the ecumenical council which last met 4,000 years ago was to have been the last if the world had improved its ways instead of becoming more wicked. He hoped the council's decisions would be guided by freedom from personal interest or passion. A majority vote would be construed as being the will of God.

"The autocephalus of Heliopolis spoke about the charge of idolatry of which we accused them. Megamicres worshipped God the creator, not his creation, he said. The appearance of truth in our religion would destroy the Megamicres' religion which was already being shaken.

"Another autocephalus rose to say that by allowing themselves to be sprinkled with holy water, the Megamicres were tacitly being made the giants' subjects. He had no quarrel with the moral value of the giants' religion but why should they think that an ablution which had meaning for themselves, would also have value for the Megamicres? Why, he asked, have they the right to make our subjects their subjects? By spreading the seed of their fanaticism, they would destroy our cult and become our masters.

"Another speaker then asked what remedies could be proposed. The discussion lasted for twenty more sessions.

"The result was a decree from the Great Spirit forbidding baptism. Reds would suffer loss of their noble status and bastards would be condemned to servitude. Reading of the giants' book was prohibited. James was deeply distressed.

"The second matter which concerned us was the distruction of serpents. When it seemed that the arguments against killing the serpents would win, I asked for time to answer. In a long harangue, I stressed our dependence on the fruit for survival, and I decried the superstition which made them venerate a species which they themselves described as cursed. We won a favorable vote.

"The subject of oracles was fiercely debated. The autocephalus explained that the oracle was the mainstay of their religion and the surest indication to the holy clergymen of God's presence. He challenged James to answer.

"Thus provoked, James argued for two hours in fluent Megamicran (his first language) that the pious drunkenness which preceded a pronouncement might be tolerated by God but not approved. The oracles themselves, if they were termed divinations, or proceeding from God, could only be fraudulent. Man could only give advice, not a direct message from God. Those who became intoxicated in order to utter so-called oracles showed by their ravaged faces that this practice was not approved.

"James continued that divination by oracle was an abuse which dishonored God. It also abused the piety of believers with the idea that God would reveal himself through a drunken ecclesiastic. If God wished to give the Megamicran world the privilege of receiving his oracle, he would have given it to the Great Spirit. This matter occupied the council for sixty-six sessions. At the end, seeing that the fathers were sitting in silent thought, undecided, the first autocephalus who had challenged James, got up in a fury. He made a speech for eight continuous hours hurling the strongest invectives at us and conjuring up divine wrath against us for daring to accuse in the presence of the Great Spirit, three hundred prelates with drunkenness.

"The speaker made one good point—like one in the Timaeus of Plato—when he said that oracles, being a species of prophecy, may have to occur when the person is in a state outside of himself. That is why the abdala or autocephalus needs to be in a condition akin to sleep. In their case sleep can only be induced by drink. Sleep therefore is an act of devotion.

"The next day, the decree on oracles was posted. The practice would be continued but only in a state of absolute sobriety, on pain of excommunication.

"But now this very autocephalus was at death's door. He was suffering from some constriction of the throat. My sons and I went to his quarters where three doctors and numerous autocephaluses surrounded his bed. He was blue, convulsive with protruding eyes. His very pretty mate, crying in a corner, looked at us with hatred as we entered.

"The doctors said they had no remedy and I understood from this that if no measures were taken, he would die. I said I would try to help even though the autocephalus had spoken with great rancor and hatred against me and my race.

"My religious beliefs required me to do what I could, in spite of his feelings. I trusted God to help me, not with any miracles however. If he were to be helped, it would be by natural remedies. The assembled Megamicres all agreed to stand by and let me do as I saw fit. I noticed that the mate now looked at me with gratitude.

"I told Theodore in English to have Elizabeth come with my surgical case and with her most valued essences. All the needed linen, bowls and hot water were already here.

"When she came, all of us helped bleed the sick man. We drew two ounces of yellowed blood. Then Theodore took some blood from a swollen vein under his tongue. Elizabeth gave him small doses of milk enemas. After a while, I

176

lanced a tumor in the back of his throat. A few hours later, I noted that his breathing was somewhat easier and the swelling of his throat a little diminished. At the end of ten hours during which he was alternately feverish and chilled, he seemed somewhat better and I began giving him gargles of sweet, then sour drinks and then a series of vapor treatments.

"When the bell announced the start of the third day, the young autocephalus—he was 34 harvests old—showed improvement. His color began to return. When he was out of danger, my wife, sons and I kneeled in a prayer of gratitude. The physicians and the others thanked me; the inseparable looked at me as if I were a God and I believe the others felt the same way.

"This astonishing cure won me the good will of all the council fathers, as well as of the ministers of the Great Spirit. At the council meeting the next day the president in a speech, thanked me, praised my heroic action to the skies and offered me on behalf of the Great Spirit an opportunity to present my own proposals.

"I acknowledged my gratitude for this chance and then I demonstrated how grateful I was by speaking for five hours. I asked for the council to approve the practice of bleeding and also for the establishment of a school for the study of anatomy. This latter proposal took several days to pass since it required discussion as to the choice of cadavers.

"I introduced a proposition to relax the prohibition against drinking plain water. James argued the point. But this wretched subject took fifteen sessions and I had to debate it myself but it finally passed.

"I further proposed that robbing a sleeper should not go unpunished. James pointed out that because the sleeper was committing an offense by getting drunk, another offense should not be tolerated. This passed, along with other legal reforms.

"My proposal that reciprocal massage after dinner be abolished failed to pass even after James made ten speeches urging the elimination of this practice.

"Then the autocephalus of Realm 83, who had never opened his mouth once, during the many long sessions, decided at the end of the second year to get up and ask me about the growth of our population. 'You came here two hundred sixty-seven years ago as two people. You now number six hundred thousand. In a short time your race will be half as numerous as ours. Will you give us a brief explanation of this?'

"Everyone was shocked. This unusual question surprised and repelled the whole council. According to their mores, such curiosity is a criminal offense. I replied at once. 'My religion does not permit me to penetrate God's secret and your religion forbids you to question me.' The president of the council hastily adjourned the meeting though it had just begun and confined the rash speaker to his quarters.

"I visited the young autocephalus who had now regained his health and was on terms of the greatest friendship with me. He showed me a letter from his brother, ruler of Realm 81, asking that one of my tribes take up residence in his kingdom on the same terms as my other tribes. The autocephalus, an altogether different person now that he was cured of his quinsy, told me that his brother had for a long time wanted to offer land to one of my tribes. He had however always objected. Now he had finally recognized his error. I assured him I would send one of my tribes to his brother as soon as I returned to Fief 216.

"The council was moving toward the end of its sessions. I could not leave the Megamicres ignorant of the fact that their belief made them idolators. I spoke for six hours making an objective analysis of the belief itself and declaring that I would consider myself damned if I left the council without obtaining the abolition of the canticle, the hymn of homage to the sun. I regarded it as an offense against God in spite of its poetry and antiquity. I prayed God to send me the direst punishment if I was mistaken and I begged that he would enlighten the minds of the Megamicres and inspire the Great Spirit to tell his people what he had always known, namely that the sun was God's creation and that the hymn of homage was in opposition to the truth.

"The next day, the canticle was by decree abolished. I was satisfied. By declaring that the hymn to the sun was anathema, idolatry was destroyed.

"The council adjourned, calling itself 'The Reform Council' and copies of its proceedings were printed and distributed world wide. After a time, the fear of punishment for baptism abated. By the time we left the inner world, scarcely ten families in our domains adhered to the old religion.

"Since five hundred eighty abdalas no longer had members, their places of worship were empty. After purification rites, I consecrated them as temples. At the cupola of each was affixed a cross. My dear son James, a very devout patriarch, maintained that he understood its meaning and he communicated his ideas in his writings and speeches. I did not wish to know his interpretation; I should have had to tell him he was wrong.

"At the beginning of my sixty-eighth year of my stay in that world, after I performed all my temple duties, I returned to my own capital. I instructed Paul and Clementine to leave for Realm 81 as I had promised the young auto-cephalus whom I had cured. I also dispatched fifteen of my younger children, sending three each to the five sectors of this new fief. This left only eight tribes at Alfredopolis with Andrew as head. He now had a population of thirty thousand and that was enough. James wrote that he had a chance to send his four oldest sons to neighboring kingdoms which asked for them. I agreed to this, reminding him to appoint the new heads as exarchs and to keep his oldest son with him. He was very much pleased since he already had a population of one hundred thousand.

"At the beginning of the sixty-ninth year, I received letters from my sons in the Republic and the nearby fief. Caesar wrote that the depravity of the Republic made him despair since corruption was finding its way into his tribe. The most attractive Megamicres of the city, mates of the most distinguished

178

and richest nobles, were seeking out giants for companions. Their own mates did not mind because they in turn found other giants. Even among the green, purple and amaranth Megamicres, the wealthy and sensual took over these same attitudes. They seduced the handsomest giants with attentions and rich gifts.

"The loud complaints of the wives who failed to become pregnant caused Caesar much sorrow. Ten of the wives had failed to conceive in the sixty-seventh year; thirteen had not conceived the year before and there would be an even greater number of discontented wives in the year to come. They felt shamed and dishonored by this terrible affront. They could not take the same action as their husbands; they did not feel any attraction for the Megamicres although the latter found them beautiful. Caesar asked for advice.

"The letter from Daniel was very similar although the circumstances were different. Daniel, a spirited and poetic man, had built a beautiful little theater and had taught his offspring to perform. The duke of the fiefdom found the theater captivating. About a year after its inception, he began giving little suppers for the actors. His other guests were like those charming Megamicres of whom we have spoken. Unfortunately, the duke himself became hopelessly enamored sometimes of one, sometimes of another giant. He easily got rid of the inseparables when their charms palled and he supped only with the poor young giants whom he enriched with gifts of precious gems.

"The wives were furious. They found love and tenderness more to their taste than all the wealth of the world. They were no longer getting pregnant and this scandal would soon become known. Daniel asked whether he should close the theater and complain to the duke. It was useless to remonstrate with the children because they said with indifference that they were not to blame. Daniel had another sorrow of which he wrote.

"One of his sons who had always given proof of the highest intelligence and prudence had been absenting himself for the last six months on the first day of each week during the hours of repose. His wife whom he loved very much did not complain. When Daniel interrogated his son, he was told that his visits though unexplained and made at unusual hours, were nevertheless innocent. He had been sworn to secrecy and could not betray this trust. Daniel concluded his letter with gloomy forebodings of the future.

"His news troubled me extremely and Elizabeth was disconsolate."

SEVENTEENTH DAY

"And odd thought occurred to me today", said Lord Chepstow. I believe those descendants of Edward's would not welcome us not even if we had a letter of introduction from him."

"I doubt that Edward would give us such a letter," Lady Rutgland remarked.

"Why do you think not?", Elizabeth asked.

"Oh, he would refuse, I'm sure...Where is he by the way?"

"In the park with the Duke of Brecnok. They don't seem to notice the heavy snowfall, they are so busy talking about electricity."

"Now there is a discovery!", Dunspili was enthusiastic. "It can be made to go far. I don't pride myself on being a great physicist but I can see that with a conductor, a bolt of lightning can be made to take another direction."

"Besides that", Lord Howard pursued Dunspili's remark, "electrification can be used to cure many illnesses."

"And there we are!" Count Bridgent said dryly. "But I see Edward coming. Remember, cousin", he turned to Lady Rutgland "ask Edward for that letter of introduction."

"Gladly", she smiled. "Edward, we have found the way to Heliopolis but we don't dare go there without a safe-conduct letter. You will give us one, I think."

"Forgive me, Milady, but I must refuse. Strangers would destroy the society I built there. They would introduce schisms into the religion which is the base for their continuing existence. If they learned the secrets I kept hidden from them, there would be dissension and division. Besides, strangers would be a threat to their political system. And remember that I am no longer the authority there. Though James is a loving son, he would not want to relinquish his power.

"Quite true. We should have to go there with a military force", Lady Rutgland teased.

Edward shook his head. "They would not be afraid. Their population as I calculate it, is now three million, nine hundred and twenty-five. Of these three hundred and ninety thousand are able to bear arms. Only five hundred and forty- nine couples are old. These act as temple functionaries."

"So the giants may live as long as the pre-flood people", Dunspili said reflectively. "It seemed that Nature retrieved her old laws in that earthly paradise. Before the deluge, people who died before four hundred were thought to have died young."

"I wonder how those worthy antediluvians kept busy all those long years." Lady Rutgland pondered.

"I know"; Dunspili replied promptly. "Scripture tells us. They were busy begetting."

Count Bridgent smiled and asked Edward, "Did you ever learn how the Republic found out about your negotiations with the duke of Fiefdom 202?"

"Spies", Edward answered without hesitation. "They have an immense network of spies, some very highly placed. The Council of Seventeen chooses three from among its own members and gives this tribunal absolute powers. The Council underwrites any decision the tribunal makes. The constitution does not provide for such a committee of three but it exists on the pretext of safeguarding the security of the state and the constitution itself. If they believe the situation warrants, they follow the maxim 'punish first, accuse later.'

"They do not tell the accused the charge and a person who very likely is innocent, no longer seems innocent after a harsh inquisition. The tribunal can always find some link, however trivial or remote or inconsequential, to connect him with the matter under inquiry.

"To return to your inquiry, Milord, the feudatory duke never learned how our business negotiation was discovered."

The company now sat down to dinner. After it was over, Edward resumed his account. "The situation in my two tribes was too serious to be disposed of in writing. I had to go there. The wives of the guilty christians were becoming sterile. If this were the way the population would decrease, then I would be unhappy indeed. Then it would be farewell to religion and tradition; farewell to peace in the home and farewell to good understanding between husbands and wives, the true guarantor of happiness in the family and the whole human race.

"Before going to the Republic, we visited Realm 81 where we settled Paul and Clementine as I had promised the young autocephalus whom I had cured of quinsy. We traveled strictly incognito until we reached our destination. Caesar and Rose came to my quarters and we discussed the situation for four hours.

"The libertines numbered twenty-three of whom two were Caesar's sons. There was reason to fear - we were already in the month of March - that forty wives would not bear children. He told me what he had done to rein in the debauchery of those stupid good-for-nothings. They seemed to become sociable and witty only in the company of those seductive Megamicres who were leading them to ruin. Caesar thought he had no other recourse but to run to the government for help. Either that or he would have to refuse admission to the

182

Megamicres in spite of their high social standing. I disapproved strongly of either plan. Instead I told Caesar to come to dinner the next day, bring the rakes and their wives and leave the rest to me.

"The dinner for fifty was not a cheerful affair. I spoke only to the wives who tried but did not succeed in hiding their sadness. After dinner, I had the twenty-three young wretches listen to a speech I addressed to them alone. I told them that they had violated the fifth article of our religion, that God had punished them by making their wives unable to conceive. If they repented, God would forgive them and perhaps their wives' fertility would be restored. If they continued to behave as they had, I warned, they would be excommunicated from the temple, deprived of their wives and families and be obliged to live apart. If the Megamicres came to visit, they were to receive them courteously but always in the presence of their wives. Further they were forbidden to leave their homes.

"Abashed and confused, they kissed my hand and left. I learned that they had been following my orders. On the first of April when I preached, they all came with their wives. Seated in the temple were also the twenty-three frolicsome madcaps who had seduced and exhausted our poor young giants. These latter kept their eyes averted from their former companions.

"That same day, the wives came to me to ask permission for their husbands to go out, saying they were truly repentant. I acceded to their wishes but I would not be convinced until I heard from Caesar that the wives had become pregnant.

"The husbands walked out the next day but only to the promenade as I learned from the polychromes whom I had put on their trail. The day after, however, to my disappointment, I learned that the first two sinners had gone by carriage to the banks of the great river. There they met their waiting Mega-micran sweethearts and they had all dived into the river, and were not seen thereafter. I surmised that they had swum into one of the underwater grottos where they spent six hours together.

"I made a sudden decision which I confided only to Caesar. Two carriages were made ready. In one of them my secretary, the two miscreants and their wives rode while Elizabeth and I took the other carriage. In twelve days, we entered the fiefdom of the prodigal duke and were warmly greeted by Daniel and Louisa. I arranged for the two couples to have a comfortable apartment where the husbands were kept under surveillance, not permitted to leave. We spent the rest of the day hearing from Daniel and Louisa about the corruption about them that was seeping into the tribe.

"Nine wives had become sterile, but their husbands argued in elaborate and artful ways that the women's infertility was not a punishment from God. The poor wives were in despair because the whole tribe knew about their misfor-tune and the reason for it. And now, jealousy, a curse hitherto unknown to our race, began to tear at the women's hearts. A remedy had to be found or we had to be prepared to see, in a few short years, this tribe scorned, its moral strength gone, my religion decried and my reputation under attack.

"The duke knew nothing about the damage which his pleasures, considered by him to be simple and innocent, were causing my family. Knowing him to be fair and reasonable, I decided to undertake the thorny task, when a favorable opportunity presented itself, of enlightening him. Nothing is so difficult as chiding a ruler for his faults and imperfections. But first I had to see for myself what was going on. I believed the guilty young men had become debauched because they were thoughtless and hare-brained. I accepted the duke's invitation to a supper to observe what I had been told were abominable orgies. We both went and saw nothing really outrageous. Perhaps our presences restrained them.

"I asked the wives of the erring husbands why they did not accompany their spouses since they were free to do so. They did go at first, they said, but were made to feel superfluous. Their presence might have embarrassed the others. At these parties, when the duke was bored and tired of restraint, he would call for strong perfumes which heated and excited the mind. Then he would sing an erotic song and the dancers were required to interpret the song in dance, executing such acts in rhythm to the music. The wives could not endure the sight nor participate. At the peak point in the dancing, the guests, following the king, would move out of the room still dancing through the gardens and to the river. There they would all plunge in. Even if they could swim, said the wives, they would not have dived in; the nature of the under water games revolted them.

"I asked Elizabeth to sound out the wives to learn if the husbands were performing their marital duties. The wives had no complaint on this score. The barren wives in the Republic also said their husbands were not remiss. I had to assume that the barrenness resulted where there was a lack of harmony between the partners. Once harmony was established, I thought, things would change. But here, if the women were barren for one year, they stayed that way. One might venture a guess and say that in this inner world with its pure air and unchanging natural laws, its total regularity, coupling alone is not enough. Harmony of feeling in the form of mutual conjugal fidelity seems required. In such a world, marital infidelity was at once exposed. I was not sure whether this was a blessing or an evil. I would use this fact however to try to find a solution to the problem.

"An unusual event provided the opportunity. Caesar wrote me that a month after I had left the capital, he was visited by the secretary from the Council of Seventeen of the Republic inquiring after the two giants who had disappeared. When Caesar told them that the two were with me, he was warned that they must return or suffer the consequences. As citizens, they could not leave without permission. The Council, he added, never refused such permission.

"I was outraged. How did the State presume to take away my rights as parent? And what kind of citizenship was this if they could not act as free men? Then I learned that the duke too had received a letter requiring the return of the giants. In a long discussion with him, I protested strongly against this action. The duke moderately explained that accepting the privileges of citizenship meant also accepting the duties of citizenship. In this case, the Republic required the giants to return when ordered to do so. The duke urged me to obey. He would be put in an awkward position if I did not return them. In the meantime, he suspended all further entertainments as I considered my position which was to ignore the demand.

"At home, Elizabeth, without arguing, simply repeated in a gentle tone 'They must be sent back.' This example, Milords, of persuasion, of not refuting, of letting me talk and listening to me without argument, had more effect on me than any reasoned debate. Coming from the lips of someone we love and respect, a simple statement surpasses the greatest eloquence. Women ought to learn this.

"The next day, I gave the duke my word that I would send my grandsons back. He praised my moderation and said he understood I had taken them away for some breach of behavior.

"Here was my opportunity to speak with him on this painful subject. I told him in detail the reasons why I had taken them away from the Republic's capital and brought them here to his fief. I described their licentious life and the unhappy consequences to their families. I spoke of the wives' despair because of their infertility. I told him of the harm to our religion, the scandal in the tribe and my own grief. I made sure to let him know that I had come to his fiefdom to see if I could remedy the same evils here.

"I observed that this talented king, who had in addition a kind heart, seemed to me extremely moved by my recital. He paced up and down thoughtfully, then asked, 'Will the wives regain their fecundity when they recover the love and fidelity of their husbands?'

"I replied that this depended on the grace of God. Only by truly repenting could the husbands hope for this favor. We parted with a cordial embrace.

"I reported my conversation to Elizabeth and I had Daniel summon his reprobates to dinner without their wives. The two from Caesar's tribe were to be present. After dinner during which complete silence prevailed, I addressed them. I first told the two that they were to be returned to their homes with the wives whom they had made sterile because of their sinning. I spoke of the law of conjugal fidelity, the punishment in the hereafter of those who disobeyed the law, of the shame in this world when they would find themselves without heirs, obliged to see their brothers rejoice at the marriage of their children while they were left desolate. Only repentance and changed behavior could restore them to God's grace. I told them to beg for forgiveness of all they had hurt by their actions.

185

"Their eyes swimming with tears, they approached, kneeled and asked forgiveness. Elizabeth wept with them. When they grew calm, I gave them my blessing. The next day, I saw on the faces of the two departing ones, evidence of true repentance. I wrote to Caesar asking him to deal gently with them. They did resume their good habits I learned but their wives failed to conceive. They did not give up hope but their wives remained barren. The fear that they will not reproduce is a most powerful curb in maintaining good behavior. There is not a one among my grandsons who does not have an ambition to become a chief of his tribe.

"During the last eleven years of my stay there, only three hundred women were barren. In a population of three to four million, that is not many.

"A month had gone by since this conversion and I was delighted to note that the court scandals had ended. The prince no longer asked for theatrical presentations; his dinners were proper and he spent his time fishing, swimming, horse racing, attending concerts and balls.

"About five or six pentamines later with everything in good order in both Daniel's and Caesar's tribes, I made plans to set out for Alfredopolis. First, though, I wanted to talk with Albert, Daniel's grandson. He was a six foot tall, dark-haired young man with a very pleasant countenance. Ordinarily, he spoke little though he was well educated in music, geometry and pyrotechnics. Both he and his cousin wife Cassandra, a dazzling blonde, were persons of splendid character. In spite of his frequent absences from home, she was pregnant.

"After dining with them, I brought up the matter of his secret absences. 'If I were free to disclose it', said Albert, 'she would know.' Cassandra declared that she would feel guilty if she made him betray a confidence. I was pleased with their answers.

"Before I set out for home in Alfredopolis, I heard from Jean, my eleventh son in Realm 87, and also from Andrew and Theodore. They all had the same problem, that of dealing with Megamicres who wished to be baptized. These were emigrating from other states to avoid the penalty of servitude or in the case of the reds to avoid losing their noble status, as had been decreed by the Great Spirit at the ecumenical council.

"In Realm 90 where my king ruled, the matter had been put to rest when he announced that as a temporal ruler, he would inflict no penalties on anyone who wished to be baptized. The clergy had objected and written to Heliopolis. But in Realm 87, the minister put the responsibility on Jean who said he had no authority. In his letter, he referred the problem to me.

"I arrived in Realm 87 in twenty days and asked for an audience with the king. When we met with the minister and the old king, I upheld Jean's position that we could not initiate an offer to baptize the Megamicres without seeming to invite them to do so. We had pledged to the Great Spirit that we would not in effect, proselytize. We would keep our word. No decision could be reached for another week. Finally, we agreed that a courier be sent to Heliopolis for an oracle and that over a period of four harvests Megamicres requesting baptism could come to us if they wished while the matter pended with the Great Spirit.

"While I was there Jean reported that a feudatory prince of this king needed a cataract operation. He had been examined two years earlier by four oculists of whom only one, the youngest, thought he was curable. Because he was a junior, they had not operated. Now when I examined this prince, he seemed to me to be a candidate for surgery. I agreed with the youngest oculist.

"When the time came for the operation, the junior whose opinion had been correct, deferred to his uncle as being the most skillful. The work was done in my presence and the successful surgeon then came to me, kneeled and kissed my hand. Both Elizabeth and I were moved and clasped him to us as my wife shed tears.

"You will pardon me, Milords, that I dwell on a detail like this. But I cannot stop myself. It is during such moments that I find myself perfectly happy, not during the times that I dispose of millions of ounces of gold, nor when I see myself master, giving orders to 300,000 men, all devoted descendants, obedient and adoring me.

"The prince, cured of his blindness, asked to have one of my tribes settle in his lands as a favor to him. I arranged for Lawrence and Lucretia my nineteenth twin to take up residence there. I wrote to Andrew at Alfredopolis to make the necessary arrangements.

"Fifteen days later, I was with Theodore in Fief 216. He introduced to me all the noble reds who had become christians and had established themselves in my fief. I met the rich merchants who had increased the prosperity of my state. I also visited the four other states of the fiefdom where my sons reigned together with the fifteen other tribes I had sent from Alfredopolis to be placed among my five sons. Everything was in order and I left them, joy and contentment in every heart.

"I finally returned to my Alfredopolis in February and Andrew prepared a welcome for us with fireworks. The royal couple had been favored with the birth of a pair of reds, thus assuring the succession for three generations.

"The city was beautiful with its quays, rivers, houses and gardens. Most wonderful in my eyes, however, were my machine shops, my forges and my arsenal on which I had spent a fortune. The arsenal consisted of a dozen armories on as many small islands along the canal. Stored in these were 200,000 rifles, the same number of pistols and numerous cannons of varying calibre. The method of casting was one I invented: five parts of silver to one of tin. I possessed several thousands of lead and iron bullets. In addition, I had all the carts and carriages necessary to transport the artillery wherever I wished. In my last storehouse, there were a hundred thousand quintals (hundred weights) of gunpowder.

"What was curious about all this accumulation of supplies was that I never once thought of its use in order to wage war. I simply enjoyed owning what in

Europe is permitted only to kings. I was rich and I enjoyed spending money on these handsome firearms and artillery pieces. If the inner world had had an ocean, I would have undertaken the construction of magnificent vessels for the pleasure of the enterprise rather than to make use of them.

"I had received a very interesting letter from my son Daniel a little while after I returned to Alfredopolis, in which he informed me that Albert and Cassandra had disappeared, leaving the care of their children to him. He had written his father a note saying that he was going on a journey which he had to make as a matter of honor and religious duty. He had a sufficient amount of money, having borrowed a substantial amount in diamonds from one of his cousins. Daniel told me that he had alerted the chiefs of all the tribes to discover his whereabouts and make him return home.

"This letter with its news did not worry me. Albert was a prudent and moral young man, intelligent and spirited. He was accompanied by his wife and he had a good supply of money. What was there to fear? I wrote at once to Daniel to respect Albert's wishes and put no obstacles in the way of his project, whatever it was, but rather to help him if he required help.

"I wrote to all my sons immediately telling them not to impede Albert in his objective but to limit themselves to prayer. A public prayer was offered up for him in all my churches. I had reason later to regret this because it was believed afterwards that I had had a hand in this mysterious affair. It is often better to pray to God in silence.

"After celebrating the religious holiday of the start of the seventy-first year, I took leave of the king and set out for my fief where I planned to spend the next three years.

"I found all my subjects content but the ten or twelve thousand Megamicran clergy were reduced to beggary. There was nothing I could do to help them even though I was sorry for their plight. They had no other profession and they were not thinking of adopting my religion since there would be no work for them in my temples.

"I observed that the new race of single birth offspring were handsome and strong. I reaffirmed the law allowing only cousins to marry but limited its tenure to twenty-nine years. I realized that by the year one hundred the law would no longer be effective. This new race would marry as they wished. Even now, their feeling of being superior was manifested in their attitude toward the offspring of twins and even in the shaky respect they showed their parents. Elizabeth and I continued to be regarded with veneration as the founders of the generations.

"In the middle of June in the seventy-second year, as I was working alone in my park on plans for a building, I saw a polychrome approach. He kneeled and gave me a letter as he had been instructed. He had obtained entry by saying I had ordered a cart of tin.

"The letter, written in English and signed 'Albert Daniel Alfred, christian,'

188

asked me to name an hour when I would be alone in the park so a carriage with ten horses carrying five persons could set down two boxes. Accommodation for the night was required. Everything would be explained later. He described the polychrome and I verified in a glance that the messenger was bona fide; he had one yellow and one jonquil eyelid.

"After the cart was unloaded of its supply, I gave the Megamicre a note with the number '14' written on it and sent him away without asking any questions, as Albert had requested.

"At the fourteenth hour, Elizabeth and I went into the park. Five minutes later, a ten horse carriage came slowly towards us. It stopped and five Megamicres got down and unloaded two large boxes. To our surprise, Albert emerged from one of them, Cassandra from the other. After kissing our hands, Albert said he needed to have three master suites in a place that was inaccessible and safe from prying eyes. I led them to a small cottage, a hundred paces from my coach house. Unobserved because the hour of repose had begun, we took our way there, followed, to my surprise, by the four Megamicre valets. Albert asked for a half hour to bathe. I showed him the baths and then Elizabeth and I spent the time walking in our kitchen garden.

"Albert and his wife reappeared and following them, to our astonishment, were four handsome reds. We hastened to render them the customary courtesy. Albert presented the first couple who were unknown to us but to our great surprise, he introduced the other couple as 'the heirs to the throne of the fief where our tribe lives.'

"This was not the place to ask questions so we invited them in as Elizabeth hastened to perfume the room with a choice fragrance. Albert asked if we had time to hear the story involved in the presence of the two couples here. I assured him this was our only interest now and that I was sure we would not be interrupted. He began to relate the story which I shall try to summarize for you. It is a long and complicated account and concerns the heir of the duke of Fiefdom 101, adjoining the Republic. In the fiefdom, my son Daniel, grandfather to Albert, resides. And in the Republic, the tribe of Caesar and Rose resides.

"When the duke and his mate (who died eight days after the birth of the unmatched pair) saw that he had a single noble heir to succeed to the throne, he made no effort to find another red, also of royal birth, with whom he could join his offspring and thus ensure a royal succession. Perhaps he was more interested in pursuing his pleasures at the time.

"A similar situation had occurred with the supervisor of canals, also of royal lineage, when he fathered a pair of whom only one was a perfect red. This red would make a perfect mate for the princeling.

"The supervisor took all the necessary steps to bring about this union. He had all the necessary papers approved by the autocephalus. Unfortunately a minister of the Republic who was visiting the autocephalus at the time,

189

overheard. He then entered into a conspiracy with the prelate to thwart the union. If the fief were left without heirs, the Republic would obtain possession. And so began a series of events which led to Albert's involvement.

"Albert had made the acquaintance of the supervisor when both were engaged in their favorite study of geometry. The princeling, the single royal red son of the duke, had been living in solitude pursuing his studies, attended by gentlemen-in-waiting from foreign states who know nothing of his background. A common interest in geometry brought Albert together with the prince through the supervisor. It was to this prince's house that Albert had been making his secret visits during the six month period when he absented himself.

"Albert had learned the identity of his royal friend after some time and he had heard also that the supervisor's offspring had been taken by the auto-cephalus on the pretext that he himself would present him to the duke as a proper mate for the heir. But a week later, the supervisor received a casket of ashes saying that these were the remains of his son who had died suddenly of an apoplexy. The griefstricken father had no recourse but to resign himself to his sorrow.

"Three days later the autocephalus also died, presumably of sorrow. The duke was angry with the supervisor for not having brought the infant directly to him and thereafter forbade him the court. Thirty-four harvests after this event, the supervisor received a letter in which was enclosed another letter signed by the autocephalus. A notary had found this letter among the effects of a deceased alfa.

"The autocephalus' letter, written as he lay dying, poisoned, begged forgive-ness for his cowardice and crime. The supervisor's young son had not died; those ashes were not his. The autocephalus had sold the baby to the minister of the Republic on his promise that he would not put the young red to death.

"Albert, to whom such villainy was incomprehensible, tried to calm the supervisor. While he did not have much hope that the young noble red might still be alive, he nevertheless agreed to help.

"He wrote first to his cherished uncle Ptolemy who lived in the Republic with Caesar's tribe. This uncle had taught the young Albert mathematics and together they had devised an unbreakable code in which they corresponded regularly. Many letters were now exchanged between Albert and his uncle who undertook to help his nephew in the search.

"In the interim, Albert visited the duke in his underwater retreat taking along with him the supervisor who had been forbidden the presence of the duke. The ruler was surprised to see Albert's companion but listened to him nevertheless. When the duke heard that the supervisor's son, destined to be his own son's inseparable, might still be alive, he agreed to cooperate. As for his own son, living alone as a student without an unseparable, he said he loved him and would be glad to have Albert pursue the search. He gave him his royal seal to indicate to the young prince that he could trust Albert in his enterprise.

190

"Meanwhile Ptolemy had been getting a great deal of information from the provost or chief of police of the prison whom he met through an acquaintance. By adroit questioning, he learned that the Republic did indeed have a noble red as a captive; that he knew he was alive since the provost had to vouch for him in order to get money for his upkeep. The young captive seemed of dull intellect; he did not speak or respond.

"Ptolemy learned that the prisoner's nourisher was an ill-bred polychrome, a deaf-mute. The young noble, though very beautiful, seemed defective. He did not know who he was and he was untaught in every respect.

"Although Ptolemy could not get into the prison itself, he succeeded in getting information about the lay-out of the building and even the location of the cell where the young red was immured. This he did partly by flattering and partly by provoking the simple provost.

"Albert and Cassandra, the supervisor and his mate, the young prince and some trustworthy servants undertook a daring plan to free the captive from a fortress prison which was said to be impregnable. No one had escaped from there in several centuries."

EIGHTEENTH DAY

After dinner, Edward took up the tale of his great-grandson's adventure.

"Albert was prowling around in the vicinity of the prison buildings. He had surveyed the area once before with his uncle Ptolemy. Not far from the buildings, he saw a small house, set apart and about forty or fifty paces from the avenue. Entering the house was a polychrome, a heavy knapsack on his back and a pair of shoes in his hand. He judged him to be a shoemaker. This house, Albert thought, would be ideal for his plan. It could be the base from which he would dig a tunnel to the cell where the red Megamicre was held captive.

"The supervisor undertook to negotiate for the purchase of the place. On the first day he ordered two pairs of shoes and looked about him. The dwelling was about twenty-four feet deep with three floors, one of which was illumined naturally. Two days later, he picked up the shoes and mentioned casually that such a place might suit his needs for his work as optician. It turned out that the polychromes were eager to sell and move to the country. On the third day, he made arrangements to buy the house and on the first day of the following pentamine, the purchase was legally consummated upon payment of eight hundred twenty ounces of gold for the house and its furnishings.

"As soon as Albert had possession, he checked the area between house and prison and satisfied himself that no masonry structure intervened. His next concern was to get exact measurements of the distance and direction for his proposed tunnel. To get this, Albert had to resort to a ruse. Ordinary means of measuring would not do here where the city walls arose nearby and where people were always milling about.

"On their holiday, the third day of every harvest, people would play at a game in which they aimed darts or arrows at a bird tied on a long cord to the summit of a tall pole. The bird had enough cord so he could fly back and forth and around as the archers tried to hit it. For a small coin, archers on the opposite bank aimed their darts at the ever-moving target. Albert promised his faithful polychrome to buy him such a pole and bird. The servant was grateful and pleased, unaware that Albert really wanted the pole to help him with his measurements.

"Ptolemy had learned from the provost some time earlier that the distance

193

from the prison courtyard to the cell was forty-eight feet. Albert, going by boat to the place where he had first surveyed the prison with his uncle, now measured the number of feet from the river bank to the prison courtyard—forty-two feet. The total, then, was ninety feet. To verify this, he had the prince who was an underwater swimmer as well as a mathematician use a rule and determine whether his figures were correct. They were. It was exactly ninety feet to the captive's cell. Albert had the polychrome put up his forty-foot bird pole at the spot where the ninety foot length began.

"Back home, Albert, with the prince's aid, planted a short pole, eight feet high, in back of his house where he planned to start his tunnel. They had the tall pole in perfect alignment with the short pole. From his calculations, Albert determined that the tunnel had to be one hundred eight feet long.

"Outside the cottage stood two vehicles with four horses each for carrying away the accumulating earth. Albert's carters would disperse the soil daily all over the countryside, being careful to flatten it out without leaving any mounds or hillocks. At hand were all the excavating tools and equipment. There were hoes and axes, shovels and levers, hatchets and hammers, baskets, barrows, and two-foot planks and six-foot laths to serve as props.

"The work began. In thirty-six days of unflagging labor, they had dug out 1272 cubic feet of earth and had opened the passage at the rate of three feet each day. A hundred planks and laths were interlocked to support the roof of the tunnel.

"It was time now to bore upwards. Albert undertook this task alone. It would be quieter with one man and, moreover, his height was needed. After two slow hours of laborious prodding with his iron-tipped tool, Albert encountered resistance. He had reached wood. To use cutting tools like an axe or a chisel would be too noisy. Albert stopped.

"He wrote to his uncle to send him a certain corrosive liquid not unlike our nitric acid which was available there. He asked for a quantity of sponges as well. As soon as he received the material, he recommenced his work. It was a slow process, requiring repetition after repetition of applications with pincers of the acid-soaked sponges to the wood surface. Then came the wait for the acid to work. Slowly the wood thinned and decomposed bit by bit, day after day.

"Albert prodded the softened wood loose. It crumbled and fell little by little. When the wood had been enough weakened and thinned by the acid eating into it, Albert began to cut out the hole.

"He glimpsed light. Now he had to learn when the prisoner would be alone. By waiting, he found out that food was brought two hours before the day's end. That would leave nineteen hours after the guard left for the rescue operation.

"Meanwhile the others had been lengthening the tunnel while he was boring upward. They had reached the wall of the canal and had broken into it so some water began to seep through. They stopped it up. But Albert had an idea and ordered the prince to unstop the hole at once. From the size of the

194

opening and the rate of flow, he estimated that the excavation could be flooded in twenty hours. This suited his purpose exactly.

"It was now past feeding time; the guard had left. Albert completed cutting around the wood and made a hole in only fifteen minutes. Staring down at him in utter astonishment were the polychrome and the captive red.

"Albert hoisted the prince to this shoulders. He in turn grasped the prisoner by the waist and handed him to Albert who placed him in the waiting arms of his father. Then Albert lifted the prince out of the dungeon. He ordered them to bring the captive to Cassandra and return at once.

"For ten hours all worked to remove the planks and laths and let the earth from above fall down into the cavity. They dug a trench strong enough to assure the flooding of the tunnel. At the house, they transformed the rescued red into a polychrome and then the two couples, all disguised as polychromes, departed for the retreat which Uncle Ptolemy had previously found for them.

"Albert locked the little house which had already been emptied of its contents and he and Cassandra went by boat to rejoin their dear friends. They lived in this retreat for two harvests, hidden from all, confident of the loyalty of their servants who, moreover, had no idea of the importance of their masters.

"Albert had heard from Ptolemy, only two days after the completion of their mission, that the flooding of one wing of the prison was discovered at once. Two Megamicres had drowned and the owners of the little house had also been drowned. The government was now presumably looking for the heirs to take possession. It was clear from these rumors that the government knew well that the red captive had been freed, that the tunnel had been built and flooded.

"Apparently silence was deemed to be the best policy at this juncture. Ptolemy wrote further that he had sent carts of merchandise to the border to see if any unusual precautions were being taken at customs but there was nothing happening there. A final letter from Ptolemy before they left the retreat notified them that the provost had disappeared from sight. Watchfulness and caution was of the utmost importance, he warned. Albert concluded the story of his adventure, worn out with hours of continuous talking.

"Albert had described the untutored and neglected captive as truly being in a state of infancy. He had had no training and no contact with others beside the deaf-mute who served him as a provider. Knowing nothing, he hoped for nothing and feared nothing. Everything was new and strange when he was restored to his parents and society. The first day, the father spent nine hours talking to him, having to digress often to explain the simplest matters. He was taught thereafter for four to five hours each day for a period of four months to give him some understanding of essentials, like the laws of nature, manners and morals, customs and laws, religion and government. He was told about his own unfortunate experience when he was kidnapped in infancy.

"As for my own contact with him, I found him surprisingly gifted. I had never met among the Megamicres one more avid for knowledge. The more he

195

learned, the more he wanted to know. In fewer than eight harvests, he had become proficient in reading, writing, music, geometry, geography and history. Perhaps the long inertia of his prison years had made him readier to ripen into perfect maturity. When I was teaching him, his questions and objections were of such a nature that I found myself as much a pupil as a teacher.

"He had a philosophical bent. In matters of religion, he could rapidly discard the non-essential and the superstitious. He understood how a mystery like the trinity and God could be a necessity without being a reality since a mystery could never be a comprehended reality.

"Later when he was established as heir in the dukedom, he put into effect a law forbidding theologians and physicists from declaring some phenomena to be miracles. Conversely he had those branded as tattlers and prattlers who sought to diminish the significance of the All Powerful.

"I thought it best for reasons of security to have Albert and Cassandra leave my house, go back home by an indirect route and then return publicly to be greeted by all members of their family. Both the duke and Daniel, being forewarned of this plan, would know how to act.

"It turned out perfectly; all played their parts well. The family members feted them, making their return an occasion for rejoicing. Meanwhile, I kept the two red couples with me, still disguised as polychromes.

"I should tell you of another event which had consequences later. The duke had just offered to Daniel the opportunity to take on the lease for collecting revenues in his fief. The duke was not satisfied with the way the former company whose lease was now expiring had handled the tax farming. They had exacted tolls on entering or leaving the dukedom, had placed import taxes on commodities to the point that commerce was impeded and many merchants suffered. The use of roads and rivers was taxed, and they had kept fifteen million ounces while paying the duke only three million. The loan of one hundred fifty million would have to be paid for the lease.

"By express courier, I told Daniel to take on the lease with two conditions: one, that the lease terminate only with the extinction of the duke's line, and two, that Daniel would have the right to make such regulations regarding taxes and fees as he thought advisable. To seal the contract, Daniel would pay the sum of fifty million ounces as a gift to be placed in the ducal treasury once the agreement was signed.

"I ordered Daniel to have a thousand copies of the contract posted after it was signed. The previous leaseholder had a three day option to meet the terms of the agreement and so did any other bidder. Daniel's manifesto would promise to end import taxes, abolish tolls on shipments, either by land or by water, of merchandise belonging to fief citizens. Further a regular accounting of all revenues would be made and any surplus returned to the duke.

"By the same courier, I sent to my fief in Heliopolis and to the Fief next to the

Republic, orders for drafts in the sum of two hundred million ounces to cover the cost of the loan and the gift. Daniel got the lease.

"I now told my illustrious reds to go by boat in their polychrome disguise to a town in my fief about a hundred leagues away. They were to wash off their disguise in the river, present themselves at the finest inn, buy a handsome coach, take on eight servants and then come to pay me a visit. I wrote out a letter which they were to present to me when they returned to pay me a formal visit.

"All was done as planned. The twentieth of January of this seventy-third year, a handsome procession appeared. My children Lucian and Ernestine presented the two reds. I pretended I had never met them and made a great show of reading the letter they handed me. Then I paid them the kind of honors I would pay a monarch to the great amazement of Theodore and his tribes who accompanied them.

"Daniel knew I was planning a state visit of the greatest pomp and solemnity to unite the duke with his heirs. In my role as prince of Alfredopolis, twice duke of two fiefdoms and grand pontiff of our religion, I would have in my train courtiers from Fiefdom One and Fiefdom 216 as well as my ministers and secretaries for ecclesiastical affairs.

"My cavalcade would include two thousand of my children and their wives as well as my retinue of four thousand servants of all colors, all on horseback behind a thousand carriages each drawn by twelve horses.

"These grand preparations were not unknown to the duke who was beside himself with delight at the thought of the huge expenditures this unheard of visit would require of him. I planned to enter the ducal palace with the greatest pomp and panoply sparing no expense. Daniel had already arranged for costly lodgings in the most beautiful houses for my courtiers, ministers and secretaries.

"I sent a messenger to the duke to expect me on the fifteenth of February at three o'clock. On the seventh of February I set out. Four hundred carriages preceded mine and four hundred followed. These carried two thousand giants and their wives. The men were nude except for a girdle, a haversack and the brodkins on their feet. The women wore the 'exomide', a haversack and similar shoes. The men carried rifles; the women carried pistols. An additional one hundred carriages conveyed my two courts with its noble Megamicres and ministers.

"In my carriage, Theodore and I sat in back with the two ducal heirs between us. In front, my wife and Theodore's wife, Frances, sat on either side of the supervisor and his inseparable. I took the most direct route. This did not require that we touch the borders of the Republic. I had provided for stops on this seven hundred mile journey. With horses covering twenty miles an hour, we did not need to change more than twenty times during the whole trip. And at each stop, pavilions had been set up where Megamicres were on hand to serve us with baskets of figs.

"The first sign of the duke's magnificence awaited us as we approached the river that separated our two fiefs. Across this body of water, sixty feet wide, a line of boats firmly joined and held fast by posts, formed the base for a bridge above. It had been constructed by one hundred thousand workers and was five hundred paces wide. Iron parapets had been built to protect its sides. Across this carpeted passage, my family and friends walked on foot, four abreast. When the entire procession of carriages had crossed, the same workmen took down the bridge.

"Our journey was made comfortable by stops at pavilions dispensing the most elegant fare. Our way had been further cleared by the action of a corps of two thousand of Daniel's giants who, at the duke's request, had destroyed all the serpents in the trees bordering our route.

"I had thought that the prodigality of my own expenditures would shock the duke. I was mistaken. Lavish expenditure is looked on askance only by those who cannot spend as much.

"The next morning, one stop before our last one, the highway had been shaded over by canopies suspended on either side over beautiful columns. And at our last stop, we were met by twelve noble couples on horseback who brought us the compliments of the duke. These then ranged themselves, six pair on each side of my carriage, to escort us to the duke. Further on, Daniel, his wife and two hundred couples of their tribe came to meet me on foot. I greeted them from my carriage and continued on.

"The duke had arranged to meet me in his gardens about a mile from the city. The procession moved ahead when my carriage stopped. Stepping out of the great portal of his pleasure palace, the duke embraced me and the others of my group. I bent low in greeting and holding the two noble reds by the hand, I presented them to the duke. With dignity and tenderness, he embraced his son and asked for his mate. 'Not yet my inseparable', the prince replied. Thereupon the duke said, 'From this moment on, he is your inseparable.'

"He thanked the supervisor for having restored his son who would , with the prince, be the legitimate heirs to the dukedom. Then he introduced the pair to his court. Though deeply astonished, they hastened to render them homage, kissing the left hand.

"The minister of the Republic abstained from this gesture since protocol forbade, but he assured them with seeming candor that no one was more aware than he of the happiness of this event. He was sure the Republic would ackowledge its pleasure by public galas. The new inseparable apparently recognized in this minister the same executioner who had spirited him away and had had the autocephalus poisoned. But he responded only with a gracious bow.

198

"The duke ordered his chancellor to register the young prince and his inseparable as the heirs by a solemn act of state. Later in a private talk with the duke, as he expressed his gratitude, I urged him to be firm in his dealings with the Republic. I would always be at hand, I assured him, to serve him with my counsel.

"There is no point in my telling you about the great galas and feasts which lasted for five pentamines in honor of the heirs. These might have gone on endlessly had not some events occurred which demanded serious attention.

"The duke's ambassador had notified the Republic about the change in succession. He heard nothing in reply. Then in August, the new heirs became the proud parents of a perfect pair of reds. The event caused much joy in the dukedom. It also proved that the two parents were nearly identical in age. In that world, the difference of even one harvest will prevent procreation. This birth occasioned much rejoicing and another round of festivities. But the minister of the Republic was called home.

"A short time later, the duke learned that five regiments of the Republic had been armed and ordered to march to the border. The replaced soldiers were to join with others in another border city so that this enlarged body was now within range of both fiefs, mine and the duke's.

"This news gave me reason for concern. I wrote at once to Andrew in Alfredopolis to send all my tribes except his, to my fief. These made up fifteen thousand armed men. My order was promptly carried out. By October, I had recruited from my twenty-five tribes, an army of three hundred thousand giants of whom sixty thousand were armed and ready.

"At the end of the year, the duke called on me for advice. He had heard from his ambassador that the Republic was sending twelve senators with two secretaries to the capital. Accompanying them was an army of 24,000 Mega-micres armed with halberds and arrows. They were bound for the city which bordered the ducal fiefdom. I advised him to receive only those who came in peace but not to receive an armed force. The duke thereupon notified the governor of the border city to keep the army from entering.

"A few days later, the duke learned from his courier that the army, having been halted at the city gates, two officers demanded to know why they had received the army of the giants and were forbidding the Republic's army admission. They then used force to enter, broke down barriers, aimed arrows at the fleeing guards and took over the city. The governor was no longer in charge.

"The duke said he would not like to use force even if he had an army. When I asked what he would do in lieu of force, he said he would appeal to the tribunal for justice. All the other nations of the world would support his stand.

"I replied that while he was waiting for justice to be done, the Republic would take possession of his person, of his heirs (who would now disappear for good), his property and his country. Then in secret maneuvers, they would convince the tribunal that the truth was falsehood and that the Republic had only taken measures which were urgent and necessary. Would the duke then congratulate himself on his confidence that justice would prevail?

"I told him that his plan was exactly what the Republic expected him to do. 'Never', I warned him, 'do what your enemies expect you to do.' This was a prickly matter. The duke had no army. I could not interfere since I had no present grievance. They had not attacked me but I wished they had. The duke admitted he was deeply upset.

"Later, at dinner a messenger came with the news that an army of 24,000 had marched on a city thirty miles inside the border. They had camped there and had even dislodged some homeowners to provide room for their higher ranking soldiers. Two officers were now on their way to the duke's palace. When they returned, the army would resume its march forward. Forty-eight vehicles had passed through this city already on the way to the duke's capital.

"A half hour before day's end, two officers, blue-gray in color, were announced. They carried halberds and cutlasses and they had safe-conduct passes from the Republic. My advice to the king was this: 'If you have the soldiers, you can and you should put them in prison.' The duke was not shocked by my words. He had a corps of eight hundred required by the state to serve him even at the cost of their lives. These were very brave fighters and were ready to die for him.

"Fifteen minutes later, he came back to tell me that the deed had been done. Then he asked me what to say to the ministers and secretaries who were coming to see him the next day. I advised him to have his soldiers arrest them even before they entered the capital gates. He should throw all of them: senators, secretaries, servants, coachmen and their baggage, all in prison.

"This action, said the duke, would be infamous, were it not for their infamous action in invading his country. The next morning I learned from him that the whole contingent, three hundred of them, were in his prison which he described as a pleasant one. He had ordered ample food for them but no perfume.

"The duke's ambassador who had returned home, having been recalled from the Republic, reported that the Republic was rife with rumors that the heirs were impostors and that the matter was of serious concern to the state. Honor required that the Republic explode this structure raised through ambition and fraud. The duke himself, so the talk went, had resigned his rights to the fief twenty years before, agreeing with them that he had no hope for heirs.

"As for Edward, the rumor continued, he was now revealed as the architect of this criminal enterprise in presenting the counterfeit couple as heirs. He had received marks of the sincerest friendship from the Republic but now his reputation was blackened. He would be deprived of his status of nobility and his tribe would be chased out. People were talking openly of not waiting for the duke to die in order to confiscate his fief.

"By now, three European months had passed without incident, since the senators and their staff had been imprisoned. The city which had been invaded and held by the Republic, remained occupied. All I knew from Caesar's coded messages was that the senate met daily. They could come to no conclusion because their numerous committees kept taking opposing positions.

"In mid-May, the duke learned that the army had begun a march. At the end of the month, three couriers arrived on the same day from three different cities with the disturbing news that the cities had been taken over. In each, a garrison of eight thousand soldiers had taken possession of the custom houses, seized the banks and arrested the Megamicres, my sons' managers. These had been replaced by their own people.

"Moreover, the Republic had mobilized an army of fifty thousand and had posted notices in every street threatening to put the entire fiefdom to fire and sword if the pretenders were not handed over. The Republic commented that they would not have resorted to such an undignified method as the use of wall posters had not the duke violated a nation's sacred rights by putting their whole embassy in prison. Seizure of the customs and businesses was a serious matter. I could not let Daniel endure this action without protest. It affected me closely, too. This action on their part was a rash one because they knew I would intervene on his behalf.

"I had Daniel send a memorandum through Caesar demanding damages, restitution and freedom for those arrested Megamicres who had been managing his businesses. After a wait of two greenwood fires, the answer, given orally, merely said that Daniel should ask for damages from the duke. At this, I lost patience. Sending a red Megamicre with a note from my own hand, I stated that I was acting in the interests of my son in requiring a redress of grievances. I did not threaten.

"The identical reply, this time in writing, said I should ask the duke for damages. I heard at the same time, that the Republic had seized stores of merchandise and had confiscated the boats belonging to the duke. They had even appropriated boats and merchandise belonging to Daniel's tribe, this confiscation having also some serious consequences for Caesar's tribe. Since Caesar was not subject to the duke, I advised he demand redress. Their actions were illegal and if he received no satisfaction, he, Caesar, would quit the Republic.

"The next day a member of the Council of Seventeen visited Caesar saying that his statement had horrified the senate body. They offered a whole city within the republic in which Daniel could settle with his tribe while he awaited the death of the duke and the confiscation of the fief. Then Daniel could succeed to the fief.

"Daniel, whom the duke loved and respected, would not consider the offer for a moment. He asked me to keep this offer concealed from the duke. He was right. It was best not to tell him; he might feel threatened. An act of virtue

201

should not be publicized. Making known to the intended victim your virtue in abstaining from hurting him, might arouse his fear anyway and perhaps put his own virtue to a test.

"Daniel could easily have sent a thousand giants armed with rifles to each border city to recover his goods. He could not make a decision for a massacre and I was careful not to give him any advice to the contrary.

"We were now well along in the seventy-fifth year; the Republic was calmly enjoying the possession of all the income from the duke's fief, with its army of fifty thousand at the borders of my fief and the duke's. It was time to strike a blow to shatter the calm. Daniel would have to be the one to do this. I ordered him to set out at once with five hundred couples of giants from my guard. He was to have Theodore put five thousand more giants under his command. In addition, the twenty thousand Megamicres I had in my guard would join his army.

"All the necessary artillery would accompany them as they made their way in flat boats to their destination. This was the fortress which they were to surround. This fort a mile and a half in circumference stood at the entrance to the rich gold and phosphorus mines of the Republic. The troops were to lay siege to the city. If the governor refused to surrender, the bombardment was to begin without delay.

"I had not told the duke about the steps I was taking. He lived happily in his court with his children, giving entertainments and amusing himself to the great astonishment of his subjects who believed hourly that they were going to have to surrender. I encouraged the prince to bring gaiety to his people, to discourage those who spoke gloomily of misfortune or urged economy. About the beginning of March, however, in the seventy-sixth year, the astonished duke heard from his spies that Daniel's army was encamped at the fortress known to be the most impregnable in their world. Hearing this, the duke felt that with such an army, the war would soon be over.

"The Republic did not have the same idea. They acted unafraid. Learning about Daniel's blockade, they had sent their army to the other side of my fief. With the system of canals in that world, it was simple to build a dam which effectively diverted water from Realm 90 into my land. I heard from Simeon that already four of his cities were inundated. The flood was rising and in one harvest, the entire fief would be under water. The peasants were fleeing, abandoning their homes. Simeon wrote that he wanted help, not advice.

"I had no time to lose. I notified the duke about this emergency. He had two thousand of my giants armed with fire power and fourteen hundred others from my guard under the command of Daniel's son. These would protect his capital and defy the army of two hundred thousand Megamicres. Then I set out with Elizabeth, Albert, Cassandra and a hundred couples from my guard."

NINETEENTH DAY

"We started out", Edward went on, "and in sixty hours, traveling at a rapid pace, we reached the border of the Republic. There, I told the officer to lower the barrier. He refused with arrogance saying he had his orders. When I threatened him with death, he lined up the soldiers of his garrison in attack positions.

"I ordered my men to fire. It was with great regret that I saw a number of Megamicres fall. The others all fled. As soon as I threw down the barrier, I put up a bridge and hastened to the second station. There I was met by a courier from Theodore. I heard the heart-breaking news that the other side of my fief was being inundated and the flooding was spreading to Realm 90.

"Without any stops, we reached Alfredopolis in three and a half days. I wrote to the king of Realm 90 explaining the situation as one from which I could not honorably withdraw. I wrote to Andrew to post notices that those who had suffered damages from the flooding of my borders would be indemnified. I wrote to Simeon to spare no expense in building dikes to halt the further flooding of the land. I ordered horses to be in readiness at the posts along my route.

"I seized and detained all boats in my ports which belonged to the Republic. I did the same with the stores and warehouses in my cities which were the property of the Republic. At the same time, I ordered Andrew to form three divisions out of three thousand troops and put a senior commander at the head of each. These were to capture three cities in the Republic near Fiefdom 109. They were to use force if necessary. Similarly I dispatched three thousand giants to three border cities in the Republic to do the same. These were to go on foot in slow marches, bypassing the capital.

"After all this, I was ready to go to the great dam in the Republic to destroy the lock and control the inundations. To assist me, I took along hydraulic engineers of my college. Fortified by a thousand men and ten cannon, we arrived by boat. It took a month of labor and cannonading to breach the dike. It took another month of slow marches (we had to commandeer the peasants' horses along the way) to get to the lock which was holding back the even flow of water from canal to canal.

"Twelve thousand Megamicres were standing fast to defend the lock. Nothing could be more unsophisticated, militarily, than the way they were lined up. They stood in twelve rows of a thousand each, one row behind the other. Since the Megamicres knew that earlier those who dared the giants' fire had been killed, I hoped they would give up. But they advanced. I had ordered half my men to charge their rifles with the blue powder which made a loud noise but was harmless; the other half had rifles with deadly bullets.

"When my corps was twenty-five paces away and they did not surrender I ordered my men to fire with the harmless powder. To my despair and horror, I saw the whole first line of the enemy fall to the earth. The eleven thousand behind them fled on foot; their officers preceded them on horse.

"Sick at heart, I proceeded with the destruction of the lock. I left when I saw the waters resuming their normal course. My geographers told me that one lock remained to be destroyed. It was a two day journey away. With the destruction of this last lock, the Republic would find itself in a pitiable state; the countryside opposite my land would become flooded and an adjacent kingdom would also receive the overflow.

"I took to heart the wise but merciless advice given to those who wage war: to wreak the greatest possible harm on the enemy.

"By now we were all tired. I, after all, had reached the grand age of ninety. Not a soul was about. The peasants' homes were abandoned. But two leagues or so in the distance, I noticed a coupola and the tips of some anaze trees. We marched there and found a dwelling. It belonged to some nobles who had retired there a hundred years earlier, having become disenchanted with the way of the Republic.

"They welcomed us courteously and offered us food so we did not have to requisition any supplies from them. I presented my sons to the noble lord, declaring that in all my three hundred and sixty years, I had never been grieved by any disobedience on their part. I could not say this anymore. Today I ordered them to frighten, not kill the subjects of the Republic, my enemy, but they killed one thousand of them. At this the commander of the first line swore that his guns had contained a harmless powder and that the Megamicres must have died of fright. The amiable lord then dispatched six horsemen to the lock. When they returned, they reported that not a single corpse was to be found on the field of battle. Halberds, arrows, knapsacks and a hundred flags were strewn about. That was all.

"Much relieved, our conversation took on a gaiety which lasted through a sumptuous repast. We spoke nothing of war or politics. I naturally made no inquiries about them but it was clear that the family was of the highest rank. We left the next day after having been entertained with the finest fare and the costliest perfume. At our first stop on our march, we had the governor of that city provide us with two hundred carriages and two thousand horses upon our threat to burn down his city. He complied promptly.

"Because we had to use the same horses sometimes for three or four days, our progress was slow. On the way, I met the army of Louis' and Caroline's tribe. I learned that they had taken over the business establishments in the city they subdued. I had not given them this order but I did not countermand it. A hundred and twenty leagues farther, I encountered the army of Jean and Tecla's tribe. They were stopping the movements of boats from one kingdom to another. Again I had not given such an order but I let it pass. And I was to learn that soldiers in the tribe of Matthew and Catherine and in that of Leopold, my fourteenth son, were all taking the same kind of actions. I wished them well, reminding them however to avoid shedding blood.

"By mid-December, I reached the fort of the mines where I was hailed with all the bellicose excitement that war inspires everywhere. Carefully examining the site where the fort stood, I satisfied myself that it could never by taken by cannonading from the river. The outside walls, twelve feet high, surrounded the fort for fifteen hundred paces.

"Fifteen towers, each twenty-four feet high, were placed at equal distances inside these ramparts. If besieged, the defenders could hurl any projectile they wished from those heights. Inside, the fort measured seventy-two feet. This fort was the invincible stronghold of the Republic and now with its weakening commerce, it was also the chief source of its wealth. I had to take it by land and I was determined to do so without sacrificing the life of any of my children.

"By the end of March in this seventy-seventh year, I received from my fief, as I had ordered, a shipment of forty cannon of twenty-four calibre gauge, a hundred mortars, a huge quantity of combustible material, fifty thousand lead bullets and all the blue powder I needed. The supplies came by boat under the escort of five thousand giants and twenty thousand Megamicres. I cordoned off a circle of six English miles to prevent anyone from entering or leaving the fort. In fewer than two months, I had broken down the fifteen towers and by early July I had breached the fortress with an opening thirty paces wide.

"I put my Megamicres to work clearing the debris. I had first sent huge numbers of leaflets flying through the fortress city announcing that I was taking possession in a few days; that no one would be deprived of his goods; that all employed would retain their jobs with a twenty percent increase in pay. The leaflet further said that my only interest was to take the fort. My soldiers, giant or Megamicre, were not to be attacked. At the first drop of blood spilled, I would order a general massacre.

"Fifteen days later, my three thousand giants marched into the fort. The debris had all been cleared and a bridge thrown across the moat. Followed by our armed guard of a hundred men, Elizabeth and I entered. In a public statement, I proclaimed that whoever would not recognize my sovereignty was free to leave and go elsewhere but without any possessions. Those who swore fidelity would keep their belongings and those who worked in the mines would get the twenty percent increase.

"All swore fealty, including the six thousand workers. I declared them all prisoners of war. I left a garrison there of three thousand giants and left twelve cannon and many mortars outside the fort. Within the ramparts, I stored those cannon for which I no longer had any use.

"Before setting out for the capital of the Republic, I had the boulevards restored which had suffered damage from the bombardment. I did not replace the towers but had a parapet constructed to surround the fort. From this shelter, my fuseliers could if necessary take cover from any archers that dared attack them.

"I heard at this time from James in Heliopolis that the Republic had avowed its submission to the Great Spirit in some matters about which it had formerly been defiant. Having thus received absolution, the Republic pleaded for strong measures against giants. The Great Spirit obliged by denouncing the giants at whose hands one hundred Megamicres had been killed. They pronounced anathema against the giants as long as they continued to support the duke's claims and anathema also against those Megamicres who supported the giants.

"I paid no attention to this and prepared to march, supplying myself with as many horses and carriages as I would need. At the beginning of July, we started. We were four hundred and fifty miles from the capital. The army preceded by the artillery was an impressive sight. Each of my warrior sons, feeling himself a prince, marched with a self-imposed discipline, each emulating the other in keeping the regiment as a whole in good order without difference in rank. They marched as a body not unlike a corps de ballet. Each regiment was distinguished by the color of its uniform from boots to their elegant caps. Each regiment was preceded by a band of Megamicre musicians and they stepped gaily in rhythmic cadence as if on a joyous hunt for serpents. But for me and Daniel and all the senior members of my family, the war was a serious business fraught with grave consequences.

"Fifty miles from the capital, we halted. The soldiers were footsore; they had marched 400 miles in 28 days. I planned to stop for a pentamine.

"Caesar had a message for me delivered by an orange-colored Megamicre. I was introduced by the orange to the governor of this pretty city where we planned to rest. The governor was a noble, a red who declared himself a friendly emissary. He asked me to meet three senators from the Republic at the city hall the next day. I replied that I would be glad to meet them but I would receive them in my quarters.

"The next day after I was suitably lodged and I had my guardsmen arrayed in the large courtyard in orderly ranks, I gave orders for the senators and the governor to be admitted to my presence. Elizabeth was with me as were Daniel and his wife.

"One of the three senators delivered a long speech which he had written out. He detailed all the injustices committed by us in killing a hundred Megamicres, in destroying their commerce, demolishing their fortress and now in marching on the capital with an army equipped with deadly fire power. The Republic, he said, had taken no retaliatory action; they had spared Caesar's tribe within their state because their religion and sense of humanity forbade it. Where, he asked, was our humanity? The Republic was offering peace, indemnity for damages, and an offer of a fief to Daniel, provided he left the ducal fief and disclaimed his alliance with the perfidious duke who had formally given up his succession rights and now again claimed it falsely.

"I wrote out a reply and had Daniel deliver it orally. I stated that the terms were unacceptable; I would make the decision, namely that the Republic recognize as legitimate, the heirs to the dukedom. The Republic knew that innocence had been oppressed and rights violated and that one of my offspring had righted this wrong. I demanded that the Republic withdraw its troops from all foreign states and indemnify the injured. Either I would return to my fief with some hostages to insure the peace or I would continue my march on the capital. The fort and the mines would be returned upon completion of all the peace terms and the restitution of all claims. The Republic had twenty days to consider my statement.

"For the next twenty days, I remained in peaceful seclusion, refusing invitations from the city's governor and keeping my armies well-behaved and disciplined.

"During this waiting period, I received another letter from James, my patriarch in Heliopolis. A situation had arisen in which the offspring of cousin marriages were now protesting any arranged unions. Up to now, he said, he had acted authoritatively but with the new seventy-eighth year approaching and marriage ceremonies imminent, he was afraid of an embarrassing confrontation. The young people - there were now more than ten thousand of them in the Ephebus - had actually sent him a signed petition complaining about restrictions. They wanted to marry of their own choice. If forbidden, they would not marry at all, they declared.

"I dispatched at once by express courier, messages to all my establishments. My new regulation forbade marriages unless by mutual consent of bride and groom. These marriages could also be made with persons from other tribes than their own. I also ruled that each person preparing to marry must travel with a Megamicran tutor chosen by the parent for a period of eight harvests before marriage. It was my idea that two years of increased maturity of the couples would add to the success of the unions and would also control the population.

"The twentieth day of the truce found Caesar in my home. He had come unexpectedly with a contingent of six senators whose ideas and decisions were unknown to him. The spokesman for the six, a senator I had not met before, addressed me. Assuring me first that the Republic wished for peace and an end to war, he explained that the council had met no less than eight times during this interval but without results. A Republic, he said, cannot come to a decision like a monarchy; each member considers himself an equal of the other and master of his own opinion. The senators needed two more months. Otherwise, they would have to say 'no' to the terms. They would have to prepare to die since they could not withstand the superior force of the giants. But their destruction would take time. They would fight from city to city and there were five hundred cities to be wiped out. In time the giants would have destroyed a world of billions, all God-created, none of whom would understand why they were being killed by a man whom they had rescued with his wife from death three hundred twelve years ago.

"The three women, my wife, and the wives of Caesar and Daniel shed warm tears at his words. I myself was moved to fear and horror at the thought. But I pulled myself together in less than a minute and wrote a reply.'I agree to an extension of two pentamines but with one irrevocable condition, that the one hundred thousand Megamicres now in my fief and the one adjoining leave there with empty knapsacks. To facilitate the peace treaty, I shall act as chief negotiator with full powers. The meetings are to take place in your capital where I shall take lodgings.' Ten days later, I heard that the reply was approved.

"Two miles before we reached the capital, I stopped to encamp the army. I ordered a grand review of my troops inviting Caesar and his tribe as well as all the nobility of the Republic to attend. From the platforms we constructed, I could see that about half a million Megamicres had gathered to view the spectacle along with more than a thousand nobles. At the end of the review, I ordered simultaneous salvos from all my artillery. The terrifying noise of the gunfire made one's hair stand on end.

"The palace designated for me, my court and my two thousand servants was both huge and magnificent. I spent much of my time at first getting acquainted with Caesar's tribe. They now numbered twenty-one thousand and ninety-five souls.

"I was gratified to learn four pentamines later that the one hundred thousand Megamicres who had been pillaging and looting in my fief had left naked and empty-handed. In the duke's fief, however, there still remained twenty-five thousand in control of Daniel's custom houses.

"Patience, I knew, was necessary until peace had been declared. For our part we still held eight cities of the Republic occupied by sixteen thousand of my giants. We still held the fort and the mines. In addition, a huge army was encamped outside the gates of the capital.

"Though I was under no obligation to do so, I nevertheless had Theodore send home about one hundred thousand of our own subject Megamicres. These had been swarming around the enemy countryside. My action, so unexpected, was met with expressions of gratitude from the Republic. This induced in me a wish to earn even greater plaudits. So I wrote to the duke asking him to release the entire embassy. They were still being held after their capture at the gates of the duke's fiefdom.

"One pentamine before the announced date of the peace conference, they all arrived under guard. I was having dinner at that time with my family and some nobles. I invited them to dine with us and they were pleased to accept. After the repast, I told the ten senators they were free to return home. The complimentary singing and dancing with which they expressed their thanks for this action did not displease me, I assure you.

"For the peace talks, I named Albert and Daniel as my secretaries. I was not unaware that my choice of Albert who had rescued the prince's mate did not sit well with some council members. At the first meeting held in the chambers of the Council of Seventeen, we all listened to a three hour harangue, read by a secretary. He read out loud the history of feudal rights up to the present. Then followed a history of the present war including an accusation against the giants. It was the giants' actions on behalf of the perfidious duke which had brought the Republic to the point of suing for peace for the sake of the innocent. The Republic hoped that the presence of the principal who had triggered the catastrophe would help resolve a matter which called on his own sense of justice, his religious beliefs and the friendship which he avowed for the Republic.

"After this speech, we three were asked to swear on our religious book that we would keep the proceedings secret. We swore. Asked to sign the statement, I demurred. My signature would mean I agreed and approved. Instead I wrote a statement over my name in which I protested the content of the harangue as having many falsehoods in it. I said I would defend the truth and the innocent by force of arms if necessary. I read this statement aloud and then delivered it into the trembling hands of the secretary.

"Caesar, waiting for me at home, asked if I thought that a peace would be concluded. I told him I had sworn to say nothing. At this, he smiled. The entire city, he declared, would know by tomorrow every word that had been spoken and so it turned out.

"The next day, a hubbub outside led me to a terrace where directly opposite my mansion, the body of a Megamicre painted polychrome was hanging. He had been strangled and impaled. His distorted visage was a horrifying sight. At this feet an inscription read, 'For the crime of high treason'.

"Caesar who had been outside talking to some reds came to me to tell me what this extraordinary spectacle meant. According to the noble reds, the deed that had been done there was intended for my eyes.

"I asked a good friend, a senator (of whom I shall speak later) what his understanding was of this act. He said that the murdered Megamicre was thought to be one of the council members who had divulged the meaning of the statement I had written at the bottom of the harangue. In that response, I had indicated knowledge of the crime done by the Republic which made me enter this war.

"Without any trial, the tribunal had made the decision to put this Megamicre to death. In this case as in others, punishment preceded trial. To the tribunal, it was evident that he had committed a crime; they needed no more information. But the judge did pay homage to justice and to the shades of the defunct by declaring that in expiating his crime, the victim was now innocent. The senator told me this without expression on his countenance.

"I had made the acquaintance of this senator on the day I was reviewing my troops. He struck me as the most agreeable person I had ever met.* He spoke well on every conceivable subject and always without pretentiousness. His speech was elegant but also playful so that a tinge of humor always brightened even the most serious discussions.

"This extremely pleasant Megamicre would poke fun at the airs some of his peers gave themselves. While they secretly conspired to keep him from filling certain important posts, he did not complain. He was cheerful and well-loved by those who were close to him, yet he went his own way. He was known for his hospitality and for the good taste of his surroundings. He had a lively and amusing coterie of friends who shared with him his enjoyment of the aspects of life which could bring them its fullest enjoyment. He was president of an academy whose selected members were devoted to wit, liveliness and urbanity. None among them shone more brightly than he.

"Although he loved luxury and magnificence, he knew how to curb this taste since he was not overly rich. He was admired for the correctness of his judgment always apparent in the results he achieved, and for his creativity which showed the marks of genius. But he did not also fail to enjoy the petty little frivolities and buffooneries of life. Amusing anecdotes, tricks including the art of legerdemain, jokes and the small gaities which lift the spirits were accommodated in his range of pleasures.

"He had enormous curiosity about strange ways and customs. If his fellows were less ignorant and complacent, they too, he believed would be eager to understand people from far-off places, hoping always to learn something new.

"This man, Milords, wanted to make my acquaintance. I could hardly believe he was a Republican. He won my friendship and I asked him to visit. He managed to know when I was free so our contacts were on an almost daily basis. Elizabeth too enjoyed his company. He could be amusing even in such matters as what made for elegance in a bonnet or gown.

"He had a distinguished and memorable appearance and the lucky gift of knowing how to be attractive to women. He enlivened the gatherings at the dinners he gave where he served exquisite food and drink.

"On one such occasion, he paid the prettiest compliments to my fourth generation grandchild whom he teased about her budding breasts. He so overwhelmed her with kisses that Leon her husband, far from being jealous,

---

*Translator's note: In the character of the senator, Casanova seems to be presenting us with a flattering self-portrait.

roared with laughter. Leon addressed a speech to the senator in such impecca-
ble Megamicran, that he was astounded. The senator's reply was worthy of a
member of that society whose hallmark is elegant and urbane wit. Indeed, he
became so enchanted with Leon's own wit that he caressed him with many and
unusual signs of affection. Leon's wife found them excessive.

"This delightful friend kept us amused and entertained during the time that
we awaited the outcome of the peace negotiations. In a serious conversation
with him one day, I learned that all of the council members did not know the
reasons for my entering the war. Those who had known or had been part of the
machinations of the Republic to imprison the duke's heir were now either dead,
had died suddenly or were in hospices awaiting their end. I could understand
better now why I was considered by some to be violent and unjust. Apparently
the strangled and hanged Megamicran put on display in front of my house was
intended to discourage inquiry.

"Eight days before the truce ended, two senators came to ask for an extension
of six months. I granted this. At the same time, I learned that the government
urgently needed the sum of fifty million ounces. One of the committee members
was studying to find out how they could obtain this sum in the least burdensome way. I offered to give this money to them in exchange for two pieces of
land bordering on Caesar's property. All three could be made one and declared
an independent principality with Caesar bearing the hereditary title of prince.

"This agreement was accepted, put into writing, signed, sealed, and registered. I allowed a paragraph which they appended, stating that the land would
revert to the Republic upon the extinction of Caesar's tribe. The money was
turned over to the Republic and Caesar was formally invested as prince of the
new enlarged principality.

"Four days after this event, a new conference was unexpectedly called
consisting of all the council members together with the reigning duke of the
Republic. Here I was lectured for three hours on a treaty, not one of whose
terms I could accept. I then took up a pen and wrote out the terms to which I
would agree. In five paragraphs, I demanded the return to Daniel of all his
custom houses, the sums received from them and the return of his banks in the
same condition they had been before seizure.

"A second paragraph demanded the release of all prisoners and the removal
of all troops from the fief.

"The third paragraph called for a delegation of twelve senators to call on the
duke and recognize as legitimate his heirs and their successors.

"A fourth paragraph required the return of all boats and businesses that had
been confiscated from the duke together with all the rights and privileges that
had been withdrawn.

"My fifth and final paragraph stated that the giants, in leaving all the
occupied cities, would not be required to return any sums they received from
customs nor would they have to rebuild any of the towers. The possessions of

the governor of the fortress city would be returned to him and the fort with all its mines would be returned to the Republic.

"A pentamine later, a vacancy occurred on the Council of Seventeen. My good friend would surely be assigned to this post. He was sad, he said, not so much because he disliked the assignment as because his duties would curtail his visits to me. I urged him to expedite the peace treaty as a member of the council. We embraced cordially and parted.

"At the beginning of the seventy-ninth year, we had the usual religious services but no marriages since the age had been increased by two years.

"In mid-June the final peace conference was held. I observed that my friend the senator was among the council members. He looked at me without recognition. The conference had accepted each of the five terms with the single exception that the twelve senators would not go to acknowledge the legitimacy of the succession until eight harvests after all the other terms of the treaty were carried out.

"I hastened to do my part, informing all my establishments of the good news. The duke of the fiefdom notified me by express courier that he requested an embassy sent him from the Republic consisting of three red couples. In this matter, I used all my efforts to have my good friend removed from his council position and placed at the head of this embassy. To his joy and mine, he was elected to that post.

"I spent the whole of that year and half of the eightieth year in receiving and returning visits. I also helped Caesar, now prince, to unite and organize his three territories into one well-organized state.

"My position which afforded me much respect and distinction did not make me especially loved but neither was I hated. I had achieved a peace without exacting too great a toll.

"And now the traveling young giants with their tutors became the novelty of the year. My new law postponing marriage and requiring a period of travel was well received by the young people. I was amused to find that their choice of visits as they voyaged was uniform; they came to visit me first; then they traveled from one set of relatives to another. Not a day passed during this year but that ten or twelve young giants, each with his tutor came to visit. More than a hundred nine and ten year olds spent this year in travel. All were beautiful, joyous and pleased to postpone the marriage and find out what was going on in their world. They flirted with all the handsome inseparables they met but their tutors kept them under strict supervision and they were obedient. By mid-July the visits had doubled with the young people coming all the way from Heliopolis. In turn, James was receiving an equal number of visitors from my part of the world. In all one hundred and forty thousand young people, age nine and ten, had made journeys during this year. In the following years the numbers increased by ten percent and in time, even the Megamicres took up the habit of voyaging.

212

"I am hardly in a position to tell you what is going on there now. Heaven alone knows what laws James will enact. As for me, I seem to have been born for the express purpose of changing the laws, the religion, the customs, the system, the nature and maybe even the tranquillity and happiness of that world. If so, I must attribute it to God's will.

"On the urgent invitation of our good friend, the senator, we left the capital on January tenth of our eighty-first year to spend some months with his family in their country house. It was a beautiful house and we were very comfortably lodged. The very next morning at his request, we arranged a serpent hunt. There were not too many left since our giants had passed through and had destroyed most of them during the war.

"Later as the senator was walking with Elizabeth and me in the meadow near the canal, he told us that the land for four miles around, belonged to him. It contained a treasure which if he could extract it, would make him the richest lord of the Republic. A cluster of mines containing red gold lay within this area. To excavate it would require more money than he had.

"We entered a cave more than five hundred feet deep which his grandfather had had dug out at enormous cost. The ground strewn with stones suggested evidence of the rich metal which filled the cave. We gathered some pebbles in a handkerchief. At the house we ground it up, added a small quantity of mercury and examined it. It seemed clear that the stone had not come from a major vein. I was determined to find the mother lode and make my friend a rich man.

"I had Cacoar send me carts containing blue and green powder. By the fifth day, I had enough powder to mine thirty miles of countryside. I began digging around the cave to form a semicircular gallery. Inside the gallery, I distributed equally four thousand pounds of powder. On the roof of the cave I cut out enough cone-shaped openings so that the explosion would affect the top of the cave too. I had seen signs of a vein above me when I explored the farthest end of the cave.

"With a long fuse, I moved a mile away before I set it afire. The noise of the blast was frightful. Twelve hundred cubic feet of earth were tossed into the air by this tremendous explosion. A rain of dust and small stones darkened the atmosphere. The sky did not clear for a full quarter hour.

"In the ensuing days I continued testing, verifying for myself that we had not yet reached the main seam. After a month of digging and blasting in every direction, vertically, horizontally and obliquely, I came upon a semicircle, sixty feet on the inside which was more than five hundred feet in diameter. I believed I was approaching the main seam. By this time, we had already uncovered enough gold ore to warrant digging, at considerable profit for a thousand years. But I was stubborn. I wanted to trace that vein of which I could see the tail, right up to where its richest and thickest part should be. In a few days, the diggers following the serpentine route of the vein came upon a natural cavern too narrow to enter and too hard to break down. I decided to blast. I filled a

213

barrel with a thousand pounds of powder, put the unlighted fuse inside and left.

"My family and the senator's family were safely distant by two miles. I began to walk in the opposite direction where two miles away, I would light the fuse. I started toward this fatal place by myself when I heard steps behind me. It was Elizabeth who smilingly said she had come to join me even though she knew there were Megamicres awaiting me. Arms linked, we walked slowly until we reached the point near the canal where I was to light the fuse. I did so and waited.

"Nothing happened; there was no explosion, no hurling of rocks and stones into the air. But suddenly, a tremendous subterranean roar accompanied by the shuddering and quaking of the earth on which we stood clasped together, tossed us violently face down. At the same time, the slab of earth on which we lay prone, gave a violent leap into the air carrying us along with such fearful speed that our chests would surely have been crushed if we had been lying instead on our backs."

TWENTIETH DAY

"You left us in mid-air yesterday." Count Bridgent complained. "I kept thinking of you two, face down holding on to that huge piece of stony earth and flying upwards. I wondered where your adventures would take you next."

"That leap into the air, Milord", replied Edward, "was the start of my return to England and the end of my story."

"Too bad", murmured the Count. "I had time to listen to you until Parliament opens."

"That vertical flight upwards", Edward went on, "lasted barely five seconds. We started straight down without a pause. Going down took a few seconds longer and was so fast at the end that I felt weightless. That 'bed' to which we clung met a solid object. It shattered into fragments and the shock of impact sent us flying up for a moment. We came down again but oddly, two thirds down, our positions seemed reversed. We were now face up instead of face down. Apparently we passed through an ascensional line which separated two opposing forces of gravity.

"Our descent was surprisingly slow and at the end, we entered an ambiance of thick dust. That, luckily lasted only an instant else we should have suffocated. We flailed about with our arms, kept our eyes closed and a handkerchief to mouth and nose.

"The ground which stopped our fall was not such as would break our backs. It began as thick dry dust like that which issues from ruined stone walls when they are knocked down. This dust was succeeded by spongy earth as flexible as any horsehair mattress and then it became the familiar ground, firm enough to walk on.

"I opened my eyes at last and found I could breathe passably well. After drawing a dozen breaths, I was restored to calm. I had glimpsed a light earlier which puzzled me until I realized it came from the ruby pin on Elizabeth's mantle. I called her name and heard her clear voice ask, 'Where are we?' She had been pressed tightly to my left side during all our travail and she had uttered no sound.

"Lying there now, we recapitulated the events of this terrible voyage which had all taken place in less than a minute. We believed that we had returned to

215

our own world and were now probably in its lowest part. We acknowledged that we would never return to that other world where our children lived.

"I asked my wife if she would not regret the step she took in abandoning her dear ones where moreover she would have been safe. Her reply moved me beyond words: 'I would have died of grief without you.'

"She comforted me further saying our situation was not so bad as it had been eighty-one years earlier. Here we were on solid ground; we could breathe freely and we had the light of our ruby to guide us, and the hope we might find again the light of day. So saying, she turned and shook off the dust from herself. I did the same and was delighted to discover that we still had three enormous rubies to serve us as torches. Unfortunately, we had lost the two biggest jewels when we were hurled into the atmosphere and beyond.

"We decided to get up, although not without some trepidation and some difficulty. On the earth were outlined the actual imprints of our bodies. For half an hour, we walked with much painfulness over the rubble and debris. When we saw that we were getting into a muddy lower level, we retraced our steps.

"Back where we started, we stopped when we heard a plaintive voice cry out in the eerie silence. More astonished than frightened we listened attentively. The words uttered in Megamicran came clearly to our ears: 'Have pity on me!' You can imagine our excitement. I knew it must be one of the workers from the place where the fuse was to be lit. I told this unfortunate man that I could not see him; he was to try to come to us. He said he was buried up to his neck and unable to extricate himself. We started out at once. Following the sound of his voice, we found him and pulled him out.

"It was a polychrome countryman. To our surprise, instead of thanking us, he threw himself on his back (the customary Megamicran attitude of adoration) and thanked the sun which had shown him mercy. His action reminded us to our shame that a humble man, an idolator, had thought first to render thanks to his deity as we had not. We hastened to imitate him, not openly or in words but 'con le ginocchia delle mente inchine.'* The countryman came to us and kissed our feet a hundred times.

"We spent the next four hours removing the debris in a circle twenty feet in radius, hoping to find other survivors, particularly the polychrome's inseparable. Just as we were about to give up the search, the poor Megamicre uncovered the leg and then the body of his mate. We were deeply distressed at his grief and we forgot our own troubles in trying to console him.

"We began to walk about without any plan other than to avoid the side where we had found the ground too soft and muddy. We knew from the deep shadows all about us that we were in a cavern so large that even the brilliance of our rubies could not reach its lofty vault. All three of us walked without any knowledge of where we were going. After two hours, we sat down, tired out.

---

*Petrarch: freely translated, it means "with inward genuflection".

216

"We had escaped death miraculously but we did not know how we would stay alive. How would we find food? As for a way out, we knew only that we had to ascend somehow. Here all was flat.

"Our Megamicre who had both courage and good sense said he would explore on his own while we rested. He wished to render us a service before he died. Since his own body contained enough nourishment for some time, he would search for some sustenance for us. He would keep us in sight, he said, because we would be wearing the rubies. The one he took would light his own way. He set out.

"What would we have done without those huge carbuncles to give us light?! We would not have dared to move in that profound darkness. Nothing lived, nor could live here. Our thoughts dwelled on the one idea, how to get out of this terrible inhuman cavern. I assumed that ninety-two miles upwards separated us from the surface of our world. How to find the way?

"It was two hours before our Megamicre returned. He told us he had traveled twelve or fourteen Megamicran leagues over flat and barren terrain. Then he came to the border of a quiet pond, three feet below the surface of the cave. He was not frightened, he said, by the blue green color of the water instead of his familiar red color. He had plunged in and had seen there numerous fish. He avoided those whose scales looked too sharp. But at the edge of the pond, he gathered up other fish.

"Emptying his basket, he showed us his catch. Among some shellfish unknown to us, were many mussels and oysters. With my knife, I opened a mussel and drank the excellent water inside. I did the same with the oysters. Then my wife and I devoured the shellfish which were six times the size of ours.

"All my efforts to make our friend eat with us were in vain. When I said he would die of starvation, he replied that he would then go to the Sun. I said this could not be since we were now outside of the world of the Great Spirit. At this news, he threw himself to the ground and began to lament and cry so bitterly that we pitied him but we did not know what to do.

"He then asked us if he could save his soul by becoming a christian. I was moved. It had not been my custom to offer baptism to any Megamicre. Further I did not believe baptism was necessary for his salvation. When I asked him what he knew about our religion, he surprised me by reciting our law and articles of faith. He had wanted to become a christian, he said, but had been frightened off by the threats of the Great Spirit.

"Both Elizabeth and I found ourselves deeply moved. Seeing Elizabeth sob, he wiped her eyes and asked her why she cried. She answered she was happy because his soul would be saved. Then she begged him to eat; his new religion required that he take care of himself. He asked how that was possible since he could not be nourished the same way as we were.

"On the way to the pond - I did not know how to baptise him other than with water - he asked whether the wrath of the Great Spirit could follow him to a world where the sun was not considered a sacred power. I replied that God was everywhere but the sun was only a creation of God. He had nothing to fear. When we arrived at the pond two hours later, I baptised him, called him my son and gave him as a gift the giant ruby. He was greatly pleased with this noble gift but begged that we take it back at his death.

"Tormented by thirst, I tasted the water of the pond. It was disgusting and I spat it out. We continued our journey along the edge of this body of water. After six hours, we flung ourselves down, exhausted. Our thirst was acute. To someone in such a state, the thought of imbibing a liquid, any liquid good or bad becomes irresistible. With no drinking vessel, we sipped some water from the tiny cupped hands of the Megamicre. We thought that the small sips would spare our palate the bad taste. But almost at once, a violent vomiting took hold of us and we did not stop until our stomachs were emptied.

"We lay by the side of the pond, stuporous and motionless, until we fell asleep. At the end of twelve hours we awoke in good and vigorous health. We reassured our friend who did not sleep, that we were well again. As we set off on our march, we saw that he was tired out. Against his protests, my wife and I insisted on carrying him, taking turns for the next six hours.

"We asked him to bring us shellfish again. He dived in and brought us a huge mollusk. If it were edible, he said, he could bring us as many as we wanted. "Inside was a soft spongy creature which moved as a single mass. I was not tempted to eat this. My wife, however suggested we use the two handsome shells as basins.

"The thought prompted her to call the Megamicre to her side. She skillfully extracted mouthfuls of milk from his breast and turned them into the basin for him to drink. She did this the customary five times.

"He tried hard to express his thanks. An hour later he found he was as well nourished as if he had received the milk from his own inseparable. He had known, he said, that he might survive another harvest by this means but he had not dared suggest what Elizabeth undertook to do for him. She assured him she would willingly do this for him every day.

"He set himself now to find food for us. He plunged into the pond three or four times, coming up each time with a knapsack full of mollusks. There was enough food for twelve. There was one splendid mollusk which he had not had the strength to bring. It was twice the size of my head, he told me. I went with him after he told me that the water was not more than thirty feet deep. Wrapping my beard and hair in a cloth, I dived in with him. We used the rubies to give us light underwater. Following his directions, I scooped up the mollusk and we swam back.

"When we opened this catch, we found that each shell held more than six pounds of water. The inside of the shells looked as shiny as the most beautiful Japanese porcelain. We discarded the flesh; it was formless and motionless. My wife and I sat down to dinner at the edge of the lake. We placed our shells on beds of algae and opened the mussels and oysters into them. We refreshed ourselves with a drink out of the porcelain-like bowls. It was delicious but of rather stronger flavor than we would have wished.

"We were grieved that our friend had to fast while we feasted but we had no way of getting any kind of grain to make him one of the soups to which he was accustomed.

"We gave ourselves over to a peaceful sleep. After a good four hours we woke rested and ready to resume our voyage. We carried our two porcelain-like bowls with us.

"Ten hours of walking showed us nothing new. We kept along the same lake in the same silence on the same flat terrain. We longed to see mountains, to know that we were getting onto higher ground. Still the lake had to have an end and the water a source. Perhaps that source would be at the foot of a mountain. So we hoped.

"Nature reminds us that we need food for strength and our man was already searching in the lake. I thought of fire and cooking and I decided to experiment. Perhaps I could light a fire under the plentiful algae. I heaped up in a semicircle what I assumed was sand. Then I placed algae on top and put some combustible powder beneath. Only a thick smoke rose from the algae. To my surprise, it was the sand that had ignited. Our Megamicran friend told us that the seeming sand was a species of pulverized naphtha. This bituminous powder gave off an unpleasant smell but such a strong fire that water did not extinguish it. We call it Greek fire.*

"I constructed a compact hearth a distance away from the lake, gathered up the bituminous material and using it as if it were wood, I set fire to the little heap and boiled water from the mussels and oysters in one of my bowls. My Megamicre friend had caught two fine fish which I cleaned and readied. The eggs I put aside with the fishmilk for boiling in one bowl; the two fish I cooked in the other bowl.

"We had a fine meal. What pleased me was that our Megamicre ate ten or twelve teaspoonsful of the cooked fish-egg mixture. We hoped it would take the place of those soups which supplemented their milk diet. When at the end of several hours, he showed no ill effects, we were full of joy. But we were deluding ourselves. The food was not suited to his physical nature and he grew thinner under our very eyes. We had to get ourselves accustomed to the idea of losing him.

"We slept for ten hours after eating then took up our journey again for another ten hours uninterruptedly, attentive all the time to a sound which came as a murmur from a distance. The sound increased gradually as we moved forward. We could not rest until we discovered its source. It was a waterfall,

---

*Translator's note - From its use by Byzantine Greeks in naval warfare.

not a rushing cascade but copious and it descended from a rise spreading alongside the lake.

"'God be praised!' I said to Elizabeth. 'Now we can start climbing.' Knowing the difficult journey which awaited us, we stopped to eat and rest. Our Megamicre brought us two dozen crustaceans which we cooked. They resembled crayfish. They were delicious as was the fresh water which he drew from the waterfall. Then we slept.

"We took along for our arduous trip as much as we could carry of naphtha powder, cooked fish and our shells. I regretted leaving behind the pure water. And I feared that food would be scarce in the mountains.

"We started our climb. In two hours the sound of the waterfall could no longer be heard. Our steps slowed; we had to catch our breath. The mountain area was ugly, arid, and barren. And always there were the caves whose vaults were either so high as to be invisible or so low that we had to bend our backs to go through.

"When we stopped to rest, we measured out an area where we could eat some of our provisions and stretch out to rest. But when we woke after ten hours, our legs had swelled right down to the ankles. We were bare-foot; our shoes had been torn in our march over the rough mountain rocks. Our thighs, arms and backs were so sore we could not move them without pain. Walking without shoes on sharp rocks was the worst torture.

"In this wretched condition, Milords, we had the will to walk for eleven more days. Our legs were swollen, our feet torn and bleeding and the inflamed areas made us fear erysipelas.

"The least of our woes was the shortage of food. Our friend who now had two portions of his milk each day managed to sustain himself though he was very thin. We ate the rest of our food and thought of seeking some comfort in sleep but looking at our feet and legs I knew we would not be able to go on. My wife then thought of the essences she always had with her. She moistened her handkerchief and applied it to the parts of our feet and legs that were in the worst condition.

"When we woke, the inflammation was gone, but the wounds around the soles of our feet were still bloody. Still we had to go on to die wherever our destiny dictated. We felt sure that we had walked, in these eleven days, at least two hundred English miles and we should be thirty miles higher than at our starting point.

"My only desire was to climb, ascend, rise higher. I had an absolute horror of the thought of going downwards. I did not mind the many turns we had to make whether to the right or left so long as it was in an upwards direction. The pain we suffered was unbelievable but we persisted, advancing very slowly. With the increasing warmth in our feet, our pain diminished somewhat.

"We had made a necessary little detour when we were all stunned by seeing light and a small piece of sky. Much encouraged we toiled upwards. I did not dare to hope that this light came from the sky of our own world; we could not be so near. What was it then? After four hours, this reddish illumination became so intense, we no longer needed our rubies. My wife hoped it was daylight; the Megamicre thought we had re-entered his world.

"Now a frightful roar reached our ears. It came at intervals. Behind was darkness; to the right and left only endless caverns; in front and above was that reddish light. We continued our tortured way but we now were chilled by a wind that caused our Megamicre to sink to the ground, incapable of moving. I lifted him to my shoulders as we pressed on. The cold wind made our sufferings unendurable but it had one advantage. It was behind us and it forced us forward.

"Suddenly we found ourselves at the summit, looking out on a vast plain of grass. To our right, perhaps three miles distant we saw the source of the red light. A huge fire extending as much as three hundred feet around and rising a hundred fifty feet high, blazed furiously as it poured forth from a cavern whose upper limits were invisible. This jagged uneven cavern with its terrifying outpouring of fire revealed to our very eyes the exact vision of Hell as it had been taught to us in childhood. And the stench of sulphur, as the air warmed, was deadly. Compared to this, the volcano Ecla which we had seen eighty years ago was a straw fire.

"But our childhood fears were not reawakened. Present real fears can occupy the mind to the exclusion of past imaginary ones and ours were very real.

"Our small friend was indeed our guardian angel. He found food for us when we could not take another step. He brought us a basket of herbs he had collected. Among them we found some fennel that we ate. There were green berries like grapes which we sucked at tentatively, then threw away for fear they were a dangerous purgative. Among the greens were some kinds of lettuce which Elizabeth sprinkled with essence and used to soothe our feet.

"We were now plagued with the presence of serpents of all sizes which hissed and slithered about us. Our Megamicre was terrified that they might be coming to take revenge for all those we had destroyed in his world. I did my best to reassure him, advising him to avoid stepping on them or otherwise provoking them.

"He found a small rise, barren of grass but also free of snakes. We crawled up here on hands and knees - our feet were too painful - and we took our rest. On other occasions, he guarded us while we slept by tossing water at the serpents if they came near us. Truthfully, both Elizabeth and I had a horror of having serpents slide over our bodies while we were asleep. Our ever wakeful friend watched over us.

"He remained under the delusion that our sleep meant the introduction into our minds of secret knowledge such as oracles were supposed to bring. I tried to give him some understanding but for the most part we were so preoccupied

221

with our need for food and water, rest for our wounded feet, and our aim to march upward, that our lessons were cursory or omitted altogether.

"On one memorable occasion, our good angel found two huge white truffles exquisite in taste. He also brought us squills or sea onions which provided us with an excellent juice.

"Our feet were still too damaged to make a long journey; they needed some protection from the rough terrain. It was then that I looked more closely at the basket of herbs and found among them small stumps of plants from which sprouted long and slender shoots. These were strong yet pliant like willow wands. It occurred to me that with diligence, patience and care, we could weave these flexible twigs into shoes.

"We set to work. Our Megamicre friend completed his pair first. Then he helped us with ours. When we were finished, we had made three pairs for each. They could not truly be called shoes, but they had sturdy soles. They fitted our feet; they were comfortable and pliant. In some respects, they resembled those sandals woven of hemp which rich Scots Highlanders wear; they call them alpargatas from the Spanish.

"If you only knew, Milords, how thankful we were! We felt the shoes were God-given. We wore out the three pairs during the rest of our arduous voyage. During those long days of suffering, we experienced cold, thirst, hunger and fatigue. We were shaken by an earthquake, nauseated by sulphurous fumes from a second volcanic eruption, surrounded by snakes, struck by blind birds until we shot them for food, all the while that we kept going through dark caverns on a bleak and brusing journey that never seemed to end.

"Most painful of all was our daily despair at seeing our small angel grow thinner and thinner until he was only skin and bones. We had probably walked a thousand miles but he had walked at least a third more than that. He was the advance scout, always returning to advise us about the best route. He made daily forays for our food and his care and watchfulness were the chief reasons we survived.

"He had explored a lake to decide if we should cross it. After swimming its width he returned to tell us we ought to get to the other side where there was an abundance of dry wood to cook the plentiful fish in its waters. With his help, we swam across, walked for four more days, then came across a narrow passageway which led us to a ruined underground building.

"Here we first saw a dilapidated stone stairway. We descended cautiously and found a ruined house with a sagging brick floor. The ceiling slanted irregularly and only one wall was supported by beams. These barely supported the rafters above, half of which had fallen to the ground. One of the two doors was blocked by stone and debris; the other led to a room holding the remains of household furniture.

"Through a window opening, we let ourselves into a small courtyard where a broken double door exposed a room which might once have been a library. Here were the remains of huge volumes, most of whose pages had crumbled to dust. I could still see the gothic type of the letters in a language unknown to me though I thought I made out half a dozen words in English. I was sure now that we were quite close to the surface of the world even though we were still buried.

"In another room, we found a stairway which led out of the house, facing a rise, which took fifteen minutes to climb. We continued on, still below the surface walking along a covered surface, like a culvert. After an hour's walk, we could hear the sound of water. Finally we saw the source. Small waterfalls spilled out, filling the ditches and seeping into the ground. We descended into what appeared to be the bottom of a dried lake and was now, we guessed, a cistern with a vaulted top. Looking up, we saw an opening perhaps six feet in diameter but the distance from our feet as we walked the bottom of the lake-cistern was at least fifty or sixty feet. How covetously I looked at that distant opening! A heap of shells in the center rose only a few feet.

"The light from that aperture was now fading. We stopped and rested and fell asleep. After another full day inside this smooth sided basin with its unreachable exit, we knew at least that we were in that part of the world where day follows night and that we were either in mid-April or mid-August.

"We wondered what country we were in but we did not really care. Even if we should find ourselves in some strange antarctic land, we would still feel no farther than fifty paces from London. We tried shouting, calling out repeatedly but it was quite useless. We had to find some other way to get out.

"Again we ate some morsels of our provisions and we slept. We were awakened by the trickling sound of water which was entering the cistern in several places. The small waterfalls we had seen before must have increased in volume because the sounds we heard were now louder and the water was coming in more plentifully.

"I realized that the peak of good fortune would be the total inundation of the basin. We could then float with the level of the water up to the opening. Never have mortals prayed so fervently to God as we did for a flood.

"By nightfall, the water had reached halfway up our legs as we sat on our little island of shells. Our good friend who had worried for us was now relieved when he saw how jubilantly we welcomed the increase. He kept swimming under the hole in the vault to report what he saw; a bluish sky with smoky masses that came and went (he had never seen clouds); a bird that fell struck by a flash of light, thus telling us that there were hunters about and we were in an inhabited country.

"Now after hours of a steadily rising level, our Megamicre swam to the opening, seized a tiny rough area on the wall, grasped it and climbed out. He came back to tell us that he had seen giants mounted on proportionately large horses. They were riding about after some animals. Some of these animals carried trees on their heads. We knew then that if these were deer, we were not in Africa.

"We were so elated that we believed no obstacle would be too great for us to surmount. Our Megamicre carried our belongings, piece by piece to the outside world.

"By nightfall, we were floating naked on the water, our heads almost touching the roof. We had to find some protrusion to grasp in order to heave ourselves out. There were none of any size. When we could no longer float, our friend moved under our bodies and sustained us with his hands. But we knew he could not keep this up very long. We swam and floated, getting more and more discouraged by our inability to reach that elusive opening. Our dear friend asked me if I could stand up in the water directly under the opening. He would then push me upwards by the soles of my feet. I did so and it worked. With a mighty effort, I raised myself up so my chest and arms attained the rim of the opening. I easily threw my leg over and got out on my knees. Leaning down I reached out for my wife.

" 'E quindi uscimmo a riveder le stelle'* With uplifted spirits, we fell to our knees, thanking God for having wrought so many miracles in keeping us alive.

"Drenched by the rain, we sat on the bare ground with no thought of getting dried. Our garments were wet and the scarfs around our hair were soaked. Our Megamicre approached bearing the two shellfish bowls. He offered them to us for hats. We burst into laughter but in that pouring rain they served us better than the best hats the factory in Kingsington could produce.

"We climbed the steep slope in a hundred paces and waited out the rain. When the weather cleared, we began our walk through the valley where grass and trees were plentiful. We could see deer, boars, many wolves and some bears too as they took their way into the deeper forest. Some halted to stare at us but they did not come close, to my relief.

"We dressed back into our wet tunics and cloaks. We needed to find food and shelter and we would not wish to frighten off any persons we met. Not far off, we saw the outlines of a sizable village with its cultivated land. And finally we came upon three men and a young lad. They were clothed in earth-colored garments of coarse fabric which folded over and were tied in the middle. They wore heavy furskin boots and large hats. Their moustaches were very long and their hair was tied back. Each carried a rifle.

"As soon as we saw them advance, we seated ourselves at the foot of a tree, arms crossed over our breast. Our Megamicre stood in the same posture. I had taken care to put all our rings into my pocket. Our attire, my beard, the naked Megamicre's striped face, the two seashells which covered our heads made

---

*"And then we came forth, once more to see the stars." Dante, *Inferno*, xxxiv, 139.

them burst into laughter. The closer they looked, the louder they laughed. When they spoke, we lowered our heads to show we did not understand their language.

"I spoke in Latin, English and a little Greek. They understood not a single word. They were most interested in the Megamicre whom they took to be a pretty little beast. I used gestures to explain our need for food, and lodging and that we would pay. They apparently understood.

"One of them sent the boy off after saying something to him. They turned their attention again to our Megamicre making small gestures such as we do with dogs when we don't quite dare caress the creatures. I gathered that they took us for a troupe of mountebanks.

"The boy returned with two men and a woman, all of whom, I guessed, had come out of curiosity. I had the Megamicre dance and sing for them as a courtesy. They were all touched but the woman was enchanted. She was quite beside herself when, following my order, he went to kiss her hand. They focussed their interest entirely on him, but my wife let them know our needs by gestures and indicated we would pay. The boy was again sent off and returned an hour later with a priest. This priest did not know Latin and he in turn sent for two Capuchin friars who did understand Latin. They arrived an hour later and I could finally make our needs known.

"The question of ability to pay was a problem so Elizabeth took a red gold cross set with diamonds from her neck and put it into the friar's hands. He kissed it but said he did not know its value. Another two hours passed and the apothecary and a doctor came. The asked us many questions. I invented a tale of a voyage from Bengal to Constantinople, of thieving servants who had taken our possessions, of wandering for many days until we arrived at this place which was unfamiliar to us. We were told we were in lower Carniola and the city in the near distance was Zirchnitz. About our Megamicre, I said he was not a species of animal as they thought but a man and a christian from a newly discovered country in the southern region of the world.

"Although they remained suspicious of us and uncertain what value the cross had, we were nevertheless allowed to take shelter in the home of the doctor. Our quarters were very poor but there was food and a fire to dry our clothing.

"I asked the priest to send for a clothing merchant. He did not understand and again referred me to the Capuchin. The latter explained that the Slavic priests used Illyrian rather than Latin in their rites.

"By now, our Megamicre was in a state of extreme emaciation. The last time Elizabeth had tried to extract milk from his breast to feed him, none was left. And now his breasts had shrunk and disappeared. I boiled rice for three hours in milk, hoping he could get some nourishment from this. He ate it but told me that a Megamicre could be sustained only by the liquid on which its life was based.

225

"This perfect creature who was gentleness itself spoke cheerfully of the glory of the after life. He said he would die in peace and contentment because he felt he had been of service to us in our long voyage. We could not restrain our tears.

"The next morning when our host woke us, I asked him to provide food only for us. Our companion could not eat and would shortly die. That I, not a doctor, should feel competent to make such a prognosis, caused him to laugh. He felt the patient's pulse and began to 'doctorise'* in the jargon of his profession. I stopped him short by telling that our Megamicre's nature was such that Hippocrates could never have believed it possible.

"I said this dying individual was a creature who never slept, whose blood was white and who was fed by his own body's substance, whose digestive system was different from ours. His interior structure was such that he was born from an egg ejected from a canal between his esophagus and trachea, the egg started in a matrix near the diaphragm.

"The good doctor was speechless. He took me for a madman or perhaps more charitably for a clever impostor with whom he could not match wits. Apparently unwilling to measure his own charlatanry against mine, he changed the subject to tell me that the Capuchins had gone off to appraise the value of the cross. He had gone to check the value of my watch and was delighted to learn it was valued at forty florins. Now that he was sure of being reimbursed for the five or six florins he had spent on our upkeep, his attitude changed. I did not blame the good doctor. He was afraid he would be cheated out of his money after he heard my description of our Megamicre. I would have been wiser to keep quiet.

"This day, I learned, was the 21st of August 1614. We had been engulfed by the Maelstrom on the 21st of August 1533. Though history furnishes us with many examples of remarkable coincidences, I felt that in this instance, God had had a hand as in so many other events in our life. There will be those who will say I am superstitious but I do not care. Every 20th of August, I will celebrate a religious service and every 21st of August, I will give a great feast.

"I kept trying to make our well-loved little friend better. Burning the Indian aloes, the Arabian myrrh, the gums and resins which I had the apothecary bring, I perfumed the sick-chamber. To no avail. I brought him outside so he could see the rising sun. He was astonished and pleased at the sight. At noon, he asked to see the sun again.

"Six days later, the two monks arrived bringing with them two nobles, the Count of Eckemberg, Governor of Croatia, and Count Prainer, commissioner to the emperor Mathias. The Count of Eckemberg was fluent in English so we could converse easily.

"The diamonds, he said, had been estimated as being worth six thousand florins, a sum one thousand florins more than usual because the diamonds had

---

*Translator's note: Casanova uses the French "doctoriser" here.

226

been so beautifully cut. He wanted to buy the red gold but I gave it to him as a present, saying that the 6,000 florins were enough for me. When he asked me courteously how I happened to be here, I told him the story I had invented but with greater detail.

"We kept the true story of our adventures until we reached our own country. I planned to write them down some day. Man has a strong need to communicate what he has learned, else he feels discontented. Seneca says somewhere that if he were offered knowledge on condition that he keep it secret, he would refuse that knowledge. Likewise Cicero tells us that if one were put in possession of marvelous understanding of the heavens and nature and could inform no one, that knowledge would be bitter. But to communicate it would be the most joyful of experiences.

"My invented tale interested the count though he had some questions about that fabled country I described where wealth and freedom abounded. I had placed it somewhere in the vicinity of New Zealand.

" 'I expect, sir', he said, 'that you will tell your King James about this discovery and will share in the glory when he takes possession of this country. It will be another jewel in Great Britain's crown.'

"He suggested that I make haste to inform the king, otherwise Holland might get there first. A rich and unknown country would interest any nation with commercial interests and a strong navy.

"The Capuchin now admitted a Jewish merchant. In less than half an hour, I had bought and paid for everything I needed in hats, shoes, hose and cloth. I turned over the bolts of cloth to the doctor with instructions to have a tailor make up the shirts, suits and coats I needed.

"The Count of Eckenberg addressed his attention to our Megamicre. Though he was cadaverous in body, yet he retained his spirit, his intelligence and a luminous brilliance in his eyes. When I told the two nobles that he had only a day to live, they were distressed. Eckemberg took him in his arms, examined his bonnet, his teeth and his color-striped skin. He caressed him and our little friend returned his kiss. Then he began to sing to him in the voice of a nightingale, one of those exquisitely beautiful songs which speak to the Mega-micres' soul and enrapture ours as well.

"The doctor could not restrain himself; he must keep this creature alive. He asked permission to give him some excellent pills which he called 'pan-chymagogues'.*

"At the whispered behest of Count Prainer, the doctor asked us to dine with him and the two nobles. This was an invitation we felt obliged to accept. And the doctor did provide a splendid dinner of game, fish and wines. We spent four hours in agreeable conversation.

"Towards evening, a servant came to tell our host that the Megamicre had

---

*Ancient Greek term: a medicine to cure all ills of the humors.

died. Excusing myself, I ran to his room. I found my angel motionless with eyes closed but still alive. After some massage, he opened his eyes, told me he was dying and asked to have his body burned. I told him to have no fear, to ask for God's pardon and to give some signs to the priest which would assure him a christian burial and eternal glory.

"The priest arrived shortly. I said our Megamicre was a Roman Catholic (I had to say so) and asked that he give him absolution on the strength of my word. Our dying friend raised his hand once to the right and then three times more as I had directed him. He pressed the priest's hand indicating contrition and a wish for absolution. Then he closed his eyes forever. I thanked God that the priest had not demanded he make the sign of the cross, a symbolic gesture which I had neglected to teach my children as well.

"Elizabeth dissolved in tears and my heart was full of anguish. Everyone left after I gave instructions for him to be embalmed. I ordered a tomb of the finest stone to be built and a casket made of the finest wood. I ordered that nearby religious communities be invited to the services and candles given out to all who accompanied his body to the church.

"Our grief, Milords, was very great. How could we not feel the greatest tenderness for this creature to whom we owed our lives. His concern for our well-being, his zeal and industry on our behalf, his good judgment, incomparable patience and unselfishness were united with a sense of morality that showed him to be unique. His was an angelic nature, surely superior to our own.

"We mourned him bitterly and we still grieve every time we think of him. On the following day, after he was embalmed, we placed him in his small coffin. Our tears fell abundantly on his cold remains. Then we carried him ourselves to the church where everyone from Carniola had come for the funeral services.

"I left a brief epitaph in Latin which the doctor was to have engraved on the stone tomb when it was placed in the cathedral. The words were simple; only 'Megamicre' was unusual.

"The funeral cost me eighteen hundred florins. I gave the priest another two hundred florins to celebrate masses and two hundred more to the order of the Capuchins. Besides that I left a thousand florins to pay for the mausoleum.

"Eight days later, the tailors had finished our clothing and we prepared to leave. I shaved and dressed in my European attire. I paid the doctor, the apothecary and the tailor and I distributed a hundred florins among the servants. I asked one favor of the count, that he send a guard of four men on horseback with us as far as Gorizia. Both the noblemen had insisted on escorting us as far as Laubac.

"When we arrived at Gorizia, I had seven hundred sequins (zecchini) in my purse.* But we had a letter from the Count of Eckemberg to his friend there

---

*Translator's Note: Sequin or zecchino is an obsolete gold coin of Italy and Turkey, valued at about $2.25 or 9s 3d.

which assured us of a courteous reception. That nobleman, the Count of Cobenzel, gave us two horsemen as escort to the city of Udine. He advised against going by sea from Trieste to Venice because the Republic was now waging war against the Eskoks**. This worthy noble gave us a letter to the doge Marc-Antonio Memmo in Venice.

'On the fifteenth of September we reached Venice and spent a whole month there without seeing anyone except for an English merchant who made us feel welcome without asking who we were or where we had come from. He helped us sell our diamond pins for eight thousand sequins (zecchini). We never showed our rubies to a soul.

"Now dressed in the English manner, we brought our letter of introduction to the Doge. We recognized in this nobleman a person of very superior quality. In spite of his age and health (at seventy-eight, he suffers occasional attacks of gout), his posture, and his countenance affirm his nobility. The most delicate courtesy and refinement emanate from his being; his affability and generosity make him much admired. When he saw that we expressed ourselves only poorly in his tongue, he turned at once to English, explaining that he had spent two years at the court of Queen Elizabeth.

"In this connection, he told us an anecdote. When the queen asked him which of two suitors he would choose for her, he replied that neither of them pleased him. Her reply was a verse from Horace.***

'Through the Doge, we became acquainted with the best thinkers in the Republic. Among these Fra Paolo (Sarpi) the monk was best known for his silence. When he did speak, he sounded like an oracle. It is said that the Holy See regards him as an enemy of the Catholic Church. Venetians say he merely opposes usurpation of civilian rights by the church.

"What I admired about these discussions was the absence of talk about politics. And remember, Milords, that in all Europe there is not another sovereign state more embroiled in international politics than Venice. Except for England, she is at peace with no one. Directly or indirectly, she is in opposition to all the other powers. But she holds her own.

"Despite these problems, I saw nothing in this beautiful capital to suggest a country at war. We saw only festivals, masquerade balls, theatre, spectacles and public entertainments. On the Grand Canal, regattas were held almost daily, watched by multitudes of joyous throngs. And in the midst of all these noisy pleasures, I never saw the least disorder. There were no murders, no thefts and, most wonderful, there were no guards, not a single armed man. It appears that these sagacious Venetians want to show foreigners how effective

---

**French "Uscoques" - Serbians fleeing from Bosnia, Herzegovina and Serbia to escape persecution from the Turks.

***The verse which reads 'prudens futuri temporis exitum caliginosa nocte premit deus.' may be translated 'the god wisely hides the future's outcome in the night time darkness.'

liberty can be. The sight of a single man in military uniform would spoil the picture and disturb the serenity of these happy people.

"Unlike the English who keep informed about politics and hence are proud, bold, unruly - and very dangerous - the Venetians do not want to know about the workings of government or about court intrigues. They want to be amused, live well at modest cost. No one may talk about state matters. Open talk is prejudicial to public tranquillity. Once talk begins, no matter how peacefully at first, it always ends in sedition. Wherever people exist, the spirit of revolt exists. It may be hidden as if asleep but that slumber is not profound. The least rumble can awaken that spirit. Then disorders result which are hard to quell.

"This unique city surrounded by water produces none of the necessities of life yet its shops are stocked with the finest foods, with an abundance of delicacies and with fish that is the best in the world. Venetians say their cuisine is so excellent because they do not use sauces. Sauce spoils good food, they contend. Good beef, whether roasted or boiled, needs only its own juices. What does a freshly caught fish or a well-cleaned bird require? A person whose health is good because of a good regimen and regular exercise does not need to have his appetite whetted by extraneous seasonings.

"Dairy products, fruits and vegetables are plentiful in the shops which keep open day and night. Greece sends Venice its good wines. The flourishing trade with the Levant provides these in abundance and inexpensively. They also have a good local wine. Yet in spite of the availablilty of good wine at low cost, I have never seen a drunkard. They are fond of a good table but they can be described without exaggeration as a sober people. From this sobriety must come their robust longevity.

"I took note of the state of their religion. No secular function in Venice is grander or more luxurious than those of religion. Rome does not worship more elaborately. The luxury of Venetian religious worship comes from the citizens who all pay the costs. The clergy does not defray any of the expenses.

"While the religion of the Venetians is Catholic, they have Jews and Turks who live in their own neighborhoods. The Greeks think as they wish and are regarded as equals. This harmonious state of affairs arises from the fact that the secular government will not allow any harsh inquisition or examination regarding religion. The Republic does not bother anyone. Religion when it is untroubled does not have to innovate any other sects.

"The government has a system of public welfare for the sick and the poor. To prevent infanticide, they have foundling homes to receive new-borns without asking where they come from.

"Knowing also that man is prone to leave the path of virtue, this wise Republic permits prostitution under police supervision. These women are obliged to receive any who come to them. Those who will not pay are not punished however; this they see as a necessary evil for the prevention of other problems which might arise as a consequence.

"After taking leave of the Doge and our other friends, we left Venice and arrived at Bologna without incident. From there, we made our way over the Apennines by mule. In the inn, we met an English sea captain who was leaving the next day for Leghorn where his vessel awaited him. He was leaving directly for London. We seized this opportunity to accompany him. After twenty-eight days of pleasant voyaging, we came at last to our dear country.

"In London we inquired about Count Bridgent and learned he would be at his residence until Parliament opened. We did not dare ask about our parents who would be over a hundred years of age now. Wishing to have no witness either to our joy if we found them alive or our sorrow if we did not, we dismissed our servitor and set out for the Count's residence.

"And here we are, at the end of our story with our dearest wishes fulfilled."

EPILOGUE

When Edward had finished his story, Lord Bridgent presented him with the written account. He did not believe he had a right to keep it without Edward's consent. He explained why he had had his secretaries take down the story covertly. Edward was grateful for this ingenious ruse and asked only for one copy. He said he could perfect and correct it should he ever publish the account. This was done but the story was never published.

The following year, Edward sold the magnificent rubies to an Armenian merchant. They passed through several hands and are now in the possesion of the Emperor of China. With the money from his sale, he purchased a noble estate in Devonshire which he willed to the great-grandson of his uncle.

Edward's father James died three years after his son's homecoming; Wilhelmina, the mother, survived her husband by four years. Edward and Elizabeth remained in the count's home where they aged with astonishing rapidity. Ten or twelve years after their return to England, they showed all the signs of great age and decrepitude. When they died, Lady Bridgent buried them as Catholics in the palace chapel. The inscription on the tomb is there for all to read follows:

HERE LIE THE BONES OF EDWARD ALFRED

AND HIS SISTER-WIFE ELIZABETH.

THEY DIED THE SAME DAY

IN THE YEAR 1629

AT ONE HUNDRED TEN YEARS OF AGE.

THEY LIVED FOR EIGHTY-ONE YEARS

IN THE INTERIOR OF THE EARTH

WHERE THEY SAW EIGHT GENERATIONS

OF THEIR CHILDREN

AND WERE ANCESTORS

OF MORE THAN FOUR MILLION SOULS.

GLOSSARY

Icosameron - Greek word for twenty days.
Protocosmos - a huge world in the interior of the earth.
Megamicres - the 30 billion tiny inhabitants of this inner world.

Megamicran Measurement of Time

A Megamicran year of 180 days is called a harvest. The year begins with the sowing of seed and ends with the harvesting of the crop. The year is divided into four seasons of 45 days each, called greenwood fires. Four harvests or 720 Megamicran days equals one of our years.

Pentamine is their 5-day week; the names of their days are:-
  First day - Cocoon or Chrysalis. Second day - Butterfly
  Third day - Death. Fourth day - Dust. Fifth day - Egg.

Metamorphosis - a day of twenty hours.
One hour consists of 36 minutes; one minute has 36 seconds.
One second equals a pulse beat. Their watches are called pulsometers.

Megamicran Religious Hierarchy

Abdala (from Arabic) - here used to mean a bishop.
Alfaquin or Alfa (from Arabic) - here used to mean a priest.
Autocephalus (from Greek) - functions as archbishop or patriarch.
Helion or Great Spirit - the Supreme Pontiff, never seen or heard and said to be ageless.

Seminaries for Education of Offspring of Edward and Elizabeth

Micropedia (from Greek) - for children aged 1 to 4.
Megalopedia (from Greek) - for children aged 4 to 8.
Ephebus (from Greek word "entering puberty") - for children aged 8 to 9 years, 3 months

THE NAMES OF
EDWARD AND ELIZABETH'S
EIGHTY CHILDREN

Elizabeth was fertile for forty years from age twelve until she was fifty-two. Each October first, she bore a twin, one male, one female, nursed them for three months, weaned them on the first of January on which day she again conceived.

Each twin married its sibling at the age of nine years, three months (they were physically more like fourteen years old). In the fifty-ninth year of their stay in Protocosmos, Edward decreed that only cousins might marry.

1. James and Wilhelmina
2. Richard and Anne
3. Adam and Eve
4. Robert and Pauline
5. William and Theresa
6. Theodore and Frances
7. Henry and Judith
8. Charles and Barbara
9. David and Joanna
10. Simeon and Faustine
11. Jean and Tecla
12. Matthew and Catherine
13. Louis and Charlotte
14. Leopold and Sophie
15. Andrew and Esther
16. Caesar and Rose
17. Daniel and Louise
18. Paul and Clementine
19. Lawrence and Lucretia
20. Stephen and Irene
21. Jules and Antoinette
22. Godfrey and Justine
23. Leon and Constance
24. Renaud and Egeria
25. Roger and Helen
26. Basil and Angelica
27. Lucian and Ernestine
28. Peter and Mathilda
29. Alexander and Eleanor
30. Albert and Clothilda
31. Hugo and Claudine
32. Guy and Rose
33. Frederick and Bertha
34. Denis and Eugenia
35. Maximilian and Josepha
36. August and Andrienne
37. Thomas and Marie
38. Octave and Cunegonde
39. Godfrey and Agnes
40. Tancred and Clorinda

SOUSCRIPTEURS.

Mad. la Comt. de Clam - Gallas, née Comt. de
Spork, pour quatorze exemplaires.

M. le Comte Charles de Spork.

M. le Comte de Kinigl.

M. le Baron de Wittdorf.

S. A. le Pr. de Reüs Henri XV.

Mad. la Comt de Nostitz, née Comt. de Kolowrat.

M. le Comte Frederic de Nostitz.

M. le Comte de Swertz.

M. le Comte Philippe de Swertz.

M. le Comte Joseph de Swertz.

M. le Comte Charles d'Harrach.

M. le Baron de Mac - neven.

M. le Comte de Millesimo.

M. le Staroste Comte de Manuzzi.

Mad. la Comt. Desfours, née Comte de Mitrowski,
pour six exemplaires.

M. le Comte Max. Desfours.

M. le Comte François Desfours.

S. A. le Marechal Pr. de Kinski.

Mad. la Comt. d'Auersberg, née Comt. de Waldstein, pour sept exemplaires.

Mad. la Comt. de Waldstein, née Comt de Sternberg.

M. le Comte Guillaume d'Auersberg.

Mad. la Comt. Chan. Sophie de Waldstein.

M. le Comte Ernest de Waldstein.

M. le Comte Emmanuel de Waldstein.

M. le Comte Joseph Desfours.

Mad. la Comt. Chan. Jos. de Lasanski.

Mad. la Comt. de Braun, née Com. de Woffskeill.

Mad. la Comt. Chan. de Kinski.

Mad. la Comt. Chan. Wal. de Martzin.

Mad. la Comt. Chan. Mar. de Martzin.

Mad. la Comt. de Przikoski, née Baron. de Wasmuth, pour six exemplaires.

S. A. la Princ. de Clary, née Princ. de Ligne, pour quatre exemplaires.

S. A. le Princ. de Clary.

S. A. la Princ. de Lichtenstein, née Comt. de Murderscheid.

S. A. le Prince Louis de Lichtenstein.

M. le Comte Max. de Lamberg, pour trois exemplaires.

M. le Comte Charles de Salm.

Mad. la Comt. Louise de Waffenberg.

S. A. la Princ. de Batthiani.

S. E. Conte Ant. Ott. di Collalto, patrizio veneto per dieci esemplari.

Il N. Signor Marchese Sbarra de Franciati.

Il Signor Abbate de Zamperoli.

Il N. Signor Conte di Ayala.

Il Signor Luigi di Cattinara.

Il N. Signor Marchese di Breme.

Il N. Signor Conte di Dietrichstein.

Il N. Signor Vettor di Gradenigo.

Il Signor Abbate de Seraffini.

Il Signor de Sumani.

M. François de Casanova pour vingt deux exemplaires.

S. A. le Prince de Kaunitz Rittberg.

M. le Baron de Switten.

M. le Comte Ernest de Kaunitz Rittberg.

M. le Comte Dominique de Kaunitz Rittberg.

M. le Baron de Guldencrone M. de D.

M. le Comte de Podevils M. de P.

M. le Ch. de Neri M. de Port.

M. le Comte de Marchall.

S. E. le Marquis de Noailles A. de Fr.

Monseigneur le N. Ap.

M. le Duc de Sicignano.

M. le Comte de Guzman.

M. le Gen. Comte de Boughaus.

Mad. la Comt. de Potocki.

S. E. M. le Comte de Kaganek A. en Esp.

Mad. la Comt. de Kaganek.

M. de Straton.

Mad. la Comt, Kinski, née Comt. de Dietrichstein.

M. le Marquis de Gallo M. de N.

Mad. la Comt. de Thunn, née Comt. d'Urfeld.

S. A. le Prince de Belaselski M. de R. à Dresde.

M. le Comte de Thurn et Valsassina.

M. Jean de Casanova.

S. A. Monseigneur le P. A. de P. pour six exemplaires.

S. A. le General Prince Christian Auguste de Waldek, pour quatre vingt exemplaires.

M. le Comte de Waldstein-Dux.

M. le Comte de Waldstein Chan. de Sal. et d'Augsb.

M. le Comte de Waldstein Ch. Teut.

M. le Comte de Waldstein Ch. de Malte.

M. le Comte de Corti Col. du R. Kinski.

M. le Comte de Serbelloni.

M. le Comte de Litta.

M. le Comte de la Perouse.

Mad. la Comt. Douairière de Wallis, née Comt. de
Schaffgotsch.

M. le Baron Dom. de Janowski.

Mad. la Comt. de Pachta, née Comt. de Canal.

M. le Comte de Salaroli.

M. le Comte de Nostitz.

M. le Comte Jean de Pachta.

M. le Comte Leopold de Spork.

M. le Comte de Thurn.

M. le Comte Christiane de Sternberg.

M. le Comte Chan. de Sternberg.

M. le Comte de Wrtby.

Mad. la Comt. Franç. Ant. Desfours, née Comt. de
Czernin.

M. le Comte de Petting.

S. A. le Pr. Philippe de Fürstenberg.

M. le Baron de Janowski.

M. de Schwaihart.

M. de Calot.

Mad. la Comt. de Hartig. née Comt. de Colloredo,
pour six exemplaires.

M. le Comte Joachim de Pachta.

M. le Comte de Saurau.

M. le Comte de Clebersberg.

S. A. le Pr. Auguste de Lobkowitz.

Mad. la Comt. Douairière de Hartig, née Comt. de Kolowrath, pour deux exempl.

M. le Comte François Colloredo.

M. le Comte François de Hartig, M. de V. à Dresde, pour douze exemplaires.

Mad. de Henet, pour sept exemplaires.

Mad. la Comt. de Schlik, née Comt. de Nostitz.

M. le Comte de Schlik.

M. de Schmitmayer.

Mad. de Ottolini, née de Henet.

M. le Marquis de Cusani.

M. de Rebach.

S. A. la Pr. de Hohenlohe, née Pr. de Reüss, pour quatre exemplaires.

Mad. la Comt. de Kinski, née Comt. d'Auersberg.

M. le Comte Joseph de Kinski.

Mad. la Comt. de Siskowics.

Mad. la Comt. de Goertz, née Comt. de Wurmser.

M. le Comte de Clam Gallas.

M. le Comte Guillaume d'Auersberg.

Mad. de Hermann.

M. le Prelat Bar. de Steimback.

Mad. la Comt. Chan. de Canal.

S. A. la Princ. de Fürstenberg, née Princ. de Fürstenberg.

M. le Comte de Caretto Millesimo.

M. le Comte Joseph d' Auersberg.

Monseigneur le Comte Emmanuel de Waldstein, Evèque de Laitmeritz.

Le très Rev. de Strahl, Chan. de Laitmeritz.

M. le Comte de Bouquoi.

M. le Comte de Lanius.

M. le Comte de Saingenois.

M. de Mayer Med. Ph.

M. de Riegger.

M. de Cornova.

M. de Roico.

M. de Trottmann.

M. de Mayer à la Cens.

M. de Mazzolà à Dresde.

M. François Duchef.

M. de Vignet.

M. d' Opitz.

M. de Cron.

M. d' O-reilli Med. Ph.

M. de Preisler Med. Ph.

M. de Przybill.

M. de Droghi.

M. de Monti.

M. da Ponte.

M. de Bruzatti Med. Ph.

M. Borneille Stephan.

M. le conseiller de Hofft.

M. Bondini.

M. Cornier correcteur à l' imprimerie.

M. Piskaczek, Facteur.

Souscripteurs
que l'éditeur avoit oublié.

Mad. la Comt. de Waldstein, née Princesse de Lichtenstein.

M. le Comte de Dietrichstein.

M. le Comte de Witzai.

M. le Comte Joseph Erdödi.

Mad. la Comt. de Zichy, née Comtesse de Kevenhüller.

S. A. le Prince de Galitzin, Amb. de R.

M. le Comte de Schönfeld, M. de Saxe.

M. le Baron d' Helsberg, M. de Bav. Pal.

Mad. Kaïser, née Rizzotti.

M. de Traumpaur.

CASANOVA'S
"RESUME OF MY LIFE"

(Casanova wrote this outline summary of his life on Nov. 17, 1797 at the request of a young woman, Cecile, Countess Roggendorff, aged 21. She had initiated a correspondence with him in February of that year on the strength of her father's friendship with Casanova.)

My mother brought me into the world on Easter day, April 2nd in 1725 in Venice. The night before, she had a craving for crayfish. I am very fond of crayfish.

I was christened Jacques Jerome. Until I was eight and a half, I was an idiot. After hemorrhaging for three months, I was sent to Padua. There, cured of my stupidity, I applied myself to my studies. At age sixteen, I was made a doctor (of church law) and given a priest's habit so I could go to Rome and make my fortune.

At Rome, the daughter of my French teacher was the reason that Cardinal Acquaviva, my patron, dismissed me.

At eighteen, I entered the military service and went to Constantinople. Two years later, I returned to Venice. I had left my honorable profession so I plucked up my courage and took on the lowly work of violin player. I horrified my friends but this occupation did not last long.

When I was twenty-one years old, one of the foremost lords of Venice adopted me as his son. Being fairly rich now, I went on visits to Italy, France, Germany, and Vienna. There I made the acquaintance of Count Roggendorff. I returned to Venice where two years later, the Inquisitors for just and wise reasons had me imprisoned under the Piombi (Leads). This is a state prison from which no one has ever escaped but with God's help I made my escape after fifteen months and fled to Paris.

In two years, I had done such good business there that I became a millionaire. But I became bankrupt, all the same. I went to Holland to make some money, then I suffered some bad luck at Stuttgart, then some good luck in Switzerland, then to visit Voltaire, then some adventures in Marseille, Genoa, Florence and Rome where the pope Rezzonico, a Venetian, created me a knight of the order of St. John Lateran and made me *pronotaire apostolique*, (apostolic porthono-tary - obsolete). This was in 1760.

In the same year, I had good luck in Naples. In Florence I eloped with a young girl and the following year, I went to the Congress of Augsburg entrusted with a commission from the king of Portugal. The Congress did not meet and after peace was declared, I went to England where a serious misadventure required that I leave the following year, 1764. I avoided the gallows. This would not have dishonored me, only hanged me.

During this same year, I sought luck in vain at Berlin and at Petersburg. But I found it in Warsaw the next year. Nine months later, I lost it again for having fought General Braniski in a pistol duel. I wounded him in the belly but he was healed in three months and I was very glad of it; he is a fine fellow.

Obliged to leave Poland, I went to Paris in 1767 where an order for my imprisonment (lettre de cachet) made me decamp for Spain where I had very bad luck. I was imprisoned in a dungeon in the citidel of Barcelona from which I got out at the end of six weeks and was exiled from Spain. My crime was that I had paid nightly visits to the villainous mistress of the viceroy. At the Spanish border, I escaped hired assassins and got to Aix en Provence. There I was overtaken by a sickness which almost brought me to my grave after eighteen days of spitting blood.

In the year 1769 I published my defense of the government of Venice against *Amelot de la Houssaye* in three large volumes. The following year, the minister of England at the court of Turin sent me, well recommended, to Leghorn. I wanted to go to Constantinople with the Russian fleet but since Admiral Orlow did not agree with the conditions I presented, I turned back and went to Rome then under the pontificate of Ganganelli.

A happy love affair made me leave Rome for Naples and three months later another love affair, this one unhappy, made me return to Rome. I had a third fencing duel with Count Medini (who died four years ago in a debtors' prison in London).

Having a good deal of money, I went to Florence. After three days there, I was exiled on Christmas Day by the Archduke Leopold, later emperor. He died four or five years ago. I had a mistress who became a Marquise by following my advice.

Tired of running all over Europe, I decided to request a pardon from the Inquisitors of Venice. For this reason I went to Trieste to establish myself. Two years later, I obtained this pardon. That was on September 14, 1774. My return to Venice was the most beautiful moment of my life.

The year 1782 found me embroiled with the entire Venetian nobility. At the beginning of 1783, I voluntarily left my ungrateful country and went to Vienna. Six months later, I went to Paris with the intention of settling there but my brother who had been living there for twenty-six years made me forget my interests in favor of his own. I rescued him from his wife and took him to Vienna where Prince Kaunitz convinced him to stay. He is still there. He is two years younger than I am.

I placed myself at the service of M. Forscarini, the Ambassador from Venice to write his dispatches. Two years later, he died in my arms killed by the gout which had gone up to his chest. I decided to go to Berlin hoping for an appointment in the Academy. Halfway there, Count Waldstein stopped me at Toeplitz and led me to Dux where I still am and where from the looks of things, I shall die.

This is the only summary of my life that I have written and I permit it to be used however one wishes.

Non erubesco evangelium

This November the 17th, 1797

Jacques Casanova

Though failing in health, the 72 year old Casanova undertook to reply to the Countess' letters — 28 of these were found in his papers at Dux —and provided her with the solace, support and advice of a kindly mentor. He even helped her towards a position with a reigning ducal family. In return, Cecile gave her friend the admiration, love and respect of a grateful heart.

Her last letter was dated April 14, 1798. He died on June 4th of that year. The young Countess had expressed a great longing to see him but she never met the man whose letters meant so much to her.

CHRONOLOGY

This Chronology and Bibliography was included in CASANOVA by J. Rives Childs, published in 1961 by George Allen & Unwin, London. We thank the author and the publisher for permission to reprint it in the ICOSAMERON.

❦

1725   Birth at Venice, April 2nd.

1734-1739   Student at Padua.

1739-1742   At Venice with occasional sojourns at Padua and Pasean. Tonsured February 14, 1740. Four minor orders January 22, 1741. Doctor of laws, 1742. Student at St Cyprian Seminary in March 1742.

1742-1743   Possibly with da Riva at Corfu from August 1742 to March 1743. Death of grandmother, March 18, 1743. Incarcerated Fort St André, Venice, from end of March to July 27, 1743. Leaves Venice with da Lezze about October 18th. Quarantined Ancona until end November. Arrives Rome about December 9th, at Naples about the 14th and at Martirano at the end of 1743.

1744   May have returned to Venice until end of April. Leaving Naples is at Marino May 31, 1744. Enters service of Cardinal Acquaviva at Rome in June.

1745   Dismissed by Acquaviva in March. Meets Bellino shortly thereafter. At Pesaro about March 20th, at Rimini about 22nd. Returns to Venice about April 2nd. Embarks for Corfu, visits Constantinople, returns to Corfu and Venice.

1746   Becomes violin player. Meets Bragadin April 21st who installs him in his palace. In office of Leze, a lawyer.

1749   Leaves Venice for Milan and Mantua early in year. Meets Henriette at Cesene in July. Accompanies her to Parma and Geneva.

1750   Returns to Venice for two months, April and May. Leaves June 1st for Paris, arriving the middle of August.

1750-1752   In Paris, leaving the middle of October for Dresden.

1753   Dresden, Prague and Vienna, returning to Venice May 29th.

1753-1756 Intrigue with C.C., M.M. and de Bernis. Arrested in the night of July 25-26, 1755, and imprisoned in the Leads. Escapes November 1, 1756, and returns a second time to Paris.

1757 Arrives in Paris January 5, 1757. Through de Bernis's influence he is sent on a secret mission to Dunkirk, August-September, and appointed a director of the French lottery. Meets Mme d'Urfé, his benefactor.

1758 To Holland about October 14th on secret French financial mission.

1759 Returns to Paris about January 7th. Imprisoned for debt in For-l'Evêque August 23rd; released the 25th. A few days later leaves on a second secret French mission for Holland.

1760 Meets St Germain in Holland. With failure of mission leaves in February for Cologne. Arrested there on February 25th on false charges, released and later completely exculpated. Elector presents him with gold snuffbox. Arrested Stuttgart for gambling debt. Escapes April 2nd to Zurich. At Soleure from end of April to end of May. Visits Voltaire early in July. Meets Mlle de Roman at Grenoble at end of July. To Avignon, Marseilles, Toulon, Antibes, Nice, Genoa, Florence and Rome.

1761 Visits Naples, Rome, Florence, Modena, Parma, Turin. At Turin from middle of March to middle of May where he is charged by Gama with representing Portugal at Augsburg Congress. Proceeds there by way of Chambery, Lyon, Paris, Chalons, Strasbourg and Munich. At Augsburg from end of August to middle of December. To Paris by Constance and Bâle.

1762 Leaves Paris January 25th for regeneration of Mme d'Urfé at Pont-Carré and Aix-la-Chapelle. Thence to Metz, Colmar, Sulzbach, Bâle, Geneva, Lyons, Chambery and Turin. Expelled from Turin early in November he awaits at Geneva and Chambery permission to return.

1763 Returns to Turin early in January. Thence to Milan. Leaves about March 20th for Genoa. Departing April 7th he arrives Marseilles April 15th for a second regenerative operation on Mme d'Urfé. From Marseilles about May 11th to Lyons and thence to Paris the end of

250

month. Leaves about June 7th, arriving London June 13th. Meets Pauline and the Charpillon.

1764 *Forced to flee London for debt about March 11th. Encounters St Germain at Tournai. Convalescent at Wesel from about April 10th to May 18th. At Wolfenbuttel about June 12-20th; in Berlin from end of June to middle of September where he meets Frederick the Great and is offered a post by him which he rejects. Arrives Riga October 20th and St Petersburg December 21st.*

1765 *After visiting Moscow and meeting Catherine the Great leaves the middle of September for Warsaw, arriving October 10th.*

1766 *Duel with Branicki, March 5th, loses him the Polish King's favour. Leaves Warsaw July 8th via Breslau for Dresden where he remains to December 16th, proceeding to Vienna.*

1767 *Expelled from Vienna end of January. To Augsburg, Schwetzingen, Mannheim, Mayence, Cologne and Spa (August 1st to end of September). Returns to Paris early in October. A lettre de cachet of Louis XV forces him to leave November 19th for Spain.*

1768 *Imprisoned in Buen Retiro, Madrid, for illegal possession of arms February 20-22nd. Leaves Madrid about September 13th for Saragossa, Valencia and Barcelona. Poaching on the governor's love preserves he is imprisoned from November 16th to December 28th.*

1769 *Through Perpignan, Narbonne, Montpellier and Nîmes to Aix-en-Provence where he meets the Marquis d'Argens and remains from end of January to May 26th. From Marseilles via Antibes, Nice, Tende and Turin to Lugano. Between July 8th to end of December he oversees publication of his Confutazione.*

1770 *Leaves Turin about March 15th for Parma, Bologna, Florence and Leghorn. Refused service in Orloff's fleet. To Pisa and Florence (April 10-29th), Rome (middle of May to June 10th), Naples (to middle of August), Salerno (early September), returning to Rome middle of September. Renews friendship with de Bernis.*

1771 *Leaves Rome in July for Florence. Expelled late in December. Arrives Bologna December 30th.*

1772 *Leaves Bologna end of September. At Ancona from*

early October to November 14th. Settles in Trieste November 15th.

1772-1774 *In Trieste with return to Venice from exile November 15th.*

1774-1783 *In Venice. Devoting himself to literary labours and as theatrical producer he becomes secret agent of the Inquisitors at end of December 1776. Forms liaison with Francesca Buschini, 1779. Publishes Ne' Amori, Ne' Donne, 1782, provoking a storm which forces him to leave Venice January 17th, 1783.*

1783 *To Vienna and return to Venice June 16, 1783, for a last few hours. Thence through Innsbruck, Augsburg and Francfort to Aix-la-Chapelle and Spa. After a month there in August to Paris (September 20th to November 24th) via the Hague, Rotterdam and Antwerp. Arrives Vienna about December 7th, thence to Dresden, Berlin and Prague.*

1784 *Returns Vienna middle of February and enters service of Venetian Ambassador as secretary. Renews acquaintance with Lorenzo Da Ponte. Meets Count Waldstein who offers him employment.*

1785 *With death of Venetian Ambassador April 23rd, 1785, and ineffectual attempts to find employment in Berlin he accepts in September service with Waldstein as librarian at Dux.*

1792 *Completes first draft of Memoirs on which he had begun work at least as early as 1790.*

1798 *June 4th, dies at Dux.*

1820 *December 13th. Manuscript of Memoirs offered to F. A. Brockhaus in Leipzig.*

1821 *January 18th, Brockhaus purchases manuscript from Carlo Angiolini for 200 thalers. Publication late in year in Urania of extracts of Memoirs in German translation.*

1960 *April 21st. Publication of the first integral text of the Memoirs by A. F. Brockhaus, Wiesbaden, and Plon, Paris.*

BIBLIOGRAPHY

This Chronology and Bibliography was included in CASANOVA by J. Rives Childs, published in 1961 by George Allen & Unwin, London. We thank the author and the publisher for permission to reprint it in the ICOSAMERON.

❦

1. BIBLIOGRAPHIES

Childs, J. Rives: *Casanoviana*, Nebehay, Vienna, 1956. Three supplements published in *Casanova Gleanings*, 1958-60, an annual review devoted to Casanova studies.

2. PRINCIPAL PUBLISHED WORKS

Zoroastro, tragedia tradotta del Francese, Dresden, 1752.

Confutazione della Storia del Governo Veneto d'Amelot de la Houssaie, Amsterdam [Lugano] 1769, 3v.

Lana Caprina [Bologna 1772]. French translation in *Pages Casanoviennes*, V.

Istoria delle turbolenze della Polonia, Gorizia, 1774, 3v.

Dell' Iliade de Omero, tradotta in ottava rima, Venedig, 1775-8, 3v.

Scrutinio del libro 'Eloges de M. de Voltaire', Venezia, 1779.

Opuscoli Miscellanei, January 1779 [1780] to July 1780, 7 parts.

Lettere della nobil donna Silvia Belegno, Venezia [1780]. Translation of Mme Riccobini's *Lettres de milady Catesby*.

Le Messager de Thalie, October 1780-January 1781, 11 numbers. Reprinted in *Pages Casanoviennes*, I.

Di Aneddoti Veneziani, Venezia, 1782. Translation of Mme de Tencin's *La siège de Calais*.

Ne' Amori, Ne' Donne ovvero la stella ripulta, Venezia, 1783. French translation in *Pages Casanoviennes*, VIII.

Lettre historico-critique, Hambourg, 12 mai, 1784.

Six untitled and unsigned articles in *Osservatore Triestino*, January 22-February 26, 1785, concerning a dispute between Venice and Holland.

---

[1] For more complete details of the works listed see *Casanoviana*, 1956.

253

Exposition raisonnée du different qui subsiste entre les deux republiques de Venise et d'Hollande, 1785. Italian translation, *Exposizione ragionata*, 1785.

Lettre à Messieurs Jean et Etienne L. 1785. Italian translation *Lettera ai Signori Giovanni e Stefano Luzac*, 1785. Dutch reprint, La Haye, 1785; Dutch translation, *Brief van eenen Venetiaan aan de Heeren J. en E.L.*, Utrecht, 1785.

Supplement à l'exposition raisonnée, 1785. Italian translation, *Supplimento alla Espozione ragionata della controversia*, 1785.

Soliloque d'un penseur, Prague, 1786. Republished in *Pages Casanoviennes*, VII. Czech translation, Prague, 1925.

Histoire de ma fuite des prisons, Leipzig [Prague] 1788 [1787].

Icosameron ou Histoire d'Edouard et d'Elisabeth qui passèrent quatre vingts un ans chez les Mégamicres habitans aborigènes du Protocosme dans l'interieur de notre globe, Prague [1788], 5v.

Solution du probleme deliaque, Dresden, 1790.

Corollaire à la duplication de l'hexaedre [Dresden, 1790].

Demonstration geometrique de la duplication du cube [Dresden, 1790].

A Leonard Snetlage [Dresden, 1797].

Aus den Memoiren des Venetianers Jacob Casanova de Seingalt, oder sein Leben, wie er es zu Dux in Böhmen niederschrieb. Nach dem Original-Manuscript bearbeitet von Wilhelm von Schütz, Leipzig, F. A. Brockhaus, 1822-8, 12v.

Mémoires du Vénitien J. Casanova de Seingalt, Tournachon-Molin, Paris, 1825-9, 14v. Corrupt translation of above. Worthless as text.

Mémoires de J. Casanova de Seingalt, écrits par lui-même, Leipsic, F. A. Brockhaus, Paris, Ponthieu et Comp 1826-38, 12v. Adaptation by Jean Laforgue. Reprinted by Garnier, Paris, 8v. 1880.

Mémoires de Jacques Casanova de Seingalt, Paris, Paulin, 1833-7, 10v. Reprinted by Rozez, Brussels, 1860-87, 6v. and by Flammarion, Paris, 1899-1928, 6v. The so-called Busoni text.

The Memoirs of Jacques Casanova Written by Himself Now for the first time translated into English [by Arthur Machen]. Privately printed [London] 1894, 12v. Numerous reprints.

Erinnerungen, übersetzt und eingeleitet von Heinrich Conrad, Müller, München und Leipzig, 1907-13, 15v. A monument of German erudition.

Mémoires de J. Casanova de Seingalt. Edition nouvelle publiée sous la direction de Raoul Vèze, d'après le texte de l'édition princeps

Leipzig-Bruxelles-Paris (1826-38). Variantes et commentaires historiques et critiques, Paris, La Sirène, 1924-35, 12v. The introductions to each volume and the voluminous notes, however demoded some cf these have become, in the light of subsequent research and publication in 1960-1 of the original Casanova text, will always give value to this monument of French erudition. The text and notes, in part, without the introductions, were published by the Limited Edition Club, N.Y., 1940, 8v.

Histoire de ma vie, édition integrale, F. A. Brockhaus, Wiesbaden, Librairie Plon, Paris, 1960-1, 12v. in 6. First publication of the original text of Casanova.

3. CORRESPONDENCE[1]

Briefwechsel (vol. XV of *Erinnerungen*, for which see above), edited by Ravà and Gugitz.

Carteggi Casanoviani, Milan, 1916, 1919, 2v. edited by P. Molmenti.

Casanova und Graf Lamberg, Vienna, 1935, edited by Gugitz.

Correspondance avec J. F. Opiz, Leipzig, 1913, 2v. Edited by Khol and Pick.

Lettere di Donne a G. Casanova, Milan, 1912. Edited by Ravà. French translation, *Lettres des femmes à J. Casanova*, Paris, 1912, by E. Maynial. Not so complete

Pages Casanoviennes, Paris, 1925-6, III-VII, edited by Pollio et Vezè.

Patrizi e avventurieri, Milan, 1930, edited by Curiel, Gugitz and Ravà.

4. BIOGRAPHIES

Endore, S. Guy, *Casanova, His Known and Unknown Life*, N.Y., 1929.

Gamba, B., *Biografia di Giacomo Casanova*, Venezia, 1835.

Gugitz, G., *Casanova und sein Lebensroman*, Vienna, 1921.

Le Gras, Joseph and Vèze, Raoul, *Casanova*, Paris, 1930.

Zottoli, Angelandrea, *Casanova*, Rome, 1945, 2v.

Zweig, Stefan, *Adepts in Self-Portraiture, Casanova, Stendhal, Tolstoy*, N.Y., 1928; London, 1929 (translated from the German).

---

[1] See also *Casanova Gleanings*, 1958-60, edited by J. Rives Childs.

Barthold, F. W. *Geschichtliche Persönlichkeiten in J. Casanova's Memoiren*, Berlin, 1846, 2v.

Baschet, Armand, 'Preuves curieuses de l'authenticité des Mémoires de J. Casanova de Seingalt', *Le Livre*, 1881.

D'Ancona, A., *Viaggiatori e avventurieri*, Firenze, 1911.

Ellis, Havelock, *Affirmations*, London, 1898.

Frenzi, Giulio de, *L'Italiano errante*, Naples, 1913.

Guède, Dr A., *J. Casanova*, Paris, 1912.

Ligne, Prince Charles de, *Melanges anecdotiques littéraires et politiques*, Paris, 1833.

Maynial, Edouard, *Casanova et son temps*, Paris, 1910. In English, *Casanova and His Time*, London, 1911.

Nettl, Paul, *The Other Casanova*, N.Y., 1950.

Pollio, Joseph (ed. with R. Vèze), *Pages Casanoviennes*, Paris, 1925-6, 8v.

Powell, Lawrence C., *Giacomo Casanova*, Pasadena, 1948. Reprinted in *Islands of Books*, Los Angeles, 1951.

Samaran, Ch., *Jacques Casanova*, Paris, 1914.

Schmidt-Pauli, E. von, *Der andere Casanova, Unveröffentlichte Dokumente aus dem Duxer Archiv*, Berlin, 1930.

Uzanne, O., 'Casanova et la posterité', *Revue du dix-huitième siècle*, Paris, 1917.

6. PARTICULAR PHASES

Ademollo, A., 'Testo dell' *Histoire de ma vie* del Casanova e la veracità dell sue Memorie', *Fanfulla della Domenica*, December 17, 1882.

Adnesse, J. F. H., *Casanova après ses Mémoires*, Bordeaux, 1919. In English, M. S. Buck, *The Life of Casanova from 1774 to 1798*, N.Y., 1924.

Belgrano, L. T., *Aneddoti e ritratti Casanoviani*, Turin, 1890.

Bleackley, H., *Casanova in England*, London, 1923.

Bocchi, A., *Brani di storia parmigana*, Parma, 1922.

Brunelli, B., *Un' Amica del G. Casanova*, Milan, 1924. In English, *Casanova Loved Her*, London, 1929.

Brunelli, B., 'Figurine Padovane nelle Memorie di G. Casanova' and 'Un mistero Casanoviano svelato', in *Atti e Memorie della R.Ac . . . in Padova*, 1933-4 and 1938.

Brunetti, M., 'I Compagni di G. Casanova sotto i "Piombi" ', *Rivista d'Italia*, June 1914; 'La fuga di G. Casanova in una narrazione contemporanea', *Nuovo Archivio Veneto*, 1917.

Contini, E., 'Uomo di Teatro', *Rivista italiana del dramma*, Rome, 1939.

Croce, Benedetto, *Anedotti di varia letteratura*, Naples, 1942, 3v.

Cucuel, G., 'La musique et les musiciens dans les Memoires de Casanova', *Revue du dix-huitième siècle*, Paris, 1913; 'La vie de société dans la Dauphiné au XVIII siècle', *ibid*, 1918.

Curiel, C. L., *Trieste Settecentesca*, Naples, 1922; 'Friuli nei "Memoires" di G. Casanova', *Ce Fastu*, Udine, 1933.

Damerini, G., *Casanova .ı Venezia, dopo il primo esilio*, Turin, 1957.

Da Ponte, L., *Memorie*, N.Y., 1823-7, 4v. In English, *Memoirs*, Philadelphia, 1929.

Frati, L., *Il Settecento a Bologna*, Milan, 1923.

Giacomo, S. di, 'Casanova a Napoli', *Nuova Antologia*, 1922.

Giulini, A., *A Milano nel Settecento*, Milan, 1926.

Givry, G. de, 'La Kabbale de J. Casanova', Sirène, III, 1926.

Grellet, P., *Les aventures de Casanova en Suisse*, Lausanne, 1919.

Haldenwang, G., *Casanova à Genève*, Paris, 1937.

Henry, Charles, *Les connaissances mathematiques de J. Casanova*, Rome, 1882; 'J. Casanova de Seingalt et la critique historique', *Revue historique*, Paris, 1889.

Ilges, F. W., *Casanova in Köln*, Cologne, 1926; 'Auf den Spuren Casanovas in Aachen', *Aachener Geschichtvereins Zeitschrift*, 1932; 'Casanova in Berlin', *Mitteilungen des Vereins für die Geschichte Berlins*, 1931; 'Casanova in Dresden', *Wissenschäftliche Beilagen des Dresdener Anzeiger*, 1931.

Lancey, C. Ver Heyden de, 'Les portraits de Jacques et de François Casanova', *Gazette des Beaux-Arts*, Paris, 1934.

Mahler, A., 'Catalogue des manuscrits de Casanova', *Revue des Bibliothèques*, Paris, 1905.

Maynial, E. (with R. Vèze), *La fin d'un aventurier. Casanova après les Mémoires*, Paris, 1952.

Messedaglia, L., 'G. Casanova e Merlin Cocai', *Nuovo Archivio Veneto*, 1938.

Mola, E., 'G. Casanova e la Repubblica di Venezia', *Rivista Europea*, 1881; 'G. Casanova all' Isola Madre', *Verbania*, July 1912; 'Casanova e le sue "Memorie" ', *Fanfulla*, May 28, 1882.

Molmenti, P., *Epistolari Veneziani nel Secolo XVIII*, Milan, 1914.

Morgulis, G., 'Musset et Casanova', *Revue des études italiennes*, Paris, 1956.

Nettl, P., 'Casanova and "Don Giovanni" ', *Saturday Review*, N.Y., January 28, 1956; 'Casanova and the Dance', *Dance*, N.Y., 1945; 'Casanova and Music', *The Musical Quarterly*, N.Y., 1929.

Nicolini, F., 'G. Casanova e il Cardinale Acquaviva d'Aragona', *Artusa*, 1945.

Ravà, Aldo, 'Casanova a Lugano', *Bolletino storico della Svizzera Italiana*, 1911; 'Come furono pubblicate le Memorie di Casanova', *Marzocco*, November 13, 1910; 'Il opere pubblicate de G. Casanova', *ibid*, October 9, 1910; 'Studi Casanoviani a Dux', *ibid*, September 18, 1910.

Rolleston, Dr J. D., 'The Medical Interest of Casanova's Memoirs', *Janus*, Leyde, 1917. French translation in Sirène, VIII.

Steiner, G., 'Songs of Experience', *The Reporter*, N.Y., October 15, 1959.

Symons, Arthur, 'Casanova at Dux', *North American Review*, 1902.

Valeri, A., 'Casanova a Roma', *Rivista d'Italia*, 1899.

Icosameron, Casanova, and Eighteenth Century Thought As College Courses

It has been suggested that Casanova's fantasy of utopia may serve as an introductory course dealing with social, cultural, religious and political mores of the 18th century.

Mara Vamos[1], a writer and Professor of French and French Literature at Fairleigh Dickinson University, evaluated the *Icosameron* as follows: "Casanova depicted not one but two utopias. He combined the tradition of describing and imaginary country for satirical purpose with the tradition of describing an ideal country. The world of the Megamicres, despite its charm and quaintness, is a world full of prejudices and injustices, dominated by a church based on superstition and by academies which indulge in scholastic, fruitless debates, an obscurantist world where experimentation is forbidden and therefore progress impossible. In short, it is a curious hybrid world, half primitive paradise, half caricature of the European institutions of the time. The actual utopia is the society and civilization developed by the alien brother and sister, the new Adam and Eve and their progeny. Edward-Casanova creates a new human race and organizes an ideal state within a state."

Francis Furlan[2] says succinctly "the universe of the Megamicres is both a critique of European society and a model of perfect social organization." Josef Polisensky[3], Professor of Modern History, comments on the upsurge of knowledge concerning all of Casanova's thinking and writing. "The main interest of Czeck historians concerns Casanova's work in its totality. It is regarded as a first class testimony on the state of European society in the 18th century. His works of historical, philosophical and even economic character are virtually unknown." Polisensky was in the midst of publishing *Casanova inconnu*, a collection with comments of Casanova's political writings. He summarized Casanova's work as "merciless mirror reflecting the varied society of the *Ancien Regime*."

The *Icosameron* would be the initial course in the study of Casanova's contribution to 18th century thought. *Die Andere Casanova⁴, Il Vero Casanova⁵, The Other Casanova⁶* are a few of the volumes on the emerging Casanova - the writer, the thinker, the scholar, the polyhistorian, "the man who delighted in frequenting libraries, who discussed politics and literature with some of the most eminent men of history...the amazing man of many sides, with his wide interests and vast knowledge..."[7]

With the publication of Willard Trask's authorized translation of Casanova's *History of my Life* and a century or more of solid verification of that life we must accept the statement of Tom Vitelli[8] that "Casanova's account is as rich and reliable a source of 18th century social history as Pepy's diary is for the history of 17th century London."

Beyond the fictional tale of a fantastic voyage and beyond the prophetic speculation of the *Icosameron*, lies a wealth of commentary by Casanova on government, economics, politics, religion, social mores and relationships. These ideas are entertainingly enmeshed within his fictional work; they would stimulate and enrich such a college course.

Notes

[1] Mara Vamos <u>communication</u> to the publisher. 1983

[2] Francis Furlan. <u>The Tradition of the Extraordinary Voyage in the Icosameron</u>. (*Casanova Gleanings*, Vol XVI, 1973)

[3] Josef Polisensky. <u>Present State of Casanova Studies in Czechoslovakia</u> *Casanova Gleanings*, Vol x, 1967, pgs 10-13)

[4] Edgar von Schmidt-Pauli. <u>Der Andere Casanova.</u> (Verlag fur Kulturpolitick Berlin, 1930)

[5] Piero Chiara. <u>Il Vero Casanova.</u> (U. Mursia, Milano, 1977)

[6] Paul Nettl. <u>The Other Casanova</u>. (Philosophical Library, New York, 1950)

[7] Angelika Huebscher. <u>Casanova on German TV.</u> (C.G. Vol XIV, pg 27)

[8] Tom Vitelli. <u>Memorialist/Diarist: The Autobiographies of Casanova and Boswell</u>. Presented at a Colloquium in Italian Studies at Brown University, 1982.

Bibliographies and References
for Graduate Students and Research

Childs, J. Rives. The Bibliography prepared by Childs for his Biography, *Casanova* is reprinted in this book on pages 253-58.

Childs' *Casanoviana*: An Annotated World Bibliography of Casanova and of Works Concerning Him (Nebehay, Vienna, 1956). A 396 page volume with several thousand references categorized into (A) Works Other Than the Memoirs (B) The Memoirs (C) Correspondence of Casanova (D) Works Relating to Casanova (E) Creative Works Inspired by Casanova.

Casanova Gleanings, a yearly supplementry publication prepared by Casanovists (in French and English) from 1958 through 1979 "devoted to the study of Casanova and his "world", or so to speak in a broader sense, to the study of almost all the Eighteenth Century he personified and pictured in so fascinating a way." During these 21 years over 900 pages were published with thousands of bibliographic references added in the same five catagories as in *Casanoviana*. (for information concerning these volumes send queries to the new Casanova publication below).

L'Intermediarie Des Casanovistes, a yearly bilingual publication was started in 1984 to continue the work of *Casanova Gleanings.* For information and subscriptions (20 Swiss Francs) write to the magazine C/O Helmut Watzlawick, 22, esplanade, CH-1214- Vernier, Switzerland.

BIOGRAPHY CUTS THROUGH MYTH
TO EXAMINE CASANOVA
Gerd Gillhoff, Bulletin, February 1978
Randoph-Macon College, Ashland, Virginia

The Walter Hines Page Library of Randolph-Macon College is the home of the world's most comprehensive Casanova collection, making it the foremost center for Caanova research in the Western Hemisphere. The collection was assembled and donated to the college by J. Rives Childs.